From Innocents to Agents

children and children's rights in New Zealand

MICHAEL REID

First published in 2006 by Maxim Institute
PO Box 49 074, Roskill South, Auckland 1445, New Zealand
Ph (0064) 9 627 3261 | Fax (0064) 9 627 3264 | www.maxim.org.nz

Copyright © 2006 Maxim Institute
ISBN 0-9582652-5-9

Design and typography by Maxim Institute
Printed in New Zealand by RED_i

"We all want a better world for children, but so far, it is the adults that have called the shots. Now we are going to build a better world with children—with you. It's high time that we adults hear what you have to say."

UN General Secretary, Kofi Annan, addressing the UN Special Session on Children, New York, May 2002

•

"This is not the final chapter in children's participation; in fact, this is where the story must begin.... Here the children will no longer hand the pens to adults; but rather, the adults will hand the pens to the children and the world will listen."

US delegate addressing the UN Special Session on Children, New York, May 2002

•

"I frankly think that children are the first big social movement of the 21ˢᵗ Century ..."

New Zealand Social Services Minister, Hon Steve Maharey's reflections on the UN Special Session on Children, New York, May 2002

•

"Another Player in the World of Lobbying"

Heading of an article on the launch of the under fives 'Littlies Lobby', in *Children,* a Newsletter from the Office of the Commissioner for Children, December 2002, p30

•

"We have reached a point in our history where perhaps the greatest goal for advancing children's rights should be a return to a time when we treated children like children; when the mistakes they made were understood to be part of the natural process of growing up; and when adults understood their obligations."

Martin Guggenheim, *What's Wrong With Children's Rights.* Massachusetts: Harvard University Press, 2005, p266

CONTENTS

FOREWORD

———————— • ————————

The atomising and alienating effects of a burgeoning 'rights culture' are particularly egregious when applied unthinkingly to families. Of particular concern, I suggest, is the prospect of children being prematurely burdened with adult-like choices and responsibilities, of being re-visioned as autonomous agents possessing rights. An unfortunate dynamic is potentially unleashed. Some parents become vulnerable to being cast as potential rights violators and not benevolent guardians guided by love and ongoing concern. Ironically, the state—traditionally the principal 'villain' in terms of trampling upon personal and communal freedoms—is now the champion of the victimised. A vast and growing network of professionals, experts, advocates and other bureaucrats to champion children is henceforth required to ensure parents do not transgress the fluid boundaries of contemporary family law—a law increasingly shaped by tendentious interpretations of international treaties.

The key international document, of course, is the United Nations Convention on the Rights of the Child, 1989. UNCROC has been promptly ratified by nearly every nation in the world—Somalia and the United States being exceptions—and New Zealand doing so in 1993. Most of the Convention's content is entirely laudable, but it is the autonomy or participation rights of the child that are the novel and potentially troublesome provisions. As Professor Cynthia Price Cohen explained, "Of the thirty-eight articles . . . devoted to substantive rights, at least ten of these have never been recognized for children in any other international instrument. They are all rights of 'individual personality', and include such civil and political rights as the right to leave and return, to privacy, to freedom of expression, assembly, association and religion, among others." (The Relevance of Theories of Natural Law and Legal Positivism, M. Freeman and P. Veerman (eds), *The Ideologies of Children's Rights* (Kluwer, 1992) chapter 5 at 61).

If the state is to honour its international treaty obligations, does this not require it to assume a more active and interventionist role in families to ensure that more than mere lip service is paid to children's fledgling rights of autonomy?

Dr Michael Reid's carefully researched and elegantly written book represents a rare and much-needed critique of the deeper philosophical forces at work in contemporary public policy on children. He does not offer glib answers nor does he indulge in petty point scoring. The subject is too important for that. Rather, he has provided New Zealand policy-makers with a thoughtful and detailed critique of the path trodden thus far. Many of his insights and observations will, in the current ideological climate, be jarring. This simply makes his searching analysis all the more valuable. *From Innocents to Agents* is an important and timely contribution to the debate; indeed, without voices such as these there really is no debate at all.

Associate Professor Rex Ahdar
Faculty of Law, University of Otago

Author's Preface

———————— • ————————

This book has grown out of many years of observation as a teacher and parent. During this time there has been a cultural redefinition of children and a concurrent growth of children's rights in New Zealand.

Much of this has been positive, and there have been many beneficial changes brought about through a greater awareness of children's developmental needs and respect for their rights. The exposure of child abuse statistics has been an ugly but necessary feature of this new environment.[1] All members of the community are being encouraged to value and protect children. But there are also less obvious implications for parents and teachers in the new rights-sensitive culture. For example, when rights clash, who's the boss? I believe that this and related philosophical issues and practical concerns are not being considered adequately.

The state in New Zealand has an honourable history of supporting children and providing for their health, welfare and education. We have led the world in many developments protecting children: the Child Welfare Act of 1925, for example, along with the work of the Department of Health and community organisations such as the Plunket Society, were all highly significant. For a long time it was assumed the state would provide for children only when intervention was necessary. Analysts were rightly critical of the official practice of taking children into custodial care and away from their families, and of anomalies surrounding adoption.

There came, however, a turning of the corner from the 1970s, as New Zealand society began to embrace a more proactive human rights culture. Children became politicised, not in the sense of making them more aware in relation to the political process itself, but as active players in advancing the interests of particular adults. With the passage of the Children, Young Persons and Their Families Act in 1989, and the ratification of the United Nations Convention on the Rights of the Child (UNCROC) in 1993, we entered into a new era of state involvement and lobbying. A particular interpretation of UNCROC has since become the yardstick in all matters regarding the welfare of the child, and accompanying this has been an enormous emphasis on the authority of international law.

Proponents for change see no conflict whatsoever when children's rights are advocated, but the reality is not that simple. Rights, once identified and empowered by government action, increase and consolidate state power. For advocates, an altruistic interest in children leads headlong into the world of group identity politics, the push for legal change, and normalising new attitudes towards children. Children's rights become a lever for social change and the people most involved are not children, but groups of reforming adults. A new dynamic emerges whereby the authority of advocates and officials, rather than that of parents, predominates.

From Innocents to Agents explores the changes in children's rights against a background of historical and international developments. I hope it will prompt a debate that extends beyond superficial and media-driven concerns.

Despite some misgivings about the direction of children's rights advocacy, I retain a respect for the expertise and concern of those involved in this work. They, as do many others, seek a nation that treats its children with respect. They are right to deplore high rates of child abuse and maltreatment and speak out on behalf of children who are victims. Recently-published findings, for example, reveal that in one year alone, 116 children were hospitalised as a result of assault; while another study found that 18 percent of all children were sexually abused, with the figure much higher for girls at 25-30 per cent.[2] Unfortunately, these statistics are all too common. While abusive parents need to be identified and held to account, we also need to consider the context in which these abuses occur, rather than focus attention on rights implications or the supposed failings of those working in state agencies. These agencies have an innately difficult job, and while this is not an excuse for non-performance, it underscores the need for a better appreciation of what is realistic to expect from them. Understanding child abuse calls for a wider grasp of family structure, parenting, and indeed, the entire experience of children within families.

Any book is the combination of many people's efforts. I acknowledge, with sincere thanks, the assistance of colleagues; those who have shared their stories and experiences of parenting, and academics and reviewers—both within New Zealand and from overseas—who have critiqued the text and added much useful comment and information. In particular I would like to thank Associate Professor Rex Ahdar, Professor Mark Henaghan, Professor Steven Nock, Dr David McKenzie, Peter Juriss, Mark Rowley, and Fiona Mackenzie. Thanks too, to Michael Bradstock for his critical insights and editing skills. Like children, we adults rely heavily on others to help us grow.

Michael Reid
June 2006

---

[1]   The hysteria surrounding child abuse and the role of men (in particular, fathers) became the corollary dimension of this awareness, see Lynley Hood, *A City Possessed: The Christchurch Civic Crèche Case – Child Abuse, Gender Politics and the Law*. Dunedin: Longacre Press, 2001, pp62-71, see also the discussion in 2.6.

[2]   *Family Voice*, Families Commission Newsletter, Issue 1, October 2005, p.3.

ABBREVIATIONS

Note: with the exception of United Nations agencies or events, all abbreviations refer to New Zealand. Abbreviations not shown here are explained as they appear in the text.

AJHR	*Appendices to the Journals of the House of Representatives*
BORA	New Zealand Bill of Rights Act 1990
CIC	Children's Issues Centre (Dunedin)
CPAG	Child Poverty Action Group (1994)
CYPA	Children and Young Persons Act 1974
CYPFA	Children, Young Persons and their Families Act 1989
DSW	Department of Social Welfare (1972)
ECC	Every Child Counts (2005)
ECE	Early Childhood Education
EPOCH	End Physical Punishment of Children (UK 1986, NZ 1997)
HRA	Human Rights Act 1993
HRC	Human Rights Commission (1978)
IYB	Independent Youth Benefit
IYC	International Year of the Child (1979) – United Nations
MFAT	Ministry of Foreign Affairs and Trade
MHR	Member of the House of Representatives (before MP was adopted)
MSD	Ministry of Social Development (2001)
NGO	Non-Governmental Organisation
NZCER	New Zealand Council for Educational Research
NZPD	*New Zealand Parliamentary Debates*
OCC	Office of the Commissioner for Children
ODT	*Otago Daily Times* (Dunedin newspaper)
s	Section (as in s59 of the Crimes Act 1961)
SNZ	*Statutes of New Zealand*
UNCROC	United Nations Convention on the Rights of the Child 1989
UNDRC	United Nations Declaration on the Rights of the Child 1959
UDHR	Universal Declaration of Human Rights 1948
UNICEF	United Nations International Children's Emergency Fund (1946)

INTRODUCTION

———————— • ————————

From *Innocents to Agents* traces the historical development of children's rights, and examines the politicisation of New Zealand's children. For much of Western history, children have been considered in the context of the family which has provided for their support, protection and care. But in the later decades of the twentieth century, children moved from being viewed as innocents in need of protection, to being politicised agents with autonomous rights guaranteed by the state.

Together with a new balance between local and international law, the state has shifted from supporting the authority and place of families to supporting the emancipation of children from their parents, and the support structures which make for their well-being. This book tells the story of that shift.

It begins with a brief historical survey of the place of children in ancient societies starting with the status of children in Hebrew, Greek, Latin and wider European thought. It then traces the rise of the first 'rescue' rights in the Victorian period, and their subsequent transplant into colonial New Zealand society.

New Zealand is small, young and geographically isolated, with a long tradition of progressive experimentation. This means that many ideas influencing our development have been imported from overseas. This is as true for ideas about childhood and children's rights as it is for economics, defence and foreign policy. Applying these ideas in a local context has always been mediated through our own experience and history, and in response to local requirements.

One of the unique and defining features of New Zealand society has been the beliefs and practices of Maori, *ahua whakaaro o te ao,* and how these have interacted with and been shaped by the later migrants, *Tauiwi,* who brought with them their own views of children and childhood.

Like Britain and America at the end of the nineteenth century, the first children's rights in New Zealand were an expression of the contemporary Victorian need to protect minors and to ensure proper legal structures were in place to 'rescue' the vulnerable. The role of the state was essentially an extension of the personal ethic of charity to provide for the needy, particularly orphans.

Slowly this extended to labour and industrial protections and then to state-sponsored education. Despite the difficulties of enforcing compulsory attendance, especially in rural areas, the Education Act 1877 initiated a long history of state schooling in New Zealand. For most children, school provided the first extensive and authoritative alternative to socialisation within the home.

During the early years of the twentieth century, the state greatly expanded its ambit to care for the health and welfare of children. Specialist facilities were established to remove 'delinquent' and criminally-prone children from the community. The state also took it upon itself to prevent children from contracting infectious and other diseases. From 1900, the Department of Health in conjunction with various education and welfare agencies, as well as the Royal New Zealand Plunket Society (from 1907), did much to promote the needs of children. International developments in education filtered through to influence policy makers, and a strong New Zealand tradition of openness to theories from abroad emerged in health, education and welfare. This continues today as ideas from abroad are adapted to local conditions and expressed in policy initiatives.

From Innocents to Agents suggests that balancing developments in international law with local needs has usually been the practice in New Zealand; as has the principle of the state and its agencies understanding and supporting the family unit. Internationally, a more conspicuous rights culture has emerged only in the wake of World War II, with the concerted effort of the United Nations to protect children from the ravages of war. As a subset of wider rights developments, children's rights—like women's rights—have developed their own momentum. The immediate post-war need to protect the freedom of all citizens, including—and perhaps especially—children, against the tyranny of the state, has given way to a more proactive understanding of state-sponsored rights. The changes are evident in comparing the text of the United Nations Declaration on the Rights of the Child 1959 (UNDRC) with that of the United Nations

Convention on the Rights of the Child 1989 (UNCROC).

The role of the state has changed from protecting children within families and intervening only when the family itself is unable to provide or protect the child, to being the central agency in identifying and legally providing empowerment or agency rights. As it was for women in the 1970s, children in the 1990s became political beings to be emancipated from what some advocates believed were oppressive family and relational structures. The role of UNCROC in the New Zealand setting has been critical to the consolidation of this interpretation and appropriation of international developments in children's rights, so that considerable space has been given to examining the Convention and how and why it was ratified by New Zealand, and the consequences of that decision.

It is argued that UNCROC has been used as a rallying point for all sorts of demands and reforms in child and family law and in social attitudes. The use of the Convention by various government agencies and NGOs has tended to polarise the debate in New Zealand, and in the process, deftly politicised the child and 'children's issues'—not in the sense of seeking to inform children and young people of the political process itself, but in the sense that the child is now political and a politicised agent.

This conclusion will be welcomed by many who have worked hard to ensure that children's concerns are a permanent item on the agenda of the nation's policy makers, but the position advanced here is that the public endorsement and advocacy of children's rights is not that simple. Not only are children—like everyone else—relational beings, with their identity and experience intricately bound up in families, but rights themselves are complex concepts which spawn a myriad of overlapping legal problems and social implications.

The political climate surrounding children's rights in New Zealand after 1993—when the Convention was ratified by the National government— has, it is argued, been replete with tension and conflict and has been characterised by a polarising of views between reformers and conservatives. Both have tended to talk over and past one another, and often in relation to consequential, rather than primary issues, e.g. the debate on section 59 of the Crimes Act 1961 (see 3.7). The increase in advocacy and groups committed to rights reform has resulted in a new role for the government that represents a discontinuity with the state's historical interest in children that was apparent until the early 1990s. From implicitly endorsing the authority of the family in the welfare of the child, the state is now positioning itself as the *avant-garde* reformer above, and sometimes against, the traditional family structure. This means the role and authority of the family in the nurture and welfare of children remains confused.

Amongst a discussion of these developments and examples of where and how children and their rights have surfaced in the media and elsewhere, is a suggestion that subsidiarity or sphere sovereignty be reconsidered by future policy makers. In essence, this is not dissimilar to the traditional understanding of children in New Zealand because it respects the authority of the family as primary, but retains roles for both the state and international instruments such as UNCROC in the protection of children. Yet by beginning at the local level, subsidiarity recognises that the primary locus of authority begins with the family, rather than with international instruments developed far from the lived experience of children, their families and communities.

CHAPTER ONE

———————— • ————————

Children in context: an historical overview

Where does authority lie when it comes to raising children? At what point does a person cease to be a child? Are children to be primarily understood through the lens of legal constructs such as *rights?*

A belief that, in New Zealand, these questions are not being debated as they need to be is the motivation for writing this book.

Before looking at the current debate, it is important to consider how views of the child have developed over time. This chapter is an overview of how past societies and eras have viewed children and their education. In some shape or form, many of these understandings persist to the present day, but our view of children is arguably evolving more rapidly now than in the past.

While later chapters will cover specific New Zealand themes, this chapter looks more widely, beginning with the world of the ancient Hebrews and Greeks—societies whose ideas predate any recorded human activity in New Zealand—it takes a quick march through history as a reminder that the way children have been understood across time has always been related to beliefs and circumstances beyond their control. Even so, the importance of the wider (intergenerational) family is an observable fact in all societies.

1.1. THE JUDEO-CHRISTIAN VIEW[1]

In the West, much of the legal and moral understanding of children is derived from ancient Jewish history and early Christian teaching contained in the

Judeo-Christian scriptures (the *Bible)* comprising the First or Old Testament and the New Testament. Strictly speaking, the Jewish *Torah* consists of the first five books of the *Bible* (the Pentateuch), but it also denotes an entire way of life, based upon the covenant that the Hebrew's God is said to have made with his people.

Considered a divinely revealed or inspired text, the Hebrew Scriptures became the foundation for all subsequent Jewish thought. Despite the variety of authors, settings and dates, certain strands stand out; notably, the belief in a single, personal God—creator of the universe and of man—caring for his creation, intervening in history, and sanctioning an elaborate code of social regulations, including instructions on matters relating to children.

To the modern secular mind, the Old Testament is polemical. The covenant revealed in the Ten Commandments (or Decalogue) led to a structured legal order in which all family members were made aware of tribal identity and genealogical roots. Children were considered a gift from God and were to be trained in moral, civil and ceremonial law. To be childless was a reproach.[2]

Children were considered a gift from God and were to be trained in moral, civil and ceremonial law. To be childless was a reproach.

Educating children was a moral duty in devotion to God's Law. The book of Deuteronomy, for example, reveals that the aim was to make men wise by training them from childhood to know the law of Moses. Zeal for the law was interwoven with a knowledge of national history, with the responsibility for raising children being laid on parents (particularly fathers) within the context of family.

This is also evident in the book of Proverbs where education for wisdom is essentially the responsibility of parents. From the prologue—and its 'advice for young men'—to the end, the child is regarded as an integral part of the family. A good son is a source of credit to his parents; an errant son is the cause of shame. The whole family is implicated in the behaviour of each of its members. Much of this learning was by rote and the repetition of precepts. While today the austerity of this society is difficult to appreciate, the law was also intended to protect the weak and vulnerable. Genuine religion, for example, was looking after widows and orphans.[3] The kind of obedience expected from the covenant people involved justice, mercy and humility.[4] Relationships were not to be exploitative, despite the prevalence of slavery in those times. Child sacrifice to foreign deities (such as Molech), common in the ancient world, was a particular abomination.[5] Children were critical to the covenantal understanding of families and their permanence, and so the *Torah* has much to say on their protection, upbringing and nurture.

An often-cited verse is Proverbs 13 verse 24: "He who spares the rod hates his son, but he who loves him is careful to discipline him." Although "rod" is commonly thought of as an instrument of punishment, it was also a symbol of both human and divine authority, and, within broader Hebrew thought and life under the *Torah*, the goal in discipline is not punishment in a vindictive sense, but rather correction and reaffirming what is right. Put another way, to leave a child to his or her own devices was to invite folly and dishonour. Unlike the Greek view, which was cyclic, the Hebrew understanding of time as a linear phenomenon adds poignancy to the notion of permanence and to the preservation of genealogical—and other—aspects of heritage.

The central personality of the New Testament and Christianity, Jesus Christ, claimed to fulfil the Torah, not by dispensing with its strict requirements, but by embodying them in a new covenant relationship, one transcending Jewry to include all gentile (non-Jewish) peoples.[6] In the Gospel accounts, Jesus clearly expressed a love and respect for children, and used their natural innocence and openness to illustrate an attitude necessary for entering 'the Kingdom of God'.[7] The early Christians, too, notably St Paul in writing to the people at Ephesus, spoke of the need for respect and mutual submission to characterise all relationships, including those in the family (husbands and wives) and towards children. Children were to obey their parents while fathers were not to exasperate or provoke their children.[8]

Child sacrifice to foreign deities (such as Molech), common in the ancient world, was a particular abomination.

These principles are no guarantee of harmony, but they present a consistent and important view of interdependence in good families. If families function well (that is, to the mutual benefit of all members), trust and respect will be evident; if not, almost certainly these elements will be lacking.

1.1. Summary

- The family, with its roots in tribal genealogy, is primary.

- In Jewish thought, children are 'a gift from God', and considered an integral part of the family.

- Education was didactic in method (e.g. rote learning but with understanding) and centred upon knowing and keeping the Mosaic law.

- Education was essentially the responsibility of parents in response to the requirements of covenant law.

- The central figure of the New Testament, Jesus Christ, accorded children a place of honour, and used their natural innocence to illustrate an attitude necessary for entering the 'Kingdom of God'.

- The later epistles (e.g. Paul's letter to the Ephesians) speak of the need for relationships between parents and children to be characterised by mutual respect.

1.2. Greek thought[9]

During the ninth and tenth centuries BC, various tribes migrated from Central Europe into Greece in successive waves. Major developments in Greek education were associated with times of political change which resulted in new ways of training the young.

The Jewish and Christian traditions were influenced by various aspects of Greek thought and culture. For example, the methods and purpose of the religious and moral instruction of the son by the father, which is a recurring theme in the book of Proverbs, is given expression in Homeric literature. Phoenix, for example, reared Achilles to manhood with love, and taught him the things that win men distinction; war and debate.[10]

For both the Spartans and Athenians, the purpose of education was not primarily intellectual curiosity, but rather the practical matter of preparing a boy physically, mentally and morally for adult activities in service as a citizen-member of the state. In the Spartan state, however, boys were trained to be soldier-citizens, with a strong emphasis on efficiency and exercise for warfare. The Athenians of the fifth century BC were more progressive, training boys not just for war, but also for peace, using literature and music to help develop a finer aesthetic sense. Athens was transformed from an agricultural community into a major maritime power, democracy was established (instead of oligarchy), and following the victory over Persia, its dominance as a major power was secured. A 'progressive education' was needed to equip youths as orators in the states of the empire. Rhetoric and the ability to read and write were necessary for democracy to work—a situation not previously faced.

The Sophists extended the range and method of ordinary state and private schools from gymnastics, music, reading and writing, to cover a demand for more intellectual subjects: dialectics, rhetoric, physical science, mathematics and philosophy. They were employed to teach young men wisdom through special training in literature and the rhetorical arts. The first Sophist was the sceptic humanist, Protagoras (490-421 BC). It was Protagoras who developed the subjectivist thesis that 'man is the measure of all things', i.e. all knowledge is relative. This was to become a significant concept in education, although it had been rejected in early Hebrew thought and would later be rejected by medieval scholars.

For both the Spartans and Athenians, the purpose of education was not primarily intellectual curiosity, but rather the practical matter of preparing a boy physically, mentally and morally for adult activities in service as a citizen-member of the state.

In his search for principles governing conduct, Socrates (469-399 BC) concluded not only that virtue *was* knowledge, but that virtue was teachable, and that men would be better citizens if they were not ignorant of what constituted a virtuous person. The methodology he developed sought to discover the true nature of an abstract thing, e.g. virtue, by searching for its correct definition and focusing on its moral rather than physical properties.

The historian, essayist and soldier, Xenophon (427-355 BC), accepted the Socratic precept that to make a man good was to make him intelligent, but goodness was defined in the more Spartan terms of practical use, rather than as a virtue. A more advanced form of Greek thought occurred in Plato's writings. For him, education was a process of interaction between the individual and society, whereby collective wisdom and virtue condition and direct individual evolution. The state is simply the soul of man writ large, and children entered into its collective wisdom through exposure to a study of literature, science and philosophy. "In childhood and youth, their study and what philosophy they should learn should be suited to their tender years; during this period while they are growing up towards manhood, the chief and special care should be given to their bodies that they may have them to use in the service of philosophy. As life advances and the intellect begins to mature, let them increase the gymnastics of the soul . . ."[11]

Despite its relative advance on Spartan thought, Plato's ideal society remained highly stratified; each person was trained to play a role in society to which they were best suited.

Another highly significant thinker in the succession of Greek writers was Aristotle (384-322 BC) who accepted many of his mentor's (Plato's) ideas but developed them in a fuller appreciation of character formation as well as in the interplay of inherited and environmental influences. Primarily, however, children were to be trained in the intellectual disciplines because they were prone to be guided by feelings rather than reason.

In the *Politics,* Aristotle explained education in relation to the state; indeed, the state is prior to family and even the individual, ". . . since [he argued] the whole is of necessity prior to the part; for example, if the whole body be destroyed, there will be no foot or hand . . . . The proof that the state is a creation of nature and prior to the individual is that the individual, when isolated, is not self-sufficing; and therefore he is like a part in relation to the whole."[12] It followed that the social element of education was subordinate to politics and public life, even though individuals may focus on personal intellectual and aesthetic development. The object was training for goodness and excellence throughout life. The state was the school of the citizen, initially emphasising physical growth before the 'irrational parts of the soul'—the appetites and passions—before (finally) focusing on reason. Character was the sum total of the acquired habits of the soul. In the Alexandrian Period (300–1 BC), Greek scholarship was fostered by the Ptolemies with the establishment of public libraries and profound intellectual inquiry. The fruits of this knowledge and wisdom were character and service.

1.2. SUMMARY

- Throughout its long history, Greece's classical writers, with wide variation, emphasised the general importance of education to the well-being of political and civil society.

- The state was primary.

- For the Spartans, the purpose of education was to prepare youths for military service.

- From the fifth century BC, however, the Sophists responded to a new desire in Athens for special training in language, rhetoric, physical science, mathematics and philosophy.

- The Sophist, Protagoras, instituted the idea that 'man is the measure of all things', thus decisively moving beyond previous epistemological notions of transcendent authority. This profoundly affected subsequent educational, political and social thought.

- The famous Athenian, Socrates, connected knowledge with virtue and sought to instruct citizens to obey the laws of the city and live moral lives, while later, Plato favoured a stratified education emphasising specific character virtues related to the role for which individuals were best suited.

- Aristotle refined many aspects of previous Greek thought. He understood that children required special training, and in order to serve the state, this process needed to accommodate physical expression, restrain appetite and passion, and culminate in an appreciation of reason (i.e. body, soul and mind).

- In the evolution of educational thought, Jewish ideas became infused with Hellenistic notions, especially the relationship between wisdom, training and social order.

1.3. EDUCATION IN THE ROMAN REPUBLIC AND EMPIRE

According to the poet and author, Virgil, Rome was founded by Romulus in 753 BC. At its height, the Roman Empire reached from the North Sea to the Atlas Mountains and from the Atlantic coast to the River Euphrates—an area today comprising 25 countries and spanning several language and people groups. The fabric of Western civilisation is interwoven with threads of Roman polity, law, language, engineering and architecture and its adoption of the Christian faith. Under Constantine, the empire also propelled Christianity from a persecuted sect to an established institutional faith.

Rome's rise was founded on discipline and virtue, including the pietas of dutiful behaviour, frugalitas and simplicitas. These were embodied in various deities e.g. Jupiter, Juno and Minerva, and merged with Hellenism—expressions of wisdom—and Christianity, as virtues of right living. In other areas too, the Romans demonstrated an ability to assimilate and absorb surrounding cultures. The cross-pollination of Greco-Roman art, for example, flourished under Octavian (Augustus) when the literature of Horace, Propertius and Virgil led to a restoration of the Golden Age of Rome and the *pax Romana*.

As with the Greeks, education in the Roman Empire was a political tool to equip citizens for public service. Whether for civil or military duties, serving the state was central. The emphasis was on grammar and rhetoric, but as the empire colonised new peoples, state support for education and the general patronage of learning increased. In civic municipalities, libraries and chairs of rhetoric were set up and funded out of the public treasury.

The new eclecticism embraced both religious and secular learning and led to education assuming a commanding importance throughout the empire.

The appropriation of Hellenistic thought and its role in advancing the intellectual and moral basis of the empire greatly assisted the spread of education. In Hadrian's era (117-138 AD), a passionate embracing of everything Greek led to the establishment of the Athenæum as a meeting place for influential men of letters, and eventually Athens became the chief centre of learning in the Roman world.

Reconciling Greek and Roman ideas with those of Christianity was a difficult task but one successfully accomplished during the time of Clement (160-215 AD).[13] This accommodation led to the formation of a Catechetical School in the cosmopolitan city of Alexandria, where the antagonisms were moderated by adopting a sympathetic attitude to the religion and culture of the past. The new eclecticism embraced both religious and secular learning and led to education assuming a commanding importance throughout the empire.

The Catechetical school assisted in reconciling the Church to scholarship and in propelling ancient learning into the Middle Ages. By the time of Constantine (320 AD), the official persecution of Christians had ended, and scholars of philosophy, grammar, rhetoric and jurisprudence excelled in the eastern city of Constantinople, the new capital of the empire. Religious and civil ideas of virtue had merged into a philosophy of schooling that decisively shaped how children were to be raised and educated.

1.3. SUMMARY

- In Roman educational thought, as it had been in Greece, individual development was secondary to serving the state. Rome expanded through conquest, making an ethic of service over self central for all citizens.

- Education was about equipping citizens to serve the state, and formal learning focused on the simple virtues of self-sacrifice and duty.

- In the long evolution from kingdom to republic and empire, Hellenistic and Christian culture were readily assimilated into Roman policy and practice—including education.

- The embracing of Christianity by imperial Rome propelled the former sect into all aspects of national polity and cultural life.

- The primacy of Christian teaching in late Roman times, including the use of grammar and rhetorical instruction from the classics as well as the Scriptures and other Christian writings, evolved into formal monastic contexts during the Middle Ages.

- Beginning with the Catechetical school in Alexandria, Roman schools laid a basis for what would later become known in the West as a classical education.

- Rome's impact in politics, law, language and architecture was extensive and indelibly woven into the tapestry of subsequent developments in Western civilisation.

1.4. MIDDLE AGES TO ENLIGHTENMENT

The Middle Ages (450–1400 AD) are often considered a period of minimal creativity, religious control and feudalism. Certainly the church was dominant with the emergence of a strong papacy, the rise of monastic orders and numerous doctrinal disputes, but there were significant developments in this period in literacy, an accompanying rise in vernacular literature— usually associated with *Bible* translation—and the beginnings of modern universities.

Thomas Aquinas (1225-1274 AD), a prominent medieval scholar, extended the Greek concept of the state beyond the secular realm. The complete human society, he believed, had an ecclesiastical as well as a secular basis, and when it came to duty and obligation, the latter was subordinate to the former. Aquinas attempted to reconcile an Aristotelian view with the spiritual and ethical requirements of Roman Catholicism. By the later Middle Ages when Aquinas was writing, learning was beginning to show signs of revival, and within the church, organised groups were meeting in institutions that later became universities. These 'schools' adopted a method combining Greek philosophy with the requirements of Catholicism, the hallmark of scholasticism.

Castiglione emphasised training in edict, manners and a sense of duty. Significantly, too, the infant became a predominant theme in Renaissance art, which often combined the themes of original sin and original innocence to great effect.

Duty, eternal and human, shaped the nurture of children in subsequent centuries, and the notions of obedience and obligation were sanctioned by Divine Law as directly relevant to the attainment of man's eternal end. In the medieval schema, a child quickly became an adult, as the French historian Philippe Ariès explains: "Medieval civilization had forgotten the Paideia of the ancients and knew nothing as yet of modern education. . . . as soon as he was weaned, or soon after, the child became the natural companion of the adult."[14]

The Renaissance, however, reconnected thinkers in the Age of Discovery with the rigours of classical Greco-Roman thought in a more secular and refined manner than the scholastics had done. Cultivating the 'man of manners', for example was a theme developed during the Renaissance. In the writings of Baldassare Castiglione (1478-1529), especially *The Book of the Courtier*, the idea of the moral character and ideal courtier were espoused. The courtier was modest, self-effacing and virtuous: ". . . Therefore little speaking, much doing, and not praising a man's own self in commendable deeds, dissembling them after an honest sort increases both the one virtue and the other in a person."[15] Castiglione emphasised training in edict, manners and a sense of duty. Significantly, too, the infant became a predominant theme in Renaissance art, which often combined the themes of original sin and original innocence to great effect.

The Reformation of the sixteenth century ritualised religious training and equated virtue with personal religious belief. Protestant fathers were encouraged to participate by catechising as well as repeating sermons to their children and household servants. During the sixteenth century, literacy was encouraged so as to promote *Bible* reading and many reformers insisted on schemes of compulsory education.

We see, then, in the 1500s the genesis of a developmental understanding of children:

> Children were subject to their parents' command until they left to take up employment or married. Urban children were often sent to serve in other households, but rural children were employed from an early age in farm labour. The concept of childhood as a carefree and innocent age developed among the privileged class only late in the century. Children were not segregated from the adult world, they dressed like adults, were addressed like adults . . . while ten- and twelve-year-olds joined in carnivals or political riots. Yet adolescence was recognized as a distinct stage of human development where youth needed outlets for its exuberant spirit. These were provided, as we have mentioned, by carnivals and other festivals.[16]

Very gradually, then, a view began to evolve that comprehended the value of children, coupled with a knowledge of how they learn.

The highly-trained and literate Jesuits of the Counter-Reformation were also serious about education and a saying ascribed to them—"show me the boy at age seven, and I'll show you the man"—captures the reinvigorated emphasis on moral and philosophical training within the church, despite the inroads of Protestantism. In the struggle for Christian Europe, Catholic and Protestant leaders alike developed principles of moral education which were remarkably similar. Behavioural training should begin in infancy and children constantly supervised to forestall immodest sexual behaviour. They should also learn to keep a respectful social distance from adults.[17]

Protecting children from their impulses and training them in modesty and conscience became distinctive features of childhood as being conceptually separated from adulthood. More significant however, in creating a new view of children, were philosophers, some of whom specifically understood that original sin—including guilt—and innocence had become impediments to an objective assessment of the nature of the child.

Although not specifically emphasising children or their education, the

English philosopher, Thomas Hobbes (1588-1679), developed a systematic—and in the present context, a helpful—theory of the 'state of nature'. His major work, *Leviathan* (1651), appeared immediately after the English Civil War and during the Interregnum. Hobbes developed a theory of the 'state of nature' which referred to what human beings would be like if they lived without any form of government or society—the concept is, of course, hypothetical as human societies have always existed in some shape or form. Even so, the state of nature provided a starting point for developing a political philosophy which specifically argued in favour of a sovereign state led by a monarch. Hobbes believed that men—in the state of nature—without the restraints of sovereign government, would be in a state of war, and for him, war (*warre*) had a specific meaning.[18]

Hobbes paints a bleak picture of men in the state of nature. Without the sovereign, there was a complete subjectivity of value, meaning each person became his own arbiter of right and wrong.[19] Without the restraint upon appetite and drives provided by political society ". . . every man is Enemy to every man . . ." and this led to the phrase often associated with Hobbes, namely, that life was ". . . solitary, poor, nasty, brutish and short".[20] Accordingly, human beings in the state of nature were not altruistic, and political society is not only necessary, but in order to be decisive, its power had to rest in the hands of the monarch. By implication, children needed to be trained, and it was significant that in his first post-Oxford employment, Hobbes was employed to tutor the son of William Cavendish, the Earl of Devonshire.

The *Leviathan* may seem far departed from the issue of children's rights in the early twenty-first century, yet the concept of a state of nature remains relevant. "What are people really like?" or more specifically, "what are children really like?" and "what is a child?"

John Locke (1632-1704), a contemporary of Hobbes, also wrote on the state of nature. It was Locke in the latter part of the seventeenth century who moved philosophy forward by initiating classical empiricism. Unlike Hobbes, however, Locke had specific things to say about children, childhood and learning. He didn't develop a theory of child nurture *per se*, but important understandings of children emerge from his wider concern for knowledge, knowing and the formation of political society.

Locke was the first Western writer to detail a theory of empirical (sensory) thought and learning. His voluminous *Essay Concerning Human*

Understanding (1690) was a critical assessment of the limits of human reason, and it is from him that we first appreciated how simple experiences became associated with a developmental understanding of learning.

In Locke's writing, the educator was to carefully observe the character of children and to guide them in the path of virtue. His focus was the training of the seventeenth century gentleman—meaning his ideas are not easily translated into the modern context of mass schooling. According to Locke, the child did not possess innate goodness or moral truth; it was education that transformed the self-centred individual into an informed and aristocratic young man. His belief in the transforming power of education was similar to Plato's, and it frequently appears today in many Western societies when 'more education' is seen to be the answer to social problems. In New Zealand, for example, 'education campaigns' are seen by many, especially politicians, to provide the solution to the road toll, reducing teenage pregnancy, and quelling tensions over the Treaty of Waitangi. For both Plato and Locke, knowledge, virtue and right action were a direct function of education. Significantly, however, the early Christian notion outlined in Paul's letter to the Romans presented an altogether different view; there was no necessary connection between knowing what was right, and doing what was right—the continual tension characterised the human condition.

According to Locke, the child did not possess innate goodness or moral truth; it was education that transformed the self-centred individual into an informed and aristocratic young man.

In the era before mass education, Locke emphasised the traditional view of education, primarily within the family and within the context of self-restraint and discipline. Children were innocent, but in need of careful training: "Liberty and Indulgence can do no Good to Children. Their Want of Judgement makes them stand in need of Restraint and Discipline."[21]

The later Enlightenment philosopher, Jean-Jacques Rousseau (1712-1778), challenged Locke's views. In rejecting the mechanistic presuppositions of Hobbes and Locke, Rousseau developed a naturalistic approach to understanding children, and proposed a different 'state of nature' in the process.[22] His major work, *Émile*, was published the same year as the *Social Contract* (1762) In essence, the child, according to Rousseau, is naturally good and made wicked only by its environment.

As with Locke, Rousseau accepted that knowledge comes from the senses, and that children should engage actively with a well-ordered environment and learn by interacting with it. He was perhaps the first thinker in Western thought to advance the virtue of learning by doing; a pragmatism more closely associated in later times with William James and John Dewey. He also understood that development refers to what happens to living things as they move forward across time. In rejecting the mechanistic assumptions of Hobbes and Locke, Rousseau saw the child as a self-regulating and self-motivating organism. Children were not merely adults in miniature, they developed according to qualitative activity and change. Nurture of the child implied a systematic drawing out of internal capacities, rather than imposition from external sources.

"the fundamental principle of all morality . . . is that man is a naturally good creature, who loves justice and order; that there is no original perversity in the human heart, and that the first movements of nature are always right."

Rousseau received little formal schooling and abandoned his five children. Nevertheless, *Émile* consolidated his fame, but led to his ostracism because its central idea was that the child is naturally good. The truly free man, Rousseau argued, ". . . wants only what he can do and does what he pleases. That is my fundamental maxim. It need only be applied to childhood for all the rules of education to flow from it."[23] The goal was autonomous agency or to be the master of one's own imagination and destiny. This strongly naturalistic philosophy angered authorities because Rousseau was effectively denying the existence of original sin. In response, he reiterated that "the fundamental principle of all morality . . . is that man is a naturally good creature, who loves justice and order; that there is no original perversity in the human heart, and that the first movements of nature are always right."[24]

He recalled, in *Confessions*, an incident that occurred in 1749. In the autumn of that year, Rousseau went to Vincennes, and in transit had an experience similar to a religious conversion. Strolling along the road, he happened to see the announcement of an essay contest on the subject, 'Has the Revival of the Sciences and the Arts helped to Purify or to Corrupt Morals?' "Instantly [he says], I saw the universe, and I became another man. . . . If only I had been able to write down a quarter of what I felt under that tree, with what clarity I would have pointed out all of the contradictions of our social system! With what force I would have exposed all the abuses of our institutions! With what simplicity I would have demonstrated that man is naturally good, and that it is only through these institutions that he becomes wicked!"[25]

This is revealing not only with respect to Rousseau, but of a belief system that has been enormously significant in shaping modern constructs of children. As will be explored in later chapters, the idea of empowerment rights rests on a state of nature very similar to that espoused by Rousseau centuries before; empowerment of the child is a self-evident good because it enables him/her to express that which is both natural and desirable, unencumbered by parental, adult, institutional or other authority.

Rousseau's belief in innate goodness, coupled with a penetrating criticism of the *ancien régime*—particularly its social and political institutions—led him to conclude that society prevented individuals from reaching their potential. It was Rousseau who first and most powerfully asserted the modern democratic belief in the infinite capacities of the ordinary man for development and improvement. Not only has this thought been the catalyst for democratic change, but it bears a striking resemblance to modern views of politicised children's rights, and the concurrent belief in theories of self-potentiation in education.[26]

While Locke positioned the child as a determining factor in the educational process, it was Rousseau who stated that belief more emphatically and arrestingly than had anyone else until that time. The *a priori* correctness of children, compared with adult 'error', was well stated in *Émile;* "We are unable to put ourselves in the child's place, we fail to enter into his thoughts, we invest him with our own ideas, and while we are following our own chain of reasoning, we merely fill his head with errors and absurdities."[27]

Of even greater significance was Rousseau's legacy: "His influence, and the influence of those whom he influenced, is at work today in every school in this country and wherever Western civilisation has penetrated. He it was who set it finally beyond question that education must accommodate itself to the child, and that the child must not be accommodated to a pre-determined, adult-centred system of education."[28]

Along with the earlier Locke and Hobbes—and many others[29]—during the eighteenth century, Rousseau helped facilitate the vast revolution in Western thought known as the Enlightenment. This was based on an ultimate reliance in the perfectibility of man through reason, and is understandably also known as the Age of Reason.[30]

The writings of German philosopher, Immanuel Kant (1724-1804), captured the Age of Reason by developing an alternative to the empiricism of Locke. For Kant, 'pure reason' was *a priori* reason, or that which can be known by reason prior to and apart from anything derived from experience. Kant's rationalism heavily influenced the eminent twentieth century developmental psychologist, Jean Piaget, who began with the central epistemological question, "What do children know and how do they acquire knowledge?" Unlike Locke, Kant asserted that the mind at birth could not be blank, for if it were, human beings could never acquire the ability to reason.

In a broader sense, the intellectual advances during this century also made possible such dramatic events as the French and American Revolutions. No less revolutionary was the new humanism which the Age of Reason fostered. Although the individual was elevated to a position of ultimate importance—resulting in a new faith in the possibilities of man—the state was the natural agent of progress. The French Encyclopaedists, for example, demanded a system of secular schools controlled by the state.[31] The influence of the church and the nobility declined in the face of such monumental change. The industrial period which followed (1750-1850) also created a need for mass schooling and new ways of understanding and nurturing children.

1.4. SUMMARY

- The medieval scholastic, Thomas Aquinas, reconciled an Aristotelian view with the spiritual and ethical requirements of Roman Catholicism. Obedience and obligation became important in the civic and spiritual training of children.

- During the Renaissance, classical (Greco-Roman) thought was 'rediscovered', and a more expansive and secular view of education emerged.

- During and after the sixteenth century, Protestantism re-emphasised the spiritual state of individuals, including the nurture and moral training of children. The need for biblical literacy resulted in new educational developments, mostly related to the churches.

- The Enlightenment of the eighteenth century drew heavily on writers such as Hobbes, Locke, and especially Rousseau. The Age of Reason, as it was also known, challenged the orthodoxy of religion and posited a new faith in the perfectibility of the human condition. This in turn led to new ways of understanding children and their schooling; processes that were aided considerably by the wider economic, political and social changes of the great industrial age which followed.

1.5. CHILD DEVELOPMENT IN THE TWENTIETH CENTURY

The phenomenon of universal schooling in the late nineteenth and early twentieth centuries was a by-product of industrialisation, urbanisation and the new demand for specialist skills to meet a mechanised labour market. Schools also assumed a new role as training agencies for both industry and academic advancement.[32] Education was to become core government business in Western societies. In the UK alone, for example, a mere £0.17m was spent on education in 1840, compared with £65m in 1940, and £16,681m in 1985.[33]

Not only was mass education assuming increasing political importance, but by the middle of the century, infant mortality was dropping and life expectancy was growing. In the Middle Ages, one child in three died in infancy and general mortality rates remained high until and during the industrial period. For example, in England and Wales in 1841-45, there were—across all age groups—21.4 deaths per 1,000 of the population, compared with 11.7 in 1981-85.[34] Advances in medicine throughout the century greatly lowered the risk of serious or fatal illness in all age groups, extended life expectancy and helped reduce infant mortality rates.

At the dawn of the new century, one educator critically aware of the scope of social and economic change—and the need for democracy to adapt—was John Dewey (1859-1952). Dewey is generally recognised as the most renowned American educator of the twentieth century. His work spanned seven decades and provided much of the philosophical framework for progressive educational reform.

Building on the insights of people like Rousseau, Dewey was a relativist. He opposed the idea of fixed-value systems; truth was conceived as a dynamic series of ideas, beliefs, and other processes which were the instruments by which the purposes of life could be achieved. The school is an organism of social change and 'progressive' if it adapts and responds to the fluidity of ever-changing needs. Dewey's focus on the instruments of social change and the need for schools to adapt means he is most closely associated with the instrumentalist-progressive educators, of whom he remains doyen.

The alternative Dewey favoured was more fluid; one in which skills and problem solving were practical responses to a changing society. In so doing he shifted the centre of gravity in education away from formalism and onto the child.

Dewey attacked the formalism of Victorian education, which in itself was an extension of the tutor/pupil approach so favoured in earlier eras by the aristocracy. This system, with its well-defined subjects, regarded knowledge as fixed units of historically tested material. The alternative Dewey favoured was more fluid; one in which skills and problem solving were practical responses to a changing society. In so doing he shifted the centre of gravity in education away from formalism and onto the child.

While primarily a philosopher, Dewey was one of many very significant theorists influencing child development. The list of others is long and includes—in no particular order—A.S. Neill, Jean Piaget, B.F. Skinner, Sigmund Freud, Percy Nunn, Cyril Burt, Benjamin Bloom, Urie Bronfrenbrenner, Albert Bandura, Lawrence Kohlberg and Carl Rogers. The spirit of educational inquiry which gained momentum with Dewey became a sustained feature of twentieth century thought.

In the voluminous writings of these theorists, the child became the subject of analysis which combined aspects of philosophical, psychological and sociological inquiry. From Freud's analysis of the subconscious, to

Skinner's programmed learning—*operant conditioning*—to Bandura's social learning theory, Neill's practical experiments in child freedom, Piaget and Bloom's insights into child learning and educational evaluation, respectively, and Rogers' *self-potentiation*, the child came of age as a distinct category of human being. The formalism which Dewey criticised was steadily displaced throughout the century, first by the 'play way' of the 1920s, then by the 'scientific' insights of a new sub-discipline, educational psychology. This continued with progressive education, beginning in the 1930s, and continued after the mid-1960s in the work of the neo-Marxists and Paulo Freire in his key work, *Pedagogy of the Oppressed*. The most recent attacks on any remaining vestiges of traditionalism have come from the poststructural deconstructionism of Michel Foucault and Jacques Derrida (see 3.6).

Despite the huge variety of theories, child development became a recognised and coherent phenomenon among behavioural psychologists. *Development*—where change is seen longitudinally—and as a result of sequential steps—is a relatively recent historical understanding. It was only during the last century that epistemological explorations into theories of learning fruitfully met with social, political, economic and demographic forces to produce the changes which resulted in categories such as 'childhood', and sub-categories such as 'adolescence' becoming recognised as distinct developmental phases in the human life cycle.

Until then, the worth of children was measured largely in terms of economic rather than educational or emotional value.[35] The close relationship between parents and children was essentially based on economic interdependence. Children played an integral part in the family economy. As soon as they were able, children would be handed a spinning card, a cleaning or a gardening tool, and expected to work. It was not until well into the twentieth century that childhood was clearly identified and seen as a period where formal education in schools needed to occur.

The battle for hearts, minds and allegiance has arisen along with the technology upon which it feeds. The modernist assumptions that emerged from writers such as Charles Darwin and Friedrich Nietzsche, in the late nineteenth century, and positivism, early in the twentieth century, seemingly dealt a decisive blow to any remaining vestiges of religion, and even classical assumptions of morality and education, while a pervasive new social ethic reduced the essence of being human more to a matter of individual choice, rather than familial or other connections.

By the end of the twentieth century, education in Western societies had become dominated by the imperatives of skills rather than content, and the formation of new attitudes, including human rights. Maximising potential became a prominent goal as did state-aided assistance for identified minorities. Curricula were tailored to meet these new goals and shape desirable social attitudes such as tolerance, diversity and inclusion.

The old certainties have been undermined, but the questions of morality that Meno raised in his dialogue with Socrates remain; namely, can virtue be taught, or is it something that arises from natural aptitude or instinct? The new foci in education may discard or obscure that question, but what it means to be human—and, by implication, how we view and understand children—remains central. To avoid society collapsing into what Hobbes described as a "war of every man against every man", an ethic of restraint has to be present. History reveals that this has primarily—but not exclusively—been attended to most closely in all societies, in the training and nurture of children.

By the end of the twentieth century, education in Western societies had become dominated by the imperatives of skills rather than content, and the formation of new attitudes, including human rights.

In the decades after World War II, children came to be understood not just as innocents requiring special protection and nurture, but as individual citizens with rights and, in philosophical parlance, as autonomous agents and rights bearers. The implications of this evolution in the New Zealand context form the substance of this book. Before shifting the focus in this direction, however, it is first helpful to consider the historical setting in which children's rights first emerged in the West towards the end of the nineteenth century.

1.5. SUMMARY

- The twentieth century understanding of child development evolved in the context of falling infant mortality rates, mass schooling, and greater investment in education as a core government activity.

- The American educator, John Dewey, was profoundly influential in rethinking schooling and its role in modern democracy. The instrumentalist view assisted in reconceptualising the child as a sensitive learner responsive to his or her environment.

- After 1945, the mature expression of these ideas resulted in a more active view of the child as an individual and citizen.

1.6. THE ORIGINS OF CHILDREN'S RIGHTS

Historically, and particularly up until the sixteenth century, Western societies depicted the child as an incapable member of the family who had little inherent value, except for his labour. In the eighteenth and nineteenth centuries, children were beginning to be seen as 'the future', but were not given individual rights. Until then they were generally considered adults in miniature, and before the abolition of slavery, children, like adults, were bought and sold in large numbers.

In the puritan New World settlements, for example, children were a ready source of cheap labour. In November 1619, a request was placed by the Virginia Company to the Lord Mayor of London for 100 children—of both sexes—aged 12 years and over. Having thanked the mayor for his previous supplies, a company spokesman made a further request for child labour:

> . . . we pray your Lordship and the rest in pursuit of your former so pious actions to renew your like favours and furnish us again with one hundred more for the next spring. Our desire is that we may have them of twelve years old and upward with allowance of three pounds apiece for their transportation and forty shillings apiece for their apparel as was formerly granted. They shall be apprentices the boys till they come to twenty-one years of age the girls till the like age or till they be married, and afterwards they shall be placed as tenants upon the public land with best conditions where they shall have houses with stock of corn or cattle to begin with, and afterward the moiety

of all increase and profit whatsoever. As so we leave this motion to your honourable and grave consideration.[36]

In a Declaration by the Privy Council the following year it was stated, ". . . if any of them [those sent to Virginia] shall be found obstinate to resist or otherwise to disobey such directions as shall be given in this behalf, we do likewise hereby authorize such as shall have the charge of this service to imprison, punish, and dispose any of those children".[37]

In relation to the wide historical coverage of this chapter, children's rights are relatively modern legal and social constructs with their origins as recent as the late 1800s.

Officially-sanctioned exploitation, as described above, was common until the Industrial Revolution, when the plight of working-class people, including and perhaps especially children, became a matter of obvious need in the newly-created centres of burgeoning population. An 1803 census of beggars in London, for example, showed that of the estimated 15,000 on the streets, more than 9,000 were children. The Poor Law provisions to rescue deprived children through day schools provided a prototype for the later English state school system, but before the era of mass schooling, attempts to deal with such a widespread problem were piecemeal.

The plight of unfortunate children trapped in circumstances beyond their control became an important theme in late Victorian literature. Life in the cities, for example, was well documented in fictional accounts such as *Oliver Twist*. Oliver's mother was unmarried, had "shoes worn to pieces", and died shortly after he was born. His prospects were pitiful—an illegitimate child, orphaned at birth, and "left to the tender mercies of churchwardens and overseers." While *Oliver Twist* is fiction, Dickens was describing a particular reality and, as an author, not alone in his criticism of the treatment of children. In Charles Kingsley's *The Water Babies,* for example, 10-year-old Tom's lot working for Mr Grimes, the chimneysweep, was not greatly different to that of Oliver, although his prospects of having apprentices and relaxing in the public house were more promising. He, too, was fatherless, at the mercy of cruel adults, and had a physically demanding job. Climbing the dark flues rubbed his knees and elbows raw and filled his eyes with soot.

The final step in response to such realities was to make schooling compulsory. The squalor made mass schooling expedient.[38] This watershed development not only kept children out of the workplace and off the streets, but also released parents from the burden of custody, and in the wider development of Western societies it consolidated a permanent separation of adulthood and childhood and gave the state a greater role in caring and providing for children.

At the beginning of the eighteenth century, with many thousands of children desperately poor, the administration of relief in Britain was still based around the outdated Poor Laws of 1597–98 and 1601. The 1597–98 Act empowered overseers to erect a poorhouse out of the poor rates. Parish overseers were to provide work for paupers and had the authority to apprentice poor children. Improvements came slowly, mainly in the form of factory and industrial legislation limiting the age and hours of work for children,[39] and through benchmark reports such as Edwin Chadwick's *Enquiry into the Sanitary Conditions of the Labouring Population of Great Britain,* in 1842.

By the mid-1850s, Britain's prosperity also meant unsafe factories, dangerous equipment, hard manual labour and abject poverty. Reform remained piecemeal,[40] and children were among those most vulnerable to exploitation and unsanitary conditions. Not surprisingly in this context, the first rights for children were protection rights—those aimed at the 'guttersnipes', as in Kingsley's novel. New understandings of rights emerged within wider and incremental social reforms.

In America, however, children's rights developed against pervasive fears of family dissolution. According to researcher Akira Morita,

> In the process of the development of the child welfare system in the United States, the concept of children's rights first arose in the wave of progressive social reform that took place at the turn of the [twentieth] century. The reformers were alarmed by the preliminary signs of trouble and breakdown they saw occurring in families against a backdrop of rapid industrialisation, urbanisation, and the influx of immigrants into the country that dated from the mid-nineteenth century.
>
> The power of the family, while the pioneering hope of twentieth-century America, was also an institution facing imminent crisis. In the midst of this duality of hope and crisis, the reformers—known as 'child savers'— concentrated all of their efforts on the establishment of a legal network (*parens patriae*) which would function as a substitute parent for the children abandoned in cities, those struggling in dark factories and coal mines, as well as for prone-delinquent [sic] children whose parents could not control them.

The reformers called the objective benefits, that should be given to children by this network, "children's rights."

Alexander McKelway, one of the reformers, defined children as having "the right to be dependent." One court practitioner cleverly described this by saying, "the juvenile's right is not the right to liberty, but the right to custody."

In other words, the child welfare laws in the first half of the twentieth century attempted to reconstruct the endangered organic parent-child structure of protection and dependence by creating a framework for the exercise of parental authority by the law. This artificial system of legal fiction was known as *parens patriae*. The right to protection in this context was therefore more accurately described as the need for protection being fulfilled within the legal framework, and can be referred to as the child's objective legal entitlement . . . these "rights" were not subjective rights in the classic sense which makes self-determination a prerequisite.

Equating children's needs with rights in this way was not limited to the United States, but developed as a common symbol of child welfare and its legal paternalism in Western countries in the twentieth century . . . [41]

The rights referred to here were protection rights. As had always been the case, children were viewed as the responsibility of their parents, but where there was abuse, or where a child was orphaned or abandoned, the state had a role to play. As in *Oliver Twist,* children in the nineteenth century were frequently portrayed as innocent and vulnerable. Many of the changes in nurture, dress, institutions, practices and in law (rights) have evolved around this image of the child. The special vulnerability of the child also resulted in the recognition that not all children were equally well cared for, and that when the family suffered the loss of a parent, external agencies may get involved. Marriage, parenting and the welfare of the child was another theme explored by Swedish pioneering rights advocate, Ellen Key.[42]

In what American historian, Linda Gordon, has called the "Progressive-era transformation of child protection" (1900-1920), child protectors adopted the framework of prevention, complete with a new medical model; child neglect was 'a preventable social disease' which could be eradicated if the health of families was improved. She explains,

. . . The new conception of neglect was diagnosed in terms of *family* pathology. Although this pathology might be seen to be rooted in poverty, racial or ethnic inferiority, and the degradation of urban life, the Progressive-era child protectors were mainly drawn to the opposite causal conclusion: that family weakness was at the root of larger social problems. Ameliorative proposals were always aimed at reforming families, not society. In this context, prevention meant protecting children from harm by disciplining parents. As a result, child-protection policy did not significantly move away from its law-enforcement emphasis.[43]

It is significant that these early responses to child care retained the primacy of the family. Neither state nor charitable bodies, it was commonly believed, would act against the widely-accepted and agreed-upon interests of the family. Gradually, however, new legal entities, children's rights, became part of a wider and evolving understanding of both families and child welfare, and with this, came greater state involvement and new law. Towards the end of the nineteenth century and in the early decades of the new century, considerable initiative concerning children's welfare lay with charitable organisations—groups that would much later be known as Non-Governmental Organisations, or NGOs; but the state played an increasing role in many Western nations—including New Zealand, as issues such as arresting childhood diseases and lowering infant mortality rates understandably came to be seen as legitimate concerns of the state, and in the public interest.

The idea of an international association to protect children was born in 1913. This was followed after the Great War with the formation in 1919 of a Committee for the Protection of Children by the newly-formed League of Nations, and with the help of the Red Cross, English woman, Eglantyne Jebb, founded the Save the Children International Union in Geneva in January 1920. Save the Children set forth five principles aimed at ensuring that every child had the essential conditions for his or her full personal development. These were formally adopted by the League as the Declaration of the Rights of the Child—also known as the Geneva Declaration—on 26 September 1924.[44] Jebb's major concern was the principle of universality according to which all children had certain rights, irrespective of their nationality or race. This was very much a forward-thinking view which led to the first expression of children's rights in international law. The Geneva Declaration, however, did not specifically mention rights—except in its title—and has been criticised as treating the child as an object rather than as a person.

By the mid-1930s, the status and care of children in the West had become the criterion for judging the worth of a society and how one generation cared for the next. The innocence of childhood routinely symbolised justice and mercy, and, in the new spirit of internationalism, children perhaps even represented a new hope of salvation. These ideals were readily expressed through the work of charitable institutions and in domestic law.

1.6. SUMMARY

- Children's rights are a relatively recent historical and legal phenomenon, coming out of the major industrialised societies of the late nineteenth century. Hitherto, children were property first and people second.

- Poverty, illness, and high mortality rates affecting families and children, characterised life in industrial societies. These conditions are well documented in contemporary fiction. The increased awareness led to wider legislative changes, including the first protection rights for children.

- Protection rights were a response to high incidences of orphaned children and their right to proper custodial care.

- These first children's rights did not negate or displace the primacy of the family in child nurture.

- The first expressions of children's rights in international law were contained in the Geneva Declaration of September 1924, which was adopted by the League of Nations.

1.7. CHILDREN'S RIGHTS AFTER 1945

The lofty protections afforded to children in the Geneva Declaration were restated by the League of Nations in 1934, but systematically disregarded by the Nazis after 1939, as were other rights throughout occupied Europe. In the USSR, the application of Joseph Stalin's New Order and the purges of the 1930s also led to a complete disregard for basic rights.

As discussed in the previous section, from the 1920s there was an increase in scholarly and public interest in children and in the formulation of human rights designed specifically for them. World War II obviously violated much of the progress, but its aftermath also helped to advance the cause of protecting and promoting human rights.

The Nuremberg War Trials of 1945–46 resulted in 24 of Germany's prominent National Socialist leaders being tried for crimes against humanity, including what had occurred in the concentration and death camps. These revelations of 'man's inhumanity to man' shocked the civilised world and created an international resolve to prevent such events recurring, and to protect individual human rights against the tyranny of the state. The failure of the League of Nations also revealed the necessity for any future international body to have the military capability to contain uprisings before they escalated into civil and/or international conflict.

The new United Nations, formed in 1946, thus needed to make more concerted efforts than its predecessor to secure world peace and protect human rights. One of the first needs was to issue a comprehensive statement on human rights for the post-war era. The Universal Declaration of Human Rights 1948 (UDHR) was the result.

Given that the Geneva Declaration had not specifically mentioned rights, the conception proper of international rights law pertaining to children began with the UN. In a veiled reference to the revelations of Nuremberg, the Preamble of the UDHR spoke of the "disregard and contempt for human rights [which] have resulted in barbarous acts which have outraged the conscience of mankind." Pre-dating the UDHR, however, was United Nations International Children's Emergency Fund (UNICEF), which had been founded by a resolution of the General Assembly on 11 December 1946. The welfare and rights of children were now a permanent and prominent aspect of international law.

Given that the Geneva Declaration had not specifically mentioned rights, the conception proper of international rights law pertaining to children began with the UN.

In addition to the formation of UNICEF and the landmark UDHR, in the spring of 1948, a Children's Charter figured for the first time on the agenda of the Social Commission, and a long series of discussions which began on 19 April eventually resulted in the Declaration on the Rights of the Child (UNDRC) in 1959.[45] This contained ten statements on the rights of children, but the focus, as at the turn of the century, remained the child's right to be protected and provided for, rather than the more pro-active civil and political rights which assumed greater importance in later decades.

UNDRC was criticised for not being legally binding on states' parties, but even so it furthered children's rights in several areas; it gave the child the right to a name and a nationality, and to be protected from discrimination—

(then understood more as unfavorable treatment or exploitation in relation to race, colour and religion (Principle 1), rather than gender or sexual orientation). The Declaration also consolidated the child's 'best interests' (Principle 7) as foundational—a phrase that would later define the essence of UNCROC.

With many regulations governing children's rights having already been asserted, there was a renewed momentum during and following the UN-sponsored International Year of the Child in 1979, and the discussions which ensued eventually led to UNCROC which has become the most widely-ratified human rights instrument in history.[46]

The shift from a focus on protection rights to civil and political rights, and more recently—following the wide ratification of UNCROC—to enabling or empowerment rights, has occurred. The change has been incremental and a consequence of wider developments, including the evolution of human rights and other fundamental changes within Western societies. The rights contained in the UDHR are universalist; they apply to the generic human family. We have rights by virtue of being human, and these rights are universal because they apply to all persons irrespective of their circumstances. The right to a name, family, shelter, nationality, to buy and sell, to free speech and so forth are basic to a common humanity. The child's primary rights, where specified, were to have parents and basic standards of care, protection, and education. As in the late nineteenth century, the legal ethos supporting these rights was complementary to, rather than in place of, the family, which was both affirmed and assumed to be the natural unit of social organisation and identity.

In simpler terms, children were no longer being seen in international law as innocent and vulnerable, but as full human beings needing support to assert rights to autonomy and independence. In decisions affecting them, children were to be consulted and their views included, especially in public policy and local government matters.

The traditional liberal view of rights that evolved from philosophers such as Locke and Kant was that the rights-bearing subject was a rational autonomous individual. Irrespective of the divide between empiricism and rationalism that contested the source of knowledge, rights were a function of capacity and maturity. For Kant, the prerequisite for holding rights was an ability to exercise them, *sui iuris,* and for Locke, children lacked maturity and independence and needed to be educated into reason. This line of argument—a capacity view—dismisses the idea of rights for children on the basis that bearers are unable to exercise them. Unlike the long struggle for industrial, women's or black civil rights, children will always lack the capacity to independently govern their own lives.

As a rationale, the capacity view is problematic because it logically excludes certain persons; e.g. the elderly and mentally infirm, from having and exercising rights.[47] If understanding what is involved and being conscious of one's rights is a requirement for exercising them, an important question arises; does one have to be developmentally mature and mentally coherent to be a bearer of rights? Even Kant's famous moral imperative, "treat other people as an end in themselves rather than as a means to an end", warns against the exploitation of others, underpinned by his wider concern for duty. For Kant, to act morally was to act for the sake of duty, and the test of a moral action was whether it was done in accordance with, and for the sake of, duty.

The view of rights emerging from Locke and Kant suggests agency and rational autonomy, but as we have seen, the first children's rights in the nineteenth century were rights of protection; the child had a 'right' to be protected from poverty and starvation, especially when orphaned or abandoned. It is an altogether different understanding that today affirms active social and cultural rights—such as the right to individuate and be independent. Whereas the UDHR was based on protecting an individual's freedom from state intrusion, the state is now frequently in the business of empowering groups it identifies as oppressed or marginalised; in the 1970s the focus was women, in the 1990s it became children.

Accordingly, modern children's rights draw more on late twentieth century social causes for inspiration than on the long philosophical tradition of the West and the writings of people like Locke and Kant. For example, in the 1970s, the theoretical quest for emancipation evident in intellectual movements such as neo-Marxism generated concerted social action in educational reform, sexuality, women's rights, and the child liberation movement. In subsequent decades, more sophisticated understandings of children's rights have emerged, and there is no shortage of new and more advanced theories (e.g. poststructuralism and deconstructionism) to pave the way for further reform.

1.7. SUMMARY

- World War II highlighted gross abuses of human rights perpetrated by the Nazis. These 'crimes against humanity' spawned a renewed desire to create international rights instruments to guard against a repeat of the atrocities. One of the early achievements of the newly-formed UN was the Universal Declaration of Human Rights in 1948, which laid the foundation for understanding rights in the post-war era.

- The UN's interest in children's rights was formalised in the Declaration on the Rights of the Child in 1959. Enabling or empowerment rights were formally expressed in UNCROC in 1989.

- UNCROC has become the most widely ratified human rights document ever, and because of this has become the benchmark for evaluating children and their rights in most contemporary societies.

- Within the Western philosophical tradition, notably Locke and Kant, the idea of children's rights is problematic. In recent decades, however, its intellectual foundation has drawn more on contemporary social causes than on Enlightenment philosophy.

ENDNOTES

CHAPTER ONE
Children in context: an historical overview

1   The pairing is for convenience: "Judeo-Christian" is often used in the West to describe an ethic that draws upon common aspects of both Jewish and Christian thought.

2   See Genesis 16 v4, *New International Version*.

3   See Psalms 68 v5, and 146 v9. An additional concept was the "Year of Jubilee" (Leviticus 25 vv8-55), when land was to be returned to original owners and slaves freed. The minor prophet, Malachi, summed up much of the law when he claimed God would testify against those who "oppress widows and the fatherless" (3 v5); while in the New Testament book of James, the writer implores readers to practice "pure and faultless" religion which looked after "orphans and widows."

4   Micah 6 v8.

5   Molech was an Ammonite deity whose worship involved child sacrifice (see Leviticus 18 v21).

6   Matthew 5 v17.

7   Matthew 18 vv2-4 and Mark 9 vv36-37.

8   Ephesians 6 vv1-4.

9   Definitions and descriptions used in this and the following section are drawn from J. Lempriere, *A Classical Dictionary: containing a copious account of all the proper names mentioned in ancient authors*. London: Milner and Sowerby, nd, c1890.

10 In *The Iliad*, Book 9, Phoenix says to Achilles: "Did not the old charioteer Peleus make me your guardian when he sent you off from Phthia to join Agamemnon? You were a mere lad, with no experience of the hazards of war, nor of debate, where people make their mark. It was to teach you all these things, to make a speaker of you and a man of action, that he sent me to you; and I could not bring myself to let you go, dear child, and stay behind, not if God himself undertook to strip me of my years and turn me into the sturdy youngster I was when I first left Hellas, the land of lovely women." E.V. Rieu (trans), London: Penguin Books, 1954, p172.

11 *The Republic* is the best known of Plato's dialogues and where he systematically attempts to apply the principles of philosophy to political affairs. This extract, however, is from Michael Foster, *Masters of Political Thought, Volume One: From Plato to Machiavelli* (London: George Harrap & Co., 1959), p94.

12 *Ibid.*, p126.

13 The tension was perhaps, not as easily resolved in Clement's time as suggested here. The difficulty in reconciling classical ideas with those of Christianity influenced the development of the school curriculum and not only what was to be taught, but by whom.

14 "Education and the Concept of Childhood", in Paula S. Fass and Mary Ann Mason (eds), *Childhood in America* (New York: New York University Press, 2000), p283.

15 This extract, rewritten in contemporary language, is from *The Second Book of the Courtier,*

but the 1561 translation can be viewed at http://darkwing.uoregon.edu/~rbear/courtier/ courtier2.html (last accessed August 2006).

[16] George Koenigsberger, George L. Mosse, and G.Q. Bowler, *Europe in the Sixteenth Century* (London & New York: Longman (second edition), 1989), p71.

[17] Philip Aries, *Centuries of Childhood* (London: Cape Publishers, 1962, pp114-19) and summarised here from Dugald McDonald's thesis, "The Governing of Children: Social policy for children and young persons in New Zealand 1840-1982", unpublished PhD thesis (Sociology), University of Canterbury, 1988, p47.

[18] Hobbes expressed it thus: "Hereby it is manifest, that during the time men live without a common Power to keep them all in awe, they are in that condition which is called Warre; and such a warre, as is of every man, against every man. For WARRE, consisteth not in Battell onely, or the act of fighting;...but in the known disposition thereto, during all the time there is no assurance to the contrary. All other time is PEACE." C.B. MacPherson (ed), Thomas Hobbes, *Leviathan* (Middlesex: Penguin Books, 1980). Part 1, Chapter 13, "Of Man", pp185-86, emphasis and spelling as in original.

[19] "For these words of Good, Evill, and Contemptible, are ever used with relation to the person that useth them: ... ." *ibid.,* Part 1, Chapter 6, p120.

[20] The original text (and spelling) reads: "In such condition, there is no place for Industry... no Culture of the Earth; no Navigation,...no commodious Building;...no Knowledge of the face of the Earth; no account of Time; no Arts; no Letters; no Society; and which is worst of all, continuall feare, and danger of violent death; And the life of man, solitary, poore, nasty, brutish and short." MacPherson (ed), *Leviathan,* Part 1, Chapter 6, p186.

[21] John W. and Jean S. Yolton (eds), John Locke, *Some Thoughts Concerning Education* (Oxford: Oxford University Press, 1989), p109, emphasis in original.

[22] Despite his notoriety, the idea that children's development was the result of activity and transition across stages (rather than being predetermined in a mechanistic manner) did not originate with Rousseau. It owed much to the earlier work of German philosopher Gottfried Leibniz (1646-1716).

[23] Joy A. Palmer (ed), *Fifty Major Thinkers on Education: From Confucius to Dewey* (London: Routledge, 2001), p56.

[24] *Ibid.,* p55, emphasis added.

[25] W.T. Jones, *Masters of Political Thought,* Vol. 2 Machiavelli to Bentham (London: George Harrap & Co. Ltd., 1959), p251.

[26] See for example, *The New Zealand Curriculum Framework Te Anga Marutanga o Aotearoa* (Wellington: Ministry of Education, 1993), p3: "The New Zealand Curriculum recognises that all students should have the opportunity to undertake study in essential areas of learning and to develop essential skills. *Such learning will enable them to develop their potential'* (emphasis added); and later in the same document: "*...the individual student is at the centre of all teaching and learning...* " (p6, emphasis added).

[27] *Émile* cited in Fass and Mason (eds), *Childhood in America (loc. cit.),* p293.

[28] H.C. Barnard, *A History of English Education from 1760* (London: University of London Press (second edition), 1963), pp33-34.

29 The Enlightenment extended to all branches of the western intellectual world. It drew upon many influential figures including Hume, Voltaire, Mendelssohn, Addison, Kant, Montesquieu, Franklin and Jefferson.

30 A useful commentary on Rousseau and the Swiss educationalists, Johann Pestalozzi, and Philipp von Fellenberg is to be found in Barnard (*op. cit.*), pp32-41.

31 Published in the period 1751-65, the *Encyclopaedia* was aimed at making recent scientific discoveries available so as to destroy superstitious notions about nature. The editor was Diderot, and among the contributors were Voltaire, Rousseau and Montesquieu.

32 The trend steadily accelerated throughout the century. See Ronald Dore, *The Diploma Disease* (London: Allen & Unwin, 1976), for more on this.

33 Chris Cook and John Stevenson, *The Longman Handbook of Modern British History 1714-1987* (London: Longman Paul, 1983), p119.

34 See "Birth-rates and death-rates in England and Wales, 1841-1985", *ibid.*, p112. It is not evident in these figures, but mortality among children and infants in the industrial period was known to be generally high.

35 On this point see Viviana Zelizer's essay "Pricing the Priceless Child," in Ann Branaman (ed), *Self and Society* (Massachusetts: Blackwell Publishers, 2001), pp54-61. Zelizer discusses "...the profound transformation in the economic and sentimental value of children—14 years of age or younger—between the 1870s and the 1930s. The emergence of this economically 'worthless' but emotionally 'priceless' child has created an essential condition of contemporary childhood." p54.

36 "Children's Involuntary Labour: Colonial Documents", in Fass and Mason (eds), *Childhood in America*, p241.

37 *Ibid.*, pp242-43.

38 The motive for these schools was more than educational, as described in the following reference to the late 1790s: "Disorders occurred in some of the big manufacturing towns, and in 1796, the mob in Manchester created a riot at a theatre during the singing of the National Anthem. Thus, over and above the idea of popular education as a humane or religious duty, there was a feeling that some modicum of education would prove a safeguard and would combat vice, irreligion, and subversive tendencies among the poor. They must be taught to live upright and industrious lives in that station of life unto which it should please God to call them. This helps to explain the great stress which was laid on so-called 'religious' education in philanthropic schools for the poor." (Barnard, A *History of English Education,* p5.)

39 See Cook and Stevenson, "Social Reform" in *The Longman Handbook*, pp121-130 for a list of principal laws.

40 *Ibid.*

41 Akira Morita, "Family Dissolution and the Concept of Children's Rights: An Historical and Culture-Comparative Analysis", unpublished paper delivered to the World Congress of Families, Prague, March 1997.

42 Key (1848-1926), a Swedish writer, was strongly influenced by the Social Darwinism of

Herbert Spencer (1820-1903). She believed marriage rested on a foundation of economic independence and easy access to divorce, which would guard against children being born into loveless marriage and where "legalised rape" was said to occur. Her bestselling book, *The Century of the Child* was published in 1900. Endorsing the ideas of the earlier Rousseau, Key believed the child was intrinsically good and has been called the "Mother of the New Education Movement" (Reformpädagogik). See Philip E. Veerman, *The Rights of the Child and the Changing Image of Childhood,* (Dordrecht: Martinus Nijhoff Publishers, 1992), p81.

[43] Linda Gordon, "The Progressive-Era Transformation of Child Protection," in Fass and Mason (eds), *Childhood in America,* p548, emphasis in original.

[44] A number of websites comment on the Declaration. A succinct statement of the main points, for example, can be found at http://www1.umn.edu/humanrts/instree/childrights.html (last accessed August 2006). It will be noted that "rights" is not used although UNDRC is generally considered the first statement specifically concerned with the rights of children.

[45] See "Declaration on the Rights of the Child, 1959," in Ian Brownlie (ed), *Basic Documents on Human Rights.* Oxford: Oxford University Press, second edition, 1981, pp108-110.

[46] A full version of UNCROC appears in the Appendix.

[47] Philosopher Peter Singer explores this further by providing a precise meaning of "person." The common meaning of the term, he says, has roots in Latin meaning a mask worn by an actor, but subsequently came to mean a rational, self-conscious being. Singer applies this to modern debates (such as euthanasia and abortion), but attributes it to "impeccable philosophical precedents," including Locke. On this reasoning, all young children, especially infants and defectives would be "non-persons" (see *Practical Ethics*, Cambridge: Cambridge University Press, 1979, pp75-6, and pp131-33). It follows that "non-persons" could not be rights bearers in the sense that persons are. This raises further issues concerning animal rights, a cause Singer argues in detail (see Chapter 3, "Equality for Animals", *ibid.*, pp48-71).

CHAPTER TWO

——————— • ———————

Children and children's rights in New Zealand to 1989

Our understanding of children has historically centred around developments in health, education and welfare; and so in this chapter, the discussion focuses on these important themes. A more identifiable children's rights advocacy did not emerge until the 1980s.

As will become evident, one of the most contentious problems in determining policy is resolving the conceptual issue between seeing a child in his or her own right or as a member of his or her family.[1] This tension is not easily resolved at either the philosophical or policy level, but is readily discernible in the following discussion.

It is appropriate to begin with some comment on what is known of the first children to inhabit New Zealand.[2]

2.1. TRADITIONAL MAORI SOCIETY

It is not possible to know in detail about the lives of pre-European Maori children. The earliest accounts date from the late eighteenth century and the interaction of Maori from that period (the 1770s) with the early European sailors—*pakeha*. The descriptions that have survived are by early European observers, and at best these provide only a partial insight.[3] Carbon dating, archaeological and genetic analysis indicates that New Zealand was first settled about the thirteenth century AD during the era of widespread Polynesian ocean voyaging.[4] What traditional Maori society and its customs were like is largely speculative because knowledge of the pre-1770 period is based on fragmented archaeological evidence and oral tradition.

Maori society of the 1770s was identifiably Polynesian but strikingly different from that of the first inhabitants. The story of the Maori before James Cook's exploration in 1769 is largely that of the adaptation of Polynesian peoples to their new island homeland. It is incorrect, therefore, to view Maori society, or the children within that society, in static terms. The evolution of iwi or tribal affiliation, and further stratification into *hapu* or sub-tribal groupings, accompanied other complex and refining aspects of technological and social change. Author Margaret Orbell explains further the concept and complexity of hapu:

> A number of closely related whānau made up a larger descent group known as a hapū . . .
>
> At every level, hapū are named for the ancestor (usually but not always male) from whom its members trace descent. This ancestral name, sometimes in shortened form, is preceded by the appellation Ngāti, or a similar expression; thus Ngāti Maru are descendants of the early ancestor Maru-tūahu (spouses from outside this descent group being excluded from membership). Within the region especially, the name Ngāti Maru often referred to Ngāti Maru 'proper' (tūturu), a senior and relatively small hapū, but for some purposes related hapū associated themselves with this descent group and all were spoken of collectively as Ngāti Maru.[5]

In common with other Polynesian peoples, family bonds and kinship, or *whanaungatanga* were a central organising feature of the *whanau,* the extended family, and there was a close affinity with the land, and honouring of ancestors.[6] The child, or *tamaiti,* was valued as part of the intergenerational web of connections as were all members of the whanau, with special reverence accorded to older and esteemed members, notably the *kaumatua* (elders), *rangatira* (chiefs), and especially the *ariki* (paramount chief). Tamariki (children) were reared on the oral traditions of the hapū which focused on cosmological accounts and creation beliefs,[7] validating genealogies (*whakapapa,* or descent lines) and on passing on practical skills. This pattern evolved over several generations, as did a more complex social organisation.[8] The isolation and physical environment also fostered distinctive regional diets and local fashions in artefacts and art styles.[9]

Alongside the peaceable activities of everyday life, inter-tribal conflict was also a feature of pre-European Maori society. Accordingly, warrior prowess was admired and valued among young males, as was training in the use of weapons; indeed, "the male and consequently the male child held special position appropriate to his fighting role."[10] With reference to extensive archaeological research of the Totaranui Maori of the West Coast of the South Island (*Te Wai Pounamu*), "Maori women began to produce children from the age of 15 years and if they survived into their 30s, they produced four or five children."[11]

In demographic terms, many pre-European Maori aged quickly:

> An average life-span of about thirty was also typical of other parts of the Pacific during pre-European times. Old age was reached at forty, and few lived beyond their fifties. . . . few people would survive long enough to become grandparents, and the extended family and frequent adoptions would ensure that children were cared for when their parents died. . . . The average number of children born to each woman was only three or four, suggesting that children were spaced at something like four-year intervals. The overall extent of infant mortality is not known, but in Palliser Bay [near Wellington], it has been estimated at 15–25 per cent, on the basis of individuals found in excavations there.[12]

This suggests that 'child' referred to very young dependents, perhaps those under 10 years of age. Beyond that it would appear that tamariki, as in western societies, adopted adult tasks and responsibilities. Lower life expectancy and inter-tribal warfare may also have meant many children were raised by adults other than their parents. Many were *atawhai* or orphans, while others served as caregivers to older members of the whanau.

As in all societies, however, it was implicitly understood that the welfare of tamariki was primary. They were to be nurtured to maturity, for their welfare determined the future: *He iti tangata, e tupu; he iti toki, e iti tonu iho*—"A little child will grow [but] a little adze will always remain small." Tamariki were intimately bound up with the whakapapa of a person's genealogy, cultural identity and family tree.

The formal settlement of New Zealand by the later Pakeha migrants or *tauiwi*[13] after 1840, had a decisive effect upon Maori. The wars from the 1860s and subsequent land taken by the Crown adversely affected traditional societies. Despite the Native Schools Act of 1867, schooling was not compulsory for Maori children, and isolation and settler prejudice worked to limit their enrolment in public schools as well.[14] Although the Maori population slowly began to recover and stabilise after 1900, an official policy of assimilation was pursued which expected full integration into Pakeha society. The post-1945 migration to urban areas created a dislocation and distance from whanau, but the closer proximity to Pakeha also brought increased awareness of the issues facing Maori. Serious consideration of Maori perspectives in relation to child welfare did not, however, emerge until the 1980s, and at that juncture, generally as part of a wider responsiveness to multicultural issues (see Chapter 3).

The plight of Maori children, identified in policy and other sociological inquiries from the 1960s, revealed disturbing statistics. For example, a national survey initiated in 1967 and published in 1970, noted that the reported rate of abuse for Maori children was six times that for Pakeha, while that of Pacific Island children was nine times as high.[15] From then until the passing of the Children, Young Persons and their Families Act (CYPFA) in 1989, there was much detailed investigation into the issues facing Maori—including children. This led to a restatement of the paramountcy principle, as one which linked the child and family as mutually inclusive; the interests of one could not be considered without reference to the other. This thinking relied heavily on the sensitivities aroused in the emerging understanding of multiculturalism—that all cultures are equally valid and cannot be critiqued by other cultural perspectives—and with respect to a reappraisal of raising children in traditional Maori society.

Although the Maori population slowly began to recover and stabilise after 1900, an official policy of assimilation was pursued which expected full integration into Pakeha society.

2.1. SUMMARY

- Arriving around 1300 AD, the first peoples to settle permanently in what was later named New Zealand came from Polynesia, and over time, complex patterns of social organisation and tribal affiliation evolved in the new land.

- Apart from what can be deduced from oral tradition and the scholarly examination of archaeological sites, little is known about Maori prior to contact with the first Europeans in the eighteenth century.

- In pre-European Maori society, the population was demographically young due to short life expectancy, and great emphasis was placed on intergenerational connection and the training and nurture of children (tamiriki).

- European settlement after 1840, the wars (1860-1872) and land confiscations that followed, adversely affected all aspects of Maori society. For much of the twentieth century, Maori were expected to assimilate; although the post-1945 movement of young Maori to cities and other urban areas created a greater awareness of their needs from the 1960s onwards. By the 1980s, a greater understanding of the Maori was exerting considerable influence on the understanding of children within families.

2.2. POST-1840 EUROPEAN SETTLEMENT AND THE WELFARE OF CHILDREN

The first recorded European contact was the 'discovery' of the islands by the Dutch explorer, Abel Tasman, in December 1642. Tasman was followed later by the British mariner, James Cook, and the Frenchman, Jean François de Surville (both in 1769), and towards the end of the eighteenth century, by an influx of sealers, and then in the early nineteenth century by shore-based whalers. The formal British annexation of New Zealand—the Anglicised version of Tasman's name, "Nieuw Zeeland"—occurred with the signing of the Treaty of Waitangi on 6 February 1840. The Treaty attempted to bring the English rule of law and unite tribal leaders. It also deftly denied the French, the competing colonial power, from establishing constitutional sovereignty.

Shortly after, on May 21, William Hobson RN declared New Zealand a British possession, claiming the South Island by right of Cook's 'discovery', and the North Island by cession. The Constitution Act of 1852 consolidated a Westminster legal and constitutional system and established six provincial governments under a Governor. From then until New Zealand achieved

Dominion status in September 1907, the country was a crown colony, and organised settlement, mostly from the British Isles, began during the 1840s, with a major wave of assisted and unassisted immigrants arriving during the public works era of the 1870s. Colonial New Zealand may have lacked the burgeoning slums of the midland cities, but breaking in the land for European settlement was no sinecure. Escaping poverty was an incentive to emigrate, but life at the other end proved equally challenging. During the three-month outward journey, shipboard diseases struck children down mercilessly, particularly measles and scarlet fever. Children's low resistance was exacerbated by dampness and poor diet. After arrival, coping with the vagaries of the antipodean climate, procuring enough food, and settling the land were equally demanding.

British entrepreneur, Edward Gibbon Wakefield's, theory of systematic colonisation attempted to forge a new society in the colonies through preservation of a hierarchical social order. The attendant idea of a 'sufficient price' for land would, he believed, lure respectable lower middle and working classes, while deterring loafers and petty criminals. The rulers, as in some pre-industrial utopia, would be the morally responsible aristocracy. The theory looked good, but Wakefield lacked understanding of conditions in Australia and New Zealand. Transplanting a stratified and 'improved' society was never going to be easy. Nevertheless, he was an able promoter and successfully established the New Zealand Company in December 1837. However, the Wakefield settlements, beginning with Port Nicholson (Wellington), suffered from a lack of planning, while in other areas, problems were compounded by financial strife, religious issues and racial conflict.

Even in the relatively well-off southern province of Canterbury, the promise of Arcadia was not realised; as late as 1853, "the hopes and dreams of the foundation seemed to clash on every hand with a rather dismaying reality."[16] For most in the first and subsequent decades of organised European settlement, creating a settler society was fraught with difficulties and, as it had been at 'Home', life was particularly hard for children. In these formative decades, provincial governments were understandably preoccupied with constitutional matters rather than social concerns. In the absence of traditional forms of support such as parish relief and philanthropic agencies, and following the abolition of the provinces in 1875, the state assumed an early responsibility for education, law and order, welfare and health. Although not fully realised in the harsh circumstances of the new colony, Wakefield's vision reinforced the optimism of creating an 'improved' society, one materially better than what the majority of migrants had known. This determination is perhaps the genesis of what evolved into the Kiwi 'can-do' attitude. Although now often the butt of stereotypes and satire, this feature of the New Zealand psyche was grounded in the need for colonists to improvise and seek pragmatic solutions to problems.[17]

The most important institution in colonial society was the family, and planners like Wakefield recognised that women had an essential role in not only being wives, but in bearing children, in being homemakers, and exerting a civilising force on men as well.[18]

For these women, bearing children was risky enough, but raising them in isolated frontier towns was even more demanding. Although European men outnumbered women at the first colony-wide census in 1851 (15,035 males to 11,672 females[19]), marriage was considered an indispensable aspect of pioneer life and having children was both desirable and expected. Women as wives, mothers and homemakers were extremely valuable in developing the colony, even though the presence of an itinerant male community persisted for some time, in particular to carry out the labour-intensive public works schemes of Julius Vogel during the 1870s.[20]

The most important institution in colonial society was the family, and planners like Wakefield recognised that women had an essential role in not only being wives, but in bearing children, in being homemakers, and exerting a civilising force on men as well.

As in past societies, children were frequently viewed as chattels to assist a family to break in and work the land. The exigencies of a frontier society placed a premium on labour and made it essential for children to contribute to the family and to the wider economy. Child labour was so important that parental rights were allowed to remain beyond the authority of external regulation or intervention. The child was a vital asset. Until overseas educational thinking began to affect local policy makers and 'cross-pollinate' through new initiatives, the availability of schooling was haphazard and reflected the capability of provincial administrations and churches to provide.[21] In the provincial era (up to 1875), provision for schooling in the respective provinces was uneven, but the situation improved quite rapidly. By 1879, two years after the Education Act of 1877, 74 per cent of 5- to 13-year-olds were attending school with some regularity, and by 1899, the figure had risen to more than 80 per cent.[22]

As in the 'Old Country', however, some children missed out on school and assumed adult responsibilities as soon as they were able, especially if the wage-earning father had been maimed or killed.

> In such circumstances, colonial children grew up very quickly. In the large families of those first decades, only the last-born had time and opportunity to be a child. In the vast majority of cases, pioneer children were expected to work and, both within and outside the home, their labour was essential to the functioning economic viability of the family enterprise. Older children fetched and carried for younger siblings from an extremely young age . . . In general terms, boys spent more time in helping their fathers and girls their mothers, but there was no rigid division. If wives worked on the farm, husbands generally helped in the house. Sons and daughters followed their example . . . For town children, too, childhood was often brief. . . . Many children in the developing townships seem to have been left largely to their own devices.[23]

Although the Education Act of 1877 stipulated compulsory attendance from seven to 13 years of age,[24] this was difficult to enforce, particularly in remote areas where there was no school to go to. Improved communications and school provision were factors behind the improved figures,[25] but acquiring credentials as a means of advance or for enhancing job prospects is a trend among developing societies which appears to have begun early in New Zealand. Improved attendance figures created momentum for wider changes in education as well. By 1910, far-sighted administrators such as the Inspector-General of Schools, George Hogben, had overseen a new syllabus for instruction (in 1904), the provision of a new reader, the *School Journal* (in 1907), and new developments in secondary schooling. Slowly, the reforming ideas of people like John Dewey also began to exert an influence on educational policy and pedagogy. Schooling in the early twentieth century also had much to do with the public spectre, conjured up by politicians and commentators, of idle youths roaming town streets, creating crime and moral dissolution.[26]

This sense of alarm also affected the state's view of welfare. From the earliest years of European settlement, the state had tried to balance its care of vulnerable and genuinely needy children with the concurrent need to punish recalcitrants, especially those deemed a threat to the moral well-being of the community. Following the Neglected and Criminal Children Act of 1867, provincial councils were able to establish industrial schools[27] to which the courts could commit neglected or delinquent children and detain them until age 21. The first school was in Caversham, Dunedin, in 1869. Early in the twentieth century, residential care was regarded as the best option for delinquents and 'larrikins'.[28] Increasingly, however, and particularly after 1916, the industrial school concept fell from favour. Probation, supervision and foster care became preferred alternatives, although it took some time to phase out industrial schools, and from 1924, a borstal system was introduced as a custodial option for serious juvenile offenders.[29]

The wide-ranging changes Hogben achieved in education were paralleled in welfare by another prominent public servant, John Beck, who later became the first Superintendent of Child Welfare in 1926.[30]

The industrial school concept was not meant to displace the centrality of the family in child welfare. It did, however, remove from circulation those whose circumstances placed them at risk, or who through their own behaviour posed a threat to society. The foundations of the Child Welfare Act of 1925 were laid almost a decade earlier when the redoubtable Josiah Hanan, Minister of Education in Thomas Mackenzie's administration in 1912, and again in the wartime Coalition Government from 1915 to 1919,[31] tabled a special report to Parliament in 1916. Hanan spoke of practical reforms in a number of areas. "I am convinced," he said, "that the education and training of the present and immediately following generations constitute the greatest reconstructive agencies at our disposal for the repair and reorganisation of national life after the present destructive upheaval."[32] This set in place a preventative philosophy of welfare which become enshrined in the 1925 Act and was skillfully developed by Beck. The family remained central in Hanan's thinking, but where the state was to be involved, 'boarding out' was preferred, with institutional care being a last resort.

The 1925 Act led to the establishment of the Children's Court and the Child Welfare Branch of the Department of Education. The Welfare Branch, as it was commonly known, "was the first semi-autonomous section of a government department devoted exclusively to welfare matters."[33] The activities of the Welfare Branch helped determine the way New Zealanders during the mid-twentieth century came to understand the nurture, education and welfare of children.

In relation to rights, universal access to schooling provided by the

Education Act of 1877 resulted in New Zealand children receiving their first individual rights, and through the schools, their first alternative to socialisation within the family. As subsequent events proved, the 1877 Act was the forerunner of an intensification of government involvement in the lives of children. By the early years of the twentieth century, the state had consolidated its authority as the chief provider of services in these areas. The Public Health Act of 1900, for example, made the nation's health and well-being a central concern of the state. The Liberal government set up the Department of Health at a time when infant welfare was assuming national importance because of concerns about 'national efficiency'. However, responsibility for infant health did not primarily lie with the new department, but rather with a voluntary agency, the Plunket Society, founded in 1907 (a unique stimulus at this time was the perceived 'decline of the British race', which had surfaced in Britain among eugenicists during the South African War of 1900-02[34]). Although strictly a charitable society, Plunket's value to the nation was soon appreciated by politicians, and it enjoyed considerable financial and moral support that transcended partisan politics.[35] For example, in 1912, the newly-elected Prime Minister, William Massey, told Plunket's founder, Dr Truby King, "[Y]ou may be certain that the Parliament of this country will always give you what you want so long as you are engaged on the good work you are now doing."[36]

In relation to rights, universal access to schooling provided by the Education Act of 1877 resulted in New Zealand children receiving their first individual rights, and through the schools, their first alternative to socialisation within the family.

During the First World War, the government was subsidising the work of Plunket to the tune of 24 shillings for every £1 of subscriptions received, up to £100.[37] The Liberal and Reform Governments (1891-1928) generally supported self-help over state intervention, so state aid to Plunket fitted comfortably within their ideologies. This level of government support helped consolidate the society's prominent status, a position it enjoyed for most of the rest of the twentieth century.

King's favourite saying encapsulates much of the official and public sentiment many felt towards the care of children. "It is wiser," he said, "to put a fence at the top of a precipice than to maintain an ambulance at the bottom."[38] This was echoed in the official statements of Josiah Hanan and the belief in many areas of public policy that prevention was better than cure.

The welfare of children was improving in other areas, too. The 'social laboratory' of the Liberal-Labour governments from the 1890s resulted in new employment and factory laws. Almost a century after the passage of the Factory Act of 1819 in Britain, New Zealand children were granted their first industrial protection rights. The New Zealand Factory Act of 1891 had a similar effect in limiting the employment of women and children.

2.2. SUMMARY

- Early views on family and child-rearing were inherited from the first European settlers, predominantly from the British Isles, who initially came to the provinces during the 1840s.

- Edward Gibbon Wakefield's vision of a transplanted and stratified English society was thwarted by the problems of establishing settlements in rugged terrain, and in some provinces, by inter-racial conflict and financial limitations.

- In colonial New Zealand, children were primarily seen as chattels of their parents, and expected to work as soon as they were able. Although the Education Act of 1877 made school attendance compulsory, this was difficult to enforce, particularly in remote rural areas where the demand for child labour remained high and communication was difficult.

- For the nation's children, universal primary schooling became a complement to socialisation within the family.

- Notable advances in educational policy and provision occurred in the early years of the twentieth century when school attendance increased, and credentials in a rapidly developing society became desirable. From this period the state also consolidated its authority in welfare and health provision, and passed several laws specifically to protect children.

- The Plunket Society, formed in May 1907, subsequently became very significant in advancing the cause of infant and child welfare in New Zealand, in effect, providing the lens through which infant welfare was understood for many decades.

- The Public Health Act of 1900 (and its consequences), the wide acceptance of Plunket's work, and far-reaching changes in industrial law, welfare policy and education combined to lay a foundation for understanding children in New Zealand in the twentieth century. The key elements of this emerging 'New Zealand way' included a compassionate view of children as protected persons, and an alliance of family, state agencies and charitable groups working in the interest of children's and the nation's future.

- The Child Welfare Act of 1925, which facilitated the establishment of the Child Welfare Branch of the Department of Education and the Children's Court, was another highly significant development.

2.3. WIDER LEGAL DEVELOPMENTS[39]

As a crown colony, New Zealand inherited a legal structure and even specific Acts from British common law. The English Laws Act 1908, for example, embodied the similar Acts of 1854 and 1858 and provided that the laws of England as existing on 18 January 1840 (almost a month before the Treaty of Waitangi) were deemed to be in force in New Zealand. This meant that landmark English legislation extending back to the Magna Carta of 1215, and including the Petition of Right 1627, the Habeas Corpus Act 1679 and the Bill of Rights 1688, were automatically valid in the new colony. However, the New Zealand General Assembly had full legislative power to make laws "for the peace, order, and good government of New Zealand", as contained in the New Zealand Constitution Act 1852 (UK) (s53).[40]

Certain assumptions about the welfare of children had grown up alongside this inherited common law. In Britain and elsewhere during the nineteenth century, there was a long-standing legal assumption that the welfare of children was essentially the concern of parents. This, it may be argued, extends beyond the history of English common law and has its ultimate origins in Judeo-Christian understandings. Parents are responsible unless circumstances render that impossible—as in the premature death of one or both, and the creation of orphaned children. In the interests of justice, the state then has a legitimate role to intervene and assist with, or even provide totally for, the welfare of children.

This thinking was apparent in New Zealand as early as 1846. In that year, the Lieutenant-Governor of the colony, George Grey, oversaw 'An Ordinance for the Support of Destitute Families and Illegitimate Children'. This stated a filial responsibility in law for children and, remarkably, extended liability for their welfare across families over five generations. Terms such as 'destitute' and 'illegitimate' reflected a growing awareness and an inclination among Victorian legislators to show compassion and even pity toward children facing such unfortunate circumstances.[41] Some children, however, needed to be 'rescued'. As migrants became settlers and the first generation of European children were born in New Zealand,[42] further laws were passed concerning the welfare of children. The Married Women's Property Act of 1860, for example, enabled deserted wives to handle their own affairs. Women could act as legitimate guardians of their children, to the exclusion of their husbands.

The first recognition of the 'separateness' of children in law, and of the state's collective responsibility for children's well-being, occurred in the Neglected and Criminal Children Act 1867. This was also notable for authorising industrial schools, but it was more about safeguarding society from vagrant children than proactively providing for child protection.

It was not until 1880 that the Education Department assumed responsibility for industrial schools which had previously been under the auspices of the Justice Department. This shift in administrative control signalled a move away from a punitive mindset towards a more educational purpose for industrial schools. The number of juveniles committed to prisons dropped steadily thereafter, from 130 in 1882 to 65 by 1891.[43] Clearly, the state was becoming responsive to its role in child welfare and looking upon disadvantaged children more altruistically.

Clearly, the state was becoming responsive to its role in child welfare and looking upon disadvantaged children more altruistically.

By 1881, two out of every five people in New Zealand were under 15 years of age, but legally children had few rights. The Adoption of Children Act, passed that year, was the first such law in the British Empire—and 45 years before .Britain. Section 8 allowed for adoption by a body corporate, which at the time was considered very progressive. The Act's sponsor, George Waterhouse MHR,[44] wanted to save children from the stigma of illegitimacy and deprivation and to protect adoptive parents from later claims for custody.[45]

Adoption subsequently became an emotive and contested area as legislation in this area inevitably intersected with wider changes in marriage, family and divorce, and more recently, with children's rights. The rationale in early law was to protect children from the stigma of illegitimacy, but it did so at the expense of shrouding adoptees from any knowledge of their birth parents. Over time, this understandably became a rights issue, but change was not evident until well over a century later, when Labour MP, Jonathan Hunt, successfully promoted the passage of the Adult Information Adoption Act in 1985.[46] This enabled adoptees to legally access records of their birth parents.

Adoption issues aside, the primacy of families in the care of children has almost always been seen as preferable to what the state saw itself providing. For this to work, however, parents had to be responsible, and Victorian legislators were quick to rail against the consequences of irresponsible parenting. In 1885, for example, Sir Robert Stout, the Premier and Minister of Education, in a speech 'Public Education in New Zealand', said in relation to industrial schools:

> What the State has to face is really this: whether it is not better to take children when young and impressionable and give them a good moral education, than to allow them to grow up criminals, and thus cost society far more than their education costs. But here I might say one word in reference to the cause of so many children being in the industrial schools. The statistics show that is mainly the fault of the parents—drunk parents, criminal parents, parents who were leading immoral lives, parents who did not recognise parental duty—it is their children who crowd our industrial schools; and I believe, there is need of some more stringent law to make parents who are criminal and neglectful do their duty.[47]

Aware perhaps of negative attitudes being attached to industrial schools, Stout reiterated the pervasively held view that inebriated and irresponsible parents, not wayward children, were the source of the problem. He also alluded to the role that law could play in shaping a social ethic of responsibility. Despite the plea for parental responsibility, most laws in the late nineteenth century were aimed at protecting and providing for children rather than correcting the dissolute habits of wayward parents.

The emerging social conscience concerning child welfare contributed to several new laws. When, for example in 1888, outspoken Dunedin Presbyterian Minister, Rutherford Waddell, preached on the 'sin of cheapness' and the exploitation of 'sweated labour', it prompted a Royal Commission which led to the Children's Protection Act in 1890. The full title of this legislation was *An Act for the Prevention of Cruelty to and Better Protection of Children*. It meant that police could now intervene directly in cases of ill-treatment, neglect, or abandonment of a child, who for the purposes of the law was defined as a boy under 14 years or a girl under 16 years.

Other legislation included the Factory Act 1891, which established a 48-hour working week for women and children (this was up-dated in 1894), the Intoxicating Liquors (Supply to Children) Act 1893, and the Infant Life Protection Act 1893. Both laws were concerned with protecting children, and the latter with guidance rather than disciplinary punishment. Section 22 of the Criminal Code Act 1893 also stipulated that a conviction could not be entered against anyone under seven years of age. Then in 1899, the Employment of Young Boys and Girls Without Protection Act made it illegal to employ children without pay, and in 1900, the Family Maintenance Act meant that deserting husbands had to pay maintenance. In the same year, the Public Health Act was passed which led to the establishment of the Department of Health. Subsequent events would prove this to be a hugely significant piece of legislation in understanding the state's obligation to care for all its citizens, including and perhaps especially, children.

It is small wonder then that the achievements of the Liberal-Labour governments from 1891, under the premierships of John Ballance and Richard Seddon, earned New Zealand a reputation for being a 'social laboratory'. The volume and scope of the reforming legislation effectively laid the foundation for the modern welfare state. As in Britain and America, the period from 1880 to 1913 may be regarded as the 'golden age' of the child rescue movement in New Zealand.[48] The state gradually moved away from the inherited and colonial view of the child as a chattel of its parents, to view the child as a person whose social rights were protected by the state. The new dynamic, however, both legal and social, did not displace the former view emphasising parents; it was complementary and based on a rationale of intervention when and as necessary depending on the circumstances.

2.3. SUMMARY

- The legal framework for understanding children was inherited from Britain when New Zealand officially became a crown colony at the signing of the Treaty of Waitangi in February 1840.

- The long-standing assumption in English law was that children were essentially the concern (and property) of their parents, unless circumstances (e.g. orphaned and destitute children) warranted intervention from other welfare providers.

- In nineteenth century Britain, charitable agencies associated with 'child rescue' often assumed the responsibility of providing for illegitimate children. From the mid-1840s, however, the welfare of such children in New Zealand was not overlooked by the state (e.g. George Grey's 1846 Ordinance).

- A raft of legislation was passed in the latter decades of the century to attend to various aspects of child welfare. By 1900, the state's role in the health, education and welfare of children was becoming more conspicuous and deliberate. The wider reforms justifiably earned New Zealand a reputation elsewhere for being a 'social laboratory'.

- Legislation helped define childhood as separate from adulthood and provided New Zealand children with their first legal protection rights.

2.4. 'TO THE FULLEST EXTENT OF HIS POWERS': 1900-1945

Sociologist, Dugald McDonald, has classified the official understanding of children in New Zealand into periods and phases beginning in 1840. This is not arbitrary in terms of dates, but is useful for tracing central elements of change.

As mentioned, in the colonial period (1840-79), children were seen as chattels of their parents, although, as in Britain, this evolved into a view of children as vulnerable and in need of basic rights; the child was a protected person guarded by the state and with limited rights (1880-1913). As welfare provision consolidated after 1918, and especially following the Great Depression, children came to be seen as important social capital and worthy of investment for the value they might return as a productive adult (1914-44).[49]

The changing economy and era of general prosperity that began in the mid-1890s and lasted until the beginning of the 1920s, resulted in improved provision for children by the state. Legislative changes kept apace of these shifts and, in some cases, pre-empted them. Along with the other legislative changes in health and education, more humane and enlightened understanding of children was emerging in early twentieth century New Zealand. One of the important changes, as McDonald notes, was that the conservative view of the age of culpability was changing.

> The two traditional common law defences, *mens rea* (guilty mind) and *doli incapax* (incapable of forming intent) had an influence on the changing legal status of children before the law. *Mens rea* had applied to children of 'tender years', on the basis that very young children, like the mentally insane, were incapable of the malicious intent to commit a crime. Even so, nineteenth century New Zealand magistrates took a rather conservative view of the age of culpability, as shown by the five- and six-[year]olds convicted of offences.[50]

The Juvenile Offenders Act 1906 (formal description: An Act to make Better Provision for the Hearing of Charges against Juvenile Offenders) provided legal recognition for those under 16 (juveniles).[51] This extended the former minimum legal age of criminal culpability (s22 of the Criminal Code Act 1893) from seven to 16 years.

Before the Child Welfare Act and the new department and Children's Court were put in place, children over the age of seven (after the Criminal Code Act 1893) but under 16 were generally considered to be as culpable as adults. Slowly, however, the procedures of arrest, arraignment, representation and custody were changing to recognise the specific predicament of children. From 1881 until 1896, young children had been imprisoned in substantial numbers, but this changed from the mid-twenties,[52] when several law changes and other new measures came into effect. Overall, there was more of a preventative focus and a favouring of welfare for young children in private homes where possible.

Commenting on the Child Welfare legislation in parliament, Sir James Parr said, "The Bill . . . proposes that Children's Courts shall be set up to deal with children, with the aim and on the principle that they require protection and guidance rather than disciplinary punishment."[53] This was followed in September 1926 by the Family Allowance Act, which provided specific funding for families with dependent children. A means-tested child allowance of two shillings per week was payable for every child after the first two children. A modified version which was universal, rather than means-tested, remained as a $6 per week Family Benefit until 1987, when it was finally abolished.

Significantly, too, the Child Welfare Amendment Act of 1927 raised the legal age of child or young person from 16 to 17, and reflected the now well-established understanding in all sectors of New Zealand society that childhood was different from adulthood.

The handling of problem children was naturally a concern for educators. In his first report to parliament, George Hogben noted that juvenile crime was not only caused by the actions of the child, but by undesirable social conditions evident in larger towns and urban centres generally.[54] His 1904 *Syllabus for Schools* retained the strong Victorian emphasis on moral instruction as a "real factor in the formation of good character", but his shift towards an understanding of wider variables in the education and understanding of the child reflected the influence of theorists like Dewey, with whom Hogben shared a belief in the importance of practical experience and 'learning by doing', especially in subjects like nature study. When explaining his new syllabus to a conference of inspectors in 1904, he said,

> We must believe with [Friedrich] Froebel and others of the most enlightened of the world's educators, that the child will learn best, not so much by reading about things in books as by doing; that is, exercising his natural activities by making things, by observing and testing things for himself; and then afterwards by reasoning about them and expressing his thoughts about them.[55]

This suggests Hogben was influenced not only by Dewey and by Froebel—who in 1886 first spoke of 'child-centred' learning—but also by the empirical epistemology of Locke. The impact of these ideas was not fully apparent until after World War I, but New Zealand educators were clearly up-to-date with the latest developments overseas. Over time, these ideas shaped a new understanding of children, or what in McDonald's typology is referred to as 'social capital'; the child was not simply a repository of factual knowledge, but an active and responsive participant in the learning process. Instruction in schools slowly came to reflect the new thinking, not only as enlightened pedagogy, but in true Deweyan fashion, to facilitate stable and productive citizenship.

These changes were accompanied by progressive developments in health and welfare. The Department of Health, augmented by the Plunket Society and the School Medical Service (from 1912), greatly improved the welfare of most children, although Maori were slower to benefit. Around the turn of the century, despite fears of being a 'dying race', the Maori population slowly recovered from the decimation of the latter half of the nineteenth century. Comparatively, however, the health and welfare of Maori, including children, lagged behind that of European New Zealanders—partly because of continued prejudice, and also because Maori predominantly lived in remote rural areas, making the provision of public services difficult.[56] All sectors of society were affected by World War I and by the influenza epidemic of 1918 in which 8,600 people died.[57] These events stimulated major domestic changes in children's health and education.

When the immediate crisis of the 1918 epidemic had passed, the state increased its role in health care. In 1920, the Public Health Act reformed the Department of Health into seven divisions, three of which were concerned with children's health: child welfare, school hygiene, and dental hygiene. Related developments were the establishment of the School Dental Service in 1921 and the appointment of Truby King as Director of Child Welfare. The idea of health camps, where undernourished children were residents in camps and provided with organised activities and nourishing food, was in line with the new direction in child welfare. The camps evolved in 1919, from the work of Elizabeth Gunn, a school medical officer at Wanganui. By 1936, a National Health Camp Federation had been formed and five permanent camps established throughout the country. These camps, along with Plunket and various other organisations, as well as the orphanages and maternity services provided by denominational churches, all augmented the state's efforts and created a comprehensive network of health and welfare services.

The aftermath of the European war stimulated important changes in education as well. New Zealanders had volunteered for overseas service in numbers proportionally higher than in any other country, and many young men had falsified their age to be part of the adventure. Although conscription had been introduced with the Defence Act 1909, most youths were keen volunteers. The reality of war, however, especially in places such as Ypres, Gallipoli, the Somme and Passchendaele, was horrendous. Not surprisingly, the aftermath spurred a world-wide movement for co-operation and brotherhood, and in educational circles there were calls for a new international language, Esperanto. In New Zealand, the fledgling Labour party came to position itself as the champion of a more progressive and enlightened education.

Despite these developments, the immediate post-1918 climate strongly endorsed the earlier jingoistic and militaristic emphases in education. The early 1920s, for example, saw new measures such as flag saluting and a loyalty oath for teachers introduced—intended to counter the Bolshevik threat.[58] But increasingly, new methods and approaches based on the emerging discipline of educational psychology and associated theories of child development were favoured. During the 1920s, pacifism and the 'play way' vied for attention with overt displays of loyalty to Empire.

The sheer numbers of children swelling the population after 1945 gave rise to a demographic phenomenon known as the baby boom, meaning the state's management of children and childhood became even more direct.

New teaching methods, for example the Dalton Plan—first used in Massachusetts—which gave pupils responsibility for completing assignments of work at their own pace, apparently aroused much interest in New Zealand.[59] In July 1937, a conference promoting the New Education Fellowship was held in New Zealand. The following year, Clarence Beeby was appointed Assistant Director of Education, and two years later, Director.

Progressive education, undergirded by a gentle, almost Fabian socialism—as typified in the Social Security Act 1938—guided educational policy and reinforced the view of the child as a developing citizen worthy of the state's attention and investment. The sheer numbers of children swelling the population after 1945 gave rise to a demographic phenomenon known as the baby boom, meaning the state's management of children and childhood became even more direct.

The more humane and progressive view of children that had evolved in New Zealand by the middle of the twentieth century is encapsulated in the now-famous statement from Peter Fraser (although attributed to the hand of Beeby), which was issued in 1939. It reads, in part:

> The government's objective, broadly expressed, is that every person, whatever his level of academic ability, whether he be rich or poor, whether he live in town or country, has a right as a citizen to a free education of the kind for

which he is best fitted, and to the fullest extent of his powers. So far is this from being a mere pious platitude that the full acceptance of the principle will involve the re-orientation of the education system.[60]

2.4. SUMMARY

- In the early and middle years of the twentieth century, perception of the child evolved from being a person with basic rights to protection, to being seen as pivotal in the overall well-being and future of the nation.

- The perception of childhood as a separate phase from adulthood became evident in a raft of legislative and policy developments, particularly in health, welfare and education.

- Because Maori children were predominantly rural dwellers throughout this period, indicators of their well-being generally lagged behind those for European children.

- World War I and its aftermath helped shape a new, liberal and progressive direction in education which rejected the formalism of the Victorian era, and reinforced the notion of childhood as a period of innocence, vulnerability and nurture. A more humane understanding of children also emerged in laws concerning child welfare and the Children's Court.

- The baby boom after 1945 meant children and children's welfare became increasingly central concerns in government policy.

2.5. 'THE COUNTRY'S RICHEST RESOURCE': CHILDREN 1945-1970

Bill Renwick, Director General of Education from 1975 to 1988, has explained the appeal of Fraser's statement of 1939. Writing many years later, he was able to offer a clear perspective afforded by the wisdom of hindsight.

His comments capture the ideas that dominated New Zealand education in the years after 1945. These fit with what McDonald referred to as a view of the child as a psychological being, whereby nurture and intervention were consciously guided not only by theories of human development and behaviour, but by the broad principles of a humane and just society. With reference to the 1939 statement, Renwick says:

Note that, as well as the commitment to equality of educational opportunity, there is a commitment to educate individual boys and girls to the fullest extent of their powers. As well as the ideal of equalizing opportunity, there is the idea of maximizing ability. This is an idea that has long won a ready response from New Zealanders. It gave assurance that the country's richest resource, its human ability, would be developed to the full. It satisfied the hankerings of very different kinds of people: those who saw it as an educational expression of the parable of the talents; social Darwinists who believed that with nations, as with species, only the strong survive; romantic liberals who saw genius and originality manifesting themselves in new ways only if all individuals were developed to the uttermost; and the defenders of the poor and oppressed who saw them rising above their inheritance only through the talented efforts of their own children.[61]

Although written in 1939, Fraser's statement carried a poignancy in the new era of international law and politics that began with the UN in 1946. It was in effect a New Zealand expression of Dewey's understanding that the best education for the defenders of democracy—an important post-war theme—would be a liberal-progressive education. Certainly the child development movement had made a lasting impact on the post-war educational consciousness, especially in the West, and New Zealand was no exception. Renwick continues:

Its research findings and teachings, and, more important, its doctrines and advocacy produced a revolution in the educational psychology taught in teachers' colleges. Where the starting point had previously been methods of teaching, it became the ways by which children grow, develop, and learn.[62]

As mentioned, the baby boom added a practical impetus and need to the new thinking. The twin forces, philosophy and demography, combined to make education one of the key instruments of social policy in a manner that it had not been before.

In 1944, secondary education was made compulsory to age 15; although by this time the need for child labour had diminished significantly and was not the issue it had been in the late nineteenth century when specific legislation (the Factory Act 1894) was needed to protect children. Labour in the buoyant post-war economy, however, remained in high demand. In establishing the leaving age at 15, the economic dependency of children and young persons was further asserted. The new leaving age reflected an economic environment that required a skilled workforce with a decreasing need for child labour.

The traditional view that marriage was the natural context for bearing and raising children was unthreatened during the early baby boom period. Marriage was still normative and the Marriage Act of 1955 reaffirmed the legal requirements of the contract. But other law, for example, the Divorce and Matrimonial Causes Amendment Act 1953, began to acknowledge the reality that marriages broke down whether or not divorce ensued. Additionally, this legislation no longer allowed one partner to prevent the other from terminating a marriage which had broken down.[63] From 1952, the Married Women's Property Act enabled married women to hold property of their own, meaning that any remaining moral strictures from the Victorian era—whereby women and children were effectively chattels of the husband and father—were virtually eliminated.

In establishing the leaving age at 15, the economic dependency of children and young persons was further asserted.

In the post-1945 period, not only were more couples divorcing, but of those with children, more were seeking divorce than in the past. In this environment the state began to take more interest in the welfare of children in matrimonial disputes. The moral framework for understanding marriage and its attendant virtues and failures was thus giving way to a more pragmatic and utilitarian perspective—at least in law, if not in custom and attitudes. With regard to children, however, the long-held assumption that a mother's nurture was primary was legally upheld. As McDonald explains:

> In custody and guardianship disputes, considerations of fault and character assumed lesser importance than continuity of adequate mothering. By a combination of these new practices, economic liberty and social mores, the unassailable position of fathers as guardians which had obtained in the 1850s had by the 1950s almost reversed completely in favour of mothers, especially, in the case of young children. Magistrates and judges adjudicating in custody disputes came to be influenced by the 'mother principle'.[64]

These legal changes did not, in themselves, undermine the primacy of marriage, but they did begin a process which, in later decades, would manifest itself in other laws less supportive of marriage.

The reality of marriage breakdown, and not just divorce, naturally affects children, as do adoption laws.[65] The Adoption Act 1955 retained the thinking behind the 1881 legislation to save children from the stigma of illegitimacy and deprivation, but it was not what in modern parlance would be called 'child friendly'. In retaining the 'complete break' principle—[66]strict confidentiality and restricted access to court records—it raised the question of the equity of rights between the parties concerned and the right to know about oneself, parents and one's children. Over time, this suppression of the birth details of adopted children created more problems than it solved.

In other areas, too, lawmakers were taking an interest in children. The 1954 inquiry into the behaviour of Lower Hutt youths emphasised the importance of parental and family control. In contrast with the legal developments discussed above, the report's authors retained a highly moral tone in describing the events that initiated the inquiry and the possible solutions. The Mazengarb Report,[67] as it was known, was sparked by newspaper reports of indecencies committed by youths on girls under 16 years of age (the age of consent). The report began with an account of revelations produced at the trial:

> The prosecuting officer was reported as saying that the police investigations revealed a shocking degree of immoral conduct which spread into sexual orgies perpetuated in several private homes during the absence of parents, and in several second-rate Hutt Valley theatres, where familiarity between youths and girls was rife and commonplace.[68]

The report went on to describe the links between sexual crime and wider juvenile delinquency as a 'world-wide problem'. It also searched for a range of influences and causes, including the changed relationship between teachers and children as a result of the effects of urbanisation and the growth of larger, inner-city schools; the pros and cons of co-education—some contributors to the inquiry felt that this could 'increase the chances of immorality'; the effects of the school-leaving age and relations with the Child Welfare Division; sex instruction in schools and possible links between the New Education and the erosion of traditional external discipline that could accompany or follow from exposure to the play way or other methods of free expression. Elsewhere, the role of the home environment, the influence of religion on morality, and the family, religion and morality were all discussed.

The Mazengarb Report provides an insight into the thinking and values influencing public morality at that time. Significantly, there was no discussion of children's rights separate from the family context; moreover, as had been the case since the colonial period, the state was still deemed to be secondary in the welfare of children, and its intervention only justified when circumstances warranted it. The authors explained that:

> The family (meaning thereby the father, mother and children) from time immemorial, has had a definite and recognised status in our national life—a place which it has not always occupied or enjoyed in other cultures and other systems of law. There is, in our culture, an air of sanctity about the home where parents and children dwell. The rights of a parent against any intrusion into his family affairs have been expressed in such statements as 'a man's home is his castle'.
>
> Our law of domestic relations centres upon the home. When the Legislature or the law courts have interfered in the conduct of the home, it has only been because one member of the family has failed to discharge the duties which an individual is required to perform towards other members of the family or towards society. Speaking generally, the rights and duties of individual members of the family have been preserved and enforced in our statute law. Illustrations are to be found in the Infants Act, the Destitute Persons Act, the Child Welfare Act, the Family Protection Act, and the Joint Family Homes Act.
>
> The policy of English law is, and always has been, to keep the family together and to uphold the rights of parents. Those rights have correlative duties attaching to them. It is the failure of some parents to perform those duties which has now become a matter of grave concern.[69]

Children's rights, except the right to be protected, clearly belonged in the future. Admittedly the view implicit in the Mazengarb Report may have concealed issues of child maltreatment and abuse which would only be aired fully in the 1970s, but it reflected a pervasive understanding of responsibility and duty upon which parental rights were conditional. The home and family were essentially private (see 4.4), but the quality of the interaction had public consequences. As we shall see, the breakdown of the family in later decades changed this by creating a greater dependency on the state and its resources when parents divorced or separated. This process coincided with a more atomistic view of children and their enabling (assertive) rights. The result has been a blurring of what was, in 1954, a much clearer delineation of private and public spheres in the welfare of children, and of course, an increase in state involvement when families fracture.

Although children's rights, as we now understand them, were not known at the time of the Mazengarb Report, the authors did affirm a modern view of the child based on the insights of progressive educational thought and educational psychology. The child needed protection because it was emotionally and psychologically vulnerable.

> A harmonious emotional development during childhood is one of the most important factors influencing human behaviour. Any child who feels unloved, unwanted, or jealous of the care and attention given to other members of the household suffers from a feeling of insecurity . . . [which] renders the child more susceptible to influences leading to delinquency.
>
> The mother's attitude to the child is of prime importance. There is a psychological link between mother and child from the very moment of birth—a link that can be substantially strengthened by breastfeeding as far as it is practicable. The attitude of the mother to the child, even before birth, may well have a marked effect upon the child's sense of security. If pregnancy was not welcomed by the mother, her child may come into the world under a distinct handicap, that of being an unwanted child. Subsequent adjustment may not be as satisfactory as she imagines it to be.[70]

Official pronouncements that the young child was innocent and vulnerable may have reached their zenith in New Zealand during the 1950s. The swelling numbers born in the first decade of the baby boom, and the flow-on effects in education and health—including the prominence of the Plunket Society—combined to create a sustained interest in the needs of children. The less desirable aspects of teenage behaviour—at least in so far as the adult population was concerned—included pre-marital sexual activity, larrikinism (the 'milkbar cowboy' or 'teddy boy' phenomenon), as well as the effects of rock and roll music later in the decade; and these further demarcated adolescence from childhood. From the time of the Mazengarb Report, adolescence came to denote a period of fraught development which signalled the physical and emotional transition between childhood proper and adulthood. The social tumult of the 1960s enhanced this perception among adults and gave rise to the generation gap which highlighted the sharp contrast in attitudes and behaviour between teenagers and their parents. The so-called 'youth culture' that emerged, however, represented more of a symbolic defiance against authority than any genuine desire for a new social order.

In the post-war period, the state embraced the psychotherapeutic ideal within the departments of welfare, education and health. Adjustment for children and adults alike became the official state goal, and psychology the instrument. In retaining a moral framework to explain the causes and effects of teenage sexual promiscuity, the Mazengarb Report appeared out of step with more modern ideas about children and child welfare. Policy changed accordingly. The formation of the Psychological Services Division of the Department of Education led to the first guidance counsellors appearing in secondary schools in 1960, and also the Visiting Teacher scheme, a support service established in 1943 (by 1971 the scheme employed 34 teachers). These services reflected a more modern belief that children involved in criminal or sexual offending were not simply moral failures, they were also victims of circumstances beyond their control.

True to Fraser's vision and in keeping with the times, the recognition of the gifted child began in 1948 when the New Zealand Council for Educational Research published George Parkyn's *Children of High Intelligence*.[71] Progressive education based on academic streaming, earlier specialisation, educational testing and the 'natural physiological and psychological changes'[72] of early adolescence also formed the rationale for intermediate schooling in New Zealand from 1922. A survey of these schools, written by Beeby in 1938, concluded that "the intermediate school system in New Zealand [should] be continued and extended."[73] This was very much the principle of educational opportunity being put into practice.

Specific legal services for children and young people were also being provided. The police established the Juvenile Crime Prevention Section in 1957 (later known as Youth Aid),[74] while for couples experiencing difficulty, "an embryonic marriage guidance movement was taken in hand by the Department of Justice and nurtured to fulfil tasks in the adjustment of disintegrating families."[75]

Young people were increasingly viewed in sociological and structural as well as psychological terms. Analysts of the emerging trends began to comment on youth issues.[76] In 1958, Auckland psychologist, A.E. Manning, published a study of juvenile abnormal psychology (*The Bodgie*). Not surprisingly, this empirical study found that 'bodgies' frequently had unhappy childhoods, came from broken homes, and lacked parental supervision, but revealingly, they were not *bad*, however repellent their behaviour appeared to others. Manning concluded, "society made these delinquents, and society has the means of curing them."[77]

This represented a shift away from previous beliefs in the moral or character failure of individuals. While parents were still culpable, a more structural understanding of causes and solutions was emerging. In a society that by the late 1950s had a well-established and relatively very large system of state welfare, the response and answers were sought in government initiatives. Not only were baby boomers maturing into awkward teenagers, but the advent of television in the 1960s promulgated images of the truculent mood among youth, and renewed fears among the older generation.

The first stirrings of a new state response were seen in 1968, when the National Development Council was set up by the government. By 1976 this had evolved into the Social Development Council, with a working party on family policy headed by economist, Brian Easton. Also in 1968, the Guardianship Act was passed and continued to give preference to the mother rather than the father for care of children in custody disputes. This legislation was also significant in restating the paramountcy principle of 'the best interests of the child'. Although times had changed, the superior nurturing qualities of the mother were still presumed in law—and have only recently been challenged by fathers' lobby groups demanding greater equality and fairness, with partial redress coming in the Care of Children Act in 2004.

Another highly significant law change was found in the Status of Children Act 1969. This was an Act to remove the legal disabilities of children born out of wedlock.

Another highly significant law change was found in the Status of Children Act 1969. This was an Act to remove the legal disabilities of children born out of wedlock. It promised all New Zealand children equal status: "For all the purposes of the law of New Zealand, the relationship between every person and his father and mother shall be determined irrespective of whether the father or the mother are or have been married to each other, and all other relationships shall be determined accordingly."[78] The second clause of Section 3 reads: "The rule of construction whereby in any instrument words of relationship signify only legitimate relationship in the absence of a contrary expression of intention is abolished."[79] Children previously considered illegitimate were to be deemed 'legitimate' irrespective of the marital status of their parents. The term 'illegitimate' was replaced by 'out of

wedlock' or 'ex-nuptial birth' in an attempt to de-stigmatise social attitudes
towards those born to unwedded parents.

The promoter of the legislation was J.R. (Ralph) Hanan, who as Minister
of Justice sought to apply the paramountcy principle which had surfaced
in the Guardianship Act 1968. The new law was considered to be a logical
extension of the principle. In what transpired to be one of his last major
speeches in parliament,[80] Hanan introduced the parameters and intent of
the Bill:

> It is an important Bill, as important as, if not more important than, any other
> Bill I have had the honour to present to the House. It is important as a
> declaration of principle. It has as its objective the final equation of the legal
> position of the illegitimate child with that of his legitimate brothers and
> sisters. More than that it cannot do. However, this is no reason why the law
> should not do whatever lies in its power to see that children themselves do
> not suffer from a situation that is certainly not of their making. This has not
> always been the general attitude. The common law approach has been a
> very harsh one. It did not recognise any ascendant or collateral relationships
> between the illegitimate and any other person; he was described as *filius
> nullius*—the child of no one. He had no rights against either parent, and they
> had no rights or obligations in respect of him. It is hard in these days to see
> what this attitude could be expected to achieve.
>
> The old law of giving the parents no responsibility meant that the parents
> had no obligations. The law has persisted for a very long time. . . . We are
> changing the law finally to equate the position of the illegitimate child with
> that of his brothers and sisters. In the last century, attitudes did begin to
> change as in other branches of family law, and this country through successive
> Governments, has shown itself quicker than most to remedy defects in its law
> in accordance with changes in public opinion. Today the child whose parents
> marry after he is born becomes legitimate as from birth on the date of the
> marriage of his parents.[81]

Hanan correctly noted that family law in New Zealand had historically stopped
short of trying to legislate explicitly for parental responsibility (despite the
intentions of some earlier politicians). His aim was simply to remove a legal
barrier and language that had existed for a long time. Those participating
in the debate were mostly lawyers, and the objections raised were not of
principle, but of legal practicalities. For example, the Labour Opposition
Justice spokesman, Dr Martyn Findlay, did not disagree with Hanan, but

spoke of the practical awkwardness of lawyers asking spouses about the issue of illegitimacy. He also drew attention to the implied redefinition of the child,[82] and Hanan's tendency to push through urgent reform. More significantly, he pointed out that getting rid of the concept of illegitimacy at a legal level would not eradicate the reality of children being born to unwed parents. He likened this to asking a group of clergymen if they thought sin existed or not.

The MPs participating in this debate[83] continued to use the term 'illegitimate' in their discussion, indicating their intention to create a legal distinction only. Over time, however, and in relation to what was to follow in the subsequent decade, this distinction, supported by other legal and social changes, attempted to remove illegitimacy not only as a legal concept, but as a reality as well.

The elimination of legal distinctions between children who have parents with a recognised relationship and those who did not proceeded with a general tone of acceptance, especially in the human-rights-sensitive society that was to emerge in the late 1970s. But there was a lot more occurring in this changed view of children than was immediately apparent in 1969. The elimination of prejudice against fatherless children was desirable, even admirable, but the de-stigmatising of fatherlessness also weakened the claims of wives to the assistance of husbands in childrearing and gave tacit approval to men—and women—to have children outside marriage with little fear of adverse consequences. Another unintended and less obvious consequence of the Bill was to diminish the importance of marriage and the desirability of being married. This was part of a slow and incremental shift, however, and was not immediately apparent. Until 1971, the marriage rate per 1,000 New Zealand women over 16 was rising (from 38.2 in 1961 to 45.5 in 1971), although it then steadily declined and has not since recovered.[84]

Northern Maori MP, Matiu (Mat) Rata, tellingly pointed out that although the Status of Children Bill would give "legal status to some 7,783 children born last year and to some 6,960 children born the year before . . . the country appears to have a much higher illegitimacy rate than other countries, and it is therefore of the greatest concern that some steps should be taken to deal with this problem. . . . Each succeeding year has seen a substantial increase in the number of illegitimate births in New Zealand, and the problem must be tackled by all sections of the community with a lead given by the Government."[85] (The number of ex-nuptial births had steadily risen from 5,967 in 1963 to 7,783 in 1967 or 8.81 per cent and 12.72 per cent of all live births respectively.[86])

Dealing with the problem at a legal level was understandable, given the focus on the rights of the individual child. Any hopes, however, that the actual incidence of illegitimacy might be reduced proved to be folly; by 1981, ex-nuptial births had climbed to 23 per cent, and by 2002, reached 44 per cent.[87] The 1969 Act ushered in a decade of significant human rights change affecting children and parents. It also helped create a legal environment which encouraged debate on marriage and family issues.

The Guardianship Act and Status of Children Act signified a new direction for the law when it came to children. Whereas previously, in marital and custody disputes, the child did not enjoy equal consideration with parents, these items of legislation were consciously tailored to their needs. Bronwyn Dalley adds:

> New Zealand also picked up the new ethos that the child had rights as an individual, with one scholar dubbing the 1970s as the era of 'children's liberation'. Legislation which removed disabilities against children, such as the Status of Children Act 1969, which eroded distinctions between the rights of those born in and out of wedlock, suggest a focus on the child *as* a child, rather than as a member of a larger unit.[88]

The law was beginning to adopt an approach that recognised children, not just in relation to their parents, but also as citizens with individual rights. Philosophically, too, children were no longer viewed solely in relation to their parents (being within families), but as individual persons. Children had agency not just because of their potential to become adults, but because of who they already were. As we have seen, this important shift was underscored by decades of psychology and understandings of how children learn, grow and develop. The tension, however, between a view of children as empowered individuals and citizens, rather than within families, and in lieu of becoming adults, remained as real as ever; indeed, as later events would prove, it was to intensify with a more concerted advocacy of children's rights.

Later in 1969, the National party signalled its intention to merge the Child Welfare Division of the Department of Education with the Social Security Department, to form a new Department of Social Welfare. This occurred following the passage of the Department of Social Welfare Bill in 1971. From April 1972, the Department of Social Welfare (DSW) heralded a new era of centralised and more specialised bureaucracies. Child welfare officers now became social workers, and the term 'child welfare' as one writer put it, "receded into history".[89] The Child Welfare Division became the Social Work Section (later Division) of the DSW.

Also in 1969, the Holyoake National government set up a Royal Commission under the chairmanship of Sir Thaddeus McCarthy to review social security in New Zealand. There was a growing concern that the existing benefit system was out of step with the buoyant economy. The Commission eventually released its report, *Social Security in New Zealand*, in March 1972, and many of the recommendations were adopted by the Kirk Labour Government after its landslide electoral win in November of that year.

One of the proposed changes accompanying the Social Security Amendment Act introduced by Labour in September 1973 (and effective from 14 November), was the introduction of a new category of benefit, the Domestic Purposes Benefit (DPB) to meet the needs of a growing number in the community who had hitherto only qualified for an emergency benefit under the Social Security Act 1964. The DPB removed any needs-based criteria and replaced it with the more contemporary understanding of a universal entitlement. It also acknowledged the growing numbers of people who had been receiving benefits, principally solo parents[90] and mothers— other than widows—with dependent children. The Social Welfare Minister, Norman King, added that it would "for the first time, . . . provide solo parents, irrespective of the cause of their sole parenthood, with defined benefit rates and income exemptions."[91] This was quite a shift from the approach of only a decade previously, where, under the Social Security Act (s74), the authorities could, at their discretion, refuse to grant a benefit, terminate an existing one, or grant a payment at a reduced rate if the applicant was not ". . . of good character and sober habits, or is living on a domestic basis as husband and wife with a person to whom he or she is not married."[92]

As in the 1969 debates, King's endorsement was shared by the National opposition. W.L. (Bill) Young said, "[T]here are good measures in this Bill, which have my full support . . . anything which is good for beneficiaries is good for the country."[93]

Unintentionally, however, the DPB fortified a culture of state entitlement and helped condone what used to be called 'illegitimacy' by effectively making the state into a surrogate parent. This was what Rata and others had feared in the Status of Children Bill debates.

In line with the rationale behind the Social Security Amendment Act and the DPB, the DSW represented a new direction for welfare and thinking about children. At one level, it embodied a necessary modernisation based on decades of experience in policy and practice since the Child Welfare Act of 1925; at another, it represented the maturity of the welfare state in New Zealand, and the culmination of the idea contained in the Social Security Act of 1938 that the state would provide 'from the cradle to the grave'. In removing the stigma of charity, Prime Minister, Michael Savage, widely believed it was the inalienable right of every person to be secured against distress in any form.

The nineteenth century concepts of 'saving' unfortunate mothers and children, of the state's duty to provide when parents could or would not, and of 'deserving', were replaced by a utilitarian approach which acknowledged changes to the family and marriage, the social sciences, and to the need for experts who were specifically trained professionals.[94] The family as a largely autonomous social institution was changing, as the state would now exercise a more proactive role in advocating for women, and later for children. This advocacy would later be invigorated by a new paradigm of children's rights.

A less significant but still important legal change around this time was the passing of the Age of Majority Act in 1970. This lowered the age of contractual adulthood from 21 to 20 and reflected a general belief in the social maturity of young adults. The age of adulthood was still ambiguous, however; 18-year-olds were able to vote, but only those aged 20 or more could legally enter licensed premises, while the 'coming of age' rite of passage remained at 21.

The exact ages were less important, however, than a century of change in education, health and welfare which had created childhood and adolescence as distinct periods in the human life cycle.

2.5. SUMMARY

- The period following World War II saw the consolidation of developmental psychology as the basis for understanding children in New Zealand. In this, the state responded to a demographic increase—the baby boom—with a raft of new thinking and initiatives, particularly in education and welfare.

- The need for child labour in New Zealand had significantly diminished by the mid-twentieth century. This economic trend helped to reinforce the understanding that childhood was distinct from adulthood.

- During the 1950s, the law became more responsive to the reality of divorce and women's needs following separation. While still favouring families, adoption laws vetoed knowledge of an adoptee's birth parents and their access to records.

- In custody disputes, the law favoured the 'mother principle', i.e. it was assumed that children—particularly young children—were better off living with their mothers rather than their fathers.

- The Mazengarb Report of 1954 highlighted the anti-social behaviour of adolescents accentuated by the emerging generation gap. Although youth behaviour was not necessarily worse than in previous decades, the baby boom, Maori urbanisation and suburban expansion created a more visible pool of teenagers than had previously been the case. A summary of the report was posted to most New Zealand homes, although welfare agencies, increasingly influenced by social science research, subsequently came to favour structural rather than moral interpretations of youth problems.

- By the 1960s, the baby boom and generation gap phenomena had stimulated specific interest in youth and youth-related policy.

- In moving beyond a moral nomenclature, the Status of Children Act 1969 was an expression of a more modern therapeutic ideal aimed at de-stigmatising the issue of illegitimacy. Children of unmarried parents were thereafter referred to as ex-nuptial rather than illegitimate. Although well-intentioned, this also implicitly weakened the responsibility and social expectations of birth parents, particularly fathers.

- The Department of Social Welfare Act 1971 created a new department in April 1972. This merged several previous agencies and was the most significant legislation concerned with children—and other recipients of welfare—since the Child Welfare Act 1925. Together with the Social Security Amendment Act 1973, it ushered in a new era of state involvement in welfare. By the beginning of the 1970s, there was growing acceptance of trained professionals as experts on children and child well-being.

2.6. PRECEDENTS AND PARALLELS: FEMINISM AND THE EMERGING RIGHTS CULTURE 1970-1986

A significant aspect of the evolving rights culture in New Zealand, and one with parallels in the development of children's rights, has been the impact of second-wave feminism since the early 1970s. Among other feminist issues, the elevation of women into a separate political constituency was a defining feature of the mid and late 1970s. 'Girls can do anything' was a popular slogan and women's new-found empowerment reinforced that belief and gave it substance in law.

The issue most closely associated with first-wave feminism was the women's franchise, which was granted in 1893 after many years of agitation.[95] The franchise movement was closely related to the Women's Christian Temperance Union, and even after the vote was granted, the National Council of Women—founded in 1896 and dubbed the 'Women's Parliament'—continued its quest to take the 'mother influence' into politics. In accordance with feminist beliefs at the time, women were seen to exert a positive moral influence on both politics and wider society. The focus was very much on improving the lot of women and children within the family context, rather than the workforce, as was the case 80 years later. That New Zealand was a single political entity rather than a confederation of states (as in Australia) helped bring about the franchise earlier than across the Tasman. Australian women got the vote immediately after the new Federal Commonwealth was established in 1901; in Britain it came at the end of the Great War, in 1918.[96]

The stated aims of second-wave feminism were to promote women's rights and re-evaluate women's role in society. The first lobbying issues were equal pay for equal work and equal employment and education opportunities. In 1972, the Australian feminist, Germaine Greer, author of *The Female Eunuch,* visited New Zealand to support the work of early local advocates such as Susan Kedgely and Sandra Coney.[97] Equal pay, particularly in the public sector, was the initial focus. In 1967, a National Advisory Council on the employment of women was established to advise the government, and in January 1971, a Royal Commission of Inquiry into Equal Pay in New Zealand was appointed. The Commission—composed of four men and one woman—reported in September that the private sector had made unsatisfactory progress towards the introduction of equal pay. After considerable public debate, the government passed the Equal Pay Act in 1972 to remove gender discrimination in the private sector, arguably the most significant law change relating to women's rights since the franchise in 1893. Occurring within the milieu of the Race Relations Act (in 1971), the formation of the DSW in April 1972 and the Royal Commission the same year, gender-based pay legislation in the public sector was part of a flourish of reforming social legislation.

By the early 1970s, the Royal Commission was recommending that social security "fit the changing pattern of society", meaning the newly-discovered emancipatory needs of women and, in particular, what were then referred to as solo parents. Engrained egalitarian beliefs were extended into new spheres, including nascent feminist concerns. Removing the stigma attached to the illegitimacy of children and solo parenthood—particularly in relation to women—buttressed perceptions of a caring and reforming state. In addition, a Select Committee on Women's Rights was set up in 1973 to investigate the extent of discrimination against women in New Zealand and to make recommendations for its elimination.

The effectiveness of the women's movement can be judged, in part, by the passage of the highly controversial Contraception, Sterilisation and Abortion Act in 1977

Despite its good intentions, the DPB soon became a considerable financial burden,[98] but the rights culture and feminist demands continued apace throughout the decade. Following the establishment of a Women's Electoral Lobby in 1975 and a greater awareness of female to male imbalance, women began to enter male-dominated professions such as mental health and dentistry in larger numbers. A further Royal Commission, this time examining contraception, sterilisation and abortion (June 1975-March 1977), sought to adjudicate on several major social issues including contraception, the status of the unborn child, and the rights of the pregnant woman.

The effectiveness of the women's movement can be judged, in part, by the passage of the highly controversial Contraception, Sterilisation and Abortion Act in 1977; the same year the Human Rights Commission Act was passed, spawning the Human Rights Commission (HRC) in September 1978. Women's advocacy had clearly been an important stimulus in the advent of the HRC.

The continuing work of the women's movement both within and

outside the HRC found a growing accommodation within the Labour party during the early 1980s, thus ensuring that the next Labour government would strengthen and institutionalise feminist issues. This occurred with the agreement in 1984 to establish the Ministry of Women's Affairs (MWA), which was officially launched two years later by the Prime Minister, David Lange. At its launch, Lange said that the MWA "must work the system. It must change the system. In the end it must challenge the system."[99]

There remained, however, a sense within the MWA that equal pay remained a legal fiction and that many areas of New Zealand society remained untouched by the reforming zeal of 1970s feminism. One of the early moves of the new Labour government was to ratify the UN Convention on the Elimination of All Forms of Discrimination Against Women (CEDAW).[100] This occurred on 10 January 1985, and provided further support for moves to keep up the pressure for domestic rights reform.

What CEDAW was to the Ministry of Women's Affairs, UNCROC would subsequently become to the New Zealand Office of the Commissioner for Children: a catalyst to more local human rights advocacy based on international law.

Women's rights gained prominence in the 1970s and children's rights in the 1990s, but both have contributed to the mature human rights culture which the HRC wants to see in early twenty-first century New Zealand. Moreover, what CEDAW was to the Ministry of Women's Affairs, UNCROC would subsequently become to the New Zealand Office of the Commissioner for Children: a catalyst to more local human rights advocacy based on international law.[101]

The language of rights is readily transferable, and mutually reinforcing to the 'race, gender and class' triumvirate. Progress in each area created momentum in the others; in relation to women's and children's rights, there is an obvious connection. Advocacy for women and their empowerment in the paid workforce readily led to calls for a state-controlled system of early childhood education in New Zealand. Early childhood author, Helen May, recalls a placard around a toddler's neck—as early as 1971—at a women's liberation protest march: FREE MUM, FREE DAD, FREE ME, FREE CHILDCARE.[102] The maternal bond meant the two causes were inextricably linked.

CEDAW and UNCROC provided an international backdrop for local debates surrounding the Treaty of Waitangi.[103] Women's and children's issues had an added urgency when linked to statistical outcomes for Maori, which in many areas of well-being were below those for Pakeha and other ethnic groups. These developments indicated a wider and more deliberate consideration of human rights issues, and the effects soon filtered down to all levels of policy making. It was no coincidence, for example, that the first Minister of Women's Affairs, Ann Hercus, called for a full review of existing Children and Young Persons legislation, especially youth justice. The Working Party, established in 1984, was the first step towards legislative change. Rights issues against the background of an emerging multiculturalism were central in the protracted process which culminated in the 1989 Act.[104]

To present women's, or any group's, agenda as human rights concerns is to give them immediacy and invoke a bureaucratic and legal structure seeking the redress of grievances. Similarly, to politicise children by viewing them primarily through the lens of human rights, rather than through lived, familial or other relationships and connections, is to invoke the authority of international and domestic statute law. If it is widely believed that children, like women, have been aggrieved by certain attitudes, prejudice and discriminatory law, the state is seen to be acting justly in correcting the situation. Like the MWA, UNCROC and the work of the Children's Commissioner rests on an understanding that there are always new issues to be addressed through affirmative government action.

Among the consciousness-raising of feminist concerns, another landmark piece of legislation affecting children, the Children and Young Persons Act (CYPA), was passed in 1974—and enacted from 1 April 1975. This defined, for the first time, the meaning of *child* as a boy or girl under the age of 14, and *young person* as a boy or girl over the age of 14 years but under the age of 17. The volume of work involving the former Child Welfare Division of the Department of Education was said to have "exploded between 1948 and 1972",[105] and this, along with the formation of the DSW in 1972, changes to child law and to the social structure of the family, made it timely for an across-the-board re-think of the services the state could provide for children.

Children's Boards were a feature of this Act,[106] and a strong emphasis was also placed on child protection, with teams based in each office. According to one commentator, however, the law adopted a "technical, conservative approach to child protection";[107] by removing children from dysfunctional families, it was implementing a child-rescue model of social work. Significantly, the DSW's interpretation of the paramountcy principle emphasised children over the interests of the family, but this was to change in the following decade, especially in relation to a policy climate sensitive to Maori understandings of whanau (extended family).

The 1974 Act was the most significant child policy legislation since the Child Welfare Act of 1925. The well-established doli *incapax* (incapable of crime) rule was upheld for children, but the new Boards were intended to divert offenders away from court where possible. This led to the Children and Young Persons Court and a more preventative and rehabilitative ethos than had been evident in the Children's Court. Young persons, however, could still be brought to court and prosecuted, although diversion was preferred. Police made use of informal warnings and diversion procedures, including the Youth Aid Section and consultation with DSW officers. This was also intended to limit the stigma attached to a court appearance and possible conviction, much as the Status of Children Act 1969 had attempted to de-stigmatise illegitimacy.

The thinking behind the Act embraced a model of welfare which saw youth justice problems as symptomatic of family difficulties, which in turn could be addressed with proper and appropriate professional intervention. In relation to the evolution of children's rights, it was significant that this approach to state welfare continued to define the child—and young person—in relation to rights of family. Empowerment and choice rights were still concepts of the future.

In practice, however, the Act failed either to reduce stigma or to adequately stem youth offending. As one commentator put it, there were "too many and inappropriate arrests of young people for minor offences and the subsequent stigmatising; the inherent injustice of open-ended sanctions and the realisation that many young people who offend do not have any special family or social problems, meaning welfare dispositions [were] thus inappropriate."[108] Other difficulties, including what to do with recidivist offenders and a perceived increase in 'street kids', led to an amendment to the Act in 1977 that allowed children to be tried for murder, and moves in the early 1980s to increase police powers to deal with loitering on streets.

Dissatisfaction with both the philosophy and practice of the 1974 Act was exacerbated throughout the 1980s by an increasing awareness of Maori cultural needs, and their disproportionate representation in youth offending—said to be six times higher than that of non-Maori in 1986.[109]

Although the paramountcy principle emphasised the well-being of children in relation to families, it did not reflect any meaningful grasp of biculturalism or multiculturalism. The problems had been evident for some time. In June 1978, for example, the Auckland Committee on Racism and Discrimination (ACORD), made allegations of inhumane treatment of young people in Auckland social welfare homes. This resulted in considerable public scrutiny of the DSW's residences, and ACORD charged the department with violating several articles of the UN Covenant on Civil and Political Rights which New Zealand had ratified that year.[110]

In view of these and other contentious race relations issues, such as the Bastion Point protests, the incoming Labour government of 1984 had pledged to honour the Treaty of Waitangi by implementing a thorough review of legislation, including the CYPA.

This process and the wider political change which accompanied the economic and social reforms of the mid-1980s had important consequences for the development of children's rights in New Zealand. The combined effect of a market economy, a trimmed-down and more accountable public service, coupled with increased calls to honour the Treaty and promote general cultural sensitivity, highlighted the inadequacies of the CYPA and the need for more satisfactory legislation. The government review was based on the assumption that deep-seated problems could not be addressed by piecemeal reform but rather warranted a comprehensive inquiry.[111]

The IYC was also a stimulus for further developments in New Zealand.

Alongside this process were a number of other important developments in children's rights. The 1979 UN International Year of the Child (IYC) was an important awareness-raising event. It provided a stimulus for the Commission on Human Rights Working Group to investigate the text of a new and binding legal instrument which would modernise and expand the 1959 Declaration. The group was composed of representatives of the 43 member states of the commission in consultation with other agencies such as UNICEF. In what became a very drawn-out process over the next decade, the group met for one week annually until a draft text was completed in 1988. This eventually formed the basis for UNCROC.

The IYC was also a stimulus for further developments in New Zealand. The 'voice for children' was increasingly being heard in forums such as the

National Council of Women,[112] while the National Symposium on Child Abuse in Dunedin in 1980 led to the formation of the National Advisory Committee for the Prevention of Child Abuse (NACPCA).[113] Another organisation, the New Zealand Committee For Children, had two goals: "1. To co-ordinate and promote the implementation of IYC Statements of Principle and underlying recommendations as approved by the National Commission in February 1980, [and] 2. To act as an advocate for and in the best interests of the children of New Zealand and the World, in the spirit of IYC."[114]

The National Advisory Committee on the Prevention of Child Abuse and Neglect, NACPCAN, was formed in 1980 by the Minister of Health, George Gair, to advocate for new child-protection legislation. In the spirit of NACPCAN, the Family Proceedings Act 1980—effective from October 1981— aimed to ensure mediation between the parties involved in matrimonial disputes and that the best possible arrangements be made for the welfare of children under 16.[115] The paramountcy principle developed a new poignancy with the introduction of no-fault divorce. Local children's rights campaigners were also viewing with interest the appointment of the world's first Ombudsman for Children, psychologist Malfrid Flekkoy, in Norway in 1981. The Committee for Children Report to the government similarly advocated having a children's ombudsman in New Zealand.[116]

As early as 1983, David Geddis of NACPCAN and Auckland lawyer, Pauline Tapp, had drawn up a Child Protection Bill. This, in effect, signalled the beginnings of the 1989 legislation. The DSW adopted many of the points in its own legislative revisions from 1984 to 1986, and these in turn helped shape the draft of a new Children and Young Persons Bill in 1986.[117] The Bill was presented by the Minister of Social Welfare in December and then referred to the Social Services Select Committee, which called for further submissions. It attracted widespread public criticism, especially for its complexity and monocultural interpretation of law. In line with calls for greater cultural sensitivity, the need for more emphasis on families (whanau) was "to meet the needs of Maori in policy, planning and service delivery in the DSW."[118] The Committee held 65 meetings on maraes and in departmental offices and institutions, and its findings were published in a report, *Puao-te-Ata-Tu*, described by a later Social Services Minister, Steve Maharey, in 2001, as "having a profound effect on the principles and objectives of what was to become the Children, Young Persons and Their Families Act 1989."[119] In *Puao-te-Ata-Tu*, the Ministerial Advisory Committee in its first recommendation stated rather bluntly that the government would endorse the following policy objective:

> To attack all forms of cultural racism in New Zealand that result in the values and lifestyle of the dominant group being regarded as superior to those of other groups, especially Maori, by
> (a) providing leadership and programs [sic] which help develop a society in which the values of all groups are of cultural importance; and
> (b) incorporating the values, cultures and beliefs of the Maori people in all policies developed for the future of New Zealand.[120]

Re-election of the Labour government in 1987 enabled the process to continue and a second Working Party review of the Bill occurred. Between 1987 and 1989, the Select Committee worked with the DSW to refine the draft, and the re-worked legislation returned to the House for its second reading in April 1989. It eventually passed into law in November 1989 as the CYPFA.[121]

This long process may have been frustrating for those involved, but it effectively kept children's issues in the parliamentary and media spotlight. Children and their rights were becoming a permanent feature of the political landscape, like women's issues nearly two decades previously. Although children and young persons didn't have the vote, they had effectively been transformed into a political constituency.

This was to develop greater intensity as the effects of the 1989 Act began to be felt in the 1990s.

Another event which kept children's issues in the spotlight when the Bill was before the select committee was the 1988 Telethon. Telethon began in 1975, and by this time, the 24-hour television event had over a decade of credibility in raising funds for community causes.[122] Its theme in 1988 was 'reducing the level of violence in our communities'. According to author, Lynley Hood, it was the publicity surrounding this Telethon that established a general mindset that 'one in four' girls in New Zealand had been sexually abused.[123] This figure had its origins in studies indicating that by age 18, one in four girls had encountered unwarranted sexual attention. In the Telethon context, however, this was extrapolated to one in four girls—including young girls—have been or will be molested, many by their own fathers. The claim allegedly appealed to the public relations manager, and, Hood claims, it ". . . leapt off the page and grabbed him by the lapels. As a result, in the month leading up to the festival, the nation was saturated with the 'one in four' claim in radio, television and print advertisements."[124] She continues:

> Two advertisements stood out. One featured a photograph of four babies. The headline read: ONE OF THESE FOUR CHILDREN WILL BE SCARRED FOR LIFE. The text began, 'One in four girls will be sexually abused before they turn 18. Half of them by their own father.' The other advertisement featured a photograph of a frightened little girl in bed. Behind her, in the darkened doorway, was the ominous silhouette of a man. The headline read: IT'S NOT THE DARK SHE'S AFRAID OF. The text began "Some children treasure Dad's good night kiss while others live to dread it. Because some fathers don't stop there."
>
> Interested parties in the fields of politics, justice, welfare and health hailed the Telethon campaign as a long-overdue attempt to make the wider community 'face cruel facts'. The wider community did not take kindly to the attempt—and given that incest convictions nationwide for the previous year totalled 19, one can hardly blame them.[125]

Support for the 'one in four' figure also benefited from a decade of children's rights advocacy, but it rested on emotive and generalised evidence by implying *all* fathers were potential abusers. Again, this had parallels in the women's movement where it was often either suggested or stated that men oppressed women and abused children.[126] Given the levels of under- and over-reporting of child abuse, Hood rightly concluded "[T]here is probably no way of ever knowing the truth."[127]

The 1988 Telethon demonstrated the way legitimate concerns for the safety of children became vulnerable to ideological capture in a society hypersensitive to rights issues.[128] Notwithstanding the abhorrence of such behaviour when it did occur, this event cast aspersions on fathers and assumed a predatory intent toward their daughters. This unreality fuelled further policy reform, rights advocacy and government intervention in the functioning of families.

2.6. SUMMARY

- Second-wave feminism was a defining motif of social change in New Zealand in the 1970s. Equality became a human rights issue, and law reform an instrument to address feminist concerns like equal pay. Advocacy later became more concrete and bureaucratic during the term of the fourth Labour government, and through the work of the Ministry of Women's Affairs in the 1980s.

- Local feminist demands were reinforced by international law; e.g. the 1978 UN Covenant on Civil and Political Rights, and the ratification of the Convention on the Elimination of All Forms of Discrimination Against Women in 1985.

- The evolution of women's rights and the transformation of women into an identifiable political constituency was a precedent for what would occur with children in the 1980s.

- The Children and Young Persons Act 1974 was landmark legislation, comparable to the Child Welfare Act 1925. Despite some improvements in policy and practice, the Act contained major deficiencies, particularly in relation to youth justice issues and the needs of Maori. A lengthy process of review began with the new Labour government in 1984, and was eventually completed with the passing of the Children Young Persons and their Families Act in 1989. The emphasis on families reflected an increased awareness of kinship, particularly in relation to multicultural understandings. In accord with the market reforms of the time, the Act also encouraged a belief that families and local communities, rather than state-funded residential institutions should be primary providers of child welfare.

- The climate of change helped raise the profile and awareness of children during the 1980s. Advocacy and efforts of interest groups were also important in the consolidation of children's rights from the early 1980s. The International Year of the Child in 1979 stimulated local advocacy and initiative. The 1988 Telethon to reduce the level of violence in the community, especially against children, ensured the momentum for rights reform was maintained, but the extrapolated 'one in four' slogan also cast aspersions on the nation's fathers.

ENDNOTES

CHAPTER TWO
Children and children's rights in New Zealand to 1989

[1] For more on this see Jean Packman, "Central issues in social policy and the rights of the child", in P. Shannon and B. Webb (eds), *Social Policy and the rights of the child* (Dunedin: University of Otago Extension Department, 1980), pp9-20.

[2] In recent decades it has become fashionable to refer to the country as "Aotearoa New Zealand" or simply "Aotearoa" to reflect the nation's bicultural history. The late nineteenth century interpretation, the "Land of the Long White Cloud", is also used, but to understand Maori society collectively may be misleading. In pre-European times, "Aotearoa" may have been used selectively and only by tribes to refer to certain areas (cf. "Gaul" in modern parlance does not mean "France").

[3] Ready examples are contained in the accounts documented by Anne Salmond in *Between Worlds: Early Exchanges Between Maori and Europeans, 1773-1815* (Auckland: Penguin Books, 1997). For example, in Samuel Marsden's reflections on the northern settlement at Rangihoua, the missionary noted that "the New Zealand chiefs are a warlike race, proud of their rank, and jealous of their dignity. They seem to be men who never forget a favour or an injury. They retain a grateful remembrance of those Europeans who have been kind and faithful to them: . . ." Chapter Eighteen, "The Mission at Rangihoua", p501. These descriptions must be seen as partial and reflecting a colonial worldview only.

[4] For general comment on first settlement see Michael King, *The Penguin History of New Zealand* (Auckland: Penguin Books, 2003), p48, and for a more specific analysis, I.C. (Ian) Campbell's *Worlds Apart: A History of the Pacific Islands* (Christchurch: Canterbury University Press, 2003), "An Eastern Polynesia Puzzle", pp40-42. Here the author notes that "[T]he earliest dates for settlements throughout the eastern Polynesian cultural area are disputed. Perhaps all that might be said with certainty is that the entire area except New Zealand was colonised during the first millennium AD, with the weight of opinion favouring the second half rather than the first half of that period. New Zealand was colonised at least partly from the Cook Islands and perhaps from elsewhere in Eastern Polynesia as well, possibly in the twelfth or thirteenth centuries, perhaps as late as the fourteenth. These estimates are generally about five hundred years later than those that were generally accepted in the 1970s and 1980s." pp40-41.

[5] Margaret Orbell, *The Illustrated Encyclopedia of Māori Myth and Legend*. Christchurch: Canterbury University Press, 1995, p8. A belief held by some in contemporary Maoridom is that there are no iwi histories, only hapu histories—a point reinforcing the inadequacy of "Aotearoa" to refer to all Maori. In common with other contemporary writers, Orbell employed the macron to assist with the pronunciation of Maori words.

[6] "As elsewhere in Polynesia", Orbell explains, "the social system was based on kinship. Extended families, or whānau, varied in size and composition but were led by a man who, if he were of good birth, would be termed a rangatira." *Ibid.*

[7] For more on this important aspect, see Orbell, *Māori Myth and Legend*, pp11-15.

8   With reference to the world of the Southern (Te Wai Pounamu) Maori, Harry Evison
     discusses the social hierarchies that evolved in Maori society. For example, "...The
     highest-born rangatira of a hapu was acknowledged as ariki. He personified the man
     of his hapu or tribe just as a European monarch personified the prestige of his nation.
     The greater his mana, the greater his tapu. There was no higher rank than ariki, but it
     was a social and religious distinction, not a political or military one." *The Long Dispute:
     Maori Land Rights and European Colonisation in Southern New Zealand*. Christchurch:
     Canterbury University Press, 1997, p22.

9   For the people of Te Wai Pounamu (as in other regions), food became an integral aspect
     of an evolving society: "[T]he distinctive flavours of local varieties of bird, eel, mollusc,
     fish and other natural foods, bound people to the land and to the waters. Infants were
     weaned on to these foods, and grew up in the love of them and of the places that
     provided them. With each succeeding generation the bonds grew stronger." *Ibid.*, p19.

10   Barry Brailsford, *The Tattooed Land: The Southern Frontiers of the Pa Maori* (Wellington:
     A.H. & A.W. Reed, 1981), p29. It should be noted that Campbell's point of caution
     concerning orthodoxy in the 1970s and 80s (see above n4) may also apply here too.

11   *Ibid.*

12   Janet Davidson, "The Polynesian Foundation", *The Oxford History of New Zealand*
     (Wellington: Oxford University Press, 1981), p8. Salmond reinforces this in her
     recollections of Marsden's observations: "[M]any of the young women seemed
     prematurely aged, which he thought was because of such exigencies." (i.e. due to tapu
     restrictions surrounding childbirth, and being left in the open air afterwards and refused
     food and drink), *Between Worlds,* pp499-500.

13   These were mostly people of European extraction also known as "Pakeha" (although
     this term, like "Aotearoa", has variable meanings depending on the context in which it is
     used).

14   For further insights into the Native School Policy up to c1900 see J.D.S. McKenzie, "More
     than a Show of Justice? The Enrolment of Maoris in European Schools prior to 1900", *New
     Zealand Journal of Educational Studies,* Vol. 17, No. 1, 1982, pp1-21.

15   Bronwyn Dalley, *Family Matters: Child Welfare in Twentieth-Century New Zealand*
     (Auckland: Auckland University Press (in association with the Historical Branch,
     Department of Internal Affairs, 1998), p252.

16   W.J. Gardiner, *A History of Canterbury* (Christchurch: Whitcombe & Tombs), Volume II,
     1971, p3.

17   This is evident throughout Jock Phillips's book, *A Man's Country?: The Image of the
     Pakeha Male—A History* (Auckland: Penguin Books, 1987).

18   *Ibid.*

19   1851 census data, cited in Phillips, *A Man's Country?*, p6

20   See Phillips, *A Man's Country?*, pp37-38 for more on the role of women in the male-
     dominated colonial society.

21   For details on the first church-run schools in Canterbury (for example), see A.G. Butchers,

A Centennial History of Education in Canterbury (Christchurch: Whitcombe & Tombs, 1950), Chapter V, "The First Schools", pp21-30, and also Chapter XI, "The Roman Catholic Education System", pp86-99. A further useful source of information regarding key developments in education in both the provincial and early centralised eras see A.E. Campbell, Educating New Zealand (Wellington: Department of Internal Affairs, 1941), Chapter 2, "The Control of Education", especially pp49-59.

[22] J.L. Ewing, *The Development of the Primary School Curriculum 1877-1970* (Wellington: NZCER, 1970), pp62-63. See also the table in Butchers, *A Centennial History*, p81; in 1900 for example, the attendance level was 81.6 per cent.

[23] Jeanine Graham, "The Pioneers, 1840-1870", in Keith Sinclair (ed), *The Oxford Illustrated History of New Zealand* (Auckland: Oxford University Press), pp66-67.

[24] See clause 89, *SNZ, Supplement to the New Zealand Gazette,* No. 96, 29 November 1877, p127.

[25] When responsibility for schooling passed from the Provincial Boards to District Education Boards (following the Education Boards Act of 1876), school attendance began to rise steeply. In 1910, for example, attendance nationally was 85.9 per cent, while by 1926, it was 89 per cent. See the tabulated data of national statistics' figures in Butchers, *A Centennial History,* p81.

[26] One of the first political figures to be aware of this was Charles Bowen, the sponsor of the 1877 Act. For more on "moral panics" and the political response see Roy Shuker, "Moral Panics and Social Control: Juvenile Delinquency in Late nineteenth Century New Zealand", in Roger Openshaw and David McKenzie (eds), *Reinterpreting the Educational Past: Essays in the History of New Zealand Education* (Wellington: NZCER Educational Research Series, No. 67, 1987), pp122-31. Mary Trewby adds that, "Although by 1881, two out of every five people in New Zealand were under 15 years of age, legally children had few rights. Primary education had become compulsory with the Education Act 1877, but the law was difficult to enforce and indeed there was little political will to do so. But in the 1890s, responding to public pressure fuelled by the street gang issues, revelations about sweated labour in Dunedin factories, and incest, 'baby farming' and infanticide scandals, the government passed a number of laws specifically enforcing children's rights." *The Best Years of Your Life: a history of New Zealand childhood* (Singapore: Viking Press, 1995), p12. The moral panic impulse in education reform was also evident in Britain, see A.J. Taylor, *Laissez-faire and State Intervention in Nineteenth-Century Britain* (London: Macmillan Press), 1978, p46.

[27] For a comprehensive study of industrial schools see J.M. Beagle, "Children of the State: A Study of the New Zealand Industrial School System 1880-1925", unpublished MA thesis (Education), University of Auckland, 1974.

[28] According to Shuker the term "larrikin" originated in Australia and is "roughly synonymous" with "juvenile delinquent" (Openshaw and McKenzie, *op. cit.,* p219).

[29] A full list of industrial schools in New Zealand is contained in Dugald McDonald, "The Governing of Children: Social policy for children and young persons in New Zealand, 1840-1982", unpublished PhD thesis (Sociology), University of Canterbury, 1988, p7. The

last industrial school in Wanganui did not close until 1952.

30 Dalley correctly asserts that Beck (1883-1926) and Hogben (1853-1920) were "the two key individuals in children's welfare during the early twentieth century", *Family Matters,* p19.

31 Hanan (1868-1954) was appointed a Minister on 28 March 1912 and held office briefly (until July 10) in the short-lived Mackenzie administration. He later held the Education and Justice portfolios between August 1915 and August 1919 in the wartime Massey-Ward coalition. A nephew, Josiah Ralph Hanan (1909-69), was MP for Invercargill from 1946 to 1969. The younger Hanan proposed the Parliamentary Commissioner (Ombudsman) Act 1962 and was a tireless crusader to abolish capital punishment. He also promoted the Status of Children Act 1969 (see 2.5). Although in 1961 he introduced the Crimes Bill, Hanan successfully persuaded government members to vote for an amendment abolishing the death penalty. It was s59 of this legislation that became a rallying point for child activists in later decades (see 3.7).

32 *AJHR,* 1916-17, E-1A, p1.

33 Dalley, *Family Matters,* p8.

34 Similar fears existed in New Zealand. The natural increase in population had significantly dropped from 29.0 persons per 1,000 of the population in 1879, to 16.2 persons per 1,000 in 1899. Lynne Milne, "The Plunket Society: an experiment in Infant Welfare", unpublished BA (Hons) dissertation (History), Otago University, 1976, p120. Milne notes the contribution of the society to a falling mortality rate for European infants from 70 per 1,000 births in 1908, to 42 per 1,000 births in 1923 (p121).

35 For a more detailed account of the relationship between Plunket and the state, including the personal approbation and patronage it received from various Prime Ministers, see Lynda Bryder's essay, "Plunket's Secret Army': The Royal New Zealand Plunket Society and the State", in Bronwyn Dalley and Margaret Tennant (eds), '*Past Judgement': Social Policy in New Zealand History* (Dunedin: University of Otago Press, 2004), Chapter 7, pp109-24.

36 Gordon Parry, *A Fence at the Top: The First 75 Years of the Plunket Society* (Dunedin: The Royal New Zealand Plunket Society, John McIndoe, 1982), p59.

37 *Ibid.,* p65.

38 *Parry,* A Fence at the Top, *frontpiece quote.*

39 Much useful material for this section was drawn from McDonald's thesis, "The Governing of Children" *(op. cit.).*

40 J.A.B. O' Keefe and W.L. Farrands, *Introduction to New Zealand Law* (Wellington: Butterworths (fourth edition), 1980), p31.

41 The pattern had been well-established in Britain at the start of the nineteenth century. A census of beggars in London in 1803, for example, showed that of the estimated 15,000 on the streets, more than 9,000 were children. See McDonald, "The Governing of Children", p48.

42 By 1880, the ratio of those born in New Zealand to those who were migrants reached an equivalence. It is hardly surprising that thinking on children was strongly influenced by contemporary British thinking in the first decades of European settlement.

43 See the tabulated data (Table 5) sourced from the *AJHR* statements 1883-1912 cited in McDonald, "The Governing of Children", p133.

44 "MHR" (Member of the House of Representatives) was used until Dominion status was granted in 1907, thereafter those elected to the House were designated "MP".

45 McDonald correctly observes that "[C]hild adoption is a field rich in fundamental questions about the human condition" (*ibid,* p266). The Adoption Act 1955, he adds, was "to change dramatically the relationship between children, their parents and the state. Most importantly, it was to become one of those items of policy initially introduced as a remedy which, in time, themselves become the problem." (p265) Changes in confidentiality and the restriction of access to court records raised the question of the equity of rights between the parties concerned and the right to know about oneself, parents and one's children.

46 Hunt, formerly a long serving MP (1966 to mid-2005), is now New Zealand's High Commissioner in London. For more on the 1985 Act and related issues see Jenny Rockel and Murray Ryburn, *Adoption Today: Change and Choice in New Zealand.* Auckland: Heinemann Reed, 1988.

47 *NZPD* cited here in "Public Education in New Zealand: A speech delivered by the Hon. Robert Stout, Minister of Education, in the House of Representatives, July 21, 1885" (Wellington: Government Printer, 1885), p24 ("The New Zealand Pamphlets, 1. Education", held in the New Zealand Room, Canterbury Public Library).

48 McDonald, "The Governing of Children", p110.

49 As mentioned in the text, the dates here are more indicative than arbitrary, i.e. 1914 was the year the conflict began, and was well before the depression of the early thirties.

50 *Ibid.,* p134.

51 McDonald, "The Governing of Children", p139.

52 See above n43.

53 *NZPD,* 1925, p585.

54 "Report on Education in Industrial Schools", AJHR, 1900, E-3, p2.

55 *AJHR,* 1904, E1-C, p2. This is similar to what Dewey had said in *The Child and the Curriculum:* "The child lives in a somewhat narrow world of personal contacts. Things hardly come within his experience unless they touch, intimately and obviously, his own well-being, or that of his family or friends. His world is a world of persons with their personal interests, rather than a realm of facts and laws." John Dewey, *The Child and the Curriculum,* and *The School and Society* (Chicago: University of Chicago Press, twelfth impression, 1974), p5. This is from *The Child and the Curriculum* which was first published in 1902.

56 See M.P.K. Sorrenson's essay, "Modern Maori: The Young Maori Party to Mana Motuhake", in Keith Sinclair (ed), *The Oxford Illustrated History of New Zealand* (Auckland: Oxford University Press, 1990), pp323-25. Over time, the situation stabilised: "Despite the influenza, the 1921 census recorded a Maori population of 56,987—an increase of some 1700 over 1916. By the mid-twenties Maori were increasing at a greater rate than Pakeha." p332.

[57] James Belich, *Paradise Reforged: A History of the New Zealanders from the 1880s to the Year 2000* (Auckland: Allen Lane-Penguin Press, 2001), p113.

[58] For more on this intriguing development see the parliamentary debates during 1919, and also Roger Openshaw's article, "The Highest Expression of Devotion: New Zealand Primary Schools and Patriotic Zeal during the early 1920s", *History of Education*, Vol. 9, No. 4, 1980, pp333-44.

[59] Ewing, *The Development of the New Zealand Primary School Curriculum*, p281.

[60] *AJHR*, E-1, 1939, pages 2 & 3. This was to become the *sans pareil* statement of progressivism in New Zealand.

[61] W.L. Renwick, *Moving Targets: Six Essays on Educational Policy*. Wellington: NZCER, 1986, p16.

[62] *Ibid.,* p105.

[63] McDonald, "The Governing of Children", p246.

[64] *Ibid,* p247, citing the future Commissioner for Children Laurie O'Reilly, "Custody: a position overview", in the HRC compendium *The Rights of the Child and the Law* (HRC 1980), p4.

[65] For example, a rigorous study showed that children growing up in single parent homes, on average, had lower academic achievements, were more likely to engage in early sexual activity, were more likely to become teenage parents, and had lower prospects of being employed following high school. See Sara McLanahan and Gary Sandefur. *Growing Up with a Single Parent: What Hurts what Helps.* (Cambridge: Harvard University Press, 1994). Furthermore, a synthesis of 92 studies on the effects of divorce on children also shows that, on average, "Children with divorced parents achieve lower levels of success at school, are more poorly behaved, exhibit more behavioural and emotional problems, have lower self-esteem, and experience more difficulties with interpersonal relationships". Paul Amato, "Children of Divorce in the 1990's: An Update of the Amato and Keith (1991) Meta-Analysis," *Journal of Marriage and the Family,* Vol. 15, No. 3, 2001, p366.

[66] McDonald, "The Governing of Children", p274.

[67] See *Report of the Special Committee on Moral Delinquency in Children and Adolescents* (Wellington: Government Printer, September 1954). This was chaired by Dr O.C. Mazengarb and is commonly referred to as the Mazengarb Report. A summary was distributed by the Social Security Department to all households receiving either a family or orphan's benefit or a war pension. By March 1955, nearly 30,000 copies had been distributed.

[68] *Ibid.*

[69] Mazengarb Report, pp41-42.

[70] *Ibid.,* p33.

[71] See Ewing, *Development of the Primary School Curriculum,* p193.

[72] These "new" discoveries were common in progressive education literature of the period. This example comes from Beeby in *The Intermediate Schools of New Zealand: a survey* (Wellington: NZCER, 1938), p166.

73   *Ibid.,* p209.

74   Juvenile crime rates were rising: during 1939-45 the figure was officially 54 per 10,000. This dropped in 1948-1951 to 33 per 10,000; but in 1968 it rose to 82 per 10,000, and by 1971, reached 114 per 10,000 crimes. (McDonald, "The Governing of Children", p258). By the early 1970s, DSW officials were concerned "there is no indication of any tendency for the rates to stabilise." *(AJHR,* 1972, E. 4, *ibid.)*

75   L.C. Clements, "Marriage guidance in New Zealand: the story of a movement", in H.S. Houston (ed), *Marriage and the Family in New Zealand,* 1970, pp157-73, and cited here in McDonald *(op.cit.),* p251.

76   See, for example, D.M. Crowther (ed), "Street Society in Christchurch, Psychological Report No. 3" (Christchurch: Department of Psychology, Canterbury University, 1956).

77   "Youth without Purpose", *New Zealand Listener,* 8 August 1958, p12.

78   Status of Children Act 1969, section 3.

79   *Ibid.*

80   Hanan died suddenly in Canberra on 24 July 1969.

81   *NZPD,* 1969, p463.

82   "Essentially, what the Bill does is to reverse a legal presumption—the presumption that the word "child" in a legal document means legal offspring. One consequence of that in terms of wills is that many thousands of wills made on the old assumption will be interpreted, if the law were changed… ." *(ibid.,* pp467-68.)

83   i.e. Hanan, Findlay, and National MPs Sir Leslie Munro and Daniel Riddiford.

84   Census figures reveal the following decline in marriage rates: 1976, 35.5 %; 1981, 29.3%; 1986, 25.3%; 1991, 19.8%; 1996, 16.5%; and 2001, 14.8%.

85   *NZPD,* vol. 360, May-June 1969, pp472-73.

86   Department of Justice H-20 Report for year ending 31 March 1964, p. 23, and H-20, 1968, p17. Commenting on official figures since 1945, Dalley *(op.cit.)* notes that ex-nuptial births "[jumped] from fewer than 2,000 in 1948-9 to more than 9,000 in 1971-2, a rise from less than ten per cent to almost 20 per cent of all live births" (p171).

87   See "Demographic Trends 2004, Live and Still Births, By nuptiality, 1962-2003", Statistics New Zealand *Tatauranga Aotearoa,* at http://www.stats.govt.nz/NR/rdonlyres/3BEED9A8-07AE-4110-9834-9AAB88CC7710/0/Fert.xls (last accessed August 2006).

88   Dalley, *Family Matters,* p250.

89   *Ibid.,* p262.

90   It is now customary to speak of "sole" or "single" rather than "solo" parents, but this was not the case when the DPB was introduced.

91   *NZPD,* 1973, p3295.

92   *SNZ,* No. 136, 1964, cited in McDonald "The Governing of Children", pp317-18.

93   *NZPD, (loc.cit.),* p3297.

94   The 1971 Act created the category of "social worker" as a State Services Occupational Classification.

95 See Tom Brooking and Paul Enright, *Milestones: Turning Points in New Zealand History* (Lower Hutt: Mills Publications, 1988), especially Chapter 12, "1893—New Zealand First: Women Win the Vote" (p102) for a discussion of moves towards the franchise prior to the 1890s.

96 The Representation of the People Act 1918 gave women over 30 the right to vote (and in local elections), and also allowed women to become MPs. The later Representation of the People Act allowed women over 21 to vote in both parliamentary and local body elections.

97 There were many others, of course. For a representative account of key women and their experiences, see Maud Cahill and Christine Dann (eds), *Changing Our Lives: Women Working in the Women's Liberation Movement, 1970-1990* (Wellington: Bridget Williams Books Ltd), 1991.

98 A Review Committee calculated from a notional base in March 1965, to March 1976, that the number of DPBs increased from 1,622 to 23,047, and expenditure in that period had risen from nearly $1 million to just on $50 million (McDonald, "The Governing of Children", p330).

99 Historical notes cited on the Ministry's website, see http://www.mwa.govt.nz/news-and-pubs/publications/panui/panui.june.2006 (last accessed September 2006). In 2004 the MWA had a budget of $3.7 million, making it one of the smaller government departments despite its on-going ideological significance in providing a "Gender Analysis" framework which all other departments must utilise.

100 CEDAW was adopted by the UN in 1979 as one of six international treaties.

101 Despite the fact the establishment of the Commissioner in 1989 pre-dated New Zealand's ratification of UNCROC. Undoubtedly, however, ratification provided a catalyst for children's advocacy.

102 Helen May, *Politics in the Playground: the world of early childhood in post-war New Zealand* (Wellington: Bridget Williams Books/NZCER, 2001), p129, emphasis in original. May was appointed Professor of Education at Otago University in early 2005.

103 The Waitangi Tribunal was established by the Treaty of Waitangi Act 1975. It is a permanent commission of inquiry charged with making recommendations on claims brought by Maori relating to actions or omissions of the Crown (commonly in relation to land confiscation), which breached promises made in the Treaty of Waitangi.

104 See the report by Emily Watt "A History of Youth Justice in New Zealand" (Part 2) at http://www.justice.govt.nz/youth/history/part2.html (last accessed August 2006). This contains helpful background including a chronology and discussion of developments leading to the 1989 Act.

105 Dalley, *Family Matters,* p172.

106 *Ibid.,* p336.

107 John Barrington, *A Voice for Children: The Office of the Commissioner for Children, 1989-2003* (Palmerston North: Dunmore Press, 2004), p13.

108 Watt, "A History of Youth Justice" (*loc. cit.*), p5.

[109] See "Te Whainga I Te Tika", in the 1987 report to the Minister of Justice, Review of the Children and Young Persons Bill, p82, and cited here in Watt, "A History of Youth Justice", p7.

[110] Dalley, *Family Matters*, pp300-01.

[111] The overseeing Minister was Ann Hercus, who was also the first Minister of Women's Affairs.

[112] Barrington, *A Voice for Children*, p15.

[113] Dalley, *loc. cit.*, p342.

[114] Barbara J. Lewis and Patricia M. Lockhart, "The IYC report: A resource for the future" (Wellington: New Zealand Commission for the International Year of the Child, 1980), and cited here in McDonald, "The Governing of Children", p369.

[115] See s45, in McDonald, "The Governing of Children", p341.

[116] Barrington, *A Voice for Children*, p16, citing an oral interview with Ludbrook in 2002.

[117] Dalley, *Family Matters*, pp351-52.

[118] Barrington, *A Voice for Children*, p15, citing report brief.

[119] *Ibid*.

[120] Cited in Marie Connolly (ed), *New Zealand Social Work: Contexts and Practice* (Auckland: Oxford University Press, 2001), p9.

[121] See Watt, "A History of Youth Justice", p8, for more details of the legislation's long and difficult passage.

[122] The first telethon, a live television fundraising event, was in 1975. At that time, there were only two television channels in New Zealand (both state-owned), "closedown" was around 11 pm, and colour transmission and colour receivers were relatively new. Causes included St. John's, the disabled, and the Mental Health Foundation. A 24-hour television variety extravaganza raising funds for a worthy cause was quickly embraced by the watching public, although (arguably) by 1988, Telethon's novelty value had waned.

[123] Hood's book, *A City Possessed: The Christchurch Civic Crèche Case – Child Abuse, Gender Politics and the Law* (Dunedin: Longacre Press, 2001) is a detailed account of events surrounding the conviction of crèche workers, and in particular, male crèche worker Peter Ellis who was imprisoned on 22 June 1993. Though not published until after Ellis's release, *A City Possessed* further stimulated interest in the case, and child abuse generally.

[124] *Ibid.*, p66.

[125] Hood, *A City Possessed*, pp66-67.

[126] The debt to feminist advocacy and the increasing awareness of child sexual abuse was sometimes directly stated, as in the preface to the 1991 resource kit (booklet and video) *Safe Before Five:* "Te Auenga acknowledges the courage of children and adults who have been abused and who have spoken out about their experiences. Without them, and without the pioneering work of feminists in exposing abuse and supporting survivors, this package could not have been made."

[127] Hood, *A City Possessed*, p71.

128 The hypersensitivity created the potential for false accusations, particularly after paediatrician David Geddis had persuaded politicians and lawyers to make child sexual abuse a special case within the justice system. Geddis was a former Chief Medical Director of the Royal New Zealand Plunket Society and on the National Advisory Committee on the Prevention of Child Abuse (1980-89). Hood adds: "As a result [of the legal and social changes] by the late '80s, white, middle-class men were suffering from white, middle-class male guilt and were anxious to atone." (*Ibid.*, p111). In more recent times, however, networks have emerged to support those falsely accused of abuse, e.g. COSA New Zealand Inc. (Casualties of false Sexual Allegations), see http://www.geocities.com/newcosanz/cosa12-01.html#Telethon (last accessed August 2006).

The evolution of UNCROC
and selected rights and policy developments in New Zealand, 1959-2001

———————— • ————————

1959   United Nations Declaration on the Rights of the Child (UNDRC)

1962   Office of the Ombudsman established (NZ)

1968   Guardianship Act (NZ)

1969   Status of Children Act (NZ)

1970   Age of Majority Act (NZ)

1972   Department of Social Welfare formed, 1 April (NZ)

1974   Children and Young Persons Act (CYPA) (NZ)

1977   Human Rights Commission Act (NZ)

1978   Poland proposed marking the 1979 International Year of the Child (IYC) with a UN Convention on the Rights of the Child, but this was met with little enthusiasm.

1979   International Year of the Child (IYC)

1980   (Early 1980s) General consensus of the Commission on Human Rights was that UNDRC would provide the starting point for discussions on a new Convention. The Commission charged an *Open-Ended Working Group* with the task of reviewing and formulating the text of the proposed Convention. The *Working Group* was made up of representatives from 43 Member States of the Commission and chaired by Adam Lopatka, the former Director of the Institute of State and Law of the Polish Academy of Sciences.

1982   The "natural family environment" was often referred to as the "biological family" in UN *Working Group* debates.

1983   NGOs co-ordinated their involvement in the drafting process by organising a mid-year Consultation for interested organisations to ensure NGO input was well-prepared and coherent. *NGO Ad-Hoc*

Group on the drafting of the Convention emerged; thereafter met twice yearly.

1984
- New Zealand ratified the UN Convention on the Elimination of All Forms of Discrimination Against Women (CEDAW); effective from 10 January 1985.
- Ministry of Women's Affairs established (1984-86)

1985
UNICEF supported the new Convention on the Rights of the Child.

1988
5 February, the Open-Ended Working Group finished the first reading of the Draft Convention. This was followed by an in-depth technical review within the UN Secretariat.

1989
- The "technically sound" UNCROC text was forwarded to the *Committee on Human Rights* (March).
- Mid-late 1989: the Third Committee of the General Assembly adopted the Convention following minor changes.
- 20 November: The 54-Article Convention was placed on the agenda of the General Assembly. After only two minutes of procedural discussion it was approved by the 158-member Assembly. The text was then officially available for ratification by individual governments, to come into force 30 days after ratification by the twentieth state.
- CYPFA and OCC established; first Commissioner, Dr Ian Hassall (NZ)

1990
- 2 September: twentieth state ratified UNCROC
- Bill of Rights Act (BORA) (NZ).
- World Summit for Children.
- Government departments and agencies were invited by the Ministry of External Relations and Trade to examine UNCROC regarding future compliance requirements.

1992
Ministerial Review of the CYPFA (NZ)

1993
- 13 March: UNCROC ratified by the New Zealand Government
- HRA (NZ)
- Privacy Act (NZ)

1994
- International Year of the Family
- CPAG formed (NZ)
- 1 September: Laurie O' Reilly became the 2nd Commissioner for Children (NZ)
- New Zealand formally recognised a diversity of family forms at the International Conference on Population and Development, in Cairo,

5-13 September 1994
- Amendments to the CYPFA passed (came into force 1995) (NZ)

1997
- First UNCROC compliance report presented to the UN (NZ)
- Ministry of Youth Affairs established (NZ)
- New Zealand branch of EPOCH formed

1998
Hon Roger McClay appointed third Commissioner for Children, 16 February (NZ)

1999
- Department of Child, Youth and Family Services (CYFS) established, 1 October (NZ)
- Conference on UNCROC hosted by Children's Issues Centre, Dunedin, July (NZ)
- Ministry of Social Policy established, 1 October (NZ)
- Election of a Labour-led coalition government, November (NZ)

2000
- The government produced a draft of second UNCROC compliance report in May: "Children in New Zealand."
- *Agenda for Children* launched at the Seminar on Children's Policy held at parliament, July
- Children's Policy Reference Group established in September to work with the Ministries of Social Policy and Youth Affairs (NZ).
- First Children's Day launched by Hon Steve Maharey and Hon Roger McClay, 29 October (NZ).
- OCC issued a comprehensive report on James Whakaruru (written by Trish Grant) (NZ).

2001
- Human Rights Amendment Act (NZ)
- Commissioner for Children Bill, 29 August (NZ)
- MSD formed, 1 October (NZ)
- *Agenda for Children* released in April and submissions received by September (NZ)
- McClay proposed "a kind of Grey Power, but for those at the other end of the age spectrum", known as the 'Littlies Lobby' (September) launched by the OCC and Plunket, December (NZ).

CHAPTER THREE

————————— • —————————

UNCROC and children's rights

The Children, Young Persons and Their Families Act (CYPFA) was passed only days before the Convention on the Rights of the Child was adopted by the UN on 20 November 1989. The passage of updated child legislation set against the international backdrop of a new UN Convention meant the stage was set in the 1990s for a decade of concerted children's rights advocacy. This chapter explores the nature of UNCROC, its origins, ratification and subsequent interpretation within the New Zealand context.

The CYPFA was hailed as a 'new paradigm' with respect to youth justice issues.[1] In relation to offending, it modified the 1974 understanding of the paramountcy principle, 'the best interests of the child', by incorporating the autonomy and responsibility of the family group.[2] As discussed in the previous chapter, much of the impetus for this came from nascent multicultural understandings of family during the 1980s.[3] The Family Court, established in 1980, also attempted to contextualise guardianship issues with respect to the wider family rather than the maternal assumptions of previous law regarding separation, divorce and the custody of children.

By including 'families' in the title, the Social Services Minister, Dr Michael Cullen, claimed the new law placed "greater emphasis on the interests and authority of families. It reduces the power of the state and of professionals to make decisions for children and young people irrespective of their families . . ."[4] The focus on families appeared to signal a return to the old idea of the state being involved in child welfare only when it necessarily had to be. Critics, however, have pointed out that a revived emphasis on family fitted comfortably with the devolution of state authority in many areas of policy, including the public sector. The motivation was more fiscal than altruistic. In *The Ministerial Review of the Department of Child, Youth and Family Services*, published in 2000, the author, Judge Michael (Mick) Brown, put it like this:

> The general principles of the Children, Young Persons and Their Families Act state that families/whanau should participate in decision-making about the welfare of their own children who are in need of care and protection. Section 13 makes it clear that the primary role in caring for children lies with the whanau/family, hapu/sub-tribe or iwi/tribe who should be given all assistance necessary to do this.
>
> The economic and political climate (as previously described), was most receptive to any cost-cutting measure and there has been a progressive lessening of State responsibility for family and child welfare. The fiscal cost of maintaining children in care was increasingly seen as unaffordable and for several years previous to the passing of the Children, Young Persons and Their Families Act, long-term foster parents had been encouraged to adopt or take legal guardianship of the children in their care, thus assuming financial responsibility.
>
> The Children, Young Persons and Their Families Act and the Public Finance Act were passed into law in 1989, and the structure imposed by the latter has had a profound influence on the operation of the former.
>
> The Mason Report (Mason, Kirby and Wary, 1992) commented on the impact of government fiscal policies on the Children, Young Persons and Their Families Act, and warned against a system that attempted to quantify social response in dollar terms . . .[5]

It may have been the case—aside from the multicultural impulse—that the state's interest in families and welfare provision was increasingly fiscal, but the new economic environment—sometimes referred to as the New Right or 'neo-liberal' reforms—of 1984-93 also provided a ready political platform to lobby for children's rights, and calls for specialist government agencies to advocate on behalf of children. The reforms were intended to create a leaner and more efficient bureaucracy, but opponents increasingly highlighted the adverse impact on children and families. By 1993 there was considerable opposition to neo-liberalism and calls for policies sensitive to social, and not just fiscal needs.

Despite the rhetoric of child-focused, family-first policy that emerged after the CYPFA, the wider changes in New Zealand society up to the early 1990s augured poorly for the cohesion of the intergenerational family.[6] The incremental changes to family and divorce law over many decades, along with developments in human rights—and not solely the reforms of 1984-93—have also played their role in contributing to a society that has become unsupportive of the intergenerational family. In New Zealand as elsewhere, 'family' has always evoked strong images of protection and nurture, but the state's new hands-off message contained in the CYPFA was hardly enhanced when Part 9 of the legislation stated there would be a Commissioner for Children. Section 411 makes no mention, however, of family, and the cause of children would now be championed by a new bureaucratic structure.

3.1. THE ORIGINS OF UNCROC

The United Nations Convention on the Rights of the Child (UNCROC)[7] was unanimously adopted by the UN General Assembly, Resolution 44/25, on 20 November 1989. This followed a meeting in Geneva on 21 February 1989, where the text had been finalised before being presented to the Human Rights Commission on 7 March.[8]

The Convention was effective from 2 September 1990, after the twentieth state had deposited its instrument of ratification with Secretary-General, Javier Perez de Cuellar. UNCROC has since become one of six core international conventions and covenants promoting and protecting human rights.[9]

Like many UN Convention documents, UNCROC is clearly laid out and easy to read. Its format follows the established pattern of a Preamble and Parts, I-III, each containing several Articles, with 54 Articles in total. It reaffirms the family "as the fundamental group of society and the natural environment for the growth and well-being of all its members",[10] but even straightforward passages such as this depend upon what is denoted by 'family'. If what constitutes a 'family' is unclear, the interpretation becomes an ideological and political battleground, as has been the experience in New Zealand.

UNCROC's appeal lies in statements which are generic in principle, to ensure universal applicability. Specific details are to be fleshed out by individual governments (properly known as ratifying states parties) interpreting each statement in relation to changing domestic law.

It should be noted, however, that within international law, a

Convention is more significant than a Declaration. The latter is a statement of principles rather than a binding document. Because of its principles, a Declaration may be developed into a Convention or Treaty to be endorsed by several states acting together. Because it is binding, a Convention carries specific obligations. It also requires the active decisions of individual states in order to be ratified. This occurs when a signatory accepts the obligations and understands the implications ratification will have on future domestic legislation.[11]

Accordingly, UNCROC carries considerable status in both international and domestic law. It is monitored regularly and member nations are held accountable. No country can ever 'arrive'—meet all obligations fully—because new issues constantly surface and need to be addressed. This is one reason why UNCROC remains a perpetual rallying point for children's advocates.

UNCROC's appeal lies in statements which are generic in principle, to ensure universal applicability.

Article 44 requires signatory states to submit to the UN Committee a statement of the measures adopted to meet the rights recognised in UNCROC. This occurs within two years of a state's ratification and thereafter every five years. They must refer in these reports to "factors and difficulties, if any, affecting the degree of fulfilment of the obligations."[12]

Despite these stringent requirements, most governments—with the notable exception of the United States—have warmly embraced the Convention.[13] Former US President, Bill Clinton, signed UNCROC in February 1995, but it was not ratified by the Senate. Generally, however, most signatory states have endeavoured to implement the Convention and it is held in high regard as setting international standards for child well-being. A Save the Children document compiled after the tenth anniversary of UNCROC boasted:

> . . . it is now the most widely ratified human rights treaty in history. The adoption of the [Convention] has marked a watershed in the recognition of children's rights, formally identifying children as the bearer of rights— rights which are distinct from those of adults. It established an international framework for the treatment of all children and created an unprecedented greater global commitment to safeguarding their rights.[14]

UNCROC had a long gestation, with its origins ultimately in the child rescue movement of the late Victorian era and the prominence of charitable groups—

later known as NGOs—committed to child protection and advocacy (see 1.7). The Convention fused long-established protection rights with choice/ enabling or empowerment rights. This is evident in the Preamble where it is stated that "childhood is entitled to special care and assistance" because of the child's vulnerability and likelihood of being exploited, while later, in Article 13, "the child shall have the right to freedom of expression; this right shall include freedom to seek, receive and impart information and ideas of all kinds."

In these positive rights, UNCROC was reflecting the way human rights generally were being understood in the latter decades of the twentieth century. As legal scholars Bruce and Jonathan Hafen explain:

> The 1989 statement [also] charts what the UN calls 'new territory' by moving beyond protection rights to choice rights for children. According to a UN description, the CRC promotes a "new concept of separate rights for children with the Government accepting . . . responsibility of protecting the child from the power of parents . . ." To this end, the CRC's proponents say it "recognizes that children should have rights identical to adults." Therefore, the CRC takes a 'quantum leap' beyond the UN's 1959 Declaration by adopting and promoting an 'autonomous' view of children's rights that is "more based on choice than needs" of children. The new 'civil rights' provisions of the CRC reject the 'integrative' character of the 1959 Declaration, which had emphasized the "integration of persons into society", and instead provides children with "a sphere of autonomy and freedom from control." [15]

While appearing to be a natural extension and evolution of earlier formulations, the new emphasis raises important issues philosophically and with regard to parental rights and authority. In later sections we will explore the tensions implicit in UNCROC and how they have been dealt with in the New Zealand setting.

3.1. SUMMARY

- UNCROC evolved from the earlier UNDRC with the IYC in 1979, providing an important stimulus for a new statement on children's rights.

- Being a Convention, UNCROC carried greater status than a Declaration because it entailed specific and on-going compliance obligations for ratifying states.

- UNCROC has become the most widely ratified human rights treaty in history.

- UNCROC expressed a new understanding of human rights in that it moved beyond protection rights to include choice, or enabling/empowerment rights.

- The new rights emphasis raises important philosophical issues in relation to parental rights and authority.

3.2. THE COMMISSIONER FOR CHILDREN AND THE RATIFICATION OF UNCROC

What eventuated in New Zealand during the late 1980s and 1990s was a response to international changes in children's rights as well as new domestic law in the shape of the CYPFA. In many respects these variables were mutually supportive: one was a major development in international law; the other, landmark statute law.

A less obvious but still important shift shaping the context of a new rights culture occurred with the end of the Cold War in 1989. This was accompanied by an easing of the ideological polarities of East and West which had dominated international relations since 1945. According to New York professor of law, Mattias Kumm, citizens in Western democracies in the Cold War period tended to rely on the resources of domestic legal systems, while international law was perceived as having serious effects on 'other people'. It made few contributions to the post-1945 struggles in constitutional democracies. However, the new climate in international law brought serious legitimacy issues to the fore. In Kumm's opinion, the emergence of a revived international legal order witnessed "if not an iron cage—[then] certainly [as] a firmly structured normative web that makes an increasingly plausible claim to authority." He continues:

It tends to exert influence on national political and legal processes and often exerts pressure on nations not in compliance with its norms. Actors in constitutional democracies are increasingly engaging seriously with international law's claim to authority. What they find once they seriously engage international law gives rise to concern. Citizens find themselves in a 'double bind': the meaning of participation in the democratic process on the domestic level is undermined as international law increasingly limits the realm in which national self-government can take place. At the same time, there are no comparable democratic institutions and practices established on the international level.[16]

This is possibly true of New Zealand which, on account of its small size and isolation, was more susceptible to international influence than many other nations; and it is certainly true with the ratification of UNCROC by an unwary National government in 1993. The drafting, writing and compliance demands of the Convention were *Children's rights* far removed from the direct democratic accountability *are not neutral;* that New Zealanders were accustomed to, yet what was being agreed to would later absorb considerable taxpayer *they can, and do,* money, new laws, and on-going compliance costs. *intersect awkwardly*

Another international development affecting the *with parental rights* evolution of children's rights in New Zealand was the *Gillick* case in the United Kingdom in 1985. The idea *and responsibilities.* that children and young persons should be given the opportunity to participate in making decisions that affect them was later enshrined in Article 12 of UNCROC, but was first evident in the case of *Gillick v West Norfolk and Wisbech Area Health Authority*.[17] This had widespread ramifications because it redefined the power parents have over children. The three major points to emerge were: 1. parents have 'power' over their children only as far as is necessary for their children's welfare, benefit and protection; 2. as children and young people mature and develop, parental power 'dwindles'; and 3. children and young people develop at different rates, meaning parental powers don't disappear at a set age, it depends upon the maturity and understanding of the individual child or young person.

Although moderate in tone, the *Gillick* case was surrounded by the type of politicking that was soon to emerge in New Zealand. Children's rights are not neutral; they can, and do, intersect awkwardly with parental rights and responsibilities. Moreover, concerted advocacy can quite deliberately work to undermine parents.

The Children's Legal Centre (CLC) was set up in England in 1979 by Peter Newell and others as an extended project of the International Year of the Child. In 1985, it unsuccessfully petitioned the House of Lords to be appointed as *amicus curiae* to represent children in the *Gillick* case, which dealt with whether doctors were allowed to prescribe the contraceptive pill to girls under 16 without their parents' knowledge or consent. Throughout the case, the CLC had been in favour of removing the right of parents to know what their underage daughters were contemplating, and when the Lords decided in favour of the family planning lobby, the centre rejoiced that 'the Victorian concept' of absolute parental authority and control had been replaced by a new concept of partnership between parents and children.

Newell went on to co-ordinate other child advocacy agencies, including STOPP, APPROACH and EPOCH,[18] and the level of activism associated with these groups has done much internationally to politicise children.

Closer to home, the CYPFA and ratification of UNCROC generated much interest in children's rights in New Zealand. The exact role of family in relation to a growing emphasis on empowerment rights remained ambivalent, but the stage was set for a decade of rights advocacy and awareness of children's issues.

The debates preceding the 1989 legislation, as well as the Act itself, heralded not only important changes for child welfare, but stimulated both a general and a specific interest in children's rights, and, as one commentator put it, "drew attention to the need for an Ombudsman type of role to safeguard these."[19]

The milieu of legal reform at this time added support to such calls. The World Declaration on the Survival, Protection and Development of Children (World Summit for Children) in September 1990, passed a Plan of Action signed by 71 Heads of State. The Plan was endorsed by 181 countries, including New Zealand. The response here was spearheaded by the Ministry of Youth Affairs (MYA) and the Commissioner for Children, who formulated a National Plan of Action for Children as required by the undertaking given by New Zealand at the World Summit.

The 1990s also saw the passage of other related and highly significant legislation in New Zealand. The New Zealand Bill of Rights Act 1990 (BORA), for example, began life as a White Paper in David Lange's government in 1985. It was originally intended by its architect, Attorney-General Geoffrey

Palmer, to be a supreme law akin to the Bill of Rights in the US Constitution. Palmer sought to entrench the Treaty of Waitangi in accordance with the new spirit of bi- and multi-culturalism, but because what eventuated was an ordinary Act of Parliament, BORA had no special authority and could be amended like any other statute. Maori believed the inclusion of the Treaty in a Bill of Rights would demean it and make it susceptible to alteration or repeal.[20]

Whereas the BORA had a 'vertical orientation' to regulate the power of the state and limit the power of executive government and departments, the Human Rights Act 1993 (HRA) was more detailed legislation concerned with addressing 'horizontal' discriminatory acts inflicted by one citizen upon another. These key pieces of human rights legislation sat comfortably alongside two Optional Protocols to the International Covenant on Civil and Political Rights which the New Zealand Government had acceded to in 1989 and 1990 respectively,[21] and of course, with the outcomes of the World Summit for Children in September 1990. Interestingly, a specific Children's Bill of Rights had been mooted in the late 1960s, possibly around the time of the Status of Children Bill in 1969, but gained little traction.[22]

Paediatrician and child advocate, Ian Hassall, was instrumental in recommending an official child advocate during the later stages of the Children and Young Persons Bill in 1989.

Paediatrician and child advocate, Ian Hassall, was instrumental in recommending an official child advocate during the later stages of the Children and Young Persons Bill in 1989. He made a submission to the select committee on 20 April pointing out that seven other countries already had such an agency. In the first of two influential papers, *A Children's Ministry for New Zealand—An Office for Children Responsible to the Minister*, Hassall noted that similar positions had been created in South Australia with the Children's Interest Bureau in 1983, and in Norway with the Children's Ombudsman's Office in 1981.[23] In a timely comment, he suggested that "children in New Zealand are at least as disadvantaged through their relative powerlessness as are women, Maori and consumers, who already have Ministries of State to pursue their interests."[24] And Hassall was not alone. In her candid account of child abuse in New Zealand and what to do about it; in 1990, Auckland journalist, Leslie Max, asked "[w]ill New Zealand be able to ratify the Convention?", and citing one of her own articles in *Metro* magazine, she lamented, "[t]here is no children's lobby. The kakapo has a lobby, the wetlands have a lobby. There are rabbit boards, electricity boards, drainage boards. There are parliamentary spokespersons for potatoes, hops and small seeds. There is no spokesperson for children . . . There is a pressing need for a body which will effectively represent children's interests. Children need their own source of advocacy and protection, unencumbered by any conflicting adult priorities."[25]

In a coalescence of 'causes', children were beginning to assume a rights status similar to other marginalised groups, notably women. Citing Human Rights Commissioner, Rae Julian, Max shared the view that the key to the advancement of women was the establishment of the Ministry of Women's Affairs.[26]

A Human Rights Commissioner for Children would, it was believed, define the work of the incumbent too narrowly. Rights issues were certainly important but advocacy needed to be positive as well and not confined solely to the legal defence of children's issues or rights. Moreover, the Office would work to balance the paramountcy principle with family considerations in accordance with the requirements of the new Act.

Even so, in his second paper to the select committee, *An Office for Children—A Solution to the Child Protection Dilemma*, Hassall pointed out that the Bill's "presumption in favour of the family . . . is seen by many in law, medicine, social work and in the community, as a retrograde step and will be the subject of controversy."[27] This suggests that the true 'experts' were trained professionals rather than parents. The title Ombudsman for Children was not favoured because a wider, more proactive role combining advocacy, research and policy development was envisaged, rather than receiving and acting upon complaints.[28]

The CYPFA accordingly provided for the appointment of a Commissioner for Children.[29] The Office of the Commissioner for Children (OCC) was set up as a Crown entity under the Public Finance Act 1989.[30]

The first Commissioner was Ian Hassall, which was not surprising given the influential nature of his submissions to the CYP Bill's select committee. He was perhaps an obvious choice—a respected medical practitioner and paediatrician,[31] and an experienced commentator on children's issues. He had been outspoken on cot death research and had advocated the fencing of private swimming pools to prevent infant deaths. He had also worked with the Plunket Society—that most venerable of charitable child welfare institutions—in South Auckland, one of the nation's most identifiable areas of need. Hassall must have been a popular choice because he was appointed four months following his second submission to the select committee, and even before the 1989 Bill had completed its passage through parliament. A former Chief Social Worker at the Department of Child, Youth and Family (CYF), Mike Doolan, later noted that Hassall's appointment was reassuring to medical and legal professionals concerned that the Act would lean too far in the direction of family responsibility without sufficient professional input.[32]

Because of its limited resources—the annual government grant for the OCC's operation in its first years was said to be 'around $500,000'[33]— and partly as a deliberate policy, the Commissioner's broad advocacy role, in reality, consisted of individual, detailed investigations into children's issues. This ensured a public profile of the Office's activities and meant that although the projects tackled were generally local in nature, they were manageable and conducted successfully within a modest budget. Among the early staff were Gabrielle Maxwell, a psychologist and university lecturer in criminology (from February 1990), and Beth Wood, a seasoned children's rights campaigner (from February 1992). Wood in particular was to be a sustained voice for children's rights, and particular causes such as the abolition of smacking later in the decade.

In their 1992 paper, *A Children's Rights Approach to Custody and Access: Time for a Radical Re-think*, Hassall and Maxwell argued in favour of children's rights, rather than wider family issues. Experience with custody and access disputes led them to believe children were suffering in the confusion between children's and parental rights. So,

> They proposed instead a 'fresh approach based firmly on a child's rights or best interests of the child perspective', applying to all proceedings [and] pointing out that Article 9 of the United Nations Convention on the Rights of the Child stated that all interested parties in court proceedings should be given an opportunity to participate.[34]

As it worked out, this statement contained two elements which set the parameters for most debates throughout the decade: children's rights were of more significance than those of parents or families, and appeals to UNCROC were the 'bottom line'—there was no greater authority. A major anomaly was that UNCROC was being cited as authoritative, when the government had yet to ratify it. This discrepancy was rectified on 13 March 1993.[35]

Despite the time lag between the advent of the Convention in 1989 and New Zealand's ratification, the Ministry of External Relations and Trade (MERT) had actively sought comment on the final text. Government agencies were invited to examine relevant provisions and consider changes needed to ensure compliance. It was MERT policy that international human rights instruments would be ratified only if existing conditions ensured compliance requirements could be met. According to lawyer, Robert Ludbrook, most government agencies were slow to respond, and those that did, did little to show whether existing laws affecting their work would comply with UNCROC. Additionally, the views of the Commissioner for Children, Youth Affairs and Women's Affairs were not sought, and only the Labour and Justice Departments along with the Human Rights Commission responded.[36] There was no attempt to consult the wider public.

In pointing out the apathy of government departments and agencies in the pre-ratification period, rights lobbyists have consequently been able not only to accentuate the need for specific reforms, e.g. to abolish smacking, but also to complain about state agencies meeting their obligations under international law.

The failure to seek comprehensive feedback or to respond clearly frustrated child advocates, but in the longer term it may have assisted their cause. In pointing out the apathy of government departments and agencies in the pre-ratification period, rights lobbyists have consequently been able not only to accentuate the need for specific reforms, e.g. to abolish smacking, but also to complain about state agencies meeting their obligations under international law. Had state agencies been informed, responsive, and committed to compliance in the first instance, the need for concerted NGO advocacy might not have been so intense. Since the initiative to implement UNCROC then rested with those most informed about and committed to it, this created a catalyst for politicising children's rights in New Zealand. It cast the nation's children in deprecating language as 'victims of tokenism and hypocrisy', and also meant the main channel for redressing 'grievances' as well as more general but proactive advocacy would lie in pressuring the state and its agencies. The context for advocacy would essentially be legal and political.

Lubrook spelled out what was entailed in ratification. It was binding on the government to:

- Respect and ensure the rights set forth in the Convention to each child within their jurisdiction without discrimination of any kind (Article 2). "Commentaries on UNCROC stress that 'to respect' means "to refrain from any actions which would violate any of the rights" and 'ensure' implies an affirmative obligation to take whatever measures are necessary to enable individual children to enjoy and exercise their Convention rights (Alston, 1991)."

- Undertake all appropriate legislative, administrative and other measures for the implementation of the rights recognised in the Convention (Article 4). "The Committee on the Rights of the Child has emphasised the particular importance that all domestic legislation be compatible with the Convention and that there is co-ordination of policy within and between all levels of government (UN Committee on the Rights of the Child, 1989, para. 12)."

- Submit regular reports to the Committee on the Rights of the Child on measures adopted to give effect to the rights set out in UNCROC and on progress made in the enjoyment by children of those rights (Article 44.1). "Such reports must indicate any factors affecting fulfilment of Convention obligations and must contain sufficient information to enable the Committee to have a comprehensive understanding of the reporting country's implementation of the Convention (UN Committee of the Rights of the Child, 1989, para. 6)." [37]

Under UNCROC the New Zealand government would become the mechanism for implementing and monitoring children's rights, but it is a daunting, if not impossible, task to meet the rights of 'each child' and "undertake all appropriate legislative, administrative and other measures."[38] The scale of what was actually entailed in delivering rights seems to have been less important than the purported benefits. The assumption of full conformity brought into sharp focus what needed to be done following ratification.[39]

The Minister of Foreign Affairs and Trade, Don McKinnon,[40] could scarcely have envisaged the import of his words when he announced that UNCROC was "an important instrument that reflected the international community's concern to promote the well-being of children through a legally binding treaty by laying down minimum standards for their protection . . . Future legislation", he said, "would need to be considered in light of the

Convention."[41] Although the National government officially ratified UNCROC, it would appear there was no compelling ideological support or knowledge of the implications of what was being done within the party at the time. There was more a feeling that this was the proper thing to do to bring New Zealand into line with international law, the BORA, and the Human Rights Bill which was then before parliament—but soon to become the HRA.[42] Up until this time—notwithstanding the work of the OCC—the initiative to articulate rights issues had lain not with the government, but with established groups such as Plunket, Barnardos and Save the Children—but this was soon to change.

"The Convention is an exciting and adaptable and powerful instrument whose power depends on the degree to which all of us take it seriously in our lives with and for our children, and work to make our governments take it seriously. The only limitations are our imagination and energy to use it."

Speaking on the tenth anniversary of UNCROC's ratification by the UN in 1999, the international child advocate and founder of EPOCH (End Physical Punishment of Children), Peter Newell, addressed a conference jointly hosted in Auckland by Action for Children in Aotearoa, the New Zealand branch of EPOCH,[43] and the Ministry of Youth Affairs (MYA). He concluded: "The Convention is an exciting and adaptable and powerful instrument whose power depends on the degree to which all of us take it seriously in our lives with and for our children, and work to make our governments take it seriously. The only limitations are our imagination and energy to use it."[44]

This is a revealing comment in light of Newell's prominence, notably in the United Kingdom. Clearly he saw UNCROC as a supra-international instrument almost possessing the ability to generate its own momentum for change.

3.2. SUMMARY

- The growth of children's rights in New Zealand reflected international and domestic developments during the 1980s. A review of the CYPA 1974 was accompanied by widespread change in understanding bi- and multi-culturalism, and specific rights for women and Maori, as well as important progress in shaping UNCROC, the outcome of the *Gillick* case in the UK, and the end of the Cold War.

- These events created a new rights-sensitive legal environment. The CYPFA of 1989 re-emphasised the importance of family and whanau in understanding and responding to children and young persons; it also created a Commissioner for Children. The new OCC, which the Commissioner led, was based firmly on UNCROC principles, with special emphasis being placed upon Article 12 and the participation of children and young people in decisions affecting them.

- The family ethos of the CYPFA, however, soon created tensions within the OCC as the rights of the child were seen in some instances to be inconsistent with family advocacy. As a result, the OCC began to place more emphasis on lobbying for children's rights.

- A major anomaly in the lobbying environment in the period 1989-1992 was that the government had not yet ratified UNCROC. Eventually, however, this occurred in March 1993, despite the then National government showing little intrinsic enthusiasm for the Convention.

- The ratification of UNCROC provided a new authority for sustained children's rights advocacy in New Zealand.

3.3. THE PRIMACY OF UNCROC

There can be little doubt that in the decade since New Zealand's ratification, long after McKinnon had left parliament to become Commonwealth Secretary-General,[45] the UNCROC legacy has been rich and the Convention remains a driving instrument of domestic public policy. Its importance has been enhanced by concerted efforts of the Commissioner for Children (now known as the Children's Commissioner[46]) and the work of numerous NGOs.[47]

From the start, Hassall as the Commissioner for Children realised the similarities between the 1989 Act and UNCROC, and he "worked hard to make UNCROC meaningful in the New Zealand context", and was "really passionate" that Article 12 would become a set of principles to guide the work of the Office.[48] Maxwell added that "[T]he compatibility between the 1989 Act and UNCROC became immediately obvious to us. It gave us an objective rather than subjective basis or benchmark for making judgements. A pattern was established where, if we did anything, we'd start with UNCROC and the Act." [49]

Accordingly, "the Office played an important role in advocating for UNCROC's ratification by New Zealand." Sensing perhaps, that some would be suspicious of what the Convention would mean for New Zealand policy and practice, Hassall attempted to allay fears by publishing a paper, *Does the Convention Go Too Far?*[50]

It was not easy to convince New Zealanders of UNCROC's validity. All subsequent Commissioners have also made it quite clear, however, that implementing the Convention was their *raison d'être*. In 2002, for example, McClay reported to parliament that that year had seen "intensive strategies to focus organisations on accepting and implementing the United Nations Convention on the Rights of the Child."[51] Elsewhere he said, "New Zealand is starting to now more proudly boast about our acceptance of the United Nations Convention on the Rights of the Child as a benchmark of what is right, fair and just for our children. But, we still have so far to go. Not all New Zealand children and young people are safe."[52] As always, this mildly self-deprecating tone helped the cause, but the extent to which UNCROC has come to be embraced in New Zealand—at least in terms of its ideals—is possibly without parallel in any country of comparable population.[53]

The passing of the BORA and the HRA made the early nineties a propitious period in advancing what was later called a 'human rights culture' in New Zealand.

UNCROC's ratification coincided with a period of frenetic development in human rights legislation, specific—and protracted—debates over the CYPFA, the tail end of a decade of economic and social change—including benefit cuts announced in the 1991 Budget, widespread reform of curricula in New Zealand schools—culminating in the New Zealand Curriculum Framework's 'seven essential learning areas', and the issuing of new curricular statements. The passing of the BORA and the HRA made the early nineties a propitious period in advancing what was later called a 'human rights culture' in New Zealand.[54]

From its rather inauspicious beginnings in March 1993, UNCROC has reached what Newell and McClay described as an exalted status.[55] Upon his retirement in July 2003, McClay proclaimed UNCROC "the bible for the office", and "how we make a judgement about what's fair and what we promise children."[56]

This elevation of UNCROC from perfunctory ratification to 'bible' is the result of many variables: New Zealand's small size and historic vulnerability to capture by the dictates of international law; the tireless efforts by NGOs to propel children's rights into the forefront of political and public policy debate; the media prominence given to high-profile and tragic cases of child abuse and maltreatment in the 1990s;[57] domestic political policy—particularly in relation to left-leaning parties—and, not least importantly, the continuing decline of marriage and family in New Zealand society with the concurrent promotion of alternative modes of cohabitation and acceptance of 'new' family forms. This trend has accelerated since the provision of no-fault divorce laws in the early 1980s.[58]

3.3. SUMMARY

- The first Commissioner for Children, Dr Ian Hassall, "worked hard to make UNCROC meaningful in the New Zealand context." As an instrument of international law, UNCROC was seen to have an objective legitimacy in guiding the work of the OCC.

- The primacy of UNCROC has provided a raison d'être for all subsequent commissioners.

- The advent of the BORA in 1990 and the HRA in 1993 augured well for UNCROC in creating a climate of receptivity for sustained children's rights advocacy in the 1990s.

3.4. FROM AXIOMATIC TO PROBLEMATIC: EXAMINING UNCROC

The New Zealand experience has demonstrated that although UNCROC may be a fairly bland document, its utility depends on how those committed to the cause choose to interpret it, and how those ideas are mediated in public debate. For example, few would disagree that the family is 'the fundamental group of society', but when the definition, form and function of family itself becomes contested, rights issues and the already inherent tension between child and parental rights become compounded; the focus shifts to ideological interpretations of what is meant.

Further to this, New Zealand formally recognised a diversity of family forms at the International Conference on Population and Development (ICPD) held in Cairo from 5 to 13 September 1994. This was the largest conference on population and development to that time, with 11,000 registered participants, including government, UN and NGO representatives and the media. More than 180 states took part in negotiations to finalise a Programme of Action for the next two decades. While the family was recognised as "the basic unit of society . . . Traditional notions of gender-based division of parental and domestic functions and participation in the paid labour force do not reflect current realities and aspirations . . . [there is an] existing diversity of family forms [and] the objectives are . . .

Extrapolated from

its original context,

UNCROC became

transformed

into a political

battleground.

To develop policies and laws that better support the family, contribute to its stability and take into account its plurality of forms."[59]

Extrapolated from its original context, UNCROC became transformed into a political battleground. In this instance, it was part of a wider attempt by certain groups to add legitimacy to their calls for a redefinition of the family, or an undermining of what some saw as oppressive parental rights to control children. In a similar manner, tensions arose in the interpretation of Articles 15 and 16—the rights of children to associate with others, the right to protection from interference, and the right to privacy—when children, especially teenagers, started: dating, engaging in sexual relations, or seeking to view objectionable material at home. As the wider rights culture moved to uphold the child's individual autonomy, this came—in the home setting at least—at the expense of a parental right to prohibit these practices. Another contentious area which surfaced recently in New Zealand, particularly during the debate on the Care of Children Bill, has been the rights of young women and girls to secure an abortion without parental knowledge or consent.[60]

These examples illustrate the susceptibility of UNCROC—or, for that matter, any ratified convention of international law—to on-going domestic interpretation and change.

Rights, in their eclectic manifestations—be they active or passive, positive or negative, abstract or concrete, group or individual—have assumed centre-stage in most Western societies, including New Zealand. As we have seen, the emergence of a rights-sensitive culture in New Zealand owes much to developments during the 1970s and the politicisation of particular causes. To assert that something is a rights issue is to transform it into a vehicle for social and legal action. An official UNCROC website, for example, confuses basic human needs with children's rights when it is claimed that "[P]reviously seen as negotiable, the child's needs have become legally binding rights. No longer the passive recipient of benefits, the child has become the subject or holder of rights."[61] When needs become rights, some agency has to monitor the provision and enforcement of those rights, and within the UNCROC rubric, the demand is clearly placed upon ratifying states.

Even so, Switzerland-based juvenile justice and children's rights attorney, Bruce Abramson,[62] argues that the jurisdiction of the state in Article 12(1), for example, "in all matters affecting the child", is not meant to be interpreted as a right against parents, nor does it apply to non-state groups (NGOs). He explains:

> There is a growing tendency to focus on the word 'all' as the basis for claiming that youngsters hold the right against their parents. Is this correct? Does Article 12 apply to non-state actors like UNICEF, the Committee on the Rights of the Child, non-governmental organizations working for children's rights, and parents?
>
> The selective focusing on the word 'all' makes the mistake of reading a legal text literally, and reading a legal provision out of context.
>
> When it comes to interpreting legal texts, the rules of legal interpretation make it clear that a literal interpretation is improper . . . The Vienna Convention on the Law of Treaties specifically addresses this issue. A word must be read according to its ordinary meanings—unless the legal document gives it a special meaning. And since all words have multiple meanings, a term's ordinary meaning is to be understood in the light of the context.
>
> There should be no dispute on this point: the State Party, and only the State Party, is the duty-bearer of the obligations imposed by CRC Articles 1 to 40. When States came together to write the treaty, they all understood that they were defining the obligations of States under international law. When States act internally, they impose legal obligations on non-state actors. They do this when parliament enacts legislation, and when authorities in the administrative branch issue regulations or directives. But when states act internationally, like when they create a treaty, they set forth the obligations

that they are willing to undertake as a part of international law . . . Article 12 does not say that every child has a right to be listened to in any matter that *anybody* takes that might affect that youngster.[63]

International law as expressed in UNCROC and intended by its framers was not imposing a legal requirement to listen at all times to the views of children, but rather "in any judicial and administrative proceedings affecting the child". In any case, this refers to the decision-making of the state party as the duty-bearer and the child as the corresponding rights holder. In New Zealand, however, Article 12 has been interpreted generically as applying to virtually *any* views the child may hold, irrespective of age or context. The clarion call has come not just from the state and its agencies, but from NGOs demanding all sectors of society listen to and promptly act upon the views of the child.

the tendency to express a range of issues as rights concerns may undermine the potency of fundamental rights

According to leading Catholic scholar, George Weigel,[64] the confusion with the contemporary view of rights lies in the errors of the UDHR. By reconceptualising social goods as human rights, he argues that the UDHR established a foundation on which many of the new understandings now rest. When, for example, the UDHR put the right to "periodic holidays with pay" on a legal plane with the fundamental right of religious freedom, it undermined the inalienability that had characterised an understanding of rights since the days of Thomas Jefferson. The ever-growing list of rights that followed the UDHR in various declarations and conventions invited the suspicion that if everything was a right, then nothing was a human right in any serious sense.[65]

This is in contrast to the views of prominent groups, notably the HRC, that human rights are inalienable, inherent, indivisible and universal. They cannot be denied to anyone because they are inherent in what it means to be human; moreover, they cannot be forfeited because they are intimately connected and form a cluster of entitlements. The point Weigel makes, however, is valid—the tendency to express a range of issues as rights concerns may undermine the potency of fundamental rights: certainly, rights-talk in war-torn nations such as Iraq or Afghanistan has an immediacy about it related to the right to live without being shot at. In the West, however, basic rights are being complemented by refined expressions concerning such diverse issues as biotechnology, mental health, public broadcasting and accident insurance.[66] The mixing of new with established rights increases the complexity of what is meant by indivisibility.

What exactly are then, the 'rights of the child'? This may seem an odd question when the whole purpose of UNCROC is to state what these rights are.

A generally useful definition of children's rights was provided by the second Commissioner for Children, Laurie O'Reilly. In a speech delivered in October 1997, he said rights could be classified in the following ways: 1. Affirmative rights, for example, freedom to express an opinion, freedom of association, privacy; 2. Entitlements, for example, rights to education and health, rights of disabled children, rights of ethnic minorities; and 3. Protections, for example, [the] right to be protected from child abuse, neglect or from harmful media.[67] While seemingly straightforward, this classification does not take into account the tensions and conflicts that occur when the expressions of rights overlap.

What happens when an expression of affirmative rights infringes upon others? When, for example, a child or young person asserts a right to be on the internet and in so doing prevents others from using the phone; or when a young person asserts his or her right to attend a particular secondary school against the right of parents to decide? (Other areas where parental rights potentially clash with those of teenagers include cell phone purchase and use, buying a car, dating, leaving home, and the particularly controversial issues of contraception and, as mentioned, for young women, abortion.)

The long history of state education in New Zealand (see Chapter 2) has traditionally upheld a parent's right to send a child to a local state school; how the newly-asserted entitlement rights of the child square with traditional parental rights adds a new dimension to current debates on school choice, and indeed, in relation to all the above-named issues.

In 1919, the American legal philosopher, Wesley N. Hohfeld, argued that 'right' could be approached from different directions.[68] It may be related to 'claim' or 'duty', but also needs to be distinguished from these terms. In a strict sense, 'right' is the correlative of 'duty' and the opposite of 'no right'. If a person knows he has a right, he can ask: "What must the other do for me?" This right is the same as 'claim'. Most of the rights in UNCROC are of this nature: the state—rather than a specific person—is required to act on behalf of the nation's children and it must not withhold its duty to so act. Duty, so defined, means that a person should be able to answer the question "What must I do for that other person?" In ratifying UNCROC, the government has taken upon itself to answer by providing a perpetual statutory duty to advocate for children.

This analytical linking is useful in considering children's rights because it demonstrates the strong and necessary relationship between rights and duties. A right is not effectual by itself—it doesn't do anything—but means something only in relation to a corresponding obligation. The utility of a right springs not from the individual who possesses it or the intended recipient, but from other persons—or organisations—who consider themselves under obligation to that individual. It is the recognition of the obligation that makes the right(s) effectual. When international conventions are ratified there will be a focus not just on the recipients of the newly articulated rights (children), but on agencies positioned to do the advocacy and 'deliver' the rights, as well.

Expressed in the language of either an individual's or a group's entitlement—as in UNCROC—rights tend to either ignore or to implicitly diminish notions of the wider public interest. This encroaches upon the problem raised earlier: do we conceive of children's rights in an individualistic sense, or do we primarily understand children relationally by defining them within, and part of, the family? UNCROC makes several references to family but the primary focus is on individual rights. The ambivalence creates a tension which is not readily resolved in any workable understanding of what it means to be a child.[69] UNCROC rights are a mix of what may be called 'passive negative rights'—the rights of freedom from interference, as in Article 16, 'passive positive rights'—the rights to receive material things such as a name, nationality, food, etc; Article 26, and the rights of autonomy—freedom to be one's own master.[70]

In *Liberalism and the Limits of Justice,* Cambridge scholar, Michael Sandel, stresses that the starting point towards the well-being of any citizen should be the well-being of the community as a whole. He contends that rights should further the goals of an entire community rather than sectional interests, and, as we have seen, this fits with the original intent of UNCROC.

This starts with realising that although a 'child' exists as an individual, it does not refer to a person in isolation. Each child is a descendent of his parents and his reality is relational within the context of family. Children's rights, therefore, should be in harmony with parental rights and understood within the context of mutual obligations.

The debates that have evolved from J.S. Mill's essays On *Liberty* and *Utilitarianism* expand on the relational nature of rights. As one writer has said in relation to Mill, "The search for a philosophical justification of children's rights might begin, for instance, with the assertion that the right to fair treatment is based on some element of human nature which is common to both adults and children."[71] For Mill, an immaturity of faculties means the child is unable to make proper judgements; it relies on the authority and direction of adults until it is capable of free and equal discussion. To claim, however, that children are not mature is not the same as saying they are incompetent; the strength of developmental psychology is that children are understood in terms of their capacities—albeit, evolving capacities—rather than their incapacities. The assumption of child immaturity has long been a rationale for protection rights as well as a basis for adult responsibility towards children.

Children's rights, therefore, should be in harmony with parental rights and understood within the context of mutual obligations.

Returning to UNCROC and contemporary understandings of rights, the Convention represented a moving away from the concept of rights as 'vertical', that is, those in which citizens are *protected from* unnecessary state intervention—as in the BORA. Children are now being *advocated for* by the state. As rights have evolved, the emphasis has moved to 'horizontal' rights which assume that children need protecting from other citizens—even parents and siblings—and that the state, in implementing the Convention, is a benign and altruistic guardian of their interests expressed as 'rights'. In this, the state comes, quite literally, to adopt a paternalistic stance, and in doing so has the potential to reorder normative family relationship dynamics by interposing new legal standards between children and parents.

The emphasis on family, including the insertion of the word in the landmark 1989 legislation, was not based on the previous understanding of family as a pivotal institution of civil society—that is, as an institution that properly and normally stands outside direct government intervention. The debates during the 1980s led to a restatement of the importance of family, but mainly through contemporary calls to better understand multiculturalism.

UNCROC thus created a new web of rights, duties and obligations by making the state a central player. The effect has been to diminish the mediating status of the intergenerational family which had hitherto been assumed in New Zealand law. The long-established principle in domestic law has been that the state should only intervene in child welfare and custody when the family was dysfunctional or rendered—through the death or separation of a parent—incapacitated or unable to provide for children. Moreover, it cannot be assumed that as the champion of children's rights, the state will act impartially or benignly, because of all the political overtones.

The ratification of UNCROC introduced a new variable into the way New Zealanders understood children. The Convention was not merely an extension of an historical response to children which, by and large, respected the autonomy and authority of families. Rather it tends to acknowledge the primacy of the state and its agencies—and NGOs demanding compliance with UNCROC. The modern obsession with human rights absorbs and replaces earlier notions.

Bureaucracy, however, lacks the simple moral understanding that parents are responsible for the care and nurture of their children.

Having introduced the state into the equation, now when things go wrong, we tend to ask: "What's the government going to do about it?" Or, more specifically with respect to high-profile child abuse cases, "Why didn't CYF intervene beforehand?", or "What's the Children's Commissioner going to do to reduce this sort of abuse?" Virtually no one asks, "Why weren't the parents being responsible?" or "Does this situation represent the state's failure to intervene, the failure of parents, or both—or neither?" The new legal environment thus makes it all too easy to blame state agencies. The normative understanding of rights and reciprocal obligations is complicated by making the state authoritative. A moral framework of rights and duties then becomes overshadowed by the expectation that an all-encompassing state will protect and provide for at-risk children.

Bureaucracy, however, lacks the simple moral understanding that parents are responsible for the care and nurture of their children.

Evidence of this was provided in Roger McClay's recommendations in a report on James Whakaruru, a four-year-old boy who died in 1999 after a long history of physical assaults perpetrated by his mother's partner. In an 88-page report, *Final Report on the Investigation into the death of James Whakaruru*, published in June 2000, McClay noted:

New Zealand has been a signatory to the United Nations Convention on the Rights of the Child since 1993. The United Nations Committee on the Rights of the Child has considered New Zealand's compliance with the Convention (report January 1997), and noted with concern that New Zealand's approach to the rights of the child appear to be somewhat fragmented due to a lack of a global policy or plan of action related to children and their rights. The Committee recommended that New Zealand prepare and adopt a comprehensive policy statement with respect to the rights of the child, (incorporating the principles and provisions of the Convention) that could provide guidance to all those involved in support services delivered or funded by Government.[72]

The conclusion he drew was that "James Whakaruru was badly let down by the state",[73] and the following agencies needed to become more active by setting in place better systems and enhanced inter-agency communication, cooperation and accountability: the Government of New Zealand (ensuring UNCROC compliance); the Minister of Social Services and Employment; the Chief Executive of the Department of Child, Youth and Family Services; the Chief Executive of the Department for Courts; the Chief Executive of the Department of Corrections; the Minister of Justice; the Commissioner of Police; the Director-General of the Ministry of Health; the Chief Executive of Healthcare Hawke's Bay; the Director of the New Zealand College of Midwives and the Chief Executive of Well Child Providers.[74] Yet nowhere was there any mention of the need for better parenting and a stable family structure.[75] Certainly the above-named agencies could and perhaps should have been more responsive, but this case shows clearly how UNCROC produces a bureaucratic response to what was essentially morally reprobate behaviour and deep-seated relational dysfunction. Moreover, the disintegrating family and increased incidence of single-parent families has provided the state with a specific reason to become more involved in the care and protection of children.[76] As in this report, the state's activities over a long period as a complicit variable in family disintegration and increasing dependency was not acknowledged. Instead the assumption is that more bureaucratic and 'inter-sectoral co-operation' will 'facilitate better outcomes' for at-risk children.

Agencies such as CYF are, of course, run by staff thoroughly committed to preventing the abuse and neglect of children. But the demand to comply with UNCROC as well as domestic political (including NGO) pressure, coupled with a disturbing rise in numbers of dysfunctional families, has created an unmanageable workload and totally unrealistic expectations of what can be achieved.[77] And there is another, less obvious drawback to the proliferation of a rights culture: the juggernaut-like growth of bureaucracy. Intimately linked with this is the way that some state agencies—under the guise of a respect for the child's rights—have militated *against* the stability and independent functioning of families.

Arguably, the most contentious problem relating to UNCROC is the paramountcy or 'best interests of the child' principle. As we have seen, this phrase is not unique to the Convention, and indeed, appears in many legal documents concerning children, including New Zealand statute law. The problem is this: even if 'best interests' can be defined clearly, who is the authority to determine those interests?

The principle assumes the child's interests are unique to each and every child. As with UNCROC generally, the vacuous nature of 'best interests' makes it vulnerable to either niche interpretations, or renders it meaningless. For example, child lobbyists wanting to ban smacking will cite as the paramountcy principle the child's right not to be harmed in any way, even—and perhaps especially—by parents. A contrary interpretation, however, might be that the occasional use of smacking or physical restraint is an appropriate and effective parenting strategy that serves the wider 'best interests of the child' by helping to maintain discipline within the home. In practice, particularly in guardianship and custody disputes, the courts decide what 'best interests' mean. Increasingly, state agencies such as the OCC and NGOs define 'best interests' according to prevailing ideological positions regarding calls to redefine the family, to ban smacking and to empower children.

The 1992 review of the CYPFA—and an amendment to the law in 1994—re-emphasised the paramountcy principle in favour of the child rather than the family. [78] The underlying concern was genuine; accusations had been made that the DSW was leaving children in abusive family situations, rather than removing them for their own safety. While this was sometimes true, restating the 'best interests' principle in this manner not only addressed a practical problem and an understandable concern, but also fitted comfortably with an ideology which sees children as autonomous rather than part of a family.

During the 1990s, UNCROC came to sit alongside increased calls for a diversity of family types and child-rearing practices,[79] MMP, and the enhanced political representation of minority interests.[80] Some NGOs were quite prepared to up the ante on children's rights. All this transformed a seemingly innocuous document into a potent tool of social reform.

Most advocates, however, did not evaluate the efficacy of UNCROC in this manner. For some, the pace of change in the 1990s was lamentably slow. In sentiments similar to those expressed by Peter Newell, New Zealand children's rights advocate and lawyer, Robert Ludbrook, was pessimistic about the progress that had been made with UNCROC. In 2000 he said:

> One can only speculate as to the government's reasons for taking its obligations so lightly. Its inaction is clearly deliberate and can probably be ascribed to a belief that it is improper for international human rights bodies to seek to influence policies of democratically elected government. The New Zealand government is obviously aware that it is likely to face criticism domestically and from the international community if it continues to defy the urgings of the United Nations committee appointed to monitor compliance with UNCROC . . . the government is more intent on providing excuses for non-compliance with UNCROC than in ensuring changes which are plainly necessary for compliance.
>
> It would be hard for the government to point to any change since ratification of UNCROC which can be demonstrated to have enhanced the rights and interests of children in this country as well as giving practical effect to the principles of UNCROC. On the other hand, there are many examples of the rights of children being ignored, overridden, or diminished as a result of government action or inaction. New Zealand's children are victims of tokenism and hypocrisy.[81]

But this is only partially correct. Although action—or inaction—by central government ired child advocates, rights-focused NGOs proliferated during the 1990s, and many took it upon themselves to actively raise an awareness of issues, publish independent reports, and above all, lobby for change. UNCROC was axiomatic and was consistently cited as *the* authority on children and their rights. Debates tended to centre around UNCROC's practical implications and the logistics of transferring the Articles into concrete policy, rather than substantive philosophical critique of its content. The relationship between international law and domestic policy, is in fact, a very important issue.

Exploring the issue of the legitimacy of international law, Mattias Kumm (see 3.2) expands on this point. He notes:

> Treaties today, though still binding only on those who ratify them, increasingly delegate powers to treaty-based bodies with a quasi-judicial character. Within their circumscribed subject-matter jurisdiction, these bodies are authorized under the treaty to develop and determine the specific content of the obligations that states are under. This means that, though states have consented to the treaty as a framework for dealing with a specified range of issues, once they have signed on, the specific rights and obligations are determined without their consent by these treaty-based bodies. The link to state consent is further attenuated by the expansive interpretation of the jurisdiction of these bodies . . .[82]

In other words, once a UN Treaty is ratified, there is real potential for legitimacy to be drawn not from the ratifying states and the participatory democracy of its citizens, but by the treaty bodies themselves. The link between consent, initially granted at the point of ratification, and on-going legal obligation, tends to widen. But, as Kumm continues:

> . . . discrepancies between international law and domestic law tend to become increasingly visible and more difficult to gloss over. In conjunction with more effective monitoring and higher reputational and other costs to non-compliance, international law in many areas and in many jurisdictions developed into a serious constraint on national political and legal processes.
> . . . The principle of international legality establishes a presumption in favour of the authority of international law.[83]

Understandably, however, most New Zealanders are unaware not only of how international law influences domestic law, they are also largely unaware of and uninterested in the lofty ideals of examples like UNCROC. Yet for child advocates, the Convention is the 'bottom line' to which they consistently refer. By ensuring UNCROC's profile is high, its authority and on-going obligations are kept alive in the public mind.

But in this task, advocates face a challenge, as was noted in the report *Children and Youth in Aotearoa 2003:*

> There remains a considerable lack of awareness of the UN Convention among the general public, adults, children and youth. There is also a perception in New Zealand that international instruments are of little practical application

to the domestic environment, to the extent where a columnist writing in New Zealand's most widely circulated newspaper, the New Zealand Herald, described the Convention as 'bureaucratic toilet paper'. While this comment can be disregarded as being deliberately sensationalist, and was made in the context of an opinion piece attacking children's rights organisations in general, it reflects a social undercurrent in New Zealand that is both opposed to and mistrustful of any notion that children are entitled to 'rights'. This is perhaps perpetuated by the fact that the mainstream media in New Zealand have done very little to dispel these prejudices, and the Government continues to make little effort to use mass media to promote the Convention.[84]

Despite these fears, and the ignorance said to be held by large sectors of the New Zealand public regarding UNCROC, the *de facto* status of the Convention, is substantial, especially in the minds of lawmakers and advocates.

Moreover, it is unlikely the general public will ever show the sort of interest in UNCROC that child advocates would desire. Ordinary citizens' lives are far removed from the machinations of international law. More importantly, in a nation state, elected representatives are directly accountable to the electorate, but in contrast, the UN is composed entirely of appointed bureaucrats/diplomats who are distant from the accountability of direct representation. International law has a trans-national authority but is not directly accountable. The New Zealand government's agreement to better implement UNCROC relies wholly on the goodwill and political resolve of elected representatives. In failing to meet the requirements of the UN Committee on the Rights of the Child, there can be no real censure beyond diplomatic disapproval and a 'can-do-better' report card.

Because of this, the work of NGOs and specific lobby groups assumes a heightened importance. The authority of international law is assumed, rather than real in any directly accountable sense, but it can and does assert a strong influence on domestic policy and law reform. Debate on these issues has not been a feature of the New Zealand experience with UNCROC: if it had, the confidence of those who so dogmatically affirm its authority might have been undermined.

A further critical issue concerns the nature and locus of authority or legitimacy. If rights are primary, how is the outcome determined when there are clashes between a child's right to be independent—or to *individuate*— and a parent's right to refuse or prohibit the expression of that right? In the

New Zealand experience, the thorny issue of the supremacy of rights has tended to be overshadowed by more specific arguments around flashpoint issues such as smacking and abortion.

3.4. SUMMARY

- As an instrument of international law, the wording of UNCROC is non-prescriptive. This has created considerable room for flexible and ideological interpretation.

- Formal recognition of a diversity of family forms by the New Zealand Government in 1994, rendered UNCROC's endorsement of the family as "the fundamental group of society" contestable.

- Rights, and children's rights in particular, are complex social and legal constructs. Natural law assumptions are readily fused with contemporary meanings and changing social attitudes. In New Zealand, human rights have assumed almost sacrosanct status. If the child is viewed in isolation, there can be little wider comprehension of what is entailed when tensions and conflicting rights occur within relationships.

- UNCROC has overturned the historical understanding of children in New Zealand. In the new legal environment since its ratification, the state has assumed a more proactive role in child welfare, making protection and intervention in families necessary. This has led to forceful lobbying, often led by the state and NGOs.

- An example of this new bureaucratic dynamic is evident in the Commissioner's report on the James Whakaruru case. The Commissioner concluded that the victim was 'badly let down by the state', without any reference to the simple fact that this boy was killed by adults who were meant to care for him.

- The meaning of UNCROC's key phrase, 'the best interests of the child', is totally dependent on ideological context.

- One of the main problems when international law is applied to the political framework of a nation state is its distance from direct representative democracy. UN committees are composed entirely of political appointees, yet their deliberations strongly influence law reform in nation states. UNCROC is a good example of this.

3.5. CHILDREN AND THE EMERGENCE OF GROUP IDENTITY POLITICS

Upon his appointment to the Office of the Commissioner for Children on 16 February 1998, former National MP and Cabinet Minister, Roger McClay, said:

> My personal goal is that during my time in office, all the articles of the UNCROC are enshrined in New Zealand law. This means that New Zealand children will be getting what they were promised when New Zealand ratified the Convention. Children represent one-third of our population but lack power and are disenfranchised. It is an honour and deep responsibility to advocate for them. And I see an awakening of public awareness about the rights of children.[85]

McClay was the third Commissioner; previous incumbents were Ian Hassall (see 3.2) and Laurie O'Reilly, a lawyer who died prematurely in 1997.[86] Like the others, McClay was deeply committed to UNCROC. He saw children's rights as *entitlements* to be presided over and monitored by the state. It is particularly revealing that McClay spoke of the nation's children as 'lacking power' and 'disenfranchised'. In the body of material consulted for the present work, there is no clearer statement than these comments in support of the thesis that children have been politicised. Politically, 'power' and 'disenfranchised' relate to the vote and voting, and there are lobbyists advocating in this direct sense for the child franchise (see below). As used here, however, McClay was probably employing the words emotively to denote a worldview of deep injustice towards children accompanied by a general call to action.

In this milieu, UNCROC became both a means to an end and an end in itself. Referring to children as a third of the country's population also identified them as a special *group*—in much the same way as women became an identifiable constituency during the 1970s. This has been part of a wider shift whereby the state increasingly redefined rights with respect to marginalised groups, rather than primarily protecting all citizens.

Few would challenge the idea that children and young people are citizens, but a caveat is needed in an ontological sense because they are both *being* and *becoming*; that is, they command respect—even special respect—by virtue of their age, immaturity and vulnerability, but at the same time they are not yet adults. The developmental theories of childhood, so dominant throughout the twentieth century, emphasised the gradual growth towards maturity—an understanding that was reinforced by social mores and rites of passage marking the transition from adolescence to full adulthood. This vast body of research told us that a *child* was below the age of puberty, an *adolescent* was between childhood and adulthood, and an *adult* was a mature grown-up. If these time-honoured understandings and practices are expunged, all children, irrespective of their age or other variables, become full citizens from infancy. This ultimate expression of egalitarianism rests on assumptions about the full autonomy and agency in a manner that makes *child* and *childhood*—as sequential developmental stages in the human life cycle—effectively redundant.

While the Child Liberation Movement never took hold in New Zealand, its ideas have not escaped the attention of local advocates.

If, in relation to children, 'disenfranchised' is taken literally—rather than generically—it raises questions as to whether they should be directly involved in the political process by being able to vote. This idea is not new and was argued by child liberation activists in America during the 1970s, notably Richard Farson and John Holt,[87] who claimed that the full equality of children would come only with a radical restructuring of the social order which eliminated all differences between children and adults. In a comment that predated UNCROC but is remarkably similar to the wording of Article 12, Farson said that "children, like adults, should have the right to decide the matters which affect them most directly. The issue of self-determination is at the heart of children's liberation. The acceptance of the child's right to self-determination is fundamental to all the rights which children are entitled."[88] Holt, too, considered it unjust that children could not vote. To have no say in the decisions affecting them was tantamount to giving children the minds and souls of slaves. "If what I think does not make a difference, why think?" is the reasoning he attributed to children.[89]

A natural consequence of this is to extend the franchise to children. While the Child Liberation Movement never took hold in New Zealand, its ideas have not escaped the attention of local advocates. Child franchise, for example, is a theme Ludbrook explored in the October 2004 issue of *Children*, the newsletter of the Children's Commissioner. He began with a sweeping claim linking the lack of child franchise with poverty: "Maybe", he said, "if Holt's ideas had been adopted we would not have a situation where 40% [*sic*] of our children live in poverty." He continued:

> The Convention on the Rights of the Child gives children who are capable of forming their own views the right to express those views freely in all matters which affect them. Despite all the talk of encouraging children's participation, children remain a disadvantaged sub-class in New Zealand society. They are denied basic human rights that adults take for granted. They are discriminated against on the grounds of their young age.
>
> Despite the proclaimed enthusiasm for child and youth participation there has been no move to give greater political power to children. An English social scientist has made the point that "consultation is often a charade: (we) let children have their say and then get on with the adult agenda." Nowhere is this more evident than in our refusal to grant children the right to vote and the right to stand as candidates in the national and local elections.
>
> . . . we rarely give thought to the fact that 27 per cent of our population are politically powerless.
>
> Research evidence suggests that by the age of 12 to 14 years children are able to make reasoned judgements about social and political matters. In any event our electoral system is based on 'one person one vote'. Voters do not have to prove their maturity or rationality before being registered on the electoral role [sic]. Imagine the uproar if we decreed that anyone over the age of 75 should not vote because some people of this age are losing their mental and physical agility!
>
> Surely it is time that the issue of lowering the voting age was taken seriously. We should not have to wait until children chain themselves to the railings of Parliament or disrupt the Ellerslie races.[90]

Interestingly, this view has moved from the radical fringe during the 1970s into an issue of mainstream rights concern in the early twenty-first century. It rests upon a notion of children as empowered and autonomous agents. Clearly, however, there could be adverse effects, for example, in relation to the age of criminal culpability and sexual consent—both of which would no longer exist. The present range of legal and other anomalies related to the age of children and young people would dissolve, but the result could render children more, rather than less, vulnerable to exploitation.[91] More importantly, the direction in which this understanding moves is consolidating the status of children as political subjects.

With UNCROC's ratification came an acknowledgement of children's rights as *bona fide* concerns in the public square. The five years from 1993 to 1998 accordingly saw many new NGOs emerge and an intensification of advocacy from more established groups. These combined to support the calls for change made by the Commissioner for Children, but had the advantage of offering specific, and in some cases more vociferous, advocacy. Without the restraints of direct accountability that the OCC was subject to, these groups demanded more immediate and widespread change.

Intertwined with a concern for children's rights, the NGOs that appeared in this period tended to embrace a structural understanding of economics which saw the role of the state to be wealth redistribution in favour of children.[92] More specific goals were the elimination of smacking—of which more will be said shortly—and child poverty. The fervour with which the elimination of child poverty has been championed must be seen in relation to the political and historical context which was, in 1994, beginning to move beyond 'New Right' or 'neo-liberal' constructs. The reforms of the previous decades were considered particularly detrimental to children, and the framework for correction relied heavily on lobbying for more state investment on the premises of redistributive justice.

Typifying this response was the Child Poverty Action Group (CPAG). Formed in 1994, CPAG is made up of academics, activists, practitioners and supporters, who

> . . . in partnership with Maori, advocate for more informed social policy to support children in Aotearoa/New Zealand, particularly the one-third of New Zealand children who presently live in relative, and occasionally, absolute poverty. CPAG believes this situation is not the result of economic necessity, but due to policy neglect. Through research and advocacy, CPAG highlights the position of tens of thousands of New Zealand children, and promotes public policies that address the underlying causes of poverty they live in.[93]

Revealing more of the organisation's philosophical stance as well as updating readers from the first edition of its publication, *Our Children: The Priority for Policy*, the CPAG writers in the preface to their 2003 booklet noted:

> Since 2001, the official discourse has changed dramatically. There have been many small policy initiatives for families and children, and a willingness on the part of politicians, the media and public policy analysts to engage in debate over the rights and needs of children. Previously, individualism, free markets

and self-responsibility were emphasised. Now, concepts such as social well-being, social capacity building and social development are freely discussed. For instance, the Ministry of Social Development has highlighted income disparity in various reports, observing that children are disproportionately among our poorest citizens, and Treasury has acknowledged the connection between economic and social policy with a raft of papers on social inclusion.[94]

The discussion that followed in the CPAG report drew extensively on overseas (primarily UNICEF) as well as locally-sourced data. What is understood by 'poverty' is broken down into absolute and relative poverty, and there can be little doubt significant numbers of children in New Zealand are adversely affected by poverty. 'Poverty' however, is a term that is objectively difficult to measure, although it does carry significant emotional weight. Some social scientists prefer 'deprivation' which has been defined as "a state of observable and demonstrable disadvantage relative to the local community or the wider society or nation to which an individual, family or group belongs."[95] Given these wide criteria, most people at some point could qualify as 'deprived'. Refining the definition by drawing a distinction between material and social deprivation, the latter is said to involve "the roles, relationships, functions, customs, rights and responsibilities of membership of society and its subgroups."[96] If this is applied to children, deprivation is increased when families split and parents re-partner, but this is not the CPAG focus; the emphasis there tends to be on the structural causes of material poverty, particularly that said to be caused by the economic reforms of the mid-1980s and beyond.

The correlation between wider family circumstances and poverty affecting children is evident in a 2002 MSD paper where researchers concluded that, "overall, the likelihood of children being in poverty has declined since the mid-1990s. However, higher proportions of children were in poor families at the end of the decade compared with at the beginning."[97] The complexity of child poverty is also acknowledged as well as multiple, rather than linear approaches to policy:

> The findings suggest a need for policies that have a wider focus than just income support. Such an expanded policy focus would incorporate recognition of the multiple sources of disadvantage of many of these children, and would explore mechanisms designed to connect parents and children to services directed at reducing the likelihood of negative child outcomes.[98]

While it cannot be denied that the reforms of the late 1980s and early 1990s created considerable hardship for some families, the effects of no-fault divorce and family dysfunction, and other variables making up 'the multiple sources of disadvantage' should also be acknowledged in the plight of children. If, as is noted in the CPAG report, "one-parent families are disproportionately represented in the bottom two income quintiles", then it follows that responsive policy should work to strengthen two-parent families.[99]

Structural and macro-economic variables constitute one level of investigation, but the micro, relational and interpersonal, and even moral dimensions, are equally important. For its part, the Green Party in the lead-up to the 2005 election was "challenging other political parties . . . to join them in pledging to eliminate child poverty in Aotearoa by the year 2010."[100]

If a child can be shown to be objectively and demonstratively poor, the context of that reality is almost, without exception, familial.

An understanding of the intergenerational family and its kinship connection, however, would approach child poverty from a very different perspective. If a child can be shown to be objectively and demonstratively poor, the context of that reality is almost, without exception, familial. Given that parents have obligations to children, 'poverty' has different meanings for both. In one sense, all children are poor—they are non-earners[101]—but their poverty occurs within families, that is, 'family poverty' rather than 'child poverty'. The CPAG philosophy is limited because it is premised on a view of children as isolated economic and political identities, rather than relational connectedness in families. It should be added that responsible government is concerned with the structural circumstances affecting children, but this analysis should not be at the expense of the relational reality that occurs within families, the place where children actually live their lives.[102]

In February 1994, Hassall wrote to the Minister of Social Welfare suggesting a national Children's Day,[103] an idea he had first mooted in 1991. Some time was to elapse before the event materialised, as explained in the official history of Children's Day:

> The initial idea for Children's Day came from a suggestion by the first Children's Commissioner, Ian Hassall, in 1991. His suggestion was developed and progressed by the Rotary Club of Wellington.

In conjunction with the next Children's Commissioner, Laurie O'Reilly, the idea was then mooted to Government.

The third Children's Commissioner and former Minister of Youth Affairs, Roger McClay, then endorsed the concept along with several other Ministers.

In 1999, the National Steering Group was established to progress the concept of Children's Day. Interested government and non-government agencies were represented on this group.

The inaugural National Children's Day was held on Sunday 29 October 2000 with the intention that Children's Day would occur on the last Sunday of October every year.

The National Steering Group established the vision and mission for National Children's Day as well as the following objectives:

- To heighten awareness of the importance and needs of children in society, and ways of promoting their development.
- To promote a national focus on children, and motivate adults towards positive appreciation and support of children.
- To promote community responses for the ongoing celebration of National Children's Day through local ownership and widespread participation.
- To embrace the National Children's Day Charter.[104]

Despite the positive and 'feel-good' nature of these objectives, the protracted government and NGO consultation which made Children's Day a reality reinforced the cumbersome bureaucratising of children's issues.

Another influential group to emerge in this period was Action for Children and Youth Aotearoa (ACYA) in 1996.[105] In 1995, the New Zealand government had submitted its first UNCROC compliance report to the UN Committee on the Rights of the Child, and ACYA was, in fact, a coalition of NGOs and individuals committed to more tangible and decisive action on children's rights than had been evident to that point. According to Gabrielle Maxwell, UNCROC had genuinely started to influence New Zealand law by this time.[106] Commissioner for Children, Laurie O'Reilly, delivered a paper to the Early Childhood Education Council in 1996, in which he said that New Zealand was slowly accepting a 'rights perspective' for children and that the Convention represented "a major leap forward in standard setting on children's issues (especially Article 12)."[107]

The Children's Issues Centre (CIC) was another significant organisation to emerge in the mid-1990s which endorsed the primacy of UNCROC. In 1995, the University of Otago in co-operation with a Children's Issues Centre

Trust established an interdisciplinary centre to provide a national forum for research into and discussion of children's issues. UNCROC was among the broad spectrum of interests. In the first issue of the Centre's journal it was stated that, "We (also) have a strong commitment to encouraging implementation of the United Nations Convention on the Rights of the Child and particularly Article 12 which says that children should have a voice and be listened to in decisions which affect them."[108]

The Centre's literature makes it clear that the intention was to present a multi-disciplinary perspective on children's issues, which involved teachers, other educators, medical personnel, lawyers and social workers, as well as numerous overseas speakers. All would contribute to the flagship journal *Childrenz Issues*, first published in 1997. This broad range of views, along with a regular schedule of colloquia and workshops, publications, a close on-going relationship with the University's Faculty of Education, as well as the OCC and other professionals, academics, policy makers, the media, parents and other members of the public, mean the Centre is highly regarded and well-positioned to speak on children's issues. Despite the eclectic range of voices, however, the theoretical framework for many of the Centre's publications is the relatively new field of sociology of childhood, coupled with a critique of developmental psychology. The guiding ethos seems to be that although developmental psychology dominated educational research last century, it is now inadequate in a postmodern age which appreciates the subjectivity of context coupled with a 'diversity of discourses' (see below).

3.5. SUMMARY

- Redefined within a new world of lobbying, children have become highly politicised in New Zealand since the 1990s. They are no longer viewed within families, but as 'lacking power' and 'disenfranchised'.

- This reflects a major shift in the wider evolution of human rights in New Zealand. Serious credence is now being given to the direct involvement of children in the political process, ideas that were associated with the fringe radicalism of child liberationists in the US in the 1970s.

- A rejection of the 'New Right' reforms of 1984-1993 also provided a stimulus for advocacy on the grounds that children were seen as particular victims of poverty.

- Among the new NGOs to emerge in the 1993-2000 period were CPAG, ACYA, and the multi-disciplinary CIC.

3.6. RE-THINKING EDUCATIONAL THEORY: FROM DEVELOPMENTAL PSYCHOLOGY TO FOUCAULT

This new philosophy referred to above—a diversity of discourses—is embraced by many education professionals[109] and owes much to the primary writings of French philosopher-historian, Michel Foucault (1926-84). Foucault is a complex writer whose ideas changed direction and emphasis over the course of a long writing career, and he doesn't fit easily into usual disciplinary categories. Even so, Foucault's influence on contemporary education theory is enormous and at least some comment on his work is relevant here.

Foucault's philosophical roots are many and varied. He drew heavily on a number of intellectuals, including the nineteenth century German writer, Friedrich Nietzsche,[110] various Marxist writers, and post-war existentialist contemporaries such as Jean-Paul Sartre.[111] Like Nietzsche, Foucault rejected the idea of objective truth, favouring instead a relativisitic individual interpretation—the core of 'perspectivism'.[112] From the Marxists he inherited an understanding of power and structures, while from the existentialists he believed in the primacy of material existence and sensation, rather than objectivity and any belief in or search for a spiritual essence. Foucault's real concern is 'power-knowledge' and how this is mediated through institutions and language—'discourse'— and expressed in the lives of individuals. He was particularly interested in the response of societies to issues of punishment and sexuality.[113]

Foucault goes beyond the Marxist critique of economic structures and even the neo-Marxist exploration of ideology. He is thus identified as a poststructural theorist. Power is embodied in 'discursive practices'—texts of meaning—and internalised in individuals who regulate their thinking and behaviour in relation to society's norms. In *Discipline and Punish,* for example, he traced the evolution of the prison from a juridical and punitive punishment focus to so-called 'humane' and 'corrective' programmes—the latter symbolising a modern, 'disciplinary' society. Across time, the dynamics within prisons shifted from overt and external measures towards more subtle and internalised thought patterns which resulted in self-regulation and 'reform'.

Power is embodied in 'discursive practices'—texts of meaning—and internalised in individuals who regulate their thinking and behaviour in relation to society's norms.

According to Foucault, power has become increasingly 'positive', meaning it is now less about coercion and external regulation and more about inducing and seducing certain forms of thought. The goal in modern disciplinary systems is not external punishment (cf. torture in premodern times), but 'reform' and acceptance of society's norms. In another context, the examination, e.g. of students in schools, or of patients in hospitals, combined what Foucault called 'hierarchical observation' with 'normative judgment'. This is a good example of power-knowledge because it elicits the truth about those who undergo the examination—reveals what they know or what their state of health is like, and controls their behaviour— by forcing them to study or directing them to a course of treatment.

In the classical age, Foucault saw madness as a legal issue, but not yet a medical one. With the birth of the asylum—in the eighteenth century—as a specific centre for treating madness came the substitution of medical for juridical power. Similarly in *The History of Sexuality*, sex came to have a close association with the power structures of modern society. The modern control of sexuality—as was evident in the history of criminality—made sex an object of scientific study; hence he speaks of the 'medicalisation of sex'. This simultaneously created knowledge and domination, and played an important role in furnishing a particular type of social control.

A number of developmental psychologists committed to children's issues and advocacy have uncritically accepted Foucauldian thought as a dominant worldview. They have abandoned the pretence that objectivity and scientific inquiry underpin behavioural or clinical psychology, in favour of a theory of social reconstruction with overt political ramifications.[114] So much so that Foucault has come to exert an almost hypnotic influence on New Zealand educators and social scientists[115] which has intensified the politicisation of children. Their lives—as well as the institutions of socialisation and nurture surrounding them—are rendered problematic and transformed into 'sites of socio-political discourse' and a 'multiplicity of discursive practices'. There are discourses which are inhibitive (there is much common ground at this point with neo-Marxist and other structural critiques of power and control), as well as those which could, in an ethically relativistic sense, be called 'liberating'. Foucault's overall goal, if it can be stated succinctly, is to facilitate 'a new economy of bodies and pleasures'.

The child is to be freed from traditional discourses of oppression, including—and perhaps especially—the authority of parents.

The intersection between the popularity of Foucault as a template for educational analysis and the politicising of children and children's rights is not immediately obvious. Foucault himself was deeply suspicious of bureaucratic structures and institutions, but his ideas add weight to new discourses about children and the possibility of autonomous agency. The implicit understanding of children that emerges from Foucault finds a natural confluence with the realised possibilities inherent in the children's rights movement and related educational notions about reaching one's potential. The child is to be freed from traditional discourses of oppression, including—and perhaps especially—the authority of parents.

In policy terms, human rights assume a heightened importance as instruments of change through their ability to assist with and facilitate (construct) new understandings. As one researcher from the CIC concluded in her Foucauldian analysis of a child in an early childhood institution: ". . . the construction of a child's subjectivity, her sense of 'who she is', 'what is and isn't possible' for her is one of the fundamentals of good practices [sic] in education . . . The images and expectations that teachers hold of and for their students are powerful normalising practices—just as they are powerful in normalising so they could be powerful in actualising and promoting alternative discourses and possibilities for students. This is the power of understanding how discourse and discursive practices act and interact with individual subjectivities which post-modern theory has given us."[116] In other words, an alternative 'discourse' could construct a new reality of interpretation; one that is both sensitive and responsive to the negative aspects of 'normalising influences'.

This approach perhaps represents the ultimate in a new understanding of children because it hints at the actualised 'child self'. There is, however, no supra or objective 'discourse' beyond convention, and constructed meaning. Poststructuralism turns human relationships into an abstract and narcissistic search ensnared in a myriad of 'normalising discursive practices'.

For ordinary parents, the esoteric world of Foucauldian discourse is a world away from the immediate challenges of raising children. In the New Zealand context, the discipline of their children has been the central issue bringing their sphere of authority into a clash with the Foucault-inspired academics, and the issue that has done it is the so-called smacking debate.

3.6. SUMMARY

- Clinical approaches to human development have been readily supplemented, and in some cases replaced, with a Foucauldian framework as a theoretical basis for contemporary educators and child professionals.

- Foucault was deeply distrustful of former understandings of objectivity and the wider search for truth that has characterised Western thought, especially since the Enlightenment. All reality is rendered a social construct and subject to on-going redefinition. The only certainties are different interpretations which make up a 'plurality of discourses', i.e. multiple viewpoints.

- Foucault's attention shifted to discourse or 'power-knowledge', and he wrote specifically on crime and punishment and sexuality as examples in history where particular discourses have exerted a strong normalising and controlling influence. As in other fields of social inquiry, Foucault is attractive to educators interested in his analysis of power and how individuals are socialised into normative thought and behaviour.

- Foucauldian theory meshes with the contemporary children's cause in its ability to suggest new discourses of child emancipation.

3.7. Case study: UNCROC, section 59 and the physical discipline of children

The best illustration of how children's rights advocates and academics have used UNCROC to advance their agenda is the debate about whether parents should be allowed to use reasonable force on their children for the purpose of correction. This debate focuses on section 59 of the Crimes Act 1961 (section 59), which applies to parents and those in the place of parents (for convenience, the term 'parents' will be used to refer to both).

Section 59 allows parents to use physical discipline as long as they satisfy both parts of a two-part test. The test is that the force used by parents (1) must be 'reasonable' and (2) must be used for the purpose of 'correction' of their children. Without the protection of section 59, parents who used physical force to discipline their children would be committing a criminal offence because the force would fall within the definition of 'assault'. An assault includes an intentional application of force, or an attempt or threat to apply force.[117] Repealing section 59 thus poses immediate problems for the concept of parental authority; without any ability to use reasonable force for disciplinary purposes, parental discipline in any form would be well-nigh impossible. Nevertheless, many children's rights advocates demand repeal of section 59, and one of their leading arguments is that the current law is inconsistent with UNCROC.[118] Since ratification of UNCROC in 1993 the push for abolition of section 59 is a theme which has repeatedly appeared in advocacy literature.[119]

In June 2005, Green MP Sue Bradford's Crimes (Abolition of Force as a Justification for Child Discipline) Amendment Bill (Crimes Amendment Bill) was drawn from the ballot of Private Member's Bills for consideration by parliament. If passed into law, the Crimes Amendment Bill would repeal section 59 of the Crimes Act 1961. It has given new impetus to the debate about the discipline of children.

Advocacy groups seeking repeal find grist for their mill in cases such as that of 33-year-old New Plymouth bar worker, Pieter Donselaar, who in March 2005 invoked section 59 in defence of hitting his four-year-old son twice for soiling his pants. The hitting was to the child's buttocks and was hard enough to leave bruising and a handprint. A jury did not accept that the defence applied and found him guilty of assault.[120] Conversely, a North Otago woman successfully cited section 59 and the exercise of 'reasonable force' for giving her teenage son 'six of the best' in May 2005. It is clear from recent surveys that a majority of parents agree with the use of physical discipline.[121]

Advocates for repeal rely on Article 19 of UNCROC, which says:

> States Parties shall take all appropriate legislative, administrative, social and educational measures to protect the child from all forms of physical or mental violence, injury or abuse, neglect or negligent treatment, maltreatment or exploitation, including sexual abuse, while in the care of parent(s), legal guardian(s) or any other person who has the care of the child.

Long-time child advocate, Beth Wood, whose work over many years has spanned involvement in UNICEF, EPOCH and Action for Children and Youth Aotearoa, was speaking on behalf of a government delegation to the UN in September 2003 when she said:

> The Committee is deeply concerned that despite a review of legislation, the State party has still not amended Section 59 of the Crimes Act 1961, which allows parents to use reasonable force to discipline their children. . . . the Committee emphasizes that the Convention requires the protection of children from all forms of violence, which includes corporal punishment in the family, and which should be accompanied by awareness-raising campaigns on the law and on children's right to protection.[122]

It will be evident the argument that Article 19 requires repeal of section 59 equates section 59's 'reasonable' force for the purpose of 'correction' with Article 19's 'violence, injury or abuse, neglect or negligent treatment, maltreatment or exploitation'. Clearly, this is a distortion of the meaning of section 59 and of Article 19 and, crucially, it illustrates the leverage which advocates for repeal try to gain from UNCROC and its aura of perceived moral and political legitimacy.

Nevertheless, it is frequently implied or asserted that section 59 permits violence against children. Consequently section 59 is often presented in the media as 'condoning abuse', as being outdated, and ignoring children's rights. But this is a very misleading slant on a law which does nothing of the sort.

In fact, the words of section 59 do not condone any of the conduct described in Article 19; they simply allow parents to use 'reasonable' force for corrective purposes. Physical restraint or smacking would usually be permitted by section 59, but every case will turn on its own facts and both parts of the two-part test must always be satisfied. This means that even a reasonable degree of force will not be protected by section 59 if it is applied in anger or for some other purpose that is not 'correction'.[123] As the *Donselaar* case indicates, section 59 is no barrier to conviction in cases of inappropriate discipline. Recent research has demonstrated that judges and juries usually recognise and punish inappropriate disciplinary force.[124]

In reality, most parents do not extract licence from this law. A range of approaches, including the positive reinforcement of good behaviour, 'time out' and the discretionary removal of privileges—among many other strategies—are employed by responsible parents. It may be true that for a minority, what begins as legitimate physical discipline degenerates into violence and maltreatment warranting legal and social agency intervention, but the constant conjunction of sporadic physical discipline with sustained or violent abuse is not the reality. Asserting that this link exists, however, is a necessary strategy for those who desire a law change and who seek to influence the public and political consciousness accordingly.

Consequently section 59 is often presented in the media as 'condoning abuse', as being outdated, and ignoring children's rights. But this is a very misleading slant on a law which does nothing of the sort.

The CIC in Dunedin also continues to lobby fervently for change, although more from an interdisciplinary research perspective. In a 2004 project which surveyed more than 300 internationally published peer-reviewed research articles, Lead Researcher, Professor Anne Smith,[125] said, "The literature is quite consistent in supporting the conclusion that there is an association between the use of parental corporal punishment and the development of antisocial behaviour in children."[126] The results were unsurprising given the strong UNCROC focus adopted by the Centre and that the project was jointly sponsored by the OCC, and released when Dr Cindy Kiro, the current Children's Commissioner, had been commenting in the media on New Zealand's position as reported in UNICEF's Innocenti Report Card of September 2003—New Zealand was third from the bottom on a league table of child maltreatment deaths in rich nations.[127] However, a 1997 New Zealand study stated that "it is misleading to imply that occasional or mild physical punishment has long term adverse consequences."[128] In a review of empirical articles dealing with parental discipline, another researcher found that the findings of the studies varied. He concluded that "the studies with stronger internal validity tended to find beneficial outcomes."[129]

Advocates for change also rely on Articles 3 and 12 of UNCROC to justify their attempts to have section 59 repealed. Again, the use of these provisions to justify repeal of section 59 is heavily influenced by a particular ideology.

Article 3 says:

> In all actions concerning children . . . the best interests of the child shall be a primary consideration.

With regard to the redefinition of family currently being promoted in New Zealand,[130] as well as the debate over section 59, UNCROC's 'best interests of the child' provides no guidance whatsoever. Lobby groups interpret the phrase as they wish; as Newell has said, "the only limitations are our imagination and energy to use it." The paramountcy principle is at risk of being seriously confused and compromised. In fact, the best interests of the child arguably require that he or she is raised in an environment where parental authority and responsibility for children are recognised. Indeed, Article 3 goes on to provide:

> States Parties undertake to ensure the child such protection and care as is necessary for his or her well-being, *taking into account the rights and duties of his or her parents, legal guardians, or other individuals legally responsible for him or her* . . . (emphasis added)

Article 12 requires ratifying states to assure to children the right to express their views freely in all matters affecting them. This Article has been used to justify repeal of section 59 on the basis that "the majority of children advised that physical punishment was the worst thing that parents could do if children transgressed."[131]

In this vein, the CIC hosted a national seminar on smacking ("Stop it, it hurts me") at Otago University in June 2004, and supervised a Master's thesis which was published in late 2005 as *Insights* (with financial assistance from Save the Children New Zealand and endorsed by Dr Kiro). The results from the focus groups, observations and questionnaires included, among other findings, that "children report heavy use of physical punishment as a primary means of discipline", and, "children report physical punishment as a negative experience."[132] The author, Terry Dobbs, concludes:

> . . . adult views have dominated the debate on family discipline. In this study, children's experiences of family discipline, especially the role of physical punishment, challenge many adult assumptions.
>
> Children's voices may temper the paternalistic, protective and primarily adult-defined perspective of past and current family discipline practices. There is a need to give real effect to children's role in issues which directly concern and affect them. Children's voices will not always prevail, but they should be heard . . . Voice implies participation, and a sense that others value one's opinions and sentiments. Indeed, we may learn much from children if only we could hear their voices.[133]

"Children", Dobbs writes, "are, in many senses, the experts on family discipline. They are experiencing it now."[134] This remarkable claim captures the essence of a rights culture which irrationally inflates the maturity and agency of children at the expense of understanding lived relationships and the mediation of parental responsibility and authority within families.

It is a considerable leap of logic to assert that Article 12 requires children's views to be treated as authoritative. It is also a selective reading of Article 12, which contains the important qualification:

> . . . the views of the child [should be] given due weight in accordance with the age and maturity of the child.

Indeed, arguments for change which are based on UNCROC usually ignore Article 5, which provides:

> States Parties shall respect the responsibilities, rights and duties of parents or, where applicable, the members of the extended family or community as provided for by local custom, legal guardians or other persons legally responsible for the child, to provide, in a manner consistent with the evolving capacities of the child, appropriate direction and guidance in the exercise by the child of the rights recognized in the present Convention.

The selective reading and interpretation of UNCROC as a justification for repeal of section 59 says much about the mindset of advocates for change and their attitude to parental authority and the parent-child relationship. In addition, the fact that repealing section 59 will criminalise parents who use physical force to discipline their children is often ignored or played down.

Repealing section 59 will result in disciplinary force being a crime because it will fall within the definition of 'assault'. Without section 59, even light smacking or picking up a child to put them into 'time out' against their wishes will be an assault, and there will be no legal protection against parents being charged by the police for such a crime. The first and most obvious problem with such a law is that it will be unworkable, criminalising, as it will, the vast majority of ordinary parents and thereby creating significant enforcement difficulties.

Supporters of repeal frequently assert that even if section 59 is repealed, the police will not prosecute parents for the use of 'minor' or 'trivial' physical discipline.[135] Even apart from the problem of defining what is 'minor' or 'trivial', it will be readily apparent that no such guarantee can be given on behalf of the police. The assertion that the police will not prosecute parents must be seen as another example of advocates presuming the facts suit their own argument. Their reliance on the police failing to prosecute parents who use physical discipline effectively advocates for selective enforcement of the law, which is a clear violation of the rule of law.

Repealing section 59 will result in disciplinary force being a crime.

Prior to the appearance of the Crimes Amendment Bill seeking outright repeal of section 59,[136] Murray Smith, a United Future list MP, proposed a compromise in his Crimes (Parental Discipline) Amendment Bill in 2003. The intended effect of this Bill was to clarify what constituted reasonable disciplinary force.[137] Rejected in principle by many child advocates, this was later overshadowed by the Crimes Amendment Bill which is being supported more enthusiastically.

Given the inevitable consequences of repeal, it is not surprising that the abolition of section 59 continues to create a dilemma for the third-term Labour-led government. Although many in the present Labour administration are in favour of abolishing section 59, it's not that simple. To do so runs the risk of alienating an important part of Labour's constituency: decent parents who are doing a good job raising their children. In the broader context, lingering controversy from the previous parliament surrounding the Care of Children, Civil Union and Relationships (Statutory References) Acts—which together extended legal recognition for same-sex and *de facto* couples[138]— meant that strategists within Labour probably did not welcome the Crimes

Amendment Bill when it appeared in June 2005, only three months out from the general election.

The political courage to repeal or even amend section 59 has remained weak within Labour. Rather, as former Justice Minister, Phil Goff, said in July 2003, the government's emphasis has been on the *quid pro quo* move to put in place "a public education campaign on alternative and more effective forms of disciplining children, rather than smacking."[139] Nevertheless, his next comment that "changes to the law on physical punishment will be considered, once the campaign is underway and has been evaluated", and recent moves to extend the powers of the Children's Commissioner—as occurred in the Children's Commissioner Act 2003—indicate that Labour has anticipated and even covertly welcomed increased lobbying on this and other children's rights issues. The point to appreciate is that the initiative is seen to come from outside government.

Like other child lobbyists sensing the government's equivocation on the issue, Cindy Kiro has risen to the challenge and been particularly critical. In an article entitled "Maharey told to get his A into G", Dr Kiro cited the government's 2001-02 *Agenda for Children* and lamented a lack of progress:

> Frustrated at a lack of action on children's issues, Dr Kiro said the lauded *Agenda for Children* [which has as its first key principle a statement that all policy will be 'consistent with UNCROC'[140]] provided an "excellent framework but so far has languished without implementation of a specific work programme . . ."
>
> The Minister has to champion (the agenda) in caucus and instruct (the Ministry of Social Development) to do it. Basically he needs to get his A into G and get it done."[141]

Notwithstanding strong support from individual members within its caucus, Labour's policy position on parental disciplinary issues has tended to be more conciliatory and less doctrinaire than that of the Greens.[142] In May 2004, for example, Labour put $11 million into a new campaign known as SKIP (Strategies for Kids—Information for Parents) to provide parents with resources on the art of parenting and, among other aims, persuade them not to physically discipline their children.[143]

Until the appearance of the Crimes Amendment Bill, the lack of political will to repeal section 59 continued to annoy groups like EPOCH. In its

Annual Report for 2003-04, for example, it was noted:

> 2003/04 has been an active year in regard to efforts to change attitudes and law on physical punishment in New Zealand. EPOCH New Zealand has continued to play a very significant part in advocating and educating for change and has been delighted to see the public support for change grow on the part of other organisations. Government support for change has on the whole been disappointing, however, with a clear indication that no further review of section 59 of the Crimes Act 1961 will take place before 2006. The Government has also backed away from the promised public education campaign on alternatives to physical punishment promised previously in public Government documents.
>
> . . . There are now three Members' Bills in the ballot in parliament. Two of these have provisions for amendment of section 59 of the Crimes Act 1961— Brian Donnelly (NZ First) and Murray Smith (United Future)—an option not supported by EPOCH New Zealand. Sue Bradford's (Green Party) bill is for full repeal.[144]

In the light of these comments, and the current Bill before parliament, the stage is clearly set for continued debate and pressure for change.

The underlying issue in this, as in other debates about children's rights, centres around where authority lies in the nurture of children. Rights advocates cite UNCROC as the ultimate legal—and moral—authority, along with ratifying states parties and their duty to enforce international law. Alternatively, if children are essentially understood as the offspring of a man and a woman, the understanding of authority changes and the main context for the nurture of children, and thus for authority, usually— but not exclusively—becomes marriage and family. From a rights-based perspective, authority rests primarily in law and its enforcement, whereas an understanding of the centrality of family relationships suggests a different locus of authority.

The political attention on family that has surfaced since Labour was first elected in 1999, and the passage of legislation which relies on an understanding of marriage and family that is rights-sensitive and 'inclusive' in nature, e.g. the Care of Children Act 2004 and the Civil Union Act 2004, affect the immediate rights debates, e.g. debates about children's rights and discipline, because they provide the context for a cultural redefinition of concepts that were legally and morally unquestioned until recent decades.

In an environment where family and marriage are rendered fluid, it becomes easier to redefine assumed roles, including parental authority and children's rights. Section 59 reflects the view that parental responsibility and authority are normative. Only in more rights-sensitive times, and as a result of concerted activism, has section 59 become vilified as a bulwark to progress.

Something that is often unarticulated in the debate about physical discipline—but that was intuitively understood in 1961 by those enacting the Crimes Act and throughout most of our history—is that parental discipline is an integral part of the unique parent-child relationship. It necessarily involves an asserting of parental will followed by action, all of which is necessary to protect from harm or correct and—ultimately—to bring the child to maturity. Physical discipline, such as smacking, is only a small component of what should be understood by parental discipline. Abuse, however, is about unjustified physical treatment of the child and by definition does not occur within a context of correction or guidance. In reality there are grey areas; where, for example, it is not obvious whether a parent acted from a motive of 'correction'. In these instances, section 59 empowers a court to establish, on a case by case basis, whether or not the discipline used is justified.

In an environment where family and marriage are rendered fluid, it becomes easier to redefine assumed roles, including parental authority and children's rights.

As is indicated in Dobbs' conclusions, the debate about section 59 opens up a plethora of very important issues which potentially have wide-reaching ramifications for how rights, children and parenting are understood. The specific issue, repeal, will continue to be the lead-in to these deeper issues, and will not go away.[145] Groups like EPOCH will ensure it stays firmly on the political agenda; EPOCH lists the support of over 40 community organisations it claims are committed to abolishing section 59.[146] Both sides of this debate will keep their concerns before the public, and UNCROC will remain an underlying issue of either credibility or criticism.

In the following letter to a newspaper editor concerning the section 59 debate, the writer correctly identifies the substantive issues to be those of parental authority, enforceability and the rule of law:

> Could we all please stop talking about smacking laws and anti-smacking laws? The abolition of section 59 of the Crimes Act would mean that parents would not be justified in using force on their children—not just smacking,

but any force. Since authority by definition is the power or right to enforce obedience, nothing and no-one would thereafter have legal authority over children except the State.

We need to get the wool off our eyes and see what is going on. All the spin about violence and positive parenting and all the rest of it is just a smokescreen. This is a formal attack on civil liberty and the rule of law.[147]

This is a reminder that the debate about discipline is of greater significance than children's welfare, or even debates on rights and parenting issues. How a society responds to it touches upon more fundamental but seldom discussed issues concerning authority in a functioning democracy.

3.7. SUMMARY

- Children's rights advocates use UNCROC to justify their demands for abolition of section 59 of the Crimes Act 1961. However, this relies on misinterpretation and selective interpretation of UNCROC.

- The use of UNCROC in this context illustrates the leverage that advocates believe can be gained from its aura of perceived political and moral legitimacy.

- In fact, the words of section 59 do not condone the type of conduct prohibited by UNCROC, nor is there any provision of UNCROC which is clearly inconsistent with section 59.

- The effect of repealing section 59 will be to criminalise the use of disciplinary force by parents, because that force will fall within the definition of 'assault' in the Crimes Act 1961. The vast majority of ordinary parents will be affected, and there can be no guarantee that the police will not prosecute these parents.

- Section 59 reflects the view that parental responsibility and authority are normative. Those advocating for repeal of section 59 and who base their arguments on UNCROC see authority as emanating from a different source, namely international law and human rights.

ENDNOTES

CHAPTER THREE
UNCROC and children's rights

1   Allison Morris and Gabrielle Maxwell, "Juvenile Justice in New Zealand: A New Paradigm" (Wellington: Victoria University of Wellington, 1990), and cited here in the summary of youth justice by researcher, Emily Watt, at http://www.justice.govt.nz/youth/history/ (last accessed August 2006) p13. The Act is divided into two broad concerns: care and protection and youth justice. One source summarises the important principles as 1. the interests of the child or young person are paramount (s6), and 2. the family should participate in decision making and be empowered to care for its children and young people, see http://www.asdin.org.nz/Advoc_Law_Govt/child_youngpersons_act.html (last accessed January 2006). This demonstrates the tension that exists in the Act between the family's and the child's interests.

2   The Act was notable in its endorsement of residential care; a philosophy which had changed markedly by the time of the 1989 legislation. The Preamble to the 1974 law reads: "An Act to make provision for preventive and social work services for children and young persons whose needs for care, protection, or control are not being met by parental or family care and who are, or are at risk of becoming, deprived, neglected, disturbed, or ill-treated, or offenders against the law" (SNZ, Vol. 2, No. 72, 8 November 1974, p1635).

3   The new emphasis on multiculturalism and families appears in the Preamble to the new Act which reads:
      "An Act to reform the law relating to Children and Young Persons who are in need of care and protection or who offend against the law, and, in particular - (a) To advance the well being of families and the well being of children and young persons as members of families, whanau, hapu, iwi and family groups: (b) To make provision for families, whanau, hapu, iwi and family groups to receive assistance in caring for their children and young persons: (c) To make provision for matters relating to children and young persons who are in need of care and protection or who have offended against the law to be resolved, wherever possible, by their own family, whanau, hapu, iwi, or family group: (d) To make provision for appointment of Commissioner of Children: [and] (e) To repeal the Children and Young Persons Act 1974" (SNZ, Vol. 1, No. 24, 27 May 1989, p448).

4   NZPD, 27 April 1989, p10246.

5   Michael J.A. Brown, Care and Protection is about adult behaviour: The Ministerial Review of the Department of Child, Youth and Family Services, report to the Minister of Social Services and Employment, Hon Steve Maharey, December 2000, pp12-13.

6   The intergenerational family is an important concept in the ensuing discussion. It embraces the traditional "nuclear family" (parents and children), but is not confined to this structure because it includes kinship ties across the generations, as well as other living relatives. It locates the nuclear family within a web of relational connectedness and

accountability. It is in accord with non-European interpretations of "family" but does not sit comfortably with contemporary multicultural understandings of a diversity of family forms.

[7] UNCROC is sometimes referred to as "the Convention", "CROC" or "CRC". The full text is contained in the Appendix.

[8] Not to be confused with the New Zealand HRC.

[9] New Zealand has ratified these six main human rights instruments: the Convention on the Elimination of All Forms of Racial Discrimination (CERD) 1965 (ratified in 1972); the Covenant on Economic, Social and Cultural Rights (1978); the Covenant on Civil and Political Rights 1966 (1978); the Convention on the Elimination of All Forms of Discrimination against Woman (CEDAW) 1979 (1985); the Convention against Torture and other Cruel, Inhuman or Degrading Treatment or Punishment (1989); and the Convention on the Rights of the Child (UNCROC) 1989 (1993). In addition, New Zealand has also signed the UN Convention on the Rights of the Child Optional Protocol on the Sale of Children, Child Prostitution and Pornography, in 2000 (this was designed to increase the international legal protection for children from sexual and other forms of exploitation across borders).

[10] See Preamble (Appendix).

[11] Material in this paragraph was gleaned from Philip E. Veerman's book *The Rights of the Child and the Changing Image of Childhood* (Dordrecht: Martinus Nijhoff Publishers, 1992), pp27-28.

[12] UNCROC Article 44. The reservations concerned Articles 22, 32(1), and 37(c).

[13] UNCROC has been ratified by 192 countries. The notable exception besides the USA is Somalia.

[14] *Children's Rights: Equal Rights?: Diversity, Difference and the Issue of Discrimination* (London: Save the Children, November 2000, Introduction), p5. This was a critical stocktake of the domestic situation for children in 25 countries, including New Zealand (see pp164-68).

[15] Bruce C. Hafen and Jonathan O. Hafen, "Abandoning Children to Their Autonomy: The United Nations Convention on the Rights of the Child", *Harvard International Law Journal*, Spring 1996, Vol. 37, No. 2, pp450-51, emphasis in original.

[16] Mattias Kumm, "The Legitimacy of International Law: A Constitutionalist Framework of Analysis", *The European Journal of International Law*, Vol. 15, No. 5, 2004, pp912-13.

[17] [1986] 1 AC 112 (HL)

[18] For an explanation of these abbreviations, see below n42.

[19] John Barrington, *A Voice for Children: The Office of the Commissioner for Children, 1989-2003* (Palmerston North: Dunmore Press, 2004), p15.

[20] The discussion in this paragraph is based on points made in Rex Ahdar's book, *Adrift in a Sea of Rights* (New Zealand Educational Development Foundation, August 2001), pp16-17.

[21] *Ibid.*, p21.

22 Barrington, *A Voice for Children*, p15.

23 In a Norwegian statement that is very similar to the rationale provided for the New Zealand Commissioner for Children, it was said that, "the task of the Commissioner for Children is to assess the impact of the societal situation on the conditions under which children grow up, and promote the interests of children both in the public and private sectors" (Veerman, The *Rights of the Child*, p114).

24 Barrington, *A Voice for Children*, p18.

25 Lesley Max, *Children: Endangered Species? How the needs of New Zealand children are being seriously neglected: a call for action* (Auckland: Penguin Books, 1990), various quotes, pp245-47.

26 *Ibid.*, p247.

27 *Ibid.*

28 Barrington, *A Voice for Children*, p19.

29 CYPFA, Part 9, s410(1).

30 Crown Entities are organisations in which the state has a controlling ownership interest. They form part of the Crown reporting entity, but are not part of the Crown itself (i.e., are non-departmental organisations).

31 Hassall was Commissioner from mid-June 1989 to August 1994. He graduated MB ChB from the University of Otago in 1965 and holds a Diploma in Child Health, and the associated professional qualifications: RCP, RCS, and MRACP. It is significant that an appointment was made some months before the legislation creating the position had been passed through parliament.

32 Barrington, *A Voice for Children*, p23.

33 *Ibid.*, p24.

34 Barrington, *A Voice for Children*, p32.

35 In May 1993 the government also accepted the Hague Convention on the Protection of Children and Co-operation in Respect of Intercountry Adoption. It was enacted in domestic law in 1997.

36 Robert Ludbrook, "Victims of tokenism and hypocrisy: New Zealand's failure to implement the United Nations Convention on the Rights of the Child", in Anne B. Smith, Megan Gollop, Kate Marshall and Karen Nairn, *Advocating for Children: International Perspectives on Children's Rights* (Dunedin: University of Otago Press, 2000), p112. Ludbrook (LLB Dip SocSc) was an experienced lawyer who had worked for the OCC for a period prior to 1998.

37 *Ibid.*, pp110-11.

38 Emphasis added.

39 See Ludbrook, "Victims of Tokenism", *op. cit.* Reservations concerning UNCROC related to the age-mixing of children with adults in prisons, the minimum age of employment, and distinguishing between people, based on their right to be in New Zealand. These may have delayed ratification but there remained widespread support for the Convention.

40 Don McKinnon entered parliament as the National MP for Albany (North Shore,

Auckland) in 1978. By 1990 he was a senior figure in the caucus and held the following positions of responsibility: Leader of the House (1993-96); Minister of Foreign Affairs and Trade (1990-99); and Deputy Prime Minister to Jim Bolger (1990-96).

[41] *The Press*, 15 March 1993, p6.

[42] The ratification of UNCROC coincided with the Human Rights Bill which was before the Justice and Law Reform Select Committee in February-March 1993 early in the new parliamentary year. The HRA came into effect almost 12 months later on 1 February 1994.

[43] Newell founded EPOCH (End Physical Punishment of Children) in the UK in 1986. He was also involved in other similar societies, including (but not exhaustively) treasurer of STOPP (Society of Teachers Opposed to Physical Punishment), founder of APROACH (Association for Protection of All Children), and chairman of the CRO (Children's Rights Office). A New Zealand branch of EPOCH was established in January 1997. "EPOCH Worldwide [the promotional website explains] is an informal alliance of organisations that share the aim of ending physical punishment of children." (http://epochnz.virtualave. net/about.html, last accessed August 2006). A government agency, the Ministry of Youth Affairs (*Te Tari Taiohi*) was also formed in 1997. According to its website the aim was "...to promote the direct participation of young people aged between 12 and 25 years in the social, educational, economic and cultural development of New Zealand, both locally and nationally."

[44] Keynote address, *The First Decade: A conference held to mark the tenth anniversary of the United Nations Convention on the Rights of the Child,* Auckland University, 25 November 1999, p7 (hereafter cited as *The First Decade)*. Newell's visit was mainly funded by the Ministry of Youth Affairs (see Beth Wood, "Peter Newell's Visit", Action for Children Aotearoa, Newsletter, June 2000, p11).

[45] McKinnon was appointed to this role in 2000 and in April 2004 was reappointed for a second four-year term.

[46] The name change is an interesting attempt to create what might be called "bureaucratic intimacy".

[47] Almost every recognised child advocacy NGO in New Zealand is a staunch supporter of UNCROC. Save the Children, for example, informs readers of its magazine that, "Everything [the International Save the Children Alliance] does is underpinned by the United Nations Convention on the Rights of the Child." World's Children, Winter 2005, p6.

[48] Barrington, *A Voice for Children*, p47.

[49] *Ibid*.

[50] Barrington, *A Voice for Children*, p48.

[51] *Commissioner's Report, 2002*, p7.

[52] "Editorial", *Children,* No. 42, June 2002, p3.

[53] This is acknowledged as conjecture, however; this claim would be difficult (if not impossible) to verify.

[54] The Human Rights Commission has five goals: "1. The human rights that underpin a fair and just society are better understood, appreciated and respected in Aotearoa/New

Zealand; 2. Economic, social and cultural rights are more fully realised in New Zealand; 3. The universality and indivisibility of human rights are supported nationally and internationally; 4. Harmonious relations between individuals and among the diverse groups in Aotearoa/New Zealand are encouraged, maintained and developed; and 5. The human rights dimensions of the Treaty of Waitangi, and their relationship with domestic and international law are better understood." *Report of the Human Rights Commission* (Te *Hahui Tika Tangata*) *and The Office of Human Rights Proceedings* (Te *Tari Whakatau Take Tika Tangata*) *for the year ended 30 June 2003* (Annual Report 2003), Wellington.

[55] McClay, a contemporary of McKinnon's, was also a National MP and former cabinet minister. A one-time primary teacher and principal, he entered parliament as MP for Taupo in 1981, and retained the seat after the renaming of the electorate as Waikaremoana before the 1984 snap election. At various times McClay was Minister of Youth Affairs, Associate Minister of Education, and Minister of Social Welfare, before leaving parliament in late 1996. He was appointed the third Commissioner for Children for a five-year term effective from 16 February 1998. The Commissioner's position came out of Part 9 (s410) of the CYPFA.

[56] See "Speaking up for children not just a job", *Otago Daily Times*, 28 July 2003, p30.

[57] These cases include a spate of infant and child deaths in horrific circumstances, often involving step, de facto and blended families. The most publicised was the death of four-year-old Riri-o-Te Rangi (James) Whakaruru, who died in April 1999 as the result of sustained abuse. His case resulted in an 88-page report issued by the Commissioner for Children (see *Final Report on the Investigation into the Death of James Whakaruru* (Wellington: Office of the Commissioner for Children, June 2000); hereafter cited as *Final Report*). McClay concluded, "New Zealand's approach to the rights of the child appear[s] to be somewhat fragmented due to a lack of global policy or plan of action related to children and their rights." (p52) His first recommendation in light of the tragedy was to urge New Zealand's closer compliance with the UN's 1997 feedback on UNCROC (see p54).

[58] Contained in the Family Proceedings Act 1980.

[59] See http://www.iisd.ca/Cairo/program/p05002.html (last accessed August 2006).

[60] This issue erupted in the media in late 2004; see, for example, "Parental guidance discretionary", *New Zealand Herald,* September 18-19, 2004, p. B3, and "Clark defends secret abortions", *ODT,* 14 September 2004, p2. Martin Guggenheim's in-depth analysis of specific legal cases in the US concerning rights and the pregnancy of minors, leads him to this conclusion: "The adolescent abortion cases are not really about children's rights. They are, instead, a well-disguised effort to settle a dispute among adults over the best rules for dealing with children who become pregnant unintentionally and do not want to become parents." *What's Wrong With Children's Rights* (Massachusetts: Harvard University Press, 2005), p243.

[61] See http://www.unicef.org/crc/crc.htm (last accessed August 2006).

[62] Bruce Abramson JD, is a Geneva-based attorney and International Human Rights Law Consultant who has published widely in the area of children's rights, including work for

the Defence of Children International, an independent NGO set-up during the IYC in 1979 to ensure the promotion and protection of the rights of the child, see: http://www. dci-is.org/Static/ijjn/jj_tuc.php?OpenDocument&menu=4 (last accessed August 2006). He was also a contributing author to *Refugee Children: Guidelines on Protection and Care* (UNHCR, Geneva, 1994), and has written over 40 papers on UNCROC, and additionally, has attended every session of the Committee on the Rights of the Child and participated in all of the Committee's days of general discussion.

[63]   "Clearing up Three Misunderstandings about the Convention on the Rights of the Child", unpublished manuscript, November 2004, various extracts pp4-7 (emphasis in original and used with permission).

[64]   For biographical details on Weigel see http://www.eppc.org/scholars/scholarID.14/scholar.asp (last accessed August 2006).

[65]   George Weigel, "Are Human Rights Still Universal?", *Commentary,* February 1995, p43.

[66]   These headings come from a list of 26 "Areas of Interest" as stated by the Human Rights Foundation of Aotearoa/New Zealand, see http://www.humanrights.co.nz/resources/ newsletters/Newsletter_November_2001.doc (last accessed August 2006).

[67]   "Advocacy on Behalf of Children", an address to the Annual General Meeting of Anglican Care, Christchurch, 14 October 1997, p2.

[68]   For a helpful discussion of Hohfeld in relation to children's rights see Veerman, *The Rights of the Child,* Chapter 2, "In Search of Workable Definitions", particularly pp13-20, and the primary text, Walter W. Cook (ed), Wesley N. Hohfeld, *Fundamental Legal Conceptions as Applied to Judicial Reasoning* (New Haven & London: Yale University Press, 1919).

[69]   Notwithstanding, of course, the legal definition as expressed in Article 1: "every human being below the age of eighteen years".

[70]   Isaiah Berlin calls this "positive liberty", but the more modern equivalent is "empowerment rights".

[71]   V.L. Worsfold, "A Philosophical Justification for Children's Rights", *Harvard Educational Review,* Vol. 44, No. 1, 1974, p146, and cited here in Ki Su Kim, "J.S. Mill's Concept of Maturity as the Criterion in Determining Children's Eligibility for Rights". *Journal of Philosophy of Education,* Vol. 24, No. 2, 1990, p242.

[72]   *Final Report,* p52.

[73]   *Ibid.*

[74]   *Final Report,* "Recommendations", pp54-60.

[75]   Two New Zealand studies have found associations between family change, single parent families and abuse, see David Fergusson and Michael Lynsky, "Physical Punishment Maltreatment During Childhood and Adjustment in Young Adulthood," *Child Abuse and Neglect,* Vol. 21, no. 7,1997, p617; David Fergusson, Michael Lynsky, and John Horwood, "Prevalence of Sexual Abuse and Factors Associated With Sexual Abuse" *Journal of the American Academy of Child and Adolescent Psychiatry,* Vol. 35, No. 10, 1996, p1355. Also, a recent ten year review of recent literature on child abuse finds that family constellation is a significant risk factor, and that the presence of a step-parent in the

home approximately doubles the chance that a girl will be sexually abused, see Frank Putnam, "Ten-Year Research Update Review: Child Sexual Abuse" *Journal of American Academy of Child and Adolescent Psychiatry*, Vol. 42, No. 3, 2003, p271. Furthermore, international research has shown strong associations between step-parent families and child abuse, see Leslie Margolin, "Child Sexual Abuse By Caretakers," *Family Relations*, Vol. 38, No. 4, 1989, p450; Leslie Margolin, "Child Abuse by Mothers Boyfriends: Why the Overrepresentation?" *Child Abuse and Neglect*, Vol. 16, No. 4, 1992, p541; Martin Daly and Margo Wilson, "Child Abuse and Other Risks Of Not Living With Both Parents," *Ethnology and Sociobiology*, Vol. 6, 1985, p197; Martin Daly and Margo Wilson, "Some Differential Attributes of Lethal Assaults On Small Children By Stepfathers Versus Genetic Fathers," *Ethnology & Sociobiology* 15 (4), 1994, p 207.

76 The increasing number of one-parent families is the most characteristic trend concerning families. According to the MSD, "[T]he most significant change in families in the past two decades has been the shift from two-parent to one-parent families. This was more pronounced in the 1980s, when the share of one-parent families increased from 14 to 24 percent, than in the 1990s, when it rose to 29 percent. One-parent families are expected to continue to increase, but at a slower rate. Family projections based on trends since 1986 suggest that by 2021, one-parent families are likely to make up around 35 percent of all families with dependent children." *2004 the Social Report: indicators of social well-being in New Zealand* (Wellington: Ministry of Social Development, 2004), p19. The disintegrating family has also affected fathers: when families break down, the state has further opportunities to intervene and be "father" (*in loco patris*).

77 The tension is even evident in CYF annual reports. In Chief Executive Jackie Pivac's opening remarks ("chief executive's overview") in 2003, for example, she admitted that "…[d]emand and financial pressures underpinned the sharp rise in turnover of field social workers, particularly senior practitioners, in the third quarter." This points to a serious difficulty in retaining competent and experienced staff. *Annual Report 2003*, Department of Child, Youth and Family Services, p1.

78 See Bronwyn Dalley, *Family Matters: Child Welfare in Twentieth-Century New Zealand* (Auckland: Auckland University Press (in association with the Historical Branch, Department of Internal Affairs), 1998), p360 for more on the review.

79 Hassall, for example, in his paper, *The New Zealand Commissioner for Children: Some relevant experiences* (Adelaide, 1992), cited three principles underpinning the implementation of UNCROC: 1. the humanity of children; 2. the individuality of children; and 3. diversity in child-rearing practices (Barrington, *op. cit.*, p25).

80 As a result of an electoral referendum in September 1992, New Zealand adopted an MMP system in preference to the "First Past the Post" system. The first MMP election was in 1996.

81 Ludbrook, "Victims of Tokenism", pages 121 and 123.

82 Kumm, "The Legitimacy of International Law: A Constitutionalist Framework of Analysis", p914.

83 *Ibid*, p915.

84   "Measures to make the principles and provisions of the Convention more widely known" in *Children and Youth in Aotearoa 2003*, http://www.acya.org.nz/Portals/0/ChildrenYouthAo tearoa2003_Appendix8.rtf p13 (unavailable November 2005), but related ACYA information can be accessed at http://www.acya.org.nz/?t=23 (last accessed August 2006).

85   Barrington, *A Voice for Children*, p83 cited from a 1998 interview with McClay.

86   Laurie O'Reilly was Commissioner from 1 September 1994 until his death in 1997. He had gained an LLB at Canterbury University in 1963, and was a family law practitioner and specialist. In 1995, his salary as Commissioner was $135,000 ("Laurie O'Reilly Keeper Of Our Kids", *North & South*, October 1995, p104).

87   Holt (1923-1985), a submariner in World War Two, later became a teacher and successful author. Most of his books on education were highly critical of formal schooling and he also wrote on children's rights and was one of the most important exponents of the Children's Liberation Movement. In *Escape from Childhood* (1974), Holt outlined 11 rights, including the right of the child to vote, the right to own property, the right to choose one's guardian, the right to drive, and the right to control one's sex life. Born in Chicago and raised in Southern California, Farson helped found the Western Behavioral Sciences Institute in 1958 in La Jolla, California (Carl Rogers also spent a number of years there as a Resident Fellow). Farson held a doctorate in psychology and in 1974 wrote *Birthrights: A Bill of Rights for Children*. He also generated a list of 10 rights, including *(inter alia)* the right of the child to alternative home environments; the right to sexual freedom, and perhaps most significantly, the right to political power.

88   Veerman, *The Rights of the Child*, pp63-64. See also Holt's key text, *Escape from Childhood: the Needs and Rights of Children* (New York: E.P. Dutton & Co. Inc., 1974).

89   Holt, *Escape from Childhood*, p115.

90   Robert Ludbrook, "Should children have the right to vote?", *Children*, No. 51, October 2004, pp6-7. Interestingly, this was reprinted verbatim the following year in No. 54 (June/July 2005, pp19-21), presumably to stimulate debate on the issue prior to the general election. In both articles, Ludbrook cites Holt's 1974 *Escape from Childhood*, and concludes that "[s]urely it is time that the issue of lowering the voting age was taken seriously . . . ." (June/July 2005, p21).

91   For a useful discussion of these issues see Rosaleen MacBrayne, "When does a child become an adult?". *New Zealand Herald*, 7 June 2000,

92   The full list of these groups would be very long, and the discussion at this point mentions only a small number considered to be "key players" in the politicisation of children.

93   Statement of aims in *Our Children: The Priority for Policy* (Auckland: CPAG, 2nd edition, 2003), p2.

94   Ibid., "Preface to the Second Edition", p5.

95   P. Townsend, "Deprivation", *Journal of Social Policy*, Vol. 16, 1987, pp125-146, and cited here in Peter Crampton, Clare Salmond, Russell Kirkpatrick, Robyn Scarborough, and Chris Skelly, *Degrees of Deprivation in New Zealand: An Atlas of Socioeconomic Difference*. Auckland: David Bateman Ltd., 2000, p13.

[96] *Ibid.*

[97] Vanessa Krishnan, John Jensen, Mike Rochford (Knowledge Group, Ministry of Social Development), "Children in Poor Families: Does the Source of Family Income Change the Picture?", *Social Policy Journal of New Zealand (Te Puna Whakaaro)*, Issue 18, June 2002, p145. Data on poverty was derived in this study from Statistics New Zealand's Household Economic Survey, and the Ministry of Social Policy's 2000 Survey of Living Standards. Another researcher, Robert Stephens, adds that by 1995, "in comparison with other OECD countries, New Zealand was not generous in its assistance to families with dependent children." "The Social Impact of Reform: Poverty in Aotearoa/New Zealand," *Social Policy and Administration,* Vol.34, No.1, March 2000, p75.

[98] *Ibid.*, p146.

[99] p11. It should be added, however, that the following sentence in this paragraph reads: "However, because overall there are more children in two parent families, there are more children from two parent families in each of the bottom quintiles" (*ibid*). This statistical qualification does not reinforce the obvious point that one parent, rather than two, is naturally at a disadvantage raising children.

[100] "Child poverty—time to act is now" in *Sue's News*, newsletter of Green MP Sue Bradford, Autumn 2005, p1. In the lead-up to the 2005 election, the Greens positioned themselves as the party most prominently committed to child welfare. More specifically, a Green Party flier from September 2005 noted that, "The [Greens] will work towards eliminating child poverty by 2010, including through [sic] a cross-party accord in Parliament". In her adjournment speech at the end of the 47th parliament, Bradford claimed, "[W]e [the Greens] kept child and adult poverty on the political agenda…" *NZPD*, 2 August 2005, p22373.

[101] It is not correct, therefore (as sometimes stated in policy papers), that it is children who receive government transfers as a source of income, but their parents/caregivers.

[102] A 1994 report by the New Zealand Council of Christian Services publication Child Poverty in Aotearoa/New Zealand in most respects endorsed the CPAG findings. Ten years later, CPAG continued to criticise Labour's Working for Families Package, announced in the 2004 budget (see 4.2). Again, children were presented in a CPAG report in November within a structural rubric, see Susan St John and David Craig, *Cut Price Kids: Does the 2004 'Working for Families' Budget work for children?* Auckland: CPAG, 2004.

[103] Barrington, A *Voice for Children*, p85.

[104.] http://www.childrensday.org.nz/about/index.html (last accessed August 2006). From 2007, Children's Day will move to March to avoid the Labour Day weekend and to take advantage of better weather (see "Change of Date", *Otago Daily Times*, 28 November 2005, p6).

[105] This had formed the year earlier as Action for Children in Aotearoa (ACA).

[106] Barrington, *A Voice for Children,* p60.

[107] Barrington pp65-66. When O'Reilly, a Roman Catholic and committed family man, said in 1997 that, "the Convention is pro-family and pro-parent", (*Childrenz Issues,* Vol. 1, No. 1, 1997, p5) there is little doubt he personally endorsed that view. Among his stated

goals was to use the experience as Commissioner to monitor and review the workings of the 1989 Act. He also spoke out on the serious issue of fatherless families. It should be added, however, that these comments were made well before the intense political debates over what was meant by family had fully surfaced in New Zealand.

[108] "About the Children's Issues Centre", *Childrenz Issues*, Vol. 1, No. 1, 1997, p34.

[109] A representative selection is contained in the Ministry of Education's 2003 booklets *Best Evidence Synthesis* (BES). BES is a summary of contemporary educational research and is replete with the assumptions of a "subject-position" analysis which, for example, dismisses "objectivity", "standards" and "excellence" in favour of more subjective and phenomenological experiences of a student's "participation" or "success". This is consequential to the embracing and promotion of a diversity ethos.

[110] Nietzsche (1844-1900) embraced "perspectivism", which is the view that the external world can only be interpreted through alternative systems of concepts and beliefs; there is no authoritative, independent criterion for determining one system as more valid than another. All claims to truth are simply "perspectives" issuing from the centre of some ascendant "will", and truth is "a mobile army of metaphors, metonyms, and anthropomorphisms". Nietzsche dismissed the idea of objective truth and embraced what we now call relativism.

[111] Sartre (1905-1980) was a leading exponent of existentialism, a philosophy concerned with the nature of human existence and the freedom of the will.

[112] See above n108.

[113] Among Foucault's main works are *Discipline and Punish: The Birth of the Prison* (New York: Vintage Books, 1977), and, *The History of Sexuality, Volume 1* (New York: Vintage Books, 1980).

[114] It should be added that Foucault himself was less interested in partisan politics than in exploring the dynamics of power. However, in a piece entitled "Polemics, Politics and Prolematisation" (1984) he did admit, "...I have in fact been situated in most squares on the political checkerboard, one after the another (sic) and simultaneously: as antichrist, leftist, ostentatious or disguised Marxist, nihilist, explicit or secret anti-Marxist, technocrat in the service of Gaullism, new liberal, etc. ...None of these descriptions is important by itself; taken together on the other hand, they mean something." *The Foucault Reader* (New York: Pantheon Books), pp383-84.

[115] But not exclusively; other influences include the discourse analysis of Roland Barthes and the deconstruction of language and meaning in the writings of Jacques Derrida.

[116] Judith Duncan, ' "She's always been what I would think, a perfect day-care child": Constructing the subjectivities of a New Zealand child.' Paper presented at the 12th Reconceptualising Early Childhood Education Conference on Research, Theory and Practice: *Troubling Identities,* Oslo University College, Oslo, Norway, 24-28 May 2004, PDF version, pp15-16, http://www.otago.ac.nz/cic/about.php (last accessed August 2006). The Children's Issues Centre is more systematic in promoting children's rights than other NGOs because it is also involved in teaching, research, making policy recommendations, and providing specific child-related qualifications. It offers an MA in Childhood and

Youth Studies, a Postgraduate Diploma in Child Advocacy, and a Postgraduate Certificate in Children's Issues. The Diploma strongly endorses UNCROC with one of the four papers (CHIX 404) seeking to bridge the Convention with contemporary theoretical models (notably Foucault). The descriptor (ibid) says, "This course links the United Nations [sic] Convention on the Rights of the Child to sociology of childhood and sociocultural theory, in order to develop implications for policies which are supportive of children's rights."

[117] Crimes Act 1961, section 2.

[118] See for example, UNCROC "Concluding observations of the Committee on the rights of the child: New Zealand" (Geneva: UN Committee on the Rights of the Child, 3 October 2003) and cited here in Terry Dobbs, *Insights: Children and young people speak out about family discipline*. Wellington: Save the Children New Zealand, 2005, p7.

[119] See, for example, *Children* (the Children's Commissioner's newsletter) and *Childrenz Issues* (a journal on children produced by the CIC at Otago University, Dunedin, since 1997).

[120] *R v Donselaar* unreported, CRI-2004-043-201, District Court New Plymouth, sentencing remarks of Judge Bidois, 14 April 2005.

[121] See *New Zealand Herald* "Smacking law – voters say leave it alone" 2 July 2005, available at http://www.nzherald.co.nz/search/story.cfm?storyid=57921F7A-39E4-11DA-8E1B-A5B353C55561 (last accessed August 2006) and *New Zealand Herald* "Government puts off move to outlaw smacking" 20 December 2001, available at http://www.nzherald.co.nz/search/story.cfm?storyid=10FC63FC-39DC-11DA-8E1B-A5B353C55561 (last accessed August 2006).

[122] Beth Wood, "How are we doing?", *Children*, No. 48, December 2003, p6.

[123] See, for example, *R v Accused* [1994] DCR, 883.

[124] Submission of Maxim Institute to the Justice and Electoral Select Committee considering the Crimes (Abolition of Force as a Justification for Child Discipline) Amendment Bill, available at http://www.maxim.org.nz/main_pages/current_page/current_parliament_main.html (last accessed August 2006).

[125] From 1974 to 1996-97 Anne Smith was a child development and educational psychology lecturer in the University of Otago's Education Department. She moved to the CIC (also based at the university) as the lead researcher in 1997. According to its own literature, the CIC has "...a strong commitment to encouraging implementation of the United Nations Convention on the Rights of the Child, and particularly Article 12 which says that children should have a voice and be listened to in decisions which affect them." "About the Children's Issues Centre", *Childrenz Issues*, Vol. 1, No. 1, 1997, p34.

[126] Media release, 25 May 2004. See also "The Discipline and Guidance of Children: A Summary of Research", Children's Issues Centre University of Otago and Office of the Children's Commissioner, June 2004.

[127] *Innocenti Report Card*. UNICEF: September 2003, Child maltreatment deaths in rich nations, see Figures 1a and 1b: Unrevised (and Revised) league table of child deaths from maltreatment.

[128] D.M Fergusson and M.T. Lynskey *Physical Punishment/Maltreatment During Childhood*

and Adjustment in Young Adulthood. Child Abuse and Neglect 21, No. 7 (1997), 628.

[129] R.E. Larzelere *A Review of the Outcomes of Parental Use of Nonabusive or Customary Physical Punishment* Pediatrics 98, No. 4 (1996) 824.

[130] Revealingly, in the Statement of Intent 2004/05 for the Families Commission presented to the House of Representatives the inclusive ethos was stated early on: "In carrying out its role the Commission is required to have regard to the kinds, structures, and diversity of families. For this purpose 'family' includes a group of people related by marriage, blood, or adoption, an extended family, two or more persons living together as a family, and a whanau or other culturally recognised family group." Families Commission: Statement of Intent 2004/05. Wellington: 2005, p7.

[131] Terry Dobbs, *Insights: children and young people speak out about family discipline.* Wellington: Save the Children New Zealand, 2005, p55.

[132] Terry Dobbs, *Insights: children and young people speak out about family discipline.* Wellington: Save the Children New Zealand, 2005, p9.

[133] *Ibid.*, p11.

[134] Dobbs, *Insights*, p13.

[135] See, for example, UNICEF's press release "Section 59 and fear of prosecution" dated 26 May 2006, available at http://www.scoop.co.nz/stories/PO0605/S00275.htm (last accessed August 2006).

[136] The selection of the Bill on 9 June 2005 happened to coincide with the beginning of Plunket's 57th National Conference being held in Palmerston North. The 560 delegates were set to debate a range of remits including "the immediate repeal of Section 59 of the Crimes Act, 1961", but the events in parliament obviously added an urgency to Plunket's voice for repeal. Kaye Crowther (president), "Our call for the repeal of Section 59", *Ray of Hope: the Littlies Lobby Newsletter*, July 2005, p1.

[137] The purpose of Smith's Bill was (in part): "to clarify the limitations on parental discipline allowed by the Crimes Act in order to prevent the Act being used to defend child abuse under the guise of parental discipline . . . ." As a result of United Future's reduced party vote at the September 2005 election, Smith was not returned to Parliament. The Bill has been overshadowed by Bradford's anyway. An amendment to section 59 was also proposed by New Zealand First list MP Brian Donnelly.

[138] There is not space here to discuss these in more detail, but along with the government's Foreshore and Seabed Act 2004 this legislation has caused greater controversy than almost any other issue since the 1985-86 homosexual law reform debates.

[139] *NZPD*, 23 July 2003, p7218.

[140] The *Agenda for Children* was a major government-initiated project in 2001-02 (see 4.1). It included an extensive number of documents for public consultation and feedback.

[141] *The Press*, 8 October 2003, pA1. Kiro was appointed on 12 August 2003. She holds a PhD in Social Policy, an MBA, and Certificate of Competency in Social Work Practice. Prior to her appointment at the OCC, Kiro had served in various health, Maori development and child advocacy roles. She was also Associate Professor and Director of the Waiora Centre for Public Health Research at Massey University's Albany campus (North Shore,

Auckland). Upon her appointment, Social Development and Employment Minister Steve Maharey said: "She herself is a mother. She has extensive working knowledge of the CYPFA. She is knowledgeable about children's rights and New Zealand's obligations under the United Nations Convention on the Rights of the Child." Press release, Hon Steve Maharey, 12 August 2003.

142 Not surprisingly, there was bloc support (nine votes) from the Greens in favour of Bradford's Bill. Bradford also made the abolition of section 59 an issue on the hustings, along with the elimination of child poverty.

143 Any references to the debate about discipline are judiciously avoided in official statements concerning SKIP. The implication is evident, however, in oblique references to "training and resources for families", as in the following from a website. SKIP, it says, "...is a strategy designed to provide parents with information about raising children to be happy, dependable adults. . . . SKIP will partner with community groups working with families and children to develop training and resources for families. SKIP will not duplicate what already exists, but will build on what's there and fill any gaps. Several groups have already approached the project team asking for support to develop initiatives." (see http://www.msd.govt.nz/media-information/press-releases/2004/pr-2004-05-06.html last accessed August 2006).

This obfuscation, however, has not satisfied NGOs vocal in their demands to repeal section 59.

144 EPOCH New Zealand Annual Report July 2003 to June 2004, Introduction, http://www.epochnz.org.nz/ (last accessed August 2006).

145 A search on *The New Zealand Herald* site revealed that 81 articles appeared on the topic of smacking and/or s59 across the period 1999-mid-2005. This averages out at 15 per year and indicates a high level of public interest in the issue.

146 The organisations which have "signed-up" in support of repealing s59 include: Action for Children and Youth Aotearoa; Ahu Whakatika Challenge Violence Trust; Amnesty International; Aotearoa New Zealand; Barnardos; Birthright; Central Plateau Reap; Child Abuse Prevention Services; Children's Agenda; Children's Issues Centre; Dannevirke Family Services Inc; Domestic Violence Centre; Dove Hawkes Bay; Education for Change; Foundation for Peace Studies; Healing and Rape Crisis Centre; Home and Family Society Inc; Horowhenua Family Violence Intervention; Kapiti Men for Non Violence Inc; La Leche League NZ; Manawatu Alternatives to Violence; Naku Enei Tamariki; National Network of Stopping Violence Services; Office of the Children's Commissioner; OMEP (World Organisation for Early Childhood); Parent and Family Counselling Service; Parent Help Wellington Inc; Parentline Hawkes Bay Inc; Parents Centre NZ Inc; Public Health Association of New Zealand Inc; Quaker Peace and Service; Rodney Stopping Violence Services; Royal New Zealand Plunket Society; Save the Children; Stopping Violence Services Nelson; Stopping Violence Services Wairarapa; Taranaki Kindergarten Association; Te Awamutu Women's Centre; Te Korowai Aroha O Ngati Whatua; UNICEF New Zealand; Wellington Community Law Centre; Whanganui Living Without Violence Trust; Women's Refuge; Youth Law/Tino Rangatiratanga; and, New Zealand Family Research Trust. (see http://www.epochnz.org.nz/index.php?option=com_content&task=view&id=26&Itemid=1 last accessed August 2006)

[147] *ODT*, 14 September 2005, p39. The point regarding "any force" was supported by an investigation into the proposed law conducted by the legal services department of the Office of the Police Commissioner. In a letter dated 11 August 2005 it was reported that, "if s59 was repealed, parents would not be authorised to use reasonable force 'by way of correction'. Parents would still be able to use force to prevent harm to their children. For instance, if a parent stopped their child from running out on to a busy road or stopped their child from climbing over a balcony on a building. 'However, smacking of a child by way of corrective action would be an assault.' " "Smacking assault if repeal Bill survives after election", *ODT*, 23 August 2005, p9.

Chapter Four

——————— • ———————

Current and future developments

As discussed in the previous chapter, debates concerning family in New Zealand society have been occurring for several decades. The lead-up to the CYPFA in 1989, brought many family-related matters into the orbit of public policy concern, although the context at that time was youth justice and the focus was bi- and multi-culturalism. The debates which preceded the Act established the parameters for debate on family over the next 20 years. The interest in multiculturalism evolved into a wider consideration of the form and function of families, and paved the way for an emphasis on diversity of family form which in 2006 still dominates policy understandings of what is denoted by family.

The passage of the 1989 legislation and ratification of UNCROC in 1993, resulted in a concurrent emphasis on families, children and children's rights. The neo-Liberal or New Right reforms led several analysts to examine the effects of those policies on both children and families from the mid-1990s. The focus, however, tended to be on children, and more specifically child poverty and a widening gap between rich and poor amidst widespread claims of government apathy and neglect. The ongoing compliance demands of UNCROC—the quinquennial reports to the UN—have added urgency and support to demands for new laws and changed social attitudes, while NGOs such as CPAG and EPOCH consistently keep up the pressure for reform in specific areas.

This chapter considers the position, in New Zealand, of children and children's rights in the early twenty-first century. If children have been politicised, where might we be heading as the cause gains momentum? Given that UNCROC is a ratified convention and firmly ensconced as a rallying point, what are the prospects for our nation's children, their parents and families? If, as this work argues, children are no longer seen as primarily deriving their identity within families, but are instead bearers of rights for which the state is responsible, what might the future hold?

These are important questions to which only partial answers can be provided. The discussion will explore current developments and tentatively suggest a way forward.

4.1. 1994-2002

The 1972 Royal Commission on Social Security brought about a major overhaul of social policy but the next revision—the Royal Commission on Social Policy—was not until 1987. The five published volumes of the 1987 Commission were issued too early to comment on the impact of the market reforms which were still in progress. The CYPFA was a major step forward in child welfare, but tensions in the new economic climate soon became apparent. Since the 1970s, a greater awareness of child physical and sexual abuse coupled with the new emphasis on family and community, rather than institutional and residential care, has underscored high-profile cases of child abuse.

Among other examples, there were allegations in 1989 of child sexual abuse occurring at Ward 24 of Christchurch Hospital; the beating to death of three-year-old Delcelia Witika by her mother's *de facto* husband in 1991, and the Christchurch Civic Creche case of 1992-93, which resulted in the conviction and incarceration of childcare worker Peter Ellis.[1] The DSW had to adhere to the Public Finance Act 1989, but when resources were stretched, Treasury officials suggested that if the Department could not work within its budget it should conduct fewer child abuse investigations.[2]

This environment was clearly unsatisfactory, and in line with the CYPFA, the Department was being accused of leaving children in abusive family situations rather than removing them for their own safety. In 1994— the International Year of the Family—a team reviewing the CYPFA was concerned by what it interpreted as the minimisation of children's rights by social workers in favour of maintaining family integrity. The tensions were not merely pragmatic and policy-related, or to do with funding; there were also conceptual and legal issues between family and children's rights.

The review resulted in the CYPF Amendment Act of 1994, which specifically reasserted the paramountcy principle in an effort to reinforce children's safety and safeguard their rights, especially in undesirable family situations. As Bronwyn Dalley explains:

> . . . Although social work staff argued that the notion of paramountcy was inherent in the [1989] legislation, the Department agreed to an amendment in 1994, which reinserted the word itself. Where the original Act stipulated that 'the welfare and interests of the child or young person shall be the deciding factor' in administering the legislation, the 1994 Amendment Act was more specific: 'In all matters relating to the administration . . . of this Act . . . the welfare and interests of the child or young person shall be the first and paramount consideration.'[3]

In light of the high notification rates of abuse, the Amendment Act also clearly defined child maltreatment as "the harming—whether physically, emotionally or sexually, ill-treatment, abuse, neglect or deprivation of any child or young person."[4]

This and subsequent amendments to the principal 1989 Act—in 1996, 1998, and 2001—attempted to provide a working balance between family and children's rights issues, although increasingly—with the general momentum in other (NGO) areas—children's rights came to predominate.

During the tenure of the third Commissioner for Children, Roger McClay (which began on 16 February 1998), and as UNCROC was approaching its tenth anniversary, the welfare orientation of the OCC gave way to a stronger focus on child and young persons' advocacy. As the above discussion illustrates, this was predictable given the preceding developments and policy direction of the period. In November 1998, Labour's Social Welfare spokesperson, Steve Maharey, unveiled a Children's Commissioner's (Convention Rights) Bill. Its main purpose was to give UNCROC "a proper place in New Zealand law," and also to strengthen the Commissioner's powers. But there was insufficient support for the Bill at the time and it did not proceed. Eventually, another Bill to empower the Commissioner and create greater legal independence was introduced by Maharey in August 2001, and was eventually passed in 2003, by the Labour-led government. The 1998 Bill was a clear indication that Labour felt both the Commissioner's and UNCROC's status needed to be consolidated in domestic law; and it would appear there was cross-party support for a re-think of the Commissioner's role and degree of independence from the Social Services Minister. Alliance MP, John Wright, sponsored a further Bill to this effect in March 1999. The Parliamentary Commissioner for Children Bill in March 1999, sought to make the Commissioner an Officer of Parliament.

The policy environment of the late 1990s and into the new decade was highly charged and intensely political. Family remained the subject of much debate, as did UNCROC and children's rights. The launch of the Ministry of Youth Affairs (MYA) in 1997, for example, ensured more debate in parliament and saw the appointment to cabinet of the New Zealand First list MP, Deborah Morris, as Minister.[5] In response to a question from Labour's Steve Maharey on 26 February 1998, regarding the extent of public consultation on UNCROC, Morris replied with a comprehensive summary of developments and events to that point:

> In addition to forums held with non-government organisations, who represent the wider public interest, the Ministry of Youth Affairs has been working with the Office of the Commissioner for Children to consult with children and young people about the Convention and their rights. Consultation with children and young people is considered a priority because they are the group most affected by the Convention. The results of this consultation will be used to inform on-going communication initiatives to raise awareness of the Convention, amongst children, young people and adults.
>
> Also, a bulletin was published by the Ministry of Foreign Affairs and Trade following presentation of New Zealand's initial report under the Convention. This report has been widely circulated and continues to be sent out to interested individuals. Other initiatives to raise awareness of the Convention and inform discussion include publication of an information page in the youth magazine *Tearaway,* and information in the Ministry of Youth Affairs and Ministry of Internal Affairs publication *Unplugged,* the newsletter for youth workers in the community.[6]

But by 2000, when the Labour government submitted its first periodic UNCROC compliance report, it was amidst familiar calls that the Convention was still undervalued in domestic policy. A CIC study published about this time found that UNCROC was mentioned in only 22 of the total 691 judgements of the courts (3.2 per cent) in the years surveyed—that was as of 1990, before New Zealand's ratification; in 1994, it was referred to in six cases, and 1998, in only 16 cases.[7]

A clear statement on what was materialising came from a group known as Children's Agenda (CA), which described itself as "a non-party-political movement of people from diverse backgrounds whose aim is a society which values children." Among the CA's principles we read: "We must *anchor child policy in the political infrastructure* so that children's interests are automatically considered when political decisions have to be made. This doesn't necessarily cost a lot of money—*it is more a question of political will.*"[8]

However, it was not until mid-2000 that the Labour-led government made children's policy based on UNCROC a more specific concern of the state. This began with a public Seminar on Children's Policy in July 2000. One outcome of this was a paper published in the *Social Policy Journal of New Zealand* which considered the research agenda for the next five years. In this, the authors alluded to one of the central concerns raised in the present study; namely, how children are conceptualised. Having discussed issues in health, education, family, peers and community factors, child protection and youth justice, it was concluded:

> Just as there was widespread agreement on the need to focus on a positive approach to child policy and child research, there was widespread agreement that greater attention needs to be given to the way we conceptualise policy and research in which children are participants. For example, is the appropriate policy concern children as vulnerable members of the population, as individuals with rights, as members of families and/or whānau, or all of these? The conceptions chosen clearly affect the design of the child research and policy.[9]

The ensuing five years have demonstrated that the government has sought to change the way children are viewed: what is sometimes referred to as the 'whole child' approach has sought to ensure that policies and practices, as well as service funding and delivery, are responsive to children's interests, rights and needs, and a concurrent emphasis on addressing child poverty and violence. Of the perspectives mentioned in the 2000 paper, however, 'individuals with rights' have tended to dominate over understandings of children as innocents or within families. Around this time, the government became committed to wide consultation, especially in seeking the views of children. A special Children's Discussion Pack, for example, was issued along with an 'adult' version of the *Agenda for Children* in April 2001.

Like much of the rhetoric concerning children's rights, the Agenda for Children was breathtakingly utopian and seemed to believe almost anything could be achieved through direct government intervention. During April to June 2001, over 7,500 children as well as large numbers of adults shared their views in the consultation process. The collated feedback was presented in a 54-page document, *Agenda for Children*, in June 2002. This contained a set of principles to guide policy affecting children; namely, the 'whole child' approach to policy and service development, and a programme of research initiatives to facilitate the vision—a Youth Development Strategy—had similar goals for young persons.

When the *Agenda* was first mooted and consultation began, it was welcomed by NGO advocates, but for some time many had been pessimistic and felt government had squandered opportunities to make a qualitative difference in these areas, particularly in relation to the perennial issues of child poverty and smacking.[10]

The frustration was understandable when, on the world stage, much was being said about giving UNCROC more acknowledgement and authority in New Zealand. For example, on 12 June 2001—around the time of the *Agenda for Children* consultation process—the Human Rights Division of MFAT issued to the UN in New York the *New Zealand Statement to the Preparatory Committee for the Special Session of the General Assembly on Children,* which read (in part): "The . . . Convention on the Rights of the Child should be the basis for all our efforts in respect of children. The Convention's ideals and objectives are universal. Unfortunately, ratification is not yet so. In our view, the Convention has more than proven its durability and worth, both as a binding international legal commitment on Governments to act in the best interests of children, and as a focal point for raising awareness of their rights."[11]

Among these developments was the establishment of the Ministry of Social Development (MSD) which assumed responsibility for a number of agencies, all within a new overarching government department.[12] Established on 1 October 2001, the MSD also replaced the DSW, which dated back to 1972. The MSD has three main roles: providing social policy advice to the government, administering income support and employment services, and maintaining the services of the Department of Child, Youth and Family (CYF). A new department was understandable given the monumental changes that had affected the DSW alone, but it hardly represented a reduction in bureaucracy.

A further important event affecting policy development in New Zealand was to be the UN Special Session on Children held in New York during 19-21 September 2001, but which was postponed owing to the terrorist attacks on the US on 11 September. Back home in that same month, however, McClay proposed a new advocacy focus to be known as the 'Littlies Lobby'. This he described as "a kind of Grey Power, but for those at the other end of the age spectrum."[13] The new lobby was launched by Plunket in association with the OCC in December 2002. An article in the *Children* newsletter at the time began with the heading "Another Player in the World of Lobbying", which in itself revealed the extent to which children had been politicised by 2002.[14] The Littlies Lobby extended a very bureaucratic and adult concern with children's rights to the youngest and most vulnerable members of society.

This he described as "a kind of Grey Power, but for those at the other end of the age spectrum."

The 2002 UNICEF Report, *When the Invisible Hand Rocks the Cradle,* "outlined how the impact on children and their parents of the economic reforms of the 1980s and 1990s were ignored",[15] and thus helped NGOs to press for programmes addressing child poverty. Other key events of that year included the release of a government plan to deal with family violence, *Te Rito: Family Violence Prevention Strategy*, in February, and the attendance of a New Zealand delegation at the UN Special Session on Children in New York, which was eventually held in May. It was organised by UNICEF, whose Executive Director, Carol Bellamy, was adamant that children would be official participants[16]. The Special Session was attended by the New Zealand Social Services Minister, Steve Maharey and youth delegates. Amidst the euphoria, the Special Session was big on promises "to create a better world for children". UN Secretary-General, Kofi Annan, delivered a speech early in the proceedings that was very much in the self-deprecating 'could-do-better' category; the UN had promised much but had to improve on its history of making decisions for children, rather than including, or even allowing them to be autonomous. He said:

We all want a better world for children, but so far, it is the adults that have called the shots. Now we are going to build a better world with children— with you. It's high time that we adults hear what you have to say.[17]

A US delegate was more specific concerning the issue of participation and the symbolic reversal of adult-child roles which would ensue, when she said:

This is not the final chapter in children's participation; in fact, this is where the story must begin. In 1990, several children were asked to participate in the World Summit for Children. Participation then was a child handing a pen to a head of State as she or he signed a document. Here the children will no longer hand the pens to adults; but rather, the adults will hand the pens to the children, and the world will listen.[18]

But perhaps most revealing, as far as developments in New Zealand were concerned, were Maharey's concluding comments. Interviewed at the end of proceedings he said:

I've moved on a notch in coming here, from a kind of intellectual commitment to a much more emotionally committed feeling about this whole notion that we have to get serious about children's issues. I frankly think that children are the first big social movement of the twenty-first century.[19]

The idea that society can find salvation in the purity of the child is an old one, but clearly it has lost none of its appeal to politicians. Here children are prophetically put into the mould of crusading historical movements, such as the philanthropists of the nineteenth century, or the suffragists early in the twentieth century.[20]

The empowering of young people that was a clear focus of the UN Special Session unsurprisingly led to the same sorts of conflicts that characterise 'adult' debates. Delegates were bitterly divided, for example, over the issues of teenagers and sex. Conservative elements within the US delegation, supported by the Vatican and delegates from Arabic and Islamic nations, wanted to promote abstinence within sexuality programmes—a move which frustrated the children's rights caucus lobbying on behalf of more than 100 national and international NGOs. The fierce arguments over family planning issues dominated the closed door debate.[21] The messy world of adult politics proved a reality check against the lofty optimism of the Session.

Mr Maharey, too, despite his new-found emotional attachment to the cause of children, is an experienced political operator aware of the pitfalls involved in facilitating social change. He has endeavoured to steer clear of the smacking debate and avoided giving NGO lobbyists any direct assurance to repeal s59 of the Crimes Act. In defending the 2004 SKIP initiative, for example, in which the government had pledged $10.8 million to assist community groups, the links with repealing s59 were inevitably made. In a radio interview, the Minister rightly sought to separate the two issues, but appeared confused when he said:

> . . . the whole thing [SKIP] . . . has been pitched as anti-smacking, but since s59 isn't about smacking, that's not what we're trying to do; we're simply trying to repeal a piece of legislation which would allow people to run a defence in court, after the police have prosecuted them for taking quite extreme action against their child. Across the other side of the policy . . . we are providing good parenting skills; but the two have got mixed all the time and that's one of the problems in presenting this policy [SKIP].
>
> . . . What we're trying to do here is spend $10.8 million on community-based programmes that do give good parenting skills, and yes, part of those parenting skills will be about trying to provide alternatives to physical discipline for everyday parents who just want to know what you do as an alternative to that. . . . s59 is something the government will revisit in its third term . . . [22]

As explained in the previous chapter, many within Maharey's caucus remain ideologically committed to banning smacking, and view the repeal of s59 as critical in bringing this about; but this is dicey political territory. Behind the scenes, many members of the Labour caucus are relieved that the lobbying is being driven by a Green Party MP, NGOs and others. An unlikely source of support for repeal came from the Governor-General, Dame Silvia Cartwright, who told a Save the Children conference in June 2002, that s59 was "a quirk in the law", whereas slapping an adult or beating an animal was a crime.[23]

A related development furthering the cause of children's rights was the Human Rights National Plan of Action, launched on 10 December 2002. This ambitious initiative has involved extensive nation-wide consultation and a general stock-take of human rights in New Zealand. Commenting on the first report released in September 2004, Chief Commissioner, Rosslyn Noonan, was reported as saying, "We should be ashamed of how the human rights of our children are neglected."[24]

Returning to mid-2002, the election in late July produced the unpredictable outcome that saw the United Future Party gain eight MPs—one electorate and seven list members—and a pledge to support the Labour and Progressive parties on confidence and supply issues. This helped the continuation of a minority Labour-led coalition, but it came at the cost of a commitment from Labour to United Future that a Commission for the Family would be established in the new parliamentary term.

4.1. SUMMARY

- Aside from UNCROC and early efforts by the OCC to get it established as a platform for children's rights reform in New Zealand, the other context for rights development in the early 1990s was the review of the CYPFA. This highlighted problems with the paramountcy principle and the tension that accompanies the assertion of children's rights within the family context.

- Within the OCC, a welfare orientation gave way to a stronger focus on advocacy issues. This coincided with attempts in parliament to provide the Commissioner for Children with greater statutory powers and independence from the DSW.

- Child policy and children's rights issues became more prominent throughout the mid and late 1990s and beyond. Both government and NGO groups introduced a number of initiatives and programmes in this period, including the launch of the MYA (in 1997) and the *Agenda for Children* (2000-02).

4.2. 2002-2004

The United Future Party's fortunes were enhanced in the run-up to the 2002 election when, in a televised debate, leader Peter Dunne spoke of 'commonsense' and 'family values'. The electronic 'worm' seen by viewers recorded the live audience's response and turned decisively in his and the party's favour. Following the election, Dunne's party entered into a confidence and supply arrangement with Labour to provide the country with stable government while giving United Future the opportunity to work within the system.

It is unlikely Labour would have pursued a family commission without United Future's push, but nevertheless it honoured the commitment and set to work early in the new term exploring the options. In fact, Labour quickly and strategically began to assimilate the family cause. The debates in parliament were therefore timely, but must be considered alongside Labour's own initiatives for reform, namely the Care of Children Bill— which was intended to update the Guardianship Act), and the Civil Union Bill—to provide legal recognition for *de facto* and same-sex couples. Both pieces of legislation rested upon modern understandings of social order, including a particular interpretation of the paramountcy principle, and related family, parenting and children's rights issues. Another initiative was the Parenting Council.

Speaking at a UNICEF forum on family violence and children's issues in July 2002, the Minister of Social Services and Employment, Steve Maharey, announced the government's intention to talk "with current providers of parenting programmes prior to establishing a Parenting Council to work on future investments in the skills that parents need, and to spell out what children can expect from their parents." He also stressed that the government "would not be taking a judgemental stance on parenting and families."[25] (This despite the previous comment that the state would now be enunciating what children could expect from parents). The emphasis on the expectation of children which would be spelled out by the state is evidence of a failure to emphasise the responsibility of parents towards their children.

The Parenting Council was launched by Mr Maharey at parliament in March 2003. As a lobby group, its aim was "to empower parents and give a higher public profile to the importance of positive parenting."[26] At the time of the launch, the government was spending $43 million in parent support and education, and it was expected that figure would rise with the formation of the Families Commission in mid-2004. The council was intended to mesh with the work of the new commission and jointly focus on 'positive parenting'.[27]

Arguably, however, the Parenting Council, like other recent government initiatives, has encouraged the state to further move into the sensitive areas of parenting and family. Although well intentioned and popularised through the rhetoric of 'partnering' with community groups, there can be little doubt that the authority for the nurture of children has continued to move decisively in the direction of the state.

Shortly after the launch of the Parenting Council, the Families Commission Bill was introduced to the House on 30 April 2003, and had its first reading on 13 May. The Care of Children Bill also had a first reading less than a month later, on 10 June. From the start, Steve Maharey made it clear which understanding of family would underpin the new commission. In December 2002 he said, "The government's decision to focus on families and parenting is not driven by concern in the decline in families with two married parents and children. Better support for parenting must and will apply equally to all family types."[28] He had long been uninterested in bolstering the two-parent family, even believing it to be in the throes of extinction. In 2000, for example, he said, "[t]he days of the nuclear European-style family unit have gone. . . . The focus of policy [has] been on the breakdown and attempted restoration of old family structures, rather than supporting the new forms existing now . . . [as long as sole parents are] able to provide love, discipline and sound nurturing, things are going to be OK."[29] The Families Commission, then, was intended to support the 'new structures'. In constitution, it would resemble the OCC as a Crown Entity with statutory independence, but be accountable to the Ministry of Social Development and its Minister. Maharey elaborates:

> The commission's main function will be to act as an advocate for the interests of families generally. The commission will not take on any individual family cases or issues. It will have additional functions to assist it to perform effectively its advocacy function, and I will list those functions now.
>
> The commission will encourage and facilitate informed debate on matters relating to the interests of families across sectors and involving the general public. It will increase public awareness and promote better understanding of families in relation to the interests of families, including the importance of stable family relationships, and the rights and responsibilities of parents.
>
> . . . Many New Zealand families are couples with nuclear families, extended families, the wider kinship groupings . . . The bill requires the Families Commission to take an inclusive approach to the family in New Zealand, and to concern itself with issues faced by all of them, whatever shape or form they take.[30]

The Leader of the Opposition, Hon Bill English, was a strong opponent of the Bill. "I give United Future credit for trying", he said, "but I give them my sympathy for having failed. . . . This commission will be praised to the skies by the Human Rights Commission and laughed at in the families of New Zealand." United Future's spokesperson, Judy Turner, replied that "we have avoided ideological definitions of the family, because the commission is not set up to serve families as they should be, but rather families as they are."[31]

Much of the debate was along the lines of what did or did not constitute a family. Judy Turner's comments, however, seemed oblivious to what would soon surface in the Care of Children Bill, which introduced concepts such as social parenting—and, until amendments were made following a political furore created by opposition parties, the possibility of 'lesbian fathers'. Social parenting introduced the idea of a day-to-day carer of the child being seen as the legal 'parent'. A former Ministry of Justice website stated there was no presumption of shared parenting, but then contradicted this by emphasising the on-going role of both parents:

> 'Shared parenting' has many meanings. In some countries it means there is a presumption in legislation that parents will have an equal share in providing a child's day-to-day care. The Bill acknowledges that the day-to-day care responsibilities for a child may be shared. Where a parent does not have a role of providing day-to-day care, the Court must consider whether that parent should have contact with the child. The Bill does not, however, create a presumption of shared parenting or a right to contact. Instead, the Bill focuses on encouraging co-operative parenting by focusing on the best interests and welfare of children, and by emphasising the ongoing role both parents have in a child's upbringing. Any presumption on the form arrangements should take would be inconsistent with the principle of taking into account the individual circumstances of each child to ensure that care arrangements are in the best interests and welfare of that child.[32]

Against such political re-jigging, UNCROC's bottom line, 'the best interests of the child', had no substance and was of little assistance. The push to normalise alternative family types in both the Families Commission Bill and the Care of Children Bill was effectively using advocacy for children as a lever to legitimise wider social change. Labour played down this charge, claiming it was simply tidying-up outdated law and keeping pace with changes that were already occurring.

National MP, Dr Nick Smith, said the Care of Children Bill, ". . . will be opposed by National because it is part of Labour's dangerous social engineering that has the State assuming more and more control and power over children's lives, at the expense of parents. The Minister [Labour MP Lianne Dalziel] stated last week: 'This legislation is getting away from the language of parents having rights. Parents have responsibilities towards their children.' We take a very different view. Only a Minister like that member who is interjecting, a member who does not have any children, could make a statement in this Parliament that parents do not have rights."[33] Being a parliamentary debate, Smith's comments were obviously intended to score political points, but for some opponents, the goal of the legislation was seen to be undermining parental authority, and not simply an extension of children's rights.

These exchanges illustrate the heated nature of the debates on children and family in recent years. In March 2004, even Treasury was considering 'Theories of the Family and Policy' as a working paper; in the same month, the Law Commission was asked by the Minister Responsible for the Law Commission, Lianne Dalziel, to review the legal rules determining parenthood.[34] Interestingly, the authors of the Treasury paper concluded, "[w]hile definitions of the family vary, its core seems to be a blood relationship. People tend to favour kin over non-kin—'blood is thicker than water'—and will take the interests of other family members into account in their decisions."[35] The debates also demonstrate that although children's rights have been a specific cause, they have been successfully interwoven with other issues as well.

Depending on the audience, it has been referred to as 'The Commission for the Family', while elsewhere the proper title, 'The Families Commission', will appear.

The Families Commission was formed in July 2004, and was allocated $28.4 million over four years. To date it has attracted few positive headlines. Chief Executive, Claire Austin, resigned in April 2005 after only five months in the position, amidst opposition claims of another golden handshake payout, the details of which were not disclosed owing to the confidentiality of her employment contract.[36] Labour is clearly sensitive to the fallout from its pluralistic redefinition of the family, as evident in the selective descriptions of the commission it employs. Depending on the audience, it has been referred to as 'The Commission for the Family', while elsewhere the proper title, 'The Families Commission', will appear.[37]

More positive for the government than the Commission has been the

Working For Families (WFF) package announced in the 2004 Budget. This is a major $3 billion initiative to be phased in over three years, which will provide extra financial assistance for families with children. While WFF is part of a wider programme of reform, it also illustrates the extent to which Labour has been prepared to appropriate and resource the families cause in addition to its concession to United Future. However it may be defined and redefined, 'family' is now a permanent feature on the agenda of most political parties.

4.2. SUMMARY

- The 2002 general election resulted in the United Future party entering into a confidence-and-supply agreement with the Labour-led coalition. The trade-off for this guaranteed support was a pledge to establish a Commission for the Family. Labour honoured the pledge but skilfully ensured that the new commission rested upon an inclusive understanding of 'family', in line with its wider ethos of diversity. In this, all social arrangements seeking to be recognised as 'family' were deemed to be functionally equivalent. The policy focus would be family function, not form.

- In the event, the Commission for the Family became the 'Families Commission', which came into being on 1 July 2004, with a budget of $28.4 million over its first four years. Its official task was to research and advocate for all New Zealand families. Its establishment also coincided with two other highly controversial pieces of legislation: the Care of Children Bill, and the Civil Union Bill.

- It was within the context of a political redefinition of the family that many issues concerning children's rights became prominent during the period 2002-04.

4.3. CHILDREN AND CHILDREN'S RIGHTS IN 2006

In early 2006, children's rights are perhaps best viewed as a subset of the wider cause of, and politicisation of, the family in New Zealand society.

The government's rejection of the Doha International Declaration on the Family in December 2004, showed a shrewd and selective appropriation of both the UN and family issues within Labour. The Declaration was the culmination of four previous regional conferences to advise the UN on the occasion of the tenth anniversary of the International Year of the Family.[38]

It was compiled in Doha, Qatar, on 29-30 November, and among other recommendations called upon all governments to protect the family and uphold man-woman marriage. The section which most likely offended reformers in New Zealand was that which called upon states to "Uphold, preserve and defend the institution of marriage; Take effective measures to strengthen the stability of marriage by, among other things, encouraging the full and equal partnership of husband and wife within a committed and enduring marital relationship."[39] To embrace this would have run counter to legislation underpinning the diversity of families, such as the Care of Children and Civil Union Acts.

Accordingly, while the Doha Declaration was supported by 139 nations, it was rejected by the New Zealand government. In explanation, career diplomat and Permanent Representative to the United Nations, Don MacKay, said this on 6 December 2004:

> New Zealand is increasingly concerned that the debate on the family is becoming a vehicle for attacking longstanding consensus agreements on tolerance of family diversity and recognising the rights of women and children. We are concerned that the Doha Declaration, for example, omits a long-standing agreed reference to the fact that many forms of the family exist, and contains no reference to the rights of women and children. The Declaration should have acknowledged that the rights of individuals within families should also be protected, and that individuals have the right to leave family environments where their well-being is at risk. Given that the Doha Declaration is inconsistent with United Nations agreements reached at Cairo, Beijing and Copenhagen, we are concerned that this is being noted in this resolution. It is particularly unusual for this Assembly to note documents that were produced by conferences to which not all governments were invited.
>
> Mr President, many forms of the family do exist. That is the reality. We cannot ignore it. In New Zealand, our families are increasingly diverse, reflecting the diversity of our people's cultures and circumstances. The Secretary-General referred to this increasing diversity of families in his statement this morning. We regret that this text and the Doha Declaration together promote only one model of the family at the expense of others, and in so doing break a longstanding consensus on such matters. New Zealand would like, therefore, to disassociate itself from the consensus on this resolution.[40]

Whereas in the past, in key areas such as CEDAW and UNCROC—women's and children's rights respectively—a huge investment was made to implement these conventions through domestic law reform, the 2002-05 Labour-led coalition was sensitive to any policy shifts in the UN, away from what it was trying to do domestically. Depending on the context, UN initiatives thus became either an expedient argument supporting government policy, or—rarely, as in this instance—something to be distanced from.

Rejecting the Doha Declaration was a rare instance of Labour distancing itself from the UN, but it did provide a further opportunity to assert a commitment to a diversity of family forms that lay at the core of domestic legislation. Foreign Affairs Minister, Phil Goff, summed it up when he said that the government's objection was ". . . not so much with what was said, but what was not said. For the first time, the resolution omitted to mention that many forms of family exist, or to refer to essential and longstanding agreements on the rights of women and children."[41] In other words, the government didn't like Doha because it was contrary to its own view of the family.

Since the 1970s, redefining the family has been a concurrent goal in the institutionalising of human rights in New Zealand, particularly in relation to left-leaning political groups. In March 1974, for example, the Socialist Action League (SAL) submitted two documents to the Parliamentary Select Committee on Women's Rights. These offered an evaluation of the trends in the women's liberation movement up to that time, and a programme and plan of action for the future. There was also an attempt to forge a link between feminist developments and the wider movement of social change. That the family was considered a locus of oppression is clear in the following extract:

> . . . we must clarify our attitude to a very important social institution: the family. Should our aim be to reinforce and maintain at all costs the family, which is itself disintegrating in so many ways under the pressures of modern society, or should our aims be broader than that?
>
> We see the family as the central institution which maintains the oppression of women as a sex in today's society. To some extent, though in a very distorted way, the patriarchal family meets various individual human needs, such as love and companionship. But fundamentally the family is an economic and social institution.
>
> It provides the means for passing on property ownership from one generation to the next—thereby perpetuating the division of society into classes. It enforces a division of labour in which women are fundamentally

reduced to a reproductive role and assigned a limited task immediately associated with this function: care of the other family members. Thus the family institution rests on and reinforces a sexual division of labour involving the domestic subjugation and economic dependence of women.

The family institution is a repressive and conservatising structure that reproduces within itself the hierarchical, authoritarian relationships necessary to the maintenance of class society as a whole. It fosters the competitive and aggressive attitudes necessary to the perpetuation of class divisions. It moulds the behaviour and character structure of children from infancy and throughout adolescence, disciplining them and teaching submission to established authority. The family represses sexuality, discouraging all sexual activity which is not within marriage. It distorts all human relationships by imposing on them the framework of economic compulsion, social dependence and sexual repression. . . . What must be done?

3. An end to coercive family laws.

    a) De facto marriage should be considered to have the same status, legally and socially, as marriage by legal contract, with no discrimination against either partner or their children . . .

    c) Divorce should be automatically available at the request of either partner . . .

    d) The rearing, social welfare and education of children should become the responsibility of society, rather than individual parents, upon whose limited resources all the burdens presently fall. All laws enforcing individual ownership of children should be abolished.

    g) All discrimination against homosexual men and women should be outlawed. In particular, the anti-homosexual laws should be repealed.

    h) All laws victimising prostitutes should be abolished . . .

6. Freedom from domestic slavery.

    a) The government should provide the finance for free child-care services, open to all children from early infancy for 24 hours a day.[42]

By 2006, the Marxist and neo-Marxist language might have gone, but the government's redefinition of the family and associated liberalisation of laws surrounding sexual morality and divorce remains thoroughly in accord with the 1974 recommendations. What many would have considered 'radical' 30 years ago has gradually gained acceptance through progressive law reform, with each of the above recommendations now implemented in policy.

Point 6 (a) was further facilitated by the Ministry of Education's takeover of ECE in 2004. This was welcomed by the primary teachers' union, the NZEI, but it has also extended the state's reach into territory traditionally governed by parents; i.e. the pre-school years. The 2004 budget promised a staggering $307 million over four years "to make [ECE] more accessible and affordable to families."[43] Much of this has been earmarked to improve teacher qualifications and reduce adult-child ratios. From 1 July 2007, three- and four-year-old children who attend teacher-led, early childhood education services will be eligible for 20 hours free education each week.[44]

The changes in ECE will bring a shift in direction, including, in the words of the Ministry:

- new funding and regulatory systems to support diverse ECE services to achieve quality ECE;
- better support for community-based ECE services;
- the introduction of professional registration requirements for all teachers in teacher-led ECE services, such as those already applying in the schools sector and kindergartens;
- better co-operation and collaboration between ECE services, parent support and development and education, health and social services to empower parents and whanau to be involved in their children's early learning;
- greater involvement by the Government in ECE, focusing particularly on communities where current participation in quality ECE is low.[45]

This last point reinforces the determination of the present administration— that is, prior to the election in September 2005—to be more involved in compulsory education, although the motive, as we have seen, is hardly altruistic. References to 'the sector' are becoming replete and indicate the extent to which bureaucracy is permeating and politicising ECE.[46]

It is tempting to see the New Zealand responses to UNCROC within this rubric of reform, and without doubt the children's rights movement has benefited from the momentum of systematic attempts at social change; e.g. the SAL's Plan of Action, and the Ministry of Education's takeover of ECE, but the links are probably more correlative than directly causal. It is significant, however, that international child advocates such as Peter Newell consistently see defenders of the family—especially if they cite religious reasons—as identifiable opponents of rights reform.

In 2006, the more usual matters concerning children's rights are smacking and child poverty. These causes found fresh articulation in the lobby group, Every Child Counts—*He Mana to ia Tamaiti,* launched in early 2005. ECC is a coalition of organisations and individuals who lobbied during the election (held on 17 September). The steering group was made up of experienced advocates including Beth Wood, Deborah Morris-Travers, Ian Hassall and Emma Davies,[47] and supported by organisations including Barnardos, the Institute of Public Policy at the Auckland University of Technology, the Plunket Society, Save the Children, and UNICEF New Zealand. ECC had its origins in a meeting in August 2004 of the major NGOs and professional bodies who endorsed the project. The aim was to 'place children at the centre' as a precondition of the nation's sustainable social and economic development. More specifically:

> Placing children at the centre of public policy development will enable New Zealand to thrive now and in the future. Childhood will be valued and respected for its own sake. Nurtured children are also a key to sustainable social and economic development of New Zealand.
>
> Research clearly shows the link between neglect, abuse and poverty in childhood and poor mental health, crime, reduced employability and lost potential in adulthood. The cost is immense, in both economic and personal terms.
>
> Developing public policy in the context of sustainable development draws attention to the importance of childhood and the social and economic consequences of child poverty and failure to care for and protect children.
>
> The development that takes place in the early years is a determinant of a person's ability to contribute to our economy and society. Unless the appropriate investment is made in the early years, New Zealand's most significant brain drain will continue to occur in the first three years of children's lives.[48]

This was much larger than a children's rights agenda because it located all things *child* in the context of 'sustainable development'. This is not fully explained in the ECC's material, but presumably the *status quo* is failing to treat children in a manner consistent with what the steering group understood by that concept. The ECC campaign appeared to be a distillation of lobbying interests which were given immediacy by a general election, where the aim—as always—was to put pressure on political parties to develop specific child-friendly policies. As has been the case since the early 1990s, child lobbying groups have been adept at creating these opportunities for structural and political reform, and ECC was essentially the latest presentation of the CPAG demands of a decade ago and the clarion calls to end child poverty. ECC rested upon a view that values families, but it endorses the diversity ethos which focuses on family function rather than form, and structural variables rather than an exploration of relational connectedness.[49]

Although specific reference to the abolition of s59 of the Crimes Act is lacking, most if not all of the personnel involved in ECC have been outspoken advocates of repeal in other roles, and it can be reasonably presumed that the group's understanding of 'sustainable development' implied the need for urgent law reform. There can also be little doubt that the leaders and supporters of ECC—which in March 2005, were said to number 250 individuals and 30 organisations[50]—genuinely desired a reappraisal of children and their role in economic and social order. The approach was one that has been repeated with monotonous regularity in calls on the state to do more. Identification of a structural problem apparently finds its 'natural' solution in state resources, but in the process it politicises children by throwing the focus almost exclusively onto the government and its agencies. Parental or family rights gradually get replaced with institutional ones.

Identification of a structural problem apparently finds its 'natural' solution in state resources, but in the process it politicises children by throwing the focus almost exclusively onto the government and its agencies.

Seen in context, ECC was a predictable extension of the 2002 *Agenda for Children,* calls to end smacking, the UN Summits, and the on-going frustrations NGOs have experienced with a government seen as unsympathetic and failing to deliver on lofty promises. Adding to the pressure is Dr Rajen Prasad, the chief commissioner of the Families Commission, who joined the chorus of groups seeking repeal of s59.[51]

Children's rights issues continue to register on the media radar screen. The following sample newspaper headlines from late 2004 to mid-2005, indicate the intense interest in children and children's rights issues in New Zealand: "Child abuse cause for shame, says watchdog";[52] "Human rights report finds wrongs";[53] "State-sanctioned secrecy cuts across parents' rights";[54] "Call for action on child poverty";[55] "Ending cycle of abuse";[56] "MPs asked to back the right to smack";[57] "Courts to keep focus on children's rights";[58] "Smacking ruling to await findings";[59] and "Saving our innocents".[60]

As always, underneath these debates lie varying understandings about what is best for children and how these beliefs translate into policy and shared notions of the public interest. As the headlines suggest, children do not exist in a vacuum; like all human beings, the choices they make and those made for them or on their behalf have wide-reaching implications. To date, the public context for understanding children has been a modern human rights worldview; one that asserts group empowerment rights first recognised and then delivered by the state.

4.3. SUMMARY

- In 2005, what is meant by 'family' continues to influence and shape current understandings of children's rights. In a rare move regarding UN proclamations, the 2004 Doha Declaration on the family was rejected by the New Zealand Government because it ran counter to the notion of diversity enshrined in a number of recent law changes.

- Political changes regarding the family are frequently made on the pretext of being "in line with modern trends", but there is clear evidence in the form of the SAL submission to parliament in 1974, that many of these changes have been the consequence of clearly determined political agenda. The Ministry of Education's takeover of ECE is among the more recent attempts to further encroach upon a domain traditionally the preserve of the family; i.e. care of the under-fives.

- The Every Child Counts campaign established in 2004 attempted to "place children at the centre" of the 2005 general election. Its goal remains to lobby all political parties to this effect. It advocates familiar children's rights themes and is staffed by personnel experienced in other NGO activities.

4.4. RE-THINKING UNCROC FROM A CIVIL SOCIETY PERSPECTIVE

It should be clear from this account that some proponents of UNCROC advance the cause with a degree of anti-parent sentiment. This is a consequence of a particular interpretation of the Convention that essentially sees the child as an autonomous bearer of rights, rather than, as historically understood both in New Zealand and elsewhere, as a person whose rights are held in guardianship within the family until maturity. Certainly, an emphasis has been placed on child rights at the expense of the wider relational context of family. The New Zealand experience bears out the assessment in other nations that UNCROC advocates have not paid enough attention to the parent/child relationship and the significant role parents play in exercising rights on behalf of children, particularly babies and infants. In his in-depth analyses, Geneva-based children's rights researcher, Bruce Abramson, argues that Article 5, for example, recognises parents as rights holders.[61]

Abramson contends that Article 5 is an umbrella right because it pertains to the 'sectoral' rights in the Convention; that is, Articles 6 through 41. The 'umbrella' provisions are in Part II, and the 'sectoral' rights in Part III; the collective or 'peoples' right of self-determination is in Part I. Conceptual clarification is difficult given that 'the child' is synecdochic: it refers to all children, but is stated in the abstract—all, yet no one in particular. If the advocacy focus is on 'the child'—where the noun is singular—it would assume only one child and no parents or other relatives worth mentioning. This is obviously not the reality, nor was it intended by the original framers that UNCROC would be interpreted with such tunnel vision. In the case of babies and infants, it is parents who make decisions on their behalf. They do not supervise the toddler's exercise of decision-making about rights: they exercise the babies' rights on their behalf. For example, parents of a six-month-old who is to enjoy the right "to the highest attainable standard of health" (under Article 24), as well as, ultimately, "the right to life" (Article 6), will seek preventative medical assistance such as immunisations. This is done without advising or seeking approval from the rights-holder. The states that wrote UNCROC recognised this and this is why Article 5 recognises the rights of parents—rights that cannot be considered in isolation from those of children.

UNCROC advocates have mostly ignored the need to empower parents.

They fear that to do so would distract from or even undermine the child's rights, but the consequences seriously weaken the holistic nature of the human condition that underlies the Convention.

In light of these points, it is evident how politicised niche rights groups such as the Littlies Lobby are in the New Zealand setting. They advocate a particular interpretation of UNCROC which shifts infants out of the family context and into the world of identity politics. This was not the intention of those who framed the Convention, but it demonstrates how international law is open to interpretation.

The Lobby is a good example of the traits that Harvard author Peter Rosenblum identifies in his article "Teaching Human Rights: Ambivalent Activism, Multiple Discourse, and Lingering Dilemmas".[62] Rosenblum makes an important distinction between human rights treaties and the human rights movement: the former are official proclamations and statements that entail on-going obligations, while the latter—although far from homogeneous—displays certain salient traits, including 'anti-sovereignty', a tendency to push arguments "beyond established boundaries"; i.e. beyond the plain meaning of treaties and the intentions of the framers; and to 'arrogance and absolutism'.[63] In the case of UNCROC, the result has been an exaggerated individualism of the child as an autonomous agent. The absolutism behind giving children 'their rights' can effectively isolate them from their families.

The New Zealand interpretation has been driven by affirmative action liberals frequently at odds with conservatives. Somewhere in between the vociferous treadmill of rights activism and the reactionary enclave of some conservatives, may lie a way ahead.

These threads run through the debates that have occurred in New Zealand, and they have given children's advocacy a particular bureaucratic and NGO character that has attempted to first legitimise and then popularise specific interpretations of UNCROC.

Despite the intensely politicised environment surrounding children's rights in New Zealand, there may be room for a new conceptual framework which accommodates the spirit of international law, honours the holistic framework of the original UNCROC framers, and respects the independence of a nation state and its domestic law while acknowledging the family as the locus of authority. Is there another way of utilising UNCROC?

The New Zealand interpretation has been driven by affirmative action liberals frequently at odds with conservatives. Somewhere in between the vociferous treadmill of rights activism and the reactionary enclave of some conservatives, may lie a way ahead. Certainly, the Convention should not be dismissed on the basis of one domineering interpretation.

The principle that one institution—such as the family—ought not to be dominated by another—such as the state—is referred to as 'subsidiarity' in Catholic social thought,[64] and elsewhere as 'sphere sovereignty', beginning with Abraham Kuyper, a Dutch writer at the turn of the twentieth century. Under both definitions, each social and political group is encouraged to help smaller or more local ones accomplish their respective ends without arrogating these tasks to itself.

Legal scholar Paolo Carozza further explains subsidiarity and its origins:

> It was only in the latter part of the nineteenth century that Catholic social theorists became the principal proponents of the idea of subsidiarity, as they sought some sort of middle way between the perceived excesses of both laissez-faire liberal capitalist society and Marxian socialist alternatives. That intellectual current led directly to the first papal encyclical on the "social question", Leo XIII's *Rerum Novarum,* in 1891. *Rerum Novarum* was primarily concerned with the conditions of workers, emphasizing the need for state intervention to protect them . . . Leo wrote, "Whenever the general interest or any particular class suffers, or is threatened with harm, which can no other way be met or prevented, the public authority must step in to deal with it"; but the limits of that intervention "must be determined by the nature of the occasion which calls for the law's interference—the principle being that the law must not undertake more, nor proceed further, than is required for the remedy of the evil or the removal of the mischief." [65]

In other words, the state is justified in intervening in specific cases like maltreatment or abuse, but as a matter of principle, it should not predominantly interfere with the largely self-regulatory institution of the family. Carozza goes on to argue that subsidiarity should be regarded as a basic principle of international law.

In more concrete terms, subsidiarity has been described as:

> . . . the principle that all social challenges should be addressed at the level of the smallest social unit possible, preferably the family. Only when a 'lower'—

i.e. smaller—level of society is manifestly incapable of handling a problem may a 'higher' level legitimately intervene. And even then, the 'higher' level may only intervene to supplement, not displace, the function of a lower level. When . . . federal government run[s] the village . . . you have completely inverted the principle of subsidiarity.

When government steps in and imposes a bureaucratic solution based on individualistic presuppositions, it removes expectations and responsibilities from smaller social units—especially the family. In effect, bureaucracy robs intermediate associations of their purpose. The stronger the tie is to the government, the weaker the ties that bind the members of a local community to one another, the weaker the social capital in a community.[66]

Throughout most of New Zealand's history, beginning with Governor George Grey's "Ordinance for the Support of Destitute Families and Illegitimate Children" in 1846, legislators have intuitively understood subsidiarity when it comes to children.[67] Only since second wave feminism in the 1970s has there really been a sustained deconstruction of marriage and the intergenerational family, with much of the impetus coming from New Zealand's alignment with international law, and the widespread influence of revisionist and poststructuralist theory on public policy and local understandings of human rights—notably the HRC.

The state, its agencies and powerful NGO groups, not the parents, are now 'the experts'.

Since the 1990s, a perception of children as politicised agents waiting for further empowerment rights has effectively shifted authority away from parents and families—despite the rhetoric about the importance of families—and on to the state. The basic notion of subsidiarity that previously pervaded New Zealand law has been displaced. The state, its agencies and powerful NGO groups, not the parents, are now 'the experts'.

In December 2000, subsidiarity formally appeared in the *Charter of Fundamental Rights of the European Union*; the preamble "reaffirms, with due regard for the powers and tasks of the Community and the Union and the principle of subsidiarity."[68] This means that the intersection of future international human rights law with a greater understanding of ordinary reality could conceivably percolate down to affect the way parties choose to view and respond to UNCROC. This perspective begins with being and actuality, rather than potentiality and abstract idealism.

To date, however, public debate has only drawn attention to what is not being done to comply with obligations under international law. The preamble of UNCROC mentions the family as "the fundamental group of society and the natural environment for the growth and well-being of all its members and particularly children", and it is timely to reassess what this might mean in a wider context. A consideration of 'kin altruism': the idea that humans invest more in those related to them, may be useful. Kin altruism is a notion stretching back to the natural law of scholasticism, and even earlier, to Aristotle.[69]

More recently, kin altruism has found support in both social psychology and evolutionary theory. A theoretical explanation by William Hamilton in the early 1960s demonstrated how a gene that predisposes its carrier to help a close relative can prosper in the population, provided that the genetic relationship between the two individuals is such that the cost to the giver is more than made up for by the benefit to the recipient multiplied by the degree of relatedness. Caution must be exercised with kin altruism, however, because it is a relative value. It would be an exaggeration to argue that biological attachment alone converts humans into good and nurturing parents; but equally, consideration of the concept could broaden currently accepted understandings of UNCROC so we at least re-evaluate what is meant in the preamble by 'the natural environment' of the family. This would not necessarily discount pluralistic family forms—and what is known as reciprocal altruism[70]—but it would reinforce the reality that those who create a child have a natural, vested and on-going interest in its nurture and well-being. Such a re-evaluation might also accommodate the complex interplay of biological and social variables that contribute to effective parenting.

A consideration of 'kin altruism': the idea that humans invest more in those related to them, may be useful.

The original understanding of sphere sovereignty was in relation to the economic realm, but later theorists, notably Peter Berger and Richard Neuhaus, have applied it to the social sphere and considered the 'mediating structures' or institutions which stand between the individual's private life and the large, formal institutions of public life.

What might subsidiarity and sphere sovereignty offer in regard to rights, and more specifically, future understandings and policy regarding children's rights in New Zealand?

This book has argued that the experience with UNCROC has been highly politicised, and driven by vocal governmental and NGO groups determined to enforce their interpretation of the Convention and of human rights generally. All indicators suggest this will continue. The HRC, for example, in September 2004, issued its first-ever comprehensive report on the state of human rights in New Zealand. This concluded that children and young people are the most at-risk group from human rights abuses. Chief HRC Commissioner Rosslyn Noonan[71] said that while New Zealand meets most international human rights standards, there are critical areas in which we are failing. Noonan claimed that some of the most pressing human rights issues in New Zealand were those relating to the poverty and abuse experienced by a large number of children and young people.[72] "We should be ashamed", she concluded, "of how the human rights of our children are neglected".[73] Accordingly, in December 2004 the HRC initiated a further action plan recommending practical steps over the next five years to improve the status of human rights in New Zealand.

Since 1993, international law has increasingly intruded upon sensitive areas such as family ethics. UNCROC has decisively shaped the prevailing intellectual and legal orthodoxy on children. Its ratification encouraged concerted child advocacy, coming in the wake of two decades of experience for feminists and other rights activists. With that in mind, the soil had historically been well tilled in New Zealand, ensuring a receptivity to international law, especially in the post-Cold War period. What distinguishes the present situation from earlier eras is the way that understandings of children and their rights have been transformed into ideological encounters, and in discourse analysis, into 'subject-positions'.[74]

Within the present human rights culture, children are being viewed as autonomous individuals and bearers of rights, rather than as individuals who exist within, and are accountable to, a family structure which gives them a name, identity, and a rich web of intergenerational connections and community. The interdependence expressed in families, and which operates at different levels of intimacy, has been described as "no mushy sentiment, but *a prime law of human motion and emotion*".[75]

The UNCROC emphasis on empowerment and participation rights has resulted in a number of interesting debates. One issue concerns the rape of a 14-year-old intellectually disabled girl who had an abortion with the knowledge of school authorities—who cited the Privacy Act 1993[76]—but without parental consent or even the parents being informed of it. This is an example of a clash between children's rights to act and parents' rights to know. The political fallout was substantial[77] because opposition parties, prompted by the media attention, successfully drew into question the ideological implications of the Care of Children Bill and exposed what they saw as state-sanctioned secrecy. National MP, Judith Collins, proposed an amendment requiring parents or guardians to be told before underage girls were referred to a consultant, but this was strenuously rejected within the Labour caucus (including the Prime Minister[78]), and by the Royal College of General Practitioners, and the New Zealand Medical Association; both citing privacy and confidentiality between doctors and patients as a non-negotiable ethical issue.[79]

Another contentious issue has been the ease with which teenagers have been able to secure the Independent Youth Benefit (IYB) without parental consent.[80] In some cases, privacy legislation has conveniently blocked inquiries from parents seeking to know how and why the IYB has been granted.[81]

Much is made in conservative circles of 'family values', but such a concept does not logically exist.

In trying to bring about a better understanding, it does not help when defenders of the family refer to it as 'the nuclear family' or present their defence within the context of a particular religious expression or a set of values sometimes described as 'traditional family values'. This feeds a stereotype which child advocates quickly label as repressive and harmful. Much is made in conservative circles of 'family values', but such a concept does not logically exist. There are values—virtues is perhaps a better concept—that find expression within families, but they are not family values *per se*. To speak of 'the intergenerational family' is more helpful because it reinforces an understanding of the biological and social links across generations which define the family and emphasise the continuity of kinship in defining human identity. If domestic law could grasp this as a foundation for thinking about rights, the local fleshing-out of UNCROC could be very different. Instead of an interpretation whereby state parties focus on changing law, there would be a fresh appreciation of the need to understand children within the intergenerational family, rather than a single-minded focus on compliance with international law and arbitrary rights.

This would also result in a different understanding of issues such as child poverty, which often miss the crucial understanding of a child's reality within the family. As discussed in 3.5, all children are 'poor' because they are non-earners, meaning we could properly refer to family poverty, rather than child poverty.[82] Does the much-repeated goal of 'eliminating child poverty' have as its goal to make children 'rich'? If so, this has a material dimension, but it also suggests relational connectedness, stability and commitment from parents and the wider family.

Subsidiarity and sphere sovereignty cast a new angle on rights and UNCROC by thinking in terms of overlapping spheres, where although the boundaries may be blurred, the family is primary and the social ethic that emerges from it would shape law, rather than the other way around. The present emphasis on embracing an inclusive and diverse definition of family (families) as a basis for public policy will only reinforce reliance on state and state agencies, while NGOs retain their strict focus on compliance with UNCROC.

For child advocates, the Convention has proved to be a potent document. However, if states' parties choose to view the intergenerational family as fundamental—as an alternative view of UNCROC could suggest and arguably, was originally intended anyway—domestic policies might be more concerned with honouring and not encroaching upon the sphere sovereignty of the family. This would place less immediate attention on UNCROC as the be-all-and-end-all, but it would remain an important international instrument to support the state and other agencies when necessary to protect children. When, as in New Zealand currently, lobbying focuses on empowerment rights, a sense of balance is lost along with understandings of parental authority and its intersection with children's rights.

Desiring a better lot for the nation's children remains a noble aim in a civil society, but in the process, the authority of parents should not be subsumed or replaced by artificial or imposed legal structures. Berger and Neuhaus expressed this and the essential problem with much contemporary rights advocacy when they wrote:

> . . . we oppose policies that expose the child directly to state intervention, without the mediation of the family. We are sceptical about much current discussion of children's rights—especially when such rights are asserted against the family. Children do have rights, among which is the right to a functionally strong family. When the rhetoric of children's rights means

transferring children from the charge of families to the charge of coteries of experts—'We know what is best for the children'—that rhetoric must be suspected of cloaking vested interests—ideological interests, to be sure, but, also, and more crudely, interest in jobs, money and power.

Our preference for the parents over the experts is more than a matter of democratic conviction—and does not ignore the existence of relevant and helpful expertise. It is based upon the simple, but often overlooked, consideration that virtually all parents love their children. Very few experts love, or can love, most of the children in their care. Not only is that emotionally difficult, but expertise generally requires a degree of emotional detachment. In addition, the parent, unlike the expert, has a long-term, open-ended commitment to the individual child.[83]

Within a sphere sovereignty framework, the sphere of government has a unique place. It possesses a threefold right and duty: whenever different spheres clash, to compel mutual regard for the boundary lines of each; to defend individuals and the weak in those spheres against the abuse of power of the rest; and thirdly, to coerce all together to bear personal and financial burdens for the maintenance of the natural unity of the state. Here the law has to indicate the rights of each party, and the rights of citizens over their own freedom must remain the bulwark against the abuse of power on behalf of the government. The government has a necessary and positive role in creating space for the different spheres to function, but this view challenges the authority of an international convention such as UNCROC as a litmus test measuring a nation's commitment to its children. Greater attention needs to be paid to maintaining the various spheres of influence and checks on state power, than on blindly accepting the authority of international law.

4.4. SUMMARY

- The concepts of subsidiarity and sphere sovereignty are helpful in defining institutions that generally lie outside the domain of direct state involvement. These institutions, among which the intergenerational family is most prominent, are relational rather than bureaucratic in nature.

- The notion of sphere sovereignty has characterised much of state policy concerning children in New Zealand since colonial times. Traditionally, state intervention was necessary only when the family experienced unfortunate circumstances; e.g. the loss of a parent, was no longer able to fulfil its obligations to its children, or when there was negligence or abuse. This assumption was seriously challenged after 1993 with the advent of a more active rights-sensitive culture.

- Sphere sovereignty presents a challenge to the primacy of UNCROC by revaluing the intergenerational family as a largely independent locus of authority and relational interconnectedness.

4.5. FUTURE PROSPECTS

Children, childhood and children's rights are now established features of public policy, in the media, and in tertiary training.[84] Child advocacy has become a big deal, and children now sit comfortably alongside other 'emancipatory' causes. The goal for many groups, as always, is to increase children's participation. The Young People's Reference Group for example, is a key aspect of the OCC's work. Nine young people have been selected to assist it in "understanding what effective youth participation actually means". Monitoring of youth justice services by child advocates will also continue, along with related calls to abolish s59 of the Crimes Act and ensure the provisions of the CYPFA are working effectively.

The ECC campaign which 'placed children at the centre' in the 2005 general election is a fitting epithet for 15 years of concerted child advocacy. It had greater import than a catchy one-liner to lobby political parties. 'Placing children at the centre' is not only vague (at the centre of what?), but it suggests everything else revolves around the child; it is also perhaps, an allusion to the fact that 'the centre' has become, in the New Zealand political context, the territory many parties now aspire to capture.[85] Either way, it captures the degree to which children have become politicised by professional lobbyists.

There is every indication that this trend will continue. NGO groups are well-organised and experienced. UNCROC will continue to supply both a *raison d'être* and methodology for all sorts of advocacy. But to date, key spokespeople in these organisations have displayed a selective indignation over things like smacking and child poverty, while saying little on other issues such as spiralling abortion rates, family breakdown and the proliferation and legitimisation of new family forms. Wider legal and philosophical issues surrounding citizenship, the child as citizen, and the relationship between domestic law, nation-state democracy, and international law, are also ignored, as are the problematic issues of primacy when rights clash—and the role of the state.

The bureaucratising of children's rights has radically reshaped the relationship between the state and the individual. The evolution from the child as chattel, to citizen, and more recently to empowered agent, has not, really been about children and young people having the right to decide for themselves. Rather, it is a question of state officials or authorised professionals deciding what is in a child's interests. Consultation with children and youth may have become the stated reason for the direction of policy, but what eventuates is still framed, shaped and put into practice by politicians and professionals—adults with particular world views.

Consultation with children and youth may have become the stated reason for the direction of policy, but what eventuates is still framed, shaped and put into practice by politicians and professionals— adults with particular world views.

A parallel process to bureaucratisation is what two British legal scholars have called 'juridification'. This is defined as "a process—or processes—by which the state intervenes in areas of social life—for example, the family—in ways which limit the autonomy of individuals or groups to determine their own affairs."[86] This is true in New Zealand where the law has played a steadily increasing role in regulating child/parent relationships.[87] If the momentum continues, there are implications for the democratic freedom of families, and potential violations of what the UDHR in 1948, considered basic human rights. As one analyst has said of the situation in Britain:

> The children's rights discourse is losing sight of the idea of civil rights as guaranteeing freedom from the state, and parents and children having a

shared interest in protection against state interference. Instead, unless there is evidence to the contrary, there is now a presumption of a conflict of interest between parents and children, rather than the state and the individual.[88]

This is at least partly due to a growing perception of children as members of a politically identifiable group.[89] In legal and policy matters they are not being understood within families, but as a group, so children's rights are therefore quite separate from those of their parents. Arguments to give children the vote, for example, effectively deny the differences between children and adults. However, unlike Farson and Holt in the 1970s—who thought children were as competent as adults, according to their vision of radical equality—present-day arguments rest on the assumption that many adults are not only power-hungry and intuitively oppressive towards children, but also incompetent. Adulthood is no longer distinctive by virtue of an attainment of rationality, maturity and independence, because if children are full citizens, adulthood as a concept effectively collapses.

Blurring the distinction between adults and children creates further problems. For example, child advocates could not make a case for a separate youth justice system based on a view of children as evolving and immature, while displacing traditional developmental and social categories between childhood and adulthood. The natural consequence, as politicians such as National Party leader, Dr Don Brash, have identified, would be to lower the age of criminal responsibility. An irony, particularly in National's proposed plan, would be that if the age of criminal responsibility were lowered, parents would still be accountable.[90]

While much policy literature discusses the evolving capacity of children, there is a strain of parallel thinking based on the assumption that adults are irresponsible and intuitively exploitative of children. A clear example of this was the decision by Qantas and Air New Zealand to ban men sitting next to unaccompanied children on flights. The response, from both liberals and conservatives was that this was taking things too far, and the action of the airlines was roundly condemned.[91]

The call to end adult tokenism towards children is only one dimension of what is going on: the other is that advocates often exhibit a paternalism towards adults. This being the case, Steve Maharey's remark that "children are the first big movement of the twenty-first century" may well prove to be true.

4.5. SUMMARY

- Children and children's rights are now firmly entrenched in the political process and policy making in New Zealand. As a result, children are no longer viewed primarily within the relational contexts of their families, but as an identifiable political constituency.

- Problems arise when children's and parental rights clash, and these will inevitably continue as overlapping spheres of authority continue to come into conflict.

- The real empowerment is not of children at all, but of adult professionals and advocates who arguably subsume the issue of children's rights to pursue their own social and political agendas.

ENDNOTES

CHAPTER FOUR
Current and future developments

[1] This, however, was very different to the other cases mentioned. There was, for example, no doubt in Delcelia Witika's killing: the conviction was based on objective forensic evidence and direct testimony, whereas in the Ellis case, the facts are more controversial (including total reliance on child rather than adult testimony). The Ward 24 case was based on the removal of children from parental care without the process of law. The point to be made is that once a case is identified as "child abuse", it is immediately stigmatised even before anything is proved. (For more on the Ellis case, see Lynley Hood, *A City Possessed: The Christchurch Civic Crèche Case – Child Abuse, Gender Politics and the Law*. Dunedin: Longacre Press, 2001.)

[2] Bronwyn Dalley, *Family Matters: Child Welfare in Twentieth-Century New Zealand* (Auckland: Auckland University Press (in association with the Historical Branch, Department of Internal Affairs), 1998), p361.

[3] *Ibid,* p360.

[4] *Child Abuse and Prevention,* (Wellington: Public Health Group, Ministry of Health, 1996), see http://econ.massey.ac.nz/cppe/papers/cppeip04/cppie4i.pdf (unavailable August 2006). Awareness of child abuse gained considerable momentum in the mid-1990s, see, for example, *Second New Zealand Conference on Child Protection. E Tipu E Rea.-* Papers Lincoln university, 15-17 February 1995.

[5] For more on Morris, see below n47.

[6] *NZPD,* 1998, p222.

[7] Part 1: "General Measures of Implementation", in *Children and Youth in Aotearoa 2003,* http://www.acya.org.nz/Portals/0/ChildrenYouthAotearoa2003_Appendix8.rtf, p26, (unavailable August 2006). The Minister of Youth Affairs, Laila Harre, oversaw the consultation process of the government's report. A draft for consultation was made available from June to July 2000, and the feedback used in the final report which was due to be submitted to the UN on 30 November. It was noted on p3 of the draft that the UN Committee had, "encouraged New Zealand to consider withdrawing reservations to the Convention...." *United Nations Convention on the Rights of the Child – First Periodic Report of New Zealand, Working Draft –* 10 May 2000, p3.

[8] Child Policy Briefing Paper, Children's Agenda, June 1999, pages 1 & 3, emphasis added.

[9] Rachel Smithies and Sue Bidrose (Ministry of Social Policy), "Debating a Research Agenda for Children for the next Five Years", *Social Policy Journal of New Zealand*, Issue 15, December 2000, p50.

[10] In June 2000, for example, Action for Children in Aotearoa (ACYA), issued a "Factsheet" tracking New Zealand's adherence to UNCROC between 1996 and May 2000 and noted that insufficient action had taken place. The following statements capture the sense of frustration: "minimal action"; "did not carry out recommendation", "situation for many

children and young people has deteriorated"; "little improvement"; "limited gains overall". ACYA, Factsheet 1, June 2000, p2.

[11] Human Rights Division of the MFAT, Newsletter, July 2001, "New Zealand Statement to the Preparatory Committee for the Special Session of the General Assembly on Children, New York, 12 June 2001", p16.

[12] That is, the New Zealand Employment Service (NZES); Te Manatu Whakahiato Ora; New Zealand Income Support Services (NZISS); the Department of Work and Income (DWI), and the Ministry of Social Policy (MSP). More recently, it was announced in April 2006, that CYF is to merge with the MSD on 1 July 2006.

[13] John Barrington, *A Voice for Children: The Office of the Commissioner for Children, 1989-2003* (Palmerston North: Dunmore Press, 2004), p104.

[14] *Children,* No. 44, December 2002, p30.

[15] *Our Children: The Priority for Policy* (Auckland: CPAG, (second edition), March 2003), p5.

[16] Carol Bellamy, a lawyer and former New York Senator, is UNICEF's fourth Executive Director. She led the organisation from 1995 to 2005.

[17] National Radio "Insight" documentary compiled and presented by Social Issues Correspondent Shona Geary, broadcast June 2003. Each country was restricted to bringing only two child/young person representatives with their governmental delegations. The New Zealand representatives were 17 year-old Te Kerei Moha from Christchurch, and 12 year-old Jessica Dewan, from Mangere, Auckland.

[18] *Ibid.*

[19] *Op. cit.,* "Insight" documentary.

[20] In his address at the Special Session on Children, Maharey clearly felt that much had already been done. He spoke of New Zealand initiatives, making specific mention of children's "direct input into policy making", the *Agenda for Children* and Youth Development Strategy; the annual Children's Day, and the work of the Commissioner for Children (McClay, who was also in attendance at the forum). "I reiterate the commitment of New Zealand to work to create a world fit for all children", he said in closing. See http://www.liveupdater.com/labourparty/LiveArticle.asp?ArtID=-1275393285 (unavailable August 2006).

[21] *Op. cit.,* "Insight" documentary.

[22] National Radio, "Nine to Noon" interview with Linda Clark, 7 May 2004.

[23] *Sunday Star Times,* 16 June 2002, p1.

[24] "Child abuse cause for shame, says watchdog", *The Press,* 1 September 2004, pA2.

[25] "Parenting Council Welcomed", Maharey Notes, Issue 85, 26 March 2003, http://www.beehive.govt.nz/ViewNewsletter.aspx?DocumentID=16332#3 (last accessed August 2006).

[26] "Labour Plans Parents Council To Promote Positive Parenting". Press Release, New Zealand Government, 1 July 2002.

[27] *Op. cit.,* "Parenting Council Welcomed".

[28] *Children,* December 2002, p31.

[29] "Major shift in traditional family values", *Christchurch Star,* Midweek Living section, 27

September 2000, pB1. Contrary to popular opinion, cohabitation and marriage are not equal, at least in terms of outcomes for children, and this has been well documented. For example, see Kathleen Lamb and Wendy Manning, "Adolescent Well-Being in Cohabiting, Married, and Single-Parent Families," *Journal of Marriage and Family,* Vol. 65, No 4, 2003; Susan Brown, "Family Structure and Child Well-Being: The Significance of Parental Cohabitation," *Journal of Marriage and Family,* Vol. 66, No. 2, 2004, p351; Wendy Manning, Pamela Smock, and Majumdar Debauren, "The Relative Stability of Cohabiting and Marital Unions for Children" *Population Research and Policy Review*, Vol. 23, No.2, 2004, p135.

30   *NZPD,* 2003, p5612.

31   *Ibid.,* p5617. For more on the Commission, see Families Commission, Statement of Intent 2004/05, presented to the House of Representatives, nd. c.November 2004.

32   See http://www.courts.govt.nz/pubs/reports/2003/care-of-children/briefing.html#top unavailable August 2006 (last accessed August 2006). More contentious was the so-called "lesbian fathers" clause, the wording of which was subsequently amended (without, however, altering the intent of the clause). The Care of Children Bill had its first reading on 1 July 2003 and passed 61 to 56 votes at that point. It clearly demonstrated the vulnerability to ideological capture of the "best interests" principle. The Bill was consistent with the family policy framework adopted in the earlier working paper, *Responsibilities for Children (especially when parents part): The Laws About Guardianship, Custody and Access* (Wellington: Ministry of Justice, August 2000); see Section 1, "The Family Policy Framework", pp5-6. The Bill passed its third reading on 9 November 2004 and the new Care of Children Act came into effect on 21 November.

33   *NZPD,* 2003, p6711. While politically such accusations constituted an attack on a member's personal life, it was ironic that Lianne Dalziel, Helen Clark, Margaret Wilson and several others in the 1999-2005 Labour caucus did not seem to consider that their level of personal experience (due to the fact they did not have children of their own) in any way diminished their authority.

34   *New Issues in Legal Parenthood: A discussion paper,* (Wellington: Law Commission, Preliminary Paper 54, March 2004). The Commissioner in charge of preparing the paper was Frances Joychild, who was assisted by the children's rights advocate and lawyer Robert Ludbrook, among others.

35   Veronica Jacobsen, Lindy Fursman, John Bryant, Megan Claridge and Benedikte Jensen, "Theories of the Family and Policy", New Zealand Treasury Working Paper 04/02. Wellington, March 2004, Conclusion, p84.

36   A new Chief Executive was announced on 3 November 2005. It is Paul Curry, formerly a General Manager of the Community Development Group at the Department of Internal Affairs. See media release "New Chief Executive for Families Commission", http://www.familiescommission.govt.nz/media/20051103.php (last accessed August 2006).

37   In a personal letter to a conservative inquirer dated 21 January 2005 the Hon Phil Goff said, "We have established a Commission for the Family", while in most other references to the commission, Labour ministers speak of "The Families Commission". See also the

comments of the Permanent Representative of New Zealand to the United Nations, Don Mackay, in "Plenary Resolution Under Item 94: Celebrating the Tenth Anniversary of the International Year of the Family New Zealand Explanation of Position" (6 December 2004) where it was said that "New Zealand has established a Commission for the Family". The reason for the variance is unclear, and may be a simple slip of the tongue, but it is worth noting that a "Commission for the Family" and "The Families Commission" carry quite different connotations.

[38] The preliminary meetings were held in Mexico City (29-31 March 2004); in Stockholm (14-15 May); in Geneva (23-25 August), and Kuala Lumpur (11-13 October).

[39] The Introduction reads: "Representatives of governments and members of civil society met in Doha, Qatar, on November 29-30, 2004, for the Doha International Conference for the Family, in commemoration of the 10th Anniversary of the International Year of the Family." See http://www.worldfamilypolicy.org/intl_conf_doha.html (last accessed August 2006).

[40] http://publications.clerk.parliament.govt.nz.clients.intergen.net.nz/Attachments/00016%20(2005)%20-%2016.doc (last accessed August 2006).

[41] Letter, see n37.

[42] "A Strategy for Women's Liberation (including the submission to a Parliamentary Select Committee on Women's Rights". Unpublished Socialist Action League paper, 1974, pp16-19.

[43] See http://www.minedu.govt.nz/index.cfm?layout=document&documentid=9637&indexid=8230&indexparentid=1095#P0_0 (last accessed August 2006)

[44] http://www.minedu.govt.nz/index.cfm?layout=document&documentid=11253&data=l (last accessed August 2006)

[45] http://www.minedu.govt.nz/index.cfm?layout=document&documentid=7648&data=l&goto=00-02#P38_4259 unavailable August 2006 (last accessed 30 August 2006)

[46] See, for example, 'Enhanced support for early childhood education', *Tukutuku Korero* (*Education Gazette*), 23 May 2005, p9.

[47] Beth Wood and Ian Hassall are both well-known and long-time campaigners for children's rights in New Zealand (see Chapter 3). Deborah Morris-Travers is a former New Zealand First list MP. She entered parliament in 1996 (as Deborah Morris) and was the youngest person to be appointed as a Minister of the Crown. Morris-Travers served as Minister of Youth Affairs, Associate Minister for the Environment and Associate Minister of Accident Rehabilitation and Compensation Insurance. She is a convenor of the New Zealand Campaign Against Landmines (CALM) and in 2005 was employed by the Plunket Society as a Marketing and Advocacy Advisor (in this role she also co-ordinates the "Littlies Lobby" launched by McClay in 2002). Emma Davies gained a doctorate from the University of Auckland in 1999 (thesis title: "Sexual abuse investigation and criminal court processes: Doing justice to the child?"), and is currently a psychologist and Programme Leader, Children and Families, at the Auckland University of Technology's (AUT's) Institute of Public Policy. She has become a frequent media commentator with several articles appearing in major New Zealand newspapers (see n55).

48   See the ECC website: http://www.everychildcounts.org.nz (last accessed August 2006).

49   The issue of family form is significant. Many studies have consistently shown that, on average, children fare better in a two-parent married family across a range of outcomes. See Kathleen Lamb and Wendy Manning, "Adolescent Well-Being in Cohabiting, Married, and Single-Parent Families" *Journal of Marriage and Family* Vol. 65, No. 4, 2003; Susan Brown, "Family Structure and Child Well-Being: The Significance of Parental Cohabitation," *Journal of Marriage and the Family,* Vol. 66, No 2, 2004, p351; Gregory Acs and Sara Nelson, "The Kids Alright? Children's Well-Being and the Rise of Cohabitation". *New Federalism National Survey of America's Families.* B-48 Urban Institute, 2002; L. Woodward, D.M. Fergusson, and L.J. Horwood, "Risk Factors and Life Processes Associated with Teenage Pregnancy: Results of a Prospective Study From Birth to 20 Years," *Journal of Marriage and Family,* Vol. 63, No. 4, 2001 p1170; Thomas Deleire and Ariel Kalil, "Good Things Come in Threes: Single-Parent Multigenerational Family Structure and Adolescent Adjustment," *Demography* Vol. 39, No. 2, 2002, p393.

50   Child care organisations seemed keen to get behind ECC prior to the election. A manager at an organisation known to the writer said this in a memorandum to staff in June 2005: "I have already signed . . . up to this initiative as an organisation, but I would now like to urge you to join it as individuals and to get as many of your friends and whanau to do the same. If you agree with the goals of the initiative, please either fill out [sic] the attached form and send it in or return it to me, and I'll do a bulk mail." This is remarkable in that the organisation lent its support without any apparent consultation with staff. The implication was that *all who worked there* supported the campaign whether or not individual members supported ECC. For a recent insider's assessment of the ECC's 2004-05 campaign see Ian Hassall's article, "The Every Child Counts Campaign—2004-05", in *Children,* No. 56, December 2005, pp4-5. Hassall, is currently employed at AUT's Institute of Public Policy.

51   As reported, "Dr Prasad believes the existence of th[is] section of the Act sends a signal to families that violence is tolerated." "Families groups supports repeal of smacking law", *ODT,* 8 July 2005, p5. See also "supporting repeal of section 59", *Family Voice,* Families Commission Newsletter, Issue 1, October 2005, p5.

52   *The Press,* 1 September 2004, pA2.

53   *Ibid.,* pA15.

54   *Christchurch Star,* 17 September 2004, pA2.

55   *The Press,* 12 October 2004, pA7.

56   Emma Davies, *The Press,* 14 October, 2004, pA13.

57   *ODT,* 4 November 2004, p32.

58   *The Press,* 26 January 2005, pA17.

59   *ODT,* 1 June 2005, p6.

60   Mike Doolan, *The Press,* 4 May 2005, pA19.

61   "Clearing Up Three Misunderstandings about the Convention on the Rights of the Child", unpublished manuscript, November 2004. A number of points in the following

paragraphs are taken from this and another recent paper by Abramson, "Why is the US having so much trouble ratifying the Convention on the Rights of the Child?: A Framework for Understanding the Ratification Debate", unpublished manuscript, January 2004.

[62] Peter Rosenblum, "Teaching Human Rights: Ambivalent Activism, Multiple Discourse, and Lingering Dilemmas", *Harvard Human Rights Journal* (Vol. 15, 2002, p301) and cited here in Abramson (*ibid,* January 2004), p4.

[63] *Ibid.*

[64] Subsidiarity also has roots in the concept of proportionalism. This holds there are certain moral rules and that it can never be right to go against those rules *unless there is a proportionate reason* which would justify it (e.g., in World War Two sheltering Jews when SS soldiers enter the house inquiring of their whereabouts). In relation to children and subsidiarity, there would be no justification for state intervention *unless* the context or situation was of sufficient magnitude to warrant intrusion into the family's sphere of authority. Proportionalism was rejected during the Vatican II reforms (1962-65), but for most of the Church's history it has been mainstream Catholic thought. See Peter Vardy and Paul Grosch, *The Puzzle of Ethics* (London: Harper-Collins, 1999), pp48-51.

[65] Paolo G. Carozza, "Subsidiarity as a Structural Principle of International Human Rights Law", *The American Journal of International Law*, Vol. 97, No. 38, 2003, p41.

[66] Rick Santorum, *It Takes a Family: Conservatism and the Common Good* (Wilmington: ISI Books, 2005), p68.

[67] In 1890, for example, the Children's Protection Act (full title: "An Act for the Prevention of Cruelty to and Better Protection of Children") meant that police could now intervene directly in cases of ill-treatment, neglect or abandonment ("child" for the purposes of this Act was defined as a boy under 14 years, or a girl under 16 years). A further example: in November 1908, a woman by the name of Sarah Jackson, from Auckland, in a letter to the Secretary of Education summed up how many in that period felt when she said, "It follows the Divine Plan of the child in the environment of home and family. For the well-being of the State it is essential that the idea of the family should be fostered. It is fundamentally right, and, being a natural law, may only, I believe, be disregarded at our peril." (*AJHR*, 1909, Section E-4, pp24-34).

[68] Carozza, *op. cit.*, p39.

[69] For more on the origins of kin altruism in Aristotle, see Don Browning, "Meaning of Family in the Universal Declaration of Human Rights", paper presented to the Asia/ Pacific Family Dialogue for The Doha International Conference for the Family, Kuala Lumpur, 12 October 2004. "Aristotle", he says, "provided much of the naturalistic and philosophical language for the centrality of kin attachment and altruism in the theory of family formation in philosophy, law, and religion." (Browning is the emeritus Alexander Campbell Professor of Religious Ethics and Social Sciences at the University of Chicago Divinity School.)

[70] Reciprocal altruism is similar behaviour between biologically un-related persons.

[71] Prior to her appointment at the HRC, Noonan had been President of the influential

primary teachers' union, the New Zealand Educational Institute (NZEI).

72   *Human Rights in New Zealand Today 2004,* HRC press release. See also "Human rights report finds wrongs", *The Press,* 1 September 2004, pA15.

73   "Child abuse cause for shame, says watchdog", *The Press (ibid),* pA2.

74   See for example, Lise Bird, "Seen and Heard? Moving Beyond Discourses about Children's Needs and Rights in Educational Policies", *New Zealand Journal of Educational Studies,* Vol. 38, No.1, 2003, p37.

75   Richard Whitfield, "Becoming and Staying Connected", paper accompanying the launch of New Zealand's Youth Development Strategy, Wellington, 11 and 12 February, 2002, p3, emphasis in original.

76   This legislation was amended later in 1993, and also in 1994.

77   The writer was involved in this debate both on National Radio's *Morning Report* (30 August 2004), and in a wider discussion in the *New Zealand Herald,* see "Parental guidance discretionary", 18-19 September, pB3.

78   "Clark defends secret abortions", *ODT,* 14 September 2004, p2. The Prime Minister was a pro-choice advocate when a political studies student at Auckland University in the early 1970s.

79   *Ibid,* editorial comment "Child abortion", 16 September 2004, p14. The results of a *New Zealand Herald* DigiPoll on 29 September indicated that seven out of 10 people would want to be told if their underage daughter had sought an abortion, even if the girl did not want them to know.

80   The IYB is administered by the MSD. Since 2001, $109.6 million has been spent on the scheme ($25 million in 2003 alone). It is available to 16-18-year-olds who claim to be having difficulties at home. In the first six months of 2004, there were 328 applications of which 205 were granted.

81   See also Mark Henderson, "Law giving parents the run-around", *Sunday Star Times,* 28 July 2002, Focus, pC5.

82   As discussed in 3.5, this point is overshadowed in CPAG material. The March 2003 *Our Children: The Priority for Policy,* for example, emphasises the rapid deregulation, privatisation and macro-economic policies as the cause of child poverty. The "Rogernomics" reforms did create hardship for some families, but so too did the on-going effects of no-fault divorce legislation and family dysfunction.

83   Peter L. Berger and Richard John Neuhaus, *To Empower People: From State to Civil Society* (Washington DC: AEI Press (second edition), 1996), p179.

84   The CIC for example, offers a certificate and postgraduate diploma as well as an MA in children's advocacy, while at the Auckland UNITEC School of Education there is now a postgraduate level 8 (30 point) course EDUC 8821, entitled "Constructions of Childhood" (for a PGDipEd or MEd). This draws heavily on feminist poststructuralist critiques of developmental psychology.

85   United Future and New Zealand First are two smaller parties both claiming "the centre" of the traditional political spectrum, while both Labour and the National parties vie

for broad-based appeal by describing themselves as "centre-left", and "centre-right" respectively.

[86] John Clark and Lord Wedderburn, "Juridification: A Universal Trend? The British Experience in Labour Law", in G. Teubner (ed), *Juridification of Social Spheres: A Comparative Analysis in the Area of Labour, Corporate, Antitrust and Social Welfare Law* (Berlin and New York: Walter de Gruyter, 1987), pp163-90 (*passim*).

[87] See for example, Hon Margaret Wilson, "A Vision for the future: New Zealand's Child Legislation in the 21st Century", speech to the Child Law Conference, 18 April 2002: http://www.beehive.govt.nz/PrintDocument.cfm?DocumentID=13767 (unavailable August 2006).

[88] Vanessa Pupavac, "Children's Rights and the Infantilisation of Citizenship: Children's Rights and New Concepts of Citizenship", unpublished paper, University of Nottingham, 1999; see also by the same author, "The International Children's Rights Regime", in David Chandler (ed), *Rethinking Human Rights: Critical Approaches to International Politics,* (Basingstoke: Palgrave, 2002), pp57-75.

[89] See the HRC's publication "Human Rights in New Zealand Today *Nga Tika Tangata O Te Motu*", Chapter 4: "The rights of children and young people", http://www.hrc.co.nz/report/chapters/chapter04/children01.html (last accessed August 2006).

[90] See "Brash wants 12-year-olds before courts". *ODT,* 22 March 2005 (no page reference).

[91] See "Airline ban may breach Human Rights Act". *ODT,* 30 November 2005, p1. According to this report, Acting Chief Human Rights Commissioner Joris de Bres said the policy was "clearly discrimination because it treated people differently on the basis of gender, which is prohibited by the Act." National Party MP Dr Wayne Mapp was more candid saying the ban was political correctness "gone mad", and added it was a gross overreaction by the airlines.

CHAPTER FIVE

———————— • ————————

Summary

The child may be either 'a gift from God' or 'a gift of nature', but childhood and children's rights are social constructions.[1] In western societies, children have had legal rights since the nineteenth century, but only since the Geneva Declaration in 1924, have they had human rights. Children's rights evolved out of the industrial period in the nineteenth century and were later specified in the 1924 and 1959 Declarations as well as in UNCROC.

The western understanding of children, inherited from ancient societies—both Judeo-Christian and pagan—placed a high premium on the value of children, but not as an end in themselves. Children had value for religious or economic purposes, or to serve the state. The idea of a 'right' emerged in the late Middle Ages when the Latin term *ius* evolved from meaning a law that was fair, to a 'right'; that is, a power that a person possesses to control or claim to do something.[2] The early evolution of rights owed much to the thirteenth century Scholastic philosopher, Thomas Aquinas, and his natural law theology, which helped dignify human beings as made in the image of God.

Although it was first introduced to the West in the seventeenth century, only with the Enlightenment—and the writings of Locke, Rousseau and Kant in particular—did a clearer distinction between childhood and adulthood emerge. It was Rousseau who first romanticised the virtue of the child and emphasised its potential in redeeming society from its corruptions—an idea which has been a powerful motivation for educational and rights reform ever since.

The separateness of childhood was subsequently refined, formalised and consolidated through the rise of human development and learning and the associated phenomenon of mass schooling. A philosophy of schooling and its connection with democratic advancement grew out of the writings of John Dewey, while behavioural psychology meshed neatly with 'scientific' and 'efficient' theories of schooling which spawned a new sub-discipline, educational psychology, in the 1920s.

Among these important developments was the growth of modern children's rights throughout the twentieth century. These owed much not only to the Enlightenment philosophers, but to the rise of developmental psychology and a new awareness—often in the context of war—of how military conflict ravaged entire populations. UNICEF and the UDHR sought to create a more prosperous post-war world and laid a foundation for more specific formulations of children's rights (UNDRC).

Children's rights in New Zealand have their origins in colonial times. Since the 1840s, legislators have attempted to provide for children when circumstances meant they were at risk. The state's response has always been motivated by a desire to protect and provide for the vulnerable and less fortunate. It did this by providing basic legal protections for at-risk children, and later, institutionalising them. In addition, charitable organisations such as the Plunket Society have played a crucial role. Since the late 1870s, all children have had access to state-funded schooling, and successive administrators have long been open to adapting ideas from overseas and applying them in New Zealand schools. This has been a major source of thinking and innovation on children, childhood and understanding the wider educational process.

Both the state response and charitable groups grew out of conditions inherited from industrial England and a belief that settlers in the new colony could create a 'better England'. The child rescue movement, although identifiably Victorian, was also a distillation of Western thought concerning human dignity and rights. A unique variable in the care of children in New Zealand has been the response to the needs of Maori, whose numbers in the nineteenth century were diminished through disease, poverty, land confiscation and the wars of the 1850s and 60s. Like indigenous people elsewhere, Maori were irrevocably affected by the arrival of European settlers.

For the first 150 years of organised settlement in New Zealand, children's rights gradually evolved. Legal provision that became more evident from the 1880s assumed that state intervention was necessary only when families could not provide—as with an orphaned child. Landmark developments such as the Child Welfare Act 1925 and revised legislation in 1974 and 1989, were always preceded by due process providing clear reasons for change. The child's 'best interests'—the paramountcy principle—has been present in domestic law for a long time, but in recent decades it has come to assume greater significance and taken on a legal and social meaning which sees children as proactive rights bearers.

The workable balance between the authority of family and state in the care of children was tipped in favour of the state in later decades of the twentieth century. After the CYPFA in 1989, incremental reform gave way to a period of frenetic change fuelled by new understandings of children's rights. It has been argued that the transformation of women from wives and homemakers into independent earners and bearers of rights during the 1970s was paralleled by the transformation of children in the 1990s. During that decade, children changed from having an identity within families to being a group identity within the body politic. The child became political. The consolidation of bureaucratic power has become very clear in recent developments such as the Labour government's increased funding of childcare, and Children's Commissioner Cindy Kiro's proposal in January 2006, to monitor with tests, all children's health, education and social situation four times up to age 18.[3]

In this consolidation process, the ratification of UNCROC in March 1993, was a very significant development. More than any other legislation, this instrument of international law precipitated a raft of domestic reform and NGO lobbying, and created a new political constituency whereby children became a permanent feature of the political agenda. This was welcomed by lobbyists, but it had an adverse and intrusive effect upon parental rights and an understanding of the parent/child relationship. It also fuelled a self-propagating bureaucracy of experts committed to children's rights.

This is not to suggest that all children's rights developments in New Zealand have been detrimental, nor that the work of lobbyists is to be dismissed. In a civilised society, it is responsible and good government to be interested in children, but this should be achieved through a respect for the reasonable sovereignty of the family, unless life circumstances or family dysfunction put the child at risk. Some legislation, such as the Adult Adoption Information Act of 1985, represented a major advance in that adopted persons could thereafter access details of their birth parents. Previous law had precluded the availability of this information. Similarly, the exposure of sexual and other child abuse was made possible only in a society that was becoming more critically self-aware and in which human rights concerns were being taken seriously. These developments were positive aspects of the rights culture that emerged during the 1970s and 80s. Unfortunately, however, rights are not a self-evident good; they emerge in particular social and political contexts and are readily infused with specific agendas. Feminist fears, for example, that men were inherently abusive created a new stereotype of male predation with wide-reaching implications extending even to the recent policy of airlines banning men from sitting next to unaccompanied children on flights.[4] Moreover, in the intense lobbying and claim to rights, the tensions, overlaps and conflict areas are often obscured.

In a civilised society, it is responsible and good government to be interested in children, but this should be achieved through a respect for the reasonable sovereignty of the family, unless life circumstances or family dysfunction put the child at risk.

Notwithstanding the occasional law thesis,[5] UNCROC's status and its implications for domestic law, parenting and parenting issues has seldom been subject to wider scrutiny or discussion in New Zealand. Its authority is presumed even though the document itself is rather vague, and certainly not prescriptive. Moreover, the symbolic image of the child as an autonomous rights bearer that has emerged in New Zealand is not only at odds with the holistic approach of other UN human rights treaties, but it also represents a break in continuity with the history of child welfare in New Zealand, which has largely respected parental authority and the assumed authority of the intergenerational family.

The interpretation of UNCROC by New Zealanders has seen it emerge as an aggressive instrument of social and legal change. It has not been championed by parents, but by child professionals; and the debates that have ensued have centred around flashpoints such as smacking and child poverty. These have sometimes been emotional, superficial and media-driven.

Who is in charge when it comes to children? This question goes to the heart of the argument advanced in this book; namely, that they are no longer innocents living within the protection of their families, but the state has assumed a new authority and controlling interest in their welfare. This has occurred through a proliferation of structures in which the state, its agencies and influential NGOs have appropriated and popularised particular understandings of children, the child development process and children's rights. But rights, and children's rights in particular, are not as conceptually straightforward as many advocates would suggest. Echoing a conclusion drawn elsewhere, it has also been argued here that:

> . . . children's agency interests are structured quite differently from those of adults. . . . this difference, in combination with children's vulnerability and dependence on adults, makes it inappropriate to think of them as bearers of fundamental agency rights, and unwise to attribute to them at least some of the legal agency rights declared in the Convention.
>
> . . . children may properly be granted agency rights which are correctly distinguished from those of adults, and when the age at which the right kicks in is clearly specified.
>
> . . . children should not be completely dominated by their parents . . . The action of the state, and the division of authority devised by it over the upbringing of children should be designed to safeguard their immediate welfare rights and their prospective autonomy.[6]

This activity and approach of the state, it has been argued, predominated in New Zealand until very recently. The redefinition of children has been part of the wider mosaic of social change in which reality itself is rendered malleable. In this poststructural worldview, everything depends on how reality is perceived and described. Hence language and the control of language are now critical in policy debates—indeed, language becomes the principal instrument in modern politics. In relation to children's rights, we have seen UNCROC being positioned alongside calls to redefine what constitutes family, what is meant by reasonable force—in s59 of the Crimes Act—and so on. If smacking and violence really are one and the same and the couplet successfully forged, the law change will be due to the demands of a minority of professionals whose view of reality has triumphed—not the result of a public outcry from hordes of parents.[7]

Writing in 1978, Serena Stier, an advocate of children's rights, touched on the basic concerns explored in this book when she said:

Attempts to expand children's legal rights so that they generally parallel those of adult citizens are confronted with the presumption of the importance of parental autonomy as a good to be preserved by the state so long as one cannot demonstrate some overriding state interest that would justify interference in the family relationship.[8]

In other words, parental autonomy can be a barrier to the expansion of children's rights. If the state has an interest in the child, but parents fail to co-operate, the state is justified in superseding parental authority. In New Zealand, the authority for children has definitely moved away from parents and onto an array of advisors.

The well-being of children is dependent on relationships, not just resources. A society that values children will place a high premium on promoting and sustaining committed and stable relationships, especially where children are involved. Mothers and fathers committed to their children generally provide a stable, secure and time-honoured context for child nurture.[9] This needs to be more fully appreciated in contemporary New Zealand society, where political understandings of family diversity have become dominant. The subsidiarity/sphere sovereignty approach which is premised on the authority of the family as normative has been proposed, and there are encouraging signs that researchers in New Zealand are beginning to consider the impact of family form on child outcomes.[10]

A society that values

children will place

a high premium

on promoting and

sustaining committed

and stable relationships,

especially where

children are involved.

Concurrently, a much wider understanding of human rights needs to pervade both intellectual and popular debate in New Zealand. The HRC and other state agencies and independent NGOs have moved beyond the UDHR concept of rights as protecting individuals and their freedoms against the intrusion of the state, to embrace group rights and the advancement of specific causes. In this, there is no truth beyond the realm of lobbying and ideological influence. The February/March 2006 issue of the newspaper *Tots to Teens (for Parents)* contains an article promoting the tenth Australasian Conference on Child Abuse and Neglect (ACCAN) held in Wellington in February 2006, and in this, the writer neatly captures the current emphasis being placed on strategic lobbying—by adults—in the children's rights agenda.[11] What is true in any objective sense is secondary to strategic advocacy in the politicising of children's rights: "[S]imply asserting children's rights is not enough. Genuine change in children's lives is more likely when advocates are strategic about the opportunities and methods they use to promote children's rights."[12] As the debate over s59 rolls on, ACCAN speakers have been very timely and strategic in their presentation of data from other countries—notably Sweden—on the need to ban smacking.[13]

In the detail of these debates there is no room, however, for constructive critiques of the status of international law documents; this too is simply assumed. If, as former Commissioner for Children, Roger McClay, believed, UNCROC is a bible for how we understand children's rights, then it is placed beyond reproach or challenge in policy making matters. At a time when the UN is itself facing sustained criticism and the possibility of widespread reform,[14] members of the present government need to be circumspect in their efforts to reform domestic child-related law.

And finally, there are, in what has been written, wider implications for democratic freedom in New Zealand society. The state interest in children has limits. Children are first and foremost members of a human family. They grow into full citizenship, and rights and responsibilities are commensurate with their development and maturity. Rights cannot be one-way traffic and centred only on children, because all other relationships are affected. The amount of bureaucracy surrounding children in New Zealand is considerable, but none of it is a substitute for loving relationships. The boundaries erected by a parent are flexible, shaped by love and a real desire to be part of the child's life.[15] Those erected by the state are uniform and loveless and no amount of new agencies or numbers of public officials in Wellington can alter that fact.

ENDNOTES

CHAPTER FIVE
Summary

[1]   David Elkind makes this point in *Reinventing Childhood* (Rosemont, New Jersey: Modern Learning Press, Inc., 1988, p1), and adds that, "[H]ow children are perceived, as opposed to how they are conceived, always reflects a social consensus.... Now that we have moved...into a post-modern era, we are reinventing childhood to reflect our contemporary perspectives and circumstances." *(Ibid.)* As suggested by their titles, it is a theme in some of Elkind's other books, viz., *The Hurried Child* (1981), and *All Grown Up and No Place to Go* (1988), that "hurrying" childhood has profound implications for families and wider society.

[2]   For further discussion on this point, see James Griffen, "Do Children Have Rights?", in David Archand and Colin MacLeod (eds), *The Moral and Political Status of Children*. (Oxford: Oxford University Press, 2002), p19.

[3]   The proposal was, however, strongly criticised by a spokesman for the New Zealand Council for Civil Liberties, see "Checks on children slammed", New Zealand Herald, 25 January 2006 http://www.nzherald.co.nz/search/story.cfm?storyid=000ECC12-DDAF-13D6-9F8E83027AF1010F (last accessed August 2006).

[4]   An obsession with safety and risk management has also impacted the number of males in the teaching profession. While those working in kindergartens and pre-school have traditionally been women, risk anxiety has been a factor in the low numbers of men entering primary teaching in recent years. According to a Ministry of Education website, as at 1 July 2001, there were 11,415 full-time teacher equivalents (FTTEs) working at licensed ECE services (excluding kohanga reo), and 98.8 percent were female; while in the primary service, 81.9 percent of teachers were women. This is higher than the OECD average of 77 percent for women, but the number of males has dropped from 1970 when the figure was around 40 percent. See http://www.stats.govt.nz/analytical-reports/human-capital-statistics/part-3-providers-of-education-and-training.htm (last accessed August 2006). For more on the cultural shift concerning physical contact and touch and the relationship between children and teachers, see Alison Jones (ed), *Touchy Subject: Teachers Touching Children*. Dunedin: University of Otago Press, 2001.

[5]   See for example, Fiona Mackenzie, "The Impact of Postmodernism upon the Doctrine of the Best Interests of the Child", unpublished LLB (Hons) dissertation, University of Otago, 2001; and, Richard McLeod, "UNCROC: Implications for Domestic Law", unpublished LLM thesis, Victoria University, 1995.

[6]   Harry Brighouse, "What Rights (if Any) do Children Have?", in David Archand and Colin MacLeod, *The Moral and Political Status of Children*. Oxford: Oxford University Press, 2002, p51.

[7]   Among the recent developments regarding s59 has been a symposium entitled "Children and Young People as Social Actors", hosted by the CIC, in Dunedin, in February 2006, and attended by about 60 people. One of the keynote speakers, an English Law

Professor from University College, London, Michael Freeman was reported as saying (in regard to s59) that "it is absolutely essential New Zealand does that [removes s59]. It is one way of tackling [child abuse] and upholding the integrity and humanity of the child." Freeman also advocated giving children citizenship rights, such as the right to vote. "Outlawing child violence in NZ 'essential' ", *Otago Daily Times,* 9 February 2006, p5. Writing some years before, however, on the "The Limits of Autonomy", and having discussed the American child liberationist pioneers Holt and Farson, Freeman appeared more circumspect when he said: "In looking for a children's rights programme we must [thus] recognize the limits of protection: we must also note the dangers inherent in the liberationist prospectus." See "The Limits of Children's Rights" in *The Moral Status of Children: Essays on the Rights of the Child.* The Hague: Martinus Nijhoff Publishers, 1997, p95.

[8]   "Children's Rights and Society's Duties", *Journal of Social Issues,* Vol. 34, No. 2, 1978, p47.

[9]   When compared with other family forms, marriage has been shown to provide a good context for child nurture. See Kathleen Lamb and Wendy Manning, "Adolescent Well-Being in Cohabiting, Married, and Single-Parent Families," *Journal of Marriage and Family* Vol. 65, No. 4, 2003; Susan Brown, "Family Structure and Child Well-Being: The Significance of Parental Cohabitation," *Journal of Marriage and Family,* Vol. 66, No. 2, 2004, p351.

[10]   See for example, Ross Mackay's paper, "The Impact of Family Structure and Family Change on Child Outcomes: A Personal Reading of the Research Literature". *Social Policy Journal of New Zealand,* Issue 24, March 2005, pp111-133. While this is a literature review only (rather than an empirical study), and the points made are from "a personal reading" (rather than articulating policy), Mackay comments upon a number of important findings from the international literature, and although the evidence obviously varies, he concludes, "…there is an abundance of evidence that children who experience a parental separation are, on average, worse off than their peers in intact families, on a number of measures of well-being. However, the scale of the differences in well-being between the two groups of children is not large and most children are not adversely affected. Parental separation then bears down most heavily on a minority of children, generally in the presence of other exacerbating factors." (p127). This would certainly be true in cases like James Whakaruru (see 3.4).

[11]   See "10th Australasian Conference on Child Abuse and Neglect", *Tots to Teens (for Parents),* February/March 2006, p10.

[12]   *Ibid.*

[13]   This event, "Kia Puawai Nga Tamariki: Blossoming of Our Children—Reliance, Rights, Responsibility", was the first ACCAN Conference to be held in New Zealand and was jointly hosted by the OCC, the MSD and CYF (with support from Plunket and the Littlies Lobby). A keynote speaker citing the Swedish experience (where smacking was banned in 1979) was Dr Joan Durrant, a child-clinical psychologist and associate professor from the University of Manitoba. Durrant's work is frequently used by researchers at the OCC and CIC. In her keynote address to the ACCAN Conference, lead CIC researcher Anne Smith was reported as saying that, "[E]ven a little smack on the hand leads to anti-social

and aggressive behaviour in children . . . [physical punishment] taught children to control others' behaviour by using violence." "Call to ban smacking", *Otago Daily Times,* 16 February 2006, p3.

[14] Although the effectiveness of the UN has long been questioned by critics, specific issues such as the oil-for-food programme in Iraq have exposed wider managerial problems. A newspaper editorial captured both the official and public sentiment when it said that the UN "grew out of a commendable desire to avert a repetition of the disaster of the 1930s and to establish a forum for finding collective solutions to problems before they became threats to global security. The UN's specialist humanitarian agencies do a lot of good work. But the world leaders collected in New York this week have their work cut out if they are to stop the organisation fading into irrelevance." "Reform the UN", *The Press,* 14 September 2005, p16.

[15] The main argument advanced in this book is that the evolution of children's rights in New Zealand has been accompanied in recent decades by an increase in state control of children. A related theme, however, is that family form matters and that children generally prosper when parents are committed to each other and their children. Commenting on the importance of fathers, for example, researchers have identified the essential interdependence of functioning families and the emotional and behavioural stability it creates. The following comments based on a number of longitudinal and empirical studies provide a useful point to conclude the present analysis: "When children feel loved and cared for by parents, their sense of emotional security is strengthened. Emotional security, in turn, helps children cope with stress and makes them less vulnerable to anxiety and depression. Furthermore, when children feel close to and respect their parents, they are more likely to obey parent rules and emulate parent behaviour, thus facilitating the internalization of social norms. Studies of two-parent families generally show that feelings of closeness between fathers and children are associated with positive outcomes, such as low levels of psychological distress and delinquency." P.R. Amato & J.G. Gilberth, "Nonresident Fathers and Children's Well-Being: A Meta Analysis." *Journal of Marriage and Family,* Vol. 61, November 1999, p559.

APPENDIX

———————— • ————————

The United Nations Convention on the Rights of the Child (UNCROC)

Introduction

The United Nations Convention on the Rights of the Child (UNCROC) was adopted and opened for signature, ratification and accession by General Assembly resolution 44/25 of 20 November 1989. It entered into force 2 September 1990, in accordance with article 49.

Preamble

The States Parties to the present Convention,

Considering that, in accordance with the principles proclaimed in the Charter of the United Nations, recognition of the inherent dignity and of the equal and inalienable rights of all members of the human family is the foundation of freedom, justice and peace in the world,

Bearing in mind that the peoples of the United Nations have, in the Charter, reaffirmed their faith in fundamental human rights and in the dignity and worth of the human person and have determined to promote social progress and better standards of life in larger freedom,

Recognising that the United Nations has, in the Universal Declaration of Human Rights and in the International Covenants on Human Rights, proclaimed and agreed that everyone is entitled to all the rights and freedoms set forth therein, without distinction of any kind, such as race, colour, sex, language, religion, political or other opinion, national or social origin, property, birth or other status,

Recalling that, in the Universal Declaration of Human Rights, the United Nations has proclaimed that childhood is entitled to special care and assistance,

Convinced that the family, as the fundamental group of society and the natural environment for the growth and well-being of all its members and particularly children, should be afforded the necessary protection and assistance so that it can fully assume its responsibilities within the community,

Recognising that the child, for the full and harmonious development of his or her personality, should grow up in a family environment, in an atmosphere of happiness, love and understanding,

Considering that the child should be fully prepared to live an individual life in society and brought up in the spirit of the ideals proclaimed in the Charter of the United Nations and in particular in the spirit of peace, dignity, tolerance, freedom, equality and solidarity,

Bearing in mind that the need to extend particular care to the child has been stated in the Geneva Declaration of the Rights of the Child of 1924 and in the Declaration of the Rights of the Child adopted by the General Assembly on 20 November 1959 and recognised in the Universal Declaration of Human Rights, in the International Covenant on Civil and Political Rights (in particular in articles 23 and 24), in the International Covenant on Economic, Social and Cultural Rights (in particular in article 10) and in the statutes and relevant instruments of specialised agencies and international organisations concerned with the welfare of children,

Bearing in mind that, as indicated in the Declaration of the Rights of the Child, "the child, by reason of his physical and mental immaturity, needs special safeguards and care, including appropriate legal protection, before as well as after birth",

Recalling the provisions of the Declaration on Social and Legal Principles relating to the Protection and Welfare of Children, with Special Reference to Foster Placement and Adoption Nationally and Internationally; the United Nations Standard Minimum Rules for the Administration of Juvenile Justice (The Beijing Rules); and the Declaration on the Protection of Women and Children in Emergency and Armed Conflict,

Recognising that, in all countries in the world, there are children living in exceptionally difficult conditions and that such children need special consideration,

Taking due account of the importance of the traditions and cultural values of each people for the protection and harmonious development of the child,

Recognising the importance of international co-operation for improving the living conditions of children in every country, in particular in the developing countries,

Have agreed as follows:

PART I

Article 1

For the purposes of the present Convention, a child means every human being below the age of eighteen years unless under the law applicable to the child, majority is attained earlier.

Article 2

1. States Parties shall respect and ensure the rights set forth in the present Convention to each child within their jurisdiction without discrimination of any kind, irrespective of the child's or his or her parent's or legal guardian's race, colour, sex, language, religion, political or other opinion, national, ethnic or social origin, property, disability, birth or other status.

2. States Parties shall take all appropriate measures to ensure that the child is protected against all forms of discrimination or punishment on the basis of the status, activities, expressed opinions, or beliefs of the child's parents, legal guardians, or family members.

Article 3

1. In all actions concerning children, whether undertaken by public or private social welfare institutions, courts of law, administrative authorities or legislative bodies, the best interests of the child shall be a primary consideration.

2. States Parties undertake to ensure the child such protection and care as is necessary for his or her well-being, taking into account the rights and duties of his or her parents, legal guardians, or other individuals legally responsible for him or her, and, to this end, shall take all appropriate legislative and administrative measures.

3. States Parties shall ensure that the institutions, services and facilities responsible for the care or protection of children shall conform with the standards established by competent authorities, particularly in the areas of safety, health, in the number and suitability of their staff, as well as competent supervision.

Article 4

States Parties shall undertake all appropriate legislative, administrative and other measures for the implementation of the rights recognised in the present Convention. With regard to economic, social and cultural rights, States Parties shall undertake such measures to the maximum extent of their available resources and, where needed, within the framework of international co-operation.

Article 5

States Parties shall respect the responsibilities, rights and duties of parents or, where applicable, the members of the extended family or community as provided for by local custom, legal guardians or other persons legally responsible for the child, to provide, in a manner consistent with the evolving capacities of the child, appropriate direction and guidance in the exercise by the child of the rights recognised in the present Convention.

Article 6

1. States Parties recognize that every child has the inherent right to life.

2. States Parties shall ensure to the maximum extent possible the survival and development of the child.

Article 7

1. The child shall be registered immediately after birth and shall have the right from birth to a name, the right to acquire a nationality and, as far as possible, the right to know and be cared for by his or her parents.

2. States Parties shall ensure the implementation of these rights in accordance with their national law and their obligations under the relevant international instruments in this field, in particular where the child would otherwise be stateless.

Article 8

1. States Parties undertake to respect the right of the child to preserve his or her identity, including nationality, name and family relations as recognised by law without unlawful interference.

2. Where a child is illegally deprived of some or all of the elements of his or her identity, States Parties shall provide appropriate assistance and protection, with a view to re-establishing speedily his or her identity.

Article 9

1. States Parties shall ensure that a child shall not be separated from his or her parents against their will, except when competent authorities subject to judicial review determine, in accordance with applicable law and procedures, that such separation is necessary for the best interests of the child. Such determination may be necessary in a particular case such as one involving abuse or neglect of the child by the parents, or one where the parents are living separately and a decision must be made as to the child's place of residence.

2. In any proceedings pursuant to paragraph 1 of the present article, all interested parties shall be given an opportunity to participate in the proceedings and make their views known.

3. States Parties shall respect the right of the child who is separated from one or both parents to maintain personal relations and direct contact with both parents on a regular basis, except if it is contrary to the child's best interests. 4. Where such separation results from any action initiated by a State Party, such as the detention, imprisonment, exile, deportation or death (including death arising from any cause while the person is in the custody of the State) of one or both parents or of the child, that State Party shall, upon request, provide the parents, the child

or, if appropriate, another member of the family with the essential information concerning the whereabouts of the absent member(s) of the family unless the provision of the information would be detrimental to the well-being of the child. States Parties shall further ensure that the submission of such a request shall of itself entail no adverse consequences for the person(s) concerned.

Article 10

1. In accordance with the obligation of States Parties under article 9, paragraph 1, applications by a child or his or her parents to enter or leave a State Party for the purpose of family reunification shall be dealt with by States Parties in a positive, humane and expeditious manner. States Parties shall further ensure that the submission of such a request shall entail no adverse consequences for the applicants and for the members of their family.

2. A child whose parents reside in different States shall have the right to maintain on a regular basis, save in exceptional circumstances personal relations and direct contacts with both parents. Towards that end and in accordance with the obligation of States Parties under article 9, paragraph 1, States Parties shall respect the right of the child and his or her parents to leave any country, including their own and to enter their own country. The right to leave any country shall be subject only to such restrictions as are prescribed by law and which are necessary to protect the national security, public order (ordre public), public health or morals or the rights and freedoms of others and are consistent with the other rights recognised in the present Convention.

Article 11

1. States Parties shall take measures to combat the illicit transfer and non-return of children abroad.

2. To this end, States Parties shall promote the conclusion of bilateral or multilateral agreements or accession to existing agreements.

Article 12

1. States Parties shall assure to the child who is capable of forming his or her own views the right to express those views freely in all matters affecting the child, the views of the child being given due weight in accordance with the age and maturity of the child.

2. For this purpose, the child shall in particular be provided the opportunity to be heard in any judicial and administrative proceedings affecting the child, either directly, or through a representative or an appropriate body, in a manner consistent with the procedural rules of national law.

Article 13

1. The child shall have the right to freedom of expression; this right shall include freedom to seek, receive and impart information and ideas of all kinds, regardless of frontiers, either orally, in writing or in print, in the form of art, or through any other media of the child's choice.

2. The exercise of this right may be subject to certain restrictions, but these shall only be such as are provided by law and are necessary:

   (a) For respect of the rights or reputations of others; or

   (b) For the protection of national security or of public order (ordre public), or of public health or morals.

Article 14

1. States Parties shall respect the right of the child to freedom of thought, conscience and religion.

2. States Parties shall respect the rights and duties of the parents and, when applicable, legal guardians, to provide direction to the child in the exercise of his or her right in a manner consistent with the evolving capacities of the child.

3. Freedom to manifest one's religion or beliefs may be subject only to such limitations as are prescribed by law and are necessary to protect public safety, order, health or morals, or the fundamental rights and freedoms of others.

Article 15

1. States Parties recognise the rights of the child to freedom of association and to freedom of peaceful assembly.

2. No restrictions may be placed on the exercise of these rights other than those imposed in conformity with the law and which are necessary in a democratic society in the interests of national security or public safety, public order (ordre public), the protection of public health or morals or the protection of the rights and freedoms of others.

Article 16

1. No child shall be subjected to arbitrary or unlawful interference with his or her privacy, family, home or correspondence, nor to unlawful attacks on his or her honour and reputation.

2. The child has the right to the protection of the law against such interference or attacks.

Article 17

States Parties recognize the important function performed by the mass media and shall ensure that the child has access to information and material from a diversity of national and international sources, especially those aimed at the promotion of his or her social, spiritual and moral well-being and physical and mental health. To this end, States Parties shall:

(a) Encourage the mass media to disseminate information and material of social and cultural benefit to the child and in accordance with the spirit of article 29;

(b) Encourage international co-operation in the production, exchange and dissemination of such information and material from a diversity of cultural, national and international sources;

(c) Encourage the production and dissemination of children's books;

(d) Encourage the mass media to have particular regard to the linguistic needs of the child who belongs to a minority group or who is indigenous;

(e) Encourage the development of appropriate guidelines for the protection of the child from information and material injurious to his or her well-being, bearing in mind the provisions of articles 13 and 18.

Article 18

1. States Parties shall use their best efforts to ensure recognition of the principle that both parents have common responsibilities for the upbringing and development of the child. Parents or, as the case may be, legal guardians, have the primary responsibility for the upbringing and development of the child. The best interests of the child will be their basic concern.

2. For the purpose of guaranteeing and promoting the rights set forth in the present Convention, States Parties shall render appropriate assistance to parents and legal guardians in the performance of their child-rearing responsibilities and shall ensure the development of institutions, facilities and services for the care of children.

3. States Parties shall take all appropriate measures to ensure that children of working parents have the right to benefit from child-care services and facilities for which they are eligible.

Article 19

1. States Parties shall take all appropriate legislative, administrative, social and educational measures to protect the child from all forms of physical or mental violence, injury or abuse, neglect or negligent treatment, maltreatment or exploitation, including sexual abuse, while in the care of parent(s), legal guardian(s) or any other person who has the care of the child.

2. Such protective measures should, as appropriate, include effective procedures for the establishment of social programmes to provide necessary support for the child and for those who have the care of the child, as well as for other forms of prevention and for identification, reporting, referral, investigation, treatment and follow-up of instances of child maltreatment described heretofore, and, as appropriate, for judicial involvement.

Article 20

1. A child temporarily or permanently deprived of his or her family environment, or in whose own best interests cannot be allowed to remain in that environment, shall be entitled to special protection and assistance provided by the State.

2. States Parties shall in accordance with their national laws ensure alternative care for such a child.

3. Such care could include, inter alia, foster placement, kafalah of Islamic law, adoption or if necessary placement in suitable institutions for the care of children. When considering solutions, due regard shall be paid to the desirability of continuity in a child's upbringing and to the child's ethnic, religious, cultural and linguistic background.

Article 21

States Parties that recognize and/or permit the system of adoption shall ensure that the best interests of the child shall be the paramount consideration and they shall:

(a) Ensure that the adoption of a child is authorised only by competent authorities who determine, in accordance with applicable law and procedures and on the basis of all pertinent and reliable information, that the adoption is permissible in view of the child's status concerning parents, relatives and legal guardians and that, if required, the persons concerned have given their informed consent to the adoption on the basis of such counselling as may be necessary;

(b) Recognise that inter-country adoption may be considered as an alternative means of child's care, if the child cannot be placed in a foster or an adoptive family or cannot in any suitable manner be cared for in the child's country of origin; (c) Ensure that the child concerned by inter-country adoption enjoys safeguards and standards equivalent to those existing in the case of national adoption;

(d) Take all appropriate measures to ensure that, in inter-country adoption, the placement does not result in improper financial gain for those involved in it;

(e) Promote, where appropriate, the objectives of the present article by concluding bilateral or multilateral arrangements or agreements and endeavour, within this framework, to ensure that the placement of the child in another country is carried out by competent authorities or organs.

Article 22

1. States Parties shall take appropriate measures to ensure that a child who is seeking refugee status or who is considered a refugee in accordance with applicable international or domestic law and procedures shall, whether unaccompanied or accompanied by his or her parents or by any other person, receive appropriate protection and humanitarian assistance in the enjoyment of applicable rights set forth in the present Convention and in other international human rights or humanitarian instruments to which the said States are Parties.

2. For this purpose, States Parties shall provide, as they consider appropriate, co-operation in any efforts by the United Nations and other competent intergovernmental organizations or non-governmental organisations co-operating with the United Nations to protect and assist such a child and to trace the parents or other members of the family of any refugee child in order to obtain information necessary for reunification with his or her family. In cases where no parents or other members of the family can be found, the child shall be accorded the same protection as any other child permanently or temporarily deprived of his or her family environment for any reason, as set forth in the present Convention.

Article 23

1. States Parties recognize that a mentally or physically disabled child should enjoy a full and decent life, in conditions which ensure dignity, promote self-reliance and facilitate the child's active participation in the community.

2. States Parties recognise the right of the disabled child to special care and shall encourage and ensure the extension, subject to available resources, to the eligible child and those responsible for his or her care, of assistance for which application is made and which is appropriate to the child's condition and to the circumstances of the parents or others caring for the child. 3. Recognising the special needs of a disabled child, assistance extended in accordance with paragraph 2 of the present article shall be provided free of charge, whenever possible, taking into account the financial resources of the parents or others caring for the child and shall be designed to ensure that the disabled child has effective access to and receives education, training, health care services, rehabilitation services, preparation for employment and recreation opportunities in a manner conducive to the child's achieving the fullest possible social integration and individual development, including his or her cultural and spiritual development

4. States Parties shall promote, in the spirit of international cooperation, the exchange of appropriate information in the field of preventive health care and of medical, psychological and functional treatment of disabled children, including dissemination of and access to information concerning methods of rehabilitation, education

and vocational services, with the aim of enabling States Parties to improve their capabilities and skills and to widen their experience in these areas. In this regard, particular account shall be taken of the needs of developing countries.

Article 24

1. States Parties recognise the right of the child to the enjoyment of the highest attainable standard of health and to facilities for the treatment of illness and rehabilitation of health. States Parties shall strive to ensure that no child is deprived of his or her right of access to such health care services.

2. States Parties shall pursue full implementation of this right and, in particular, shall take appropriate measures:

   (a) To diminish infant and child mortality;

   (b) To ensure the provision of necessary medical assistance and health care to all children with emphasis on the development of primary health care;

   (c) To combat disease and malnutrition, including within the framework of primary health care, through, inter alia, the application of readily available technology and through the provision of adequate nutritious foods and clean drinking-water, taking into consideration the dangers and risks of environmental pollution;

   (d) To ensure appropriate pre-natal and post-natal health care for mothers;

   (e) To ensure that all segments of society, in particular parents and children, are informed, have access to education and are supported in the use of basic knowledge of child health and nutrition, the advantages of breastfeeding, hygiene and environmental sanitation and the prevention of accidents;

   (f) To develop preventive health care, guidance for parents and family planning education and services.

3. States Parties shall take all effective and appropriate measures with a view to abolishing traditional practices prejudicial to the health of children.

4. States Parties undertake to promote and encourage international co-operation with a view to achieving progressively the full realization of the right recognised in the present article. In this regard, particular account shall be taken of the needs of developing countries.

Article 25

States Parties recognize the right of a child who has been placed by the competent authorities for the purposes of care, protection or treatment of his or her physical or mental health, to a periodic review of the treatment provided to the child and all other circumstances relevant to his or her placement.

Article 26

1. States Parties shall recognise for every child the right to benefit from social security, including social insurance and shall take the necessary measures to achieve the full realization of this right in accordance with their national law.

2. The benefits should, where appropriate, be granted, taking into account the resources and the circumstances of the child and persons having responsibility for the maintenance of the child, as well as any other consideration relevant to an application for benefits made by or on behalf of the child.

Article 27

1. States Parties recognise the right of every child to a standard of living adequate for the child's physical, mental, spiritual, moral and social development.

2. The parent(s) or others responsible for the child have the primary responsibility to secure, within their abilities and financial capacities, the conditions of living necessary for the child's development.

3. States Parties, in accordance with national conditions and within their means, shall take appropriate measures to assist parents and others responsible for the child to implement this right and shall in case of need provide material assistance and support programmes, particularly with regard to nutrition, clothing and housing.

4. States Parties shall take all appropriate measures to secure the recovery of maintenance for the child from the parents or other persons having financial responsibility for the child, both within the State Party and from abroad. In particular, where the person having financial responsibility for the child lives in a State different from that of the child, States Parties shall promote the accession to international agreements or the conclusion of such agreements, as well as the making of other appropriate arrangements.

Article 28

1. States Parties recognise the right of the child to education and with a view to achieving this right progressively and on the basis of equal opportunity, they shall, in particular:

   (a) Make primary education compulsory and available free to all;

   (b) Encourage the development of different forms of secondary education, including general and vocational education, make them available and accessible to every child and take appropriate measures such as the introduction of free education and offering financial assistance in case of need;

   (c) Make higher education accessible to all on the basis of capacity by every appropriate means;

(d) Make educational and vocational information and guidance available and accessible to all children;

(e) Take measures to encourage regular attendance at schools and the reduction of drop-out rates.

2. States Parties shall take all appropriate measures to ensure that school discipline is administered in a manner consistent with the child's human dignity and in conformity with the present Convention

3. States Parties shall promote and encourage international cooperation in matters relating to education, in particular with a view to contributing to the elimination of ignorance and illiteracy throughout the world and facilitating access to scientific and technical knowledge and modern teaching methods. In this regard, particular account shall be taken of the needs of developing countries.

Article 29

1. States Parties agree that the education of the child shall be directed to:

(a) The development of the child's personality, talents and mental and physical abilities to their fullest potential;

(b) The development of respect for human rights and fundamental freedoms, and for the principles enshrined in the Charter of the United Nations;

(c) The development of respect for the child's parents, his or her own cultural identity, language and values, for the national values of the country in which the child is living, the country from which he or she may originate, and for civilisations different from his or her own;

(d) The preparation of the child for responsible life in a free society, in the spirit of understanding, peace, tolerance, equality of sexes, and friendship among all peoples, ethnic, national and religious groups and persons of indigenous origin;

(e) The development of respect for the natural environment.

2. No part of the present article or article 28 shall be construed so as to interfere with the liberty of individuals and bodies to establish and direct educational institutions, subject always to the observance of the principle set forth in paragraph 1 of the present article and to the requirements that the education given in such institutions shall conform to such minimum standards as may be laid down by the State.

Article 30

In those States in which ethnic, religious or linguistic minorities or persons of indigenous origin exist, a child belonging to such a minority or who is indigenous shall not be denied the right, in community with other members of his or her group, to enjoy his or her own culture, to profess and practise his or her own religion, or to use his or her own language.

Article 31

1. States Parties recognize the right of the child to rest and leisure, to engage in play and recreational activities appropriate to the age of the child and to participate freely in cultural life and the arts.

2. States Parties shall respect and promote the right of the child to participate fully in cultural and artistic life and shall encourage the provision of appropriate and equal opportunities for cultural, artistic, recreational and leisure activity.

Article 32

1. States Parties recognize the right of the child to be protected from economic exploitation and from performing any work that is likely to be hazardous or to interfere with the child's education, or to be harmful to the child's health or physical, mental, spiritual, moral or social development.

2. States Parties shall take legislative, administrative, social and educational measures to ensure the implementation of the present article. To this end and having regard to the relevant provisions of other international instruments, States Parties shall in particular:

    (a) Provide for a minimum age or minimum ages for admission to employment;

    (b) Provide for appropriate regulation of the hours and conditions of employment;

    (c) Provide for appropriate penalties or other sanctions to ensure the effective enforcement of the present article.

Article 33

States Parties shall take all appropriate measures, including legislative, administrative, social and educational measures, to protect children from the illicit use of narcotic drugs and psychotropic substances as defined in the relevant international treaties and to prevent the use of children in the illicit production and trafficking of such substances.

Article 34

States Parties undertake to protect the child from all forms of sexual exploitation and sexual abuse. For these purposes, States Parties shall in particular take all appropriate national, bilateral and multilateral measures to prevent:

    (a) The inducement or coercion of a child to engage in any unlawful sexual activity;

    (b) The exploitative use of children in prostitution or other unlawful sexual practices;

(c) The exploitative use of children in pornographic performances and materials.

Article 35

States Parties shall take all appropriate national, bilateral and multilateral measures to prevent the abduction of, the sale of or traffic in children for any purpose or in any form.

Article 36

States Parties shall protect the child against all other forms of exploitation prejudicial to any aspects of the child's welfare.

Article 37

States Parties shall ensure that:

(a) No child shall be subjected to torture or other cruel, inhuman or degrading treatment or punishment. Neither capital punishment nor life imprisonment without possibility of release shall be imposed for offences committed by persons below eighteen years of age;

(b) No child shall be deprived of his or her liberty unlawfully or arbitrarily. The arrest, detention or imprisonment of a child shall be in conformity with the law and shall be used only as a measure of last resort and for the shortest appropriate period of time;

(c) Every child deprived of liberty shall be treated with humanity and respect for the inherent dignity of the human person and in a manner which takes into account the needs of persons of his or her age. In particular, every child deprived of liberty shall be separated from adults unless it is considered in the child's best interest not to do so and shall have the right to maintain contact with his or her family through correspondence and visits, save in exceptional circumstances;

(d) Every child deprived of his or her liberty shall have the right to prompt access to legal and other appropriate assistance, as well as the right to challenge the legality of the deprivation of his or her liberty before a court or other competent, independent and impartial authority and to a prompt decision on any such action.

Article 38

1. States Parties undertake to respect and to ensure respect for rules of international humanitarian law applicable to them in armed conflicts which are relevant to the child.

2. States Parties shall take all feasible measures to ensure that persons who have not attained the age of fifteen years do not take a direct part in hostilities.

3. States Parties shall refrain from recruiting any person who has not attained the age of fifteen years into their armed forces. In recruiting among those persons who have attained the age of fifteen years but who have not attained the age of eighteen years, States Parties shall endeavour to give priority to those who are oldest.

4. In accordance with their obligations under international humanitarian law to protect the civilian population in armed conflicts, States Parties shall take all feasible measures to ensure protection and care of children who are affected by an armed conflict.

Article 39

States Parties shall take all appropriate measures to promote physical and psychological recovery and social reintegration of a child victim of: any form of neglect, exploitation, or abuse; torture or any other form of cruel, inhuman or degrading treatment or punishment; or armed conflicts. Such recovery and reintegration shall take place in an environment which fosters the health, self-respect and dignity of the child.

Article 40

1. States Parties recognise the right of every child alleged as, accused of, or recognized as having infringed the penal law to be treated in a manner consistent with the promotion of the child's sense of dignity and worth, which reinforces the child's respect for the human rights and fundamental freedoms of others and which takes into account the child's age and the desirability of promoting the child's reintegration and the child's assuming a constructive role in society.

2. To this end and having regard to the relevant provisions of international instruments, States Parties shall, in particular, ensure that:

    (a) No child shall be alleged as, be accused of, or recognized as having infringed the penal law by reason of acts or omissions that were not prohibited by national or international law at the time they were committed;

    (b) Every child alleged as or accused of having infringed the penal law has at least the following guarantees:

        (i)   To be presumed innocent until proven guilty according to law;

        (ii) To be informed promptly and directly of the charges against him or her, and, if appropriate, through his or her parents or legal guardians and to have legal or other appropriate assistance in the preparation and presentation of his or her defence;

        (iii) To have the matter determined without delay by a competent, independent and impartial authority or judicial body in a fair hearing according to law, in the presence of legal or other appropriate assistance and, unless it is considered not to be in the best interest of the child, in particular, taking into account his or her age or situation, his or her parents or legal guardians;

(iv) Not to be compelled to give testimony or to confess guilt; to examine or have examined adverse witnesses and to obtain the participation and examination of witnesses on his or her behalf under conditions of equality;

(v) If considered to have infringed the penal law, to have this decision and any measures imposed in consequence thereof reviewed by a higher competent, independent and impartial authority or judicial body according to law;

(vi) To have the free assistance of an interpreter if the child cannot understand or speak the language used;

(vii) To have his or her privacy fully respected at all stages of the proceedings.

3. States Parties shall seek to promote the establishment of laws, procedures, authorities and institutions specifically applicable to children alleged as, accused of, or recognised as having infringed the penal law, and, in particular:

(a) The establishment of a minimum age below which children shall be presumed not to have the capacity to infringe the penal law;

(b) Whenever appropriate and desirable, measures for dealing with such children without resorting to judicial proceedings, providing that human rights and legal safeguards are fully respected.

4. A variety of dispositions, such as care, guidance and supervision orders; counselling; probation; foster care; education and vocational training programmes and other alternatives to institutional care shall be available to ensure that children are dealt with in a manner appropriate to their well-being and proportionate both to their circumstances and the offence.

Article 41

Nothing in the present Convention shall affect any provisions which are more conducive to the realisation of the rights of the child and which may be contained in:

(a) The law of a State party; or

(b) International law in force for that State.

PART II

Article 42

States Parties undertake to make the principles and provisions of the Convention widely known, by appropriate and active means, to adults and children alike.

Article 43

1. For the purpose of examining the progress made by States Parties in achieving the realisation of the obligations undertaken in the present Convention, there shall be established a Committee on the Rights of the Child, which shall carry out the functions hereinafter provided.

2. The Committee shall consist of ten experts of high moral standing and recognized competence in the field covered by this Convention. The members of the Committee shall be elected by States Parties from among their nationals and shall serve in their personal capacity, consideration being given to equitable geographical distribution, as well as to the principal legal systems.

3. The members of the Committee shall be elected by secret ballot from a list of persons nominated by States Parties. Each State Party may nominate one person from among its own nationals.

4. The initial election to the Committee shall be held no later than six months after the date of the entry into force of the present Convention and thereafter every second year. At least four months before the date of each election, the Secretary-General of the United Nations shall address a letter to States Parties inviting them to submit their nominations within two months. The Secretary-General shall subsequently prepare a list in alphabetical order of all persons thus nominated, indicating States Parties which have nominated them and shall submit it to the States Parties to the present Convention.

5. The elections shall be held at meetings of States Parties convened by the Secretary-General at United Nations Headquarters. At those meetings, for which two thirds of States Parties shall constitute a quorum, the persons elected to the Committee shall be those who obtain the largest number of votes and an absolute majority of the votes of the representatives of States Parties present and voting.

6. The members of the Committee shall be elected for a term of four years. They shall be eligible for re-election if renominated. The term of five of the members elected at the first election shall expire at the end of two years; immediately after the first election, the names of these five members shall be chosen by lot by the Chairman of the meeting.

7. If a member of the Committee dies or resigns or declares that for any other cause he or she can no longer perform the duties of the Committee, the State Party which nominated the member shall appoint another expert from among its nationals to serve for the remainder of the term, subject to the approval of the Committee.

8. The Committee shall establish its own rules of procedure.

9. The Committee shall elect its officers for a period of two years.

10. The meetings of the Committee shall normally be held at United Nations Headquarters or at any other convenient place as determined by the Committee. The Committee shall normally meet annually. The duration of the meetings of the Committee shall be determined and reviewed, if necessary, by a meeting of the States Parties to the present Convention, subject to the approval of the General Assembly.

11. The Secretary-General of the United Nations shall provide the necessary staff and facilities for the effective performance of the functions of the Committee under the present Convention.

12. With the approval of the General Assembly, the members of the Committee established under the present Convention shall receive emoluments from United Nations resources on such terms and conditions as the Assembly may decide.

Article 44

1. States Parties undertake to submit to the Committee, through the Secretary-General of the United Nations, reports on the measures they have adopted which give effect to the rights recognised herein and on the progress made on the enjoyment of those rights:

   (a) Within two years of the entry into force of the Convention for the State Party concerned;

   (b) Thereafter every five years.

2. Reports made under the present article shall indicate factors and difficulties, if any, affecting the degree of fulfilment of the obligations under the present Convention. Reports shall also contain sufficient information to provide the Committee with a comprehensive understanding of the implementation of the Convention in the country concerned.

3. A State Party which has submitted a comprehensive initial report to the Committee need not, in its subsequent reports submitted in accordance with paragraph 1 (b) of the present article, repeat basic information previously provided.

4. The Committee may request from States Parties further information relevant to the implementation of the Convention.

5. The Committee shall submit to the General Assembly, through the Economic and Social Council, every two years, reports on its activities.

6. States Parties shall make their reports widely available to the public in their own countries.

Article 45

In order to foster the effective implementation of the Convention and to encourage international co-operation in the field covered by the Convention:

(a) The specialised agencies, the United Nations Children's Fund and other United Nations organs shall be entitled to be represented at the consideration of the implementation of such provisions of the present Convention as fall within the scope of their mandate. The Committee may invite the specialised agencies, the United Nations Children's Fund and other competent bodies as it may consider appropriate to provide expert advice on the implementation of the Convention in areas falling within the scope of their respective mandates. The Committee may invite the specialised agencies, the United Nations Children's Fund and other United Nations organs to submit reports on the implementation of the Convention in areas falling within the scope of their activities;

(b) The Committee shall transmit, as it may consider appropriate, to the specialised agencies, the United Nations Children's Fund and other competent bodies, any reports from States Parties that contain a request, or indicate a need, for technical advice or assistance, along with the Committee's observations and suggestions, if any, on these requests or indications;

(c) The Committee may recommend to the General Assembly to request the Secretary-General to undertake on its behalf studies on specific issues relating to the rights of the child;

(d) The Committee may make suggestions and general recommendations based on information received pursuant to articles 44 and 45 of the present Convention. Such suggestions and general recommendations shall be transmitted to any State Party concerned and reported to the General Assembly, together with comments, if any, from States Parties.

PART III

Article 46

The present Convention shall be open for signature by all States.

Article 47

The present Convention is subject to ratification. Instruments of ratification shall be deposited with the Secretary-General of the United Nations.

Article 48

The present Convention shall remain open for accession by any State. The instruments of accession shall be deposited with the Secretary-General of the United Nations.

Article 49

1. The present Convention shall enter into force on the thirtieth day following the date of deposit with the Secretary-General of the United Nations of the twentieth instrument of ratification or accession.

2. For each State ratifying or acceding to the Convention after the deposit of the twentieth instrument of ratification or accession, the Convention shall enter into force on the thirtieth day after the deposit by such State of its instrument of ratification or accession.

Article 50

1. Any State Party may propose an amendment and file it with the Secretary-General of the United Nations. The Secretary-General shall thereupon communicate the proposed amendment to States Parties, with a request that they indicate whether they favour a conference of States Parties for the purpose of considering and voting upon the proposals. In the event that, within four months from the date of such communication, at least one third of the States Parties favour such a conference, the Secretary-General shall convene the conference under the auspices of the United Nations. Any amendment adopted by a majority of States Parties present and voting at the conference shall be submitted to the General Assembly for approval.

2. An amendment adopted in accordance with paragraph 1 of the present article shall enter into force when it has been approved by the General Assembly of the United Nations and accepted by a two-thirds majority of States Parties.

3. When an amendment enters into force, it shall be binding on those States Parties which have accepted it, other States Parties still being bound by the provisions of the present Convention and any earlier amendments which they have accepted.

Article 51

1. The Secretary-General of the United Nations shall receive and circulate to all States the text of reservations made by States at the time of ratification or accession.

2. A reservation incompatible with the object and purpose of the present Convention shall not be permitted.

3. Reservations may be withdrawn at any time by notification to that effect addressed to the Secretary-General of the United Nations, who shall then inform all States. Such notification shall take effect on the date on which it is received by the Secretary-General.

Article 52

A State Party may denounce the present Convention by written notification to the Secretary-General of the United Nations. Denunciation becomes effective one year after the date of receipt of the notification by the Secretary-General.

Article 53

The Secretary-General of the United Nations is designated as the depositary of the present Convention.

Article 54

The original of the present Convention, of which the Arabic, Chinese, English, French, Russian and Spanish texts are equally authentic, shall be deposited with the Secretary-General of the United Nations.

IN WITNESS THEREOF the undersigned plenipotentiaries, being duly authorised thereto by their respective governments, have signed the present Convention.

(*Convention on the Rights of the Child: Presentation of the Initial Report of the Government of New Zealand*, Wellington: Human Rights Division Bulletin of the Ministry of Foreign Affairs and Trade, No. 2, May 1997, pp37-59)

BIBLIOGRAPHY

——————— • ———————

Note: Electronic sources are not included here but are referenced in the Endnotes.

PRIMARY SOURCES

OFFICIAL PUBLICATIONS

2004 the Social Report: indicators of social well-being in New Zealand. Wellington: Ministry of Social Development

2005 the Social Report: indicators of social well-being in New Zealand. Wellington: Ministry of Social Development

Agenda for Children Discussion Paper. Wellington: Ministry of Social Policy, April 2001

Annual Report 2003. Department of Child, Youth and Family Services

Appendices to the Journals of the House of Representatives

Best Evidence Synthesis. Wellington: Ministry of Education, 2003

Michael J.A. Brown, *Care and Protection is about Adult Behaviour: The Ministerial Review of the Department of Child, Youth and Family Services.* Report to the Minister of Social Services and Employment, Hon Steve Maharey, December 2000

Commissioner's Report. Office of the Commissioner for Children, 2002

Convention on the Rights of the Child: Presentation of the Initial Report of the Government of New Zealand. Wellington: Human Rights Division Bulletin of the Ministry of Foreign Affairs and Trade, No. 2, May 1997

Families Commission (Kōmihana ā-Whānau): *Statement of Intent, 2004/05.* Wellington: 2005

Final Report on the Investigation into the Death of James Whakaruru. Wellington: Office of the Commissioner for Children, June 2000

New Issues in Legal Parenthood: A discussion paper. Wellington: Ministry of Justice Preliminary Paper 54, March 2004

New Zealand Families Today: A Briefing for the Families Commission. Wellington: Ministry of Social Development, July 2004

New Zealand Parliamentary Debates (Hansard)

New Zealand's Agenda for Children (Mahere rautaki mā te Hunga Tamariki) Making Life better for all Children. Wellington: Ministry of Social Development, June 2002

Report of the Human Rights Commission (Te Hahui Tika Tangata) and The Office of Human Rights Proceedings (Te Tari Whakatau Take Tika Tangata) for the year ended 30 June 2003 (Annual Report 2003), Wellington

Report of the Special Committee on Moral Delinquency in Children and Adolescents. Wellington: Government Printer, September 1954 (*Mazengarb Report*)

Responsibilities for Children (Especially When Parents Part): The Laws About Guardianship, Custody and Access. Discussion Paper. Wellington: Ministry of Justice, August 2000

Statutes of New Zealand

"Te Whainga I Te Tika," report to the Minister of Justice, Review of the Children and Young Persons Bill, 1987

The New Zealand Curriculum Framework (Te Anga Marutanga o Aotearoa). Wellington: Ministry of Education, 1993

"Theories of the Family and Policy," New Zealand Treasury Working Paper 04/02. Wellington: March 2004

United Nations Convention on the Rights of the Child, First Periodic Report of New Zealand, Working Draft – 10 May 2000

PERIODICALS

Childrenz Issues, Dunedin: Children's Issues Centre, 1997 - 2005

New Zealand Listener, 8 August 1958

North & South, October 1995

Tukutuku Korero (Education Gazette), 23 May 2005

NEWSLETTERS

Action for Children Aotearoa, Newsletter, June 2000

Children (Newsletter of the Commissioner for Children/Children's Commissioner)

Family Voice, Families Commission Newsletter, Issue 1, October 2005

"New Zealand Statement to the Preparatory Committee for the Special Session of the General Assembly on Children," New York, 12 June 2001. Human Rights Division of the Ministry of Foreign Affairs and Trade, Newsletter, July 2001

Ray of Hope: the Littlies Lobby Newsletter, July 2005

World's Children (Save the Children), Winter 2005

NEWSPAPERS

Christchurch Star

Dominion Post (Wellington)

New Zealand Herald (Auckland)

Otago Daily Times (Dunedin)

Sunday Star Times

The Press (Christchurch)

MISCELLANEOUS PAPERS, REPORTS AND SPEECHES

Action for Children in Aotearoa, Factsheet 1, June 2000

Terry Dobbs, *Insights: children and young people speak out about family discipline.* Wellington: Save the Children New Zealand, 2005

Judith Duncan, '"She's always been what I would think, a perfect day-care child": Constructing the subjectivities of a New Zealand child.' Paper presented at the 12th Reconceptualising Early Childhood Education Conference on Research, Theory and Practice: *Troubling Identities,* Oslo University College, Oslo, Norway, 24-28 May 2004

Child Policy Briefing Paper, Children's Agenda, June 1999

Children's Commissioner (Manaakitia a Tatou Tamariki), *Annual Report 2004*

Children and Youth in Aotearoa 2003: The second non-governmental organisations' report from Aotearoa New Zealand to the United Nations Committee on the Rights of the Child. Wellington: Action for Children and Youth Aotearoa, March 2003

Children's Rights: Equal Rights?: Diversity, Difference and the Issue of Discrimination. London: Save the Children, November 2000

EPOCH New Zealand, *Annual Report, July 2003 to June 2004*

Human Rights in New Zealand Today 2004. Human Rights Commission press release, September 2004

Peter Newell, "The First Decade: Keynote Address," in *The First Decade: A conference held to mark the tenth anniversary of the United Nations Convention on the Rights of the Child*. Auckland: Action for Children Aotearoa, Auckland University, 25 November 1999 (Proceedings edited by Beth Wood and Alison Blaiklock)

Laurie O'Reilly, "Advocacy on Behalf of Children," an address to the Annual General Meeting of Anglican Care, Christchurch, 1997

Our Children: The Priority for Policy. Auckland: Child Poverty Action Group, 2nd edition, 2003

"Protect and Treasure New Zealand's Children: Repeal Section 59 and stop an act of violence." Pamphlet issued on behalf of 24 children's rights' groups, Wellington: 2004

Second New Zealand Conference on Child Protection, E Tipu E Rea – Papers. Christchurch: Lincoln University, 14-17 February 1995

Susan St John and David Craig, *Cut Price Kids: Does the 2004 'Working for Families' Budget Work for Children?* Auckland: Child Poverty Action Group, 2004

"The Discipline and Guidance of Children: A Summary of Research," Children's Issues Centre University of Otago and Office of the Children's Commissioner, June 2004

The Rights of the Child and the Law. Human Rights Commission, 1980

Tots to Teens (for Parents), Christchurch edition, February/March 2006

Richard Whitfield, "Becoming and Staying Connected." Address to the Launch of New Zealand's Youth Development Strategy, Wellington: 11-12 February 2002

SECONDARY SOURCES

REFERENCE WORKS

Josephine Bacon (author) and Martin Gilbert (consulting ed), *The Illustrated Atlas of Jewish Civilization*. London: André Deutsch Ltd., 1990

Ian Brownlie (ed), *Basic Documents on Human Rights*. Oxford: Oxford University Press, second edition, 1981

Chris Cook and John Stevenson, *The Longman Handbook of Modern British History 1714-1987*. London: Longman Paul, 1983

Peter Crampton, Clare Salmond, Russell Kirkpatrick, Robyn Scarborough, and Chris Skelly, *Degrees of Deprivation in New Zealand: an atlas of socioeconomic difference*. Auckland: David Bateman Ltd., 2000

J.A.B. O' Keefe and W.L. Farrands, *Introduction to New Zealand Law*. Wellington: Butterworths, fourth edition, 1980

J. Lempriere, *A Classical Dictionary: containing a copious account of all the proper names mentioned in ancient authors*. London: Milner and Sowerby, nd, c1890

Margaret Orbell, *The Illustrated Encyclopedia of Māori Myth and Legend*. Christchurch: Canterbury University Press, 1995

Joy A. Palmer (ed), *Fifty Major Thinkers on Education: from Confucius to Dewey*. London: Routledge, 2001

Youth and the Law 2003: A comprehensive guide to the law relating to young people from birth to adulthood. Wellington: Educational Resources, September 2002

CHAPTERS IN BOOKS

Phillippe Ariès, "Education and the Concept of Childhood," in Paula S. Fass and Mary Ann Mason (eds), *Childhood in America*. New York: New York University Press, 2000

Harry Brighouse, "What Rights (if Any) do Children Have?" in David Archand and Colin MacLeod (eds), *The Moral and Political Status of Children*. Oxford: Oxford University Press, 2002

Lynda Bryder, "Plunket's Secret Army: The Royal New Zealand Plunket Society and the State", in Bronwyn Dalley and Margaret Tennant (eds), *'Past Judgement': social policy in New Zealand history*. Dunedin: University of Otago Press, 2004

John Clark and Lord Wedderburn, "Juridification: A Universal Trend? The British Experience in Labour Law", in G. Teubner (ed), *Juridification of Social Spheres: a comparative analysis in the area of labour, corporate, antitrust and social welfare law*. Berlin and New York: Walter de Gruyter, 1987

Janet Davidson, "The Polynesian Foundation," *The Oxford History of New Zealand*. Wellington: Oxford University Press, 1981

Michel Foucault, "Polemics, Politics and Prolematisation," *The Foucault Reader*. New York: Pantheon Books, 1984

James Griffen, "Do Children Have Rights?" in David Archand and Colin MacLeod (eds), *The Moral and Political Status of Children*. Oxford: Oxford University

Press, 2002

Jean Packman, "Central Issues in Social Policy and the Rghts of the Child," in P. Shannon and B. Webb (eds), *Social Policy and the rights of the child*. Dunedin: University of Otago Extension Department, 1980

Vanessa Pupavac, "The International Children's Rights Regime," in David Chandler (ed), *Rethinking Human Rights: Critical Approaches to International Politics*. Basingstoke: Palgrave, 2002

Michael I. Sandel, *Liberalism and the Limits of Justice*. Cambridge: Cambridge University Press, 1982, in Phillip E. Veerman, *The Rights of the Child and the Changing Image of Childhood*. Dordrecht: Martinus Nijhoff Publishers, 1992

Roy Shuker, "Moral Panics and Social Control: Juvenile Delinquency in Late 19th Century New Zealand," in Roger Openshaw and David McKenzie (eds), *Reinterpreting the Educational Past: essays in the history of New Zealand education*. Wellington: NZCER Educational Research Series, No. 67, 1987

Viviana Zelizer, "Pricing the Priceless Child," in Ann Branaman (ed), *Self and Society*. Massachusetts: Blackwell Publishers, 2001

BOOKS

Rex Ahdar, *Adrift in a Sea of Rights*. New Zealand Educational Development Foundation, August 2001

_____, *Worlds Colliding: conservative christians and the law*. Burlington: Ashgate Publishing, 2001

Ernest Barker, *Social Contract: essays by Locke, Hume and Rousseau*. London: Oxford University Press, 1958

H.C. Barnard, *A History of English Education from 1760*. London: University of London Press (second edition), 1963

John Barrington, *A Voice for Children: The Office of the Commissioner for Children, 1989-2003*. Palmerston North: Dunmore Press, 2004

C.E. Beeby, *The Intermediate Schools of New Zealand: a survey*. Wellington: NZCER, 1938

James Belich, *Paradise Reforged: a history of the New Zealanders from the 1880s to the Year 2000*. Auckland: Allen Lane-Penguin Press, 2001

Peter L. Berger and Richard John Neuhaus, *To Empower People: from state to civil society*. Washington DC: AEI Press (second edition), 1996

William Boyd, *The History of Western Education*. London: Adam & Charles Black, sixth edition, 1952

Barry Brailsford, *The Tattooed Land: the southern frontiers of the Pa Maori*. Wellington: A.H. & A.W. Reed, 1981

Tom Brooking and Paul Enright, *Milestones: turning points in New Zealand history*. Lower Hutt: Mills Publications, 1988

Lynette Burrows, *The Fight for the Family: the adults behind children's rights*. Oxford: Family Education Trust, 1998

A.G. Butchers, *A Centennial History of Education in Canterbury*. Christchurch: Whitcombe & Tombs, 1950

Maud Cahill and Christine Dann (eds), *Changing Our Lives: women working in the women's liberation movement, 1970-1990*. Wellington: Bridget Williams Books Ltd., 1991

A.E. Campbell, *Educating New Zealand*. Wellington: Department of Internal Affairs, 1941

I.C. Campbell, *World's Apart: a history of the Pacific Islands*. Christchurch: Canterbury University Press, 2003

Leonard Carmichael, *John Dewey: the child and the curriculum, the school and society*. Chicago: University of Chicago Press, twelfth impression, 1974

Marie Connolly (ed), *New Zealand Social Work: contexts and practice*. Auckland: Oxford University Press, 2001

Walter W. Cook (ed), Wesley N. Hohfeld, *Fundamental Legal Conceptions as Applied to Judicial Reasoning*. New Haven & London: Yale University Press, 1919

Ian Cumming and Alan Cumming, *History of State Education in New Zealand: 1840-1975*. Wellington: Pitman Publishing, 1978

Bronwyn Dalley, *Family Matters: child welfare in twentieth-century New Zealand*. Auckland: Auckland University Press (in association with the Historical Branch, Department of Internal Affairs), 1998

Charles Dickens, *Oliver Twist*. London: Heron Books, nd, c1965

Ronald Dore, *The Diploma Disease*. London: Allen & Unwin, 1976

David Elkind, *Reinventing Childhood*. Rosemont, New Jersey: Modern Learning Press, Inc., 1988

Harry C. Evison, *The Long Dispute: Maori land rights and European colonisation in southern New Zealand*. Christchurch: Canterbury University Press, 1997

J.L. Ewing, *The Development of the Primary School Curriculum 1877-1970*. Wellington: NZCER, 1970

Richard Farson, *Birthrights: a bill of rights for children*. New York: Macmillan, 1974

Paula S. Fass and Mary Ann Mason (eds) *Childhood in America*. New York: New York University Press, 2000

Michael Foster, *Masters of Political Thought, Volume One: from Plato to Machiavelli*. London: George Harrap & Co., 1959

Michel Foucault, *Discipline and Punish: the birth of the prison*. New York: Vintage Books, 1977

_____, *The History of Sexuality, Volume 1*. New York: Vintage Books, 1980

B. Foxley (trans), *J.J. Rousseau: Émile*. London: Dent Publishers, 1969

Michael D.A. Freeman, *The Moral Status of Children: essays on the rights of the child*. The Hague: Martinus Nijhoff Publishers, 1997

W.J. Gardiner, *A History of Canterbury*. Christchurch: Whitcombe & Tombs, Volume II, 1971

Martin Guggenheim, *What's Wrong With Children's Rights*. Massachusetts: Harvard University Press, 2005

John Holt, *Escape from Childhood: the needs and rights of children*. New York: E.P. Dutton & Co. Inc., 1974

Lynley Hood, *A City Possessed: The Christchurch Civic Crèche Case – child abuse, gender politics and the law*. Dunedin: Longacre Press, 2001

Alison Jones (ed), *Touchy Subject: teachers touching children*. Dunedin: University of Otago Press, 2001

W.T. Jones, *Masters of Political Thought, Volume Two: Machiavelli to Bentham*. London: George Harrap & Co., 1959

Michael King, *The Penguin History of New Zealand*. Auckland: Penguin Books, 2003

George Koenigsberger, George L. Mosse, and G.Q. Bowler, *Europe in the Sixteenth Century*. London & New York: Longman (second edition), 1989

Harold J. Laski, *Political Thought in England: Locke to Bentham*. London: Oxford University Press, 1955

Desmond Lee (trans), *Plato: the republic*. Middlesex: Penguin Books, second edition, 1974

Sara McLanahan and Gary Sandefur, *Growing Up with a Single Parent: What Hurts what Helps*, Cambridge: Harvard University Press, 1994

C.B. MacPherson (ed), Thomas Hobbes, *Leviathan*. Middlesex: Penguin Books, 1980

Martin McQuillan (ed), *Deconstruction: a reader*. Edinburgh: Edinburgh University Press, 2000

Barry Maley, *Children's Rights: where the law is heading and what it means for families*. St Leonards, Australia: Centre for Independent Studies, Policy Monograph 43, 1999

Lesley Max, *Children: Endangered Species? How the needs of New Zealand children are being seriously neglected: a call for action*. Auckland: Penguin Books, 1990

Helen May, *Politics in the Playground: the world of early childhood in postwar New Zealand*. Wellington: Bridget Williams Books/NZCER, 2001

Gordon Parry, *A Fence at the Top: the first 75 years of the plunket society*. Dunedin: The Royal New Zealand Plunket Society, John McIndoe, 1982

Thomas P. Peardon (ed), *John Locke: the second treatise of government*. Indianapolis: The Bobbs-Merrill Company, twentieth printing, 1979

Jock Phillips, *A Man's Country?: the image of the Pakeha male—a history*. Auckland: Penguin Books, 1987

Harris Rackham, *Aristotle: the Nicomachean ethics*. Hertfordshire: Wordsworth Editions Limited, 1996

W.L. Renwick, *Moving Targets: six essays on educational policy*. Wellington: NZCER, 1986

E.V. Rieu (trans), *The Iliad*. London: Penguin Books, 1954

Jenny Rockel and Murray Ryburn, *Adoption Today: change and choice in New Zealand*. Auckland: Heinemann Reed, 1988

George H. Sabine, *A History of Political Theory*. London: George Harrop & Co., third edition, 1951

Anne Salmond, *Between Worlds: early exchanges between Maori and Europeans, 1773-1815*. Auckland: Penguin Books, 1997

Rick Santorum, *It Takes a Family: conservatism and the common good*. Wilmington: ISI Books, 2005

Keith Sinclair (ed) *The Oxford Illustrated History of New Zealand*. Auckland: Oxford University Press, 1990

T.A. Sinclair (trans), *Aristotle: the politics*. Middlesex: Penguin Books, 1980

Peter Singer, *Practical Ethics*. Cambridge: Cambridge University Press, 1979

Anne B. Smith, Megan Gollop, Kate Marshall and Karen Nairn (eds), *Advocating for Children: international perspectives on children's rights*. Dunedin: University of Otago Press, 2000

A.J. Taylor, *Laissez-faire and State Intervention in Nineteenth-Century Britain*. London: Macmillan Press, 1978

Hugh Tredennick, *Plato: the last days of Socrates*. Middlesex: Penguin Books, 1984

Mary Trewby, *The Best Years of Your Life: a history of New Zealand childhood*. Singapore: Viking Press, 1995

Peter Vardy and Paul Grosch, *The Puzzle of Ethics*. London: Harper-Collins, 1999

Philip E. Veerman, *The Rights of the Child and the Changing Image of Childhood*. Dordrecht: Martinus Nijhoff Publishers, 1992

John P. Wynne, *The Theories of Education: an introduction to the foundations of education*. New York: Harper & Row, 1963

John W. and Jean S. Yolton (eds), John Locke, *Some Thoughts Concerning Education*. Oxford: OUP, 1989

JOURNAL ARTICLES

Paul Amato and Joan Gilberth, "Non-resident Fathers and Children's Well-Being: A Meta Analysis," *Journal of Marriage and Family*, Vol. 61, November 1999, 557-573

Paul Amato, "Children of Divorce in the 1990's: An Update of the Amato and Keith (1991) Meta-Analysis," *Journal of Marriage and the Family*, Vol. 15, No. 3, 2001, 366

Gregory Acs and Sara Nelson, "The Kids Alright? Children's Well-Being and the Rise of Cohabitation," New Federalism National Survey of America's Families, B-48, Urban Institute, 2002

Lise Bird, "Seen and Heard? Moving Beyond Discourses about Children's Needs and Rights in Educational Policies," *New Zealand Journal of Educational Studies*, Vol. 38, No.1, 2003, 37-48

Susan Brown, "Family Structure and Child Well-Being: The Significance of Parental Cohabitation," *Journal of Marriage and Family*, Vol. 66, No. 2, 2004, 351

Paolo G. Carozza, "Subsidiarity as a Structural Principle of International Human Rights Law," *The American Journal of International Law*, Vol. 97, No. 38, 2003, 38-79

Martin Daly and Margo Wilson, "Child Abuse and Other Risks Of Not Living With Both Parents," *Ethnology and Sociobiology,* Vol. 6, 1985, 197

Martin Daly and Margo Wilson, "Some Differential Attributes of Lethal Assaults On Small Children By Stepfathers Versus Genetic Fathers," *Ethnology & Sociobiology,* 15 (4), 1994, 207

Thomas Deleire and Ariel Kalil, "Good Things Come in Threes: Single-Parent Multigenerational Family Structure and Adolescent Adjustment," *Demography,* Vol. 39, No. 2, 2002

David Fergusson and Michael Lynsky, "Physical Punishment Maltreatment During Childhood and Adjustment in Young Adulthood," *Child Abuse and Neglect,* Vol. 21, No. 7, 1997, 617

David Fergusson, Michael T. Lynsky and John L. Horwood, "Prevalence of Sexual Abuse and Factors Associated With Sexual Abuse," *Journal of the American Academy of Child and Adolescent Psychiatry,* Vol. 35, No. 10, 1996, 1355

David Fergusson, "The Christchurch Health and Development Study: an Overview and Some Key Findings," *Social Policy Journal of New Zealand,* Issue 10, June 1998, 154-176

David Fergusson and Michael Lynskey, "Physical Punishment During Childhood and Adjustment in Young Adulthood," *Child Abuse & Neglect,* Vol. 21, No. 7, 1997, 617-630

Bruce C. Hafen and Jonathan O. Hafen, "Abandoning Children to Their Autonomy: The United Nations Convention on the Rights of the Child," *Harvard International Law Journal,* Spring 1996, Vol. 37, No. 2, 449-491

Ki Su Kim, "J.S. Mill's Concept of Maturity as the Criterion in Determining Children's Eligibility for Rights," *Journal of Philosophy of Education,* Vol. 24, No. 2, 1990, 235-244

Vanessa Krishnan, John Jensen, Mike Rochford (Knowledge Group, Ministry of Social Development), "Children in Poor Families: Does the Source of Family Income Change the Picture?" *Social Policy Journal of New Zealand (Te Puna Whakaaro),* Issue 18, June 2002, 118-147

Mattias Kumm, "The Legitimacy of International Law: A Constitutionalist Framework of Analysis," *The European Journal of International Law,* Vol. 15, No. 5, 2004, 907-931

Kathleen Lamb and Wendy Manning "Adolescent Well-Being in Cohabiting, Married, and Single-Parent Families," *Journal of Marriage and Family,* Vol. 65, No 4, 2003

Lingxin, Hao and Guihua, Xie, "The Complexity and Endogeneity of Family

Structure in Explaining Children's Misbehavior," *Social Science Research*, Vol. 31, No.1, 2001

Ross Mackay, "The Impact of Family Structure and Family Change on Child Outcomes: A Personal Reading of the Research Literature," *Social Policy Journal of New Zealand*, Issue 24, March 2005, 111-133

J.D.S. McKenzie, "More than a Show of Justice? The Enrolment of Maoris in European Schools prior to 1900," *New Zealand Journal of Educational Studies*, Vol. 17, No. 1, 1982, 1-21

Wendy Manning, Pamela Smock and Majumdar Debauren, "The Relative Stability of Cohabiting and Marital Unions for Children," *Population Research and Policy Review*, Vol. 23, No.2, 2004, 135

Leslie Margolin, "Child Sexual Abuse By Caretakers," *Family Relations*, Vol. 38, No. 4, 1989, 450

Leslie Margolin, "Child Abuse by Mothers' Boyfriends: Why the Overrepresentation?" *Child Abuse and Neglect*, Vol. 16, No. 4, 1992, 541

Roger Openshaw, "The Highest Expression of Devotion: New Zealand Primary Schools and Patriotic Zeal during the early 1920s," *History of Education*, Vol. 9, No. 4, 1980, 333-334

Frank, W, Putnam, "Ten-Year Research Update Review: Child Sexual Abuse," *Journal of American Academy of Child and Adolescent Psychiatry*, Vol. 42, No. 3, 2003, 271

Peter Rosenblum, "Teaching Human Rights: Ambivalent Activism, Multiple Discourse, and Lingering Dilemmas," *Harvard Human Rights Journal*, Vol. 15, 2002

Rachel Smithies and Sue Bidrose (Ministry of Social Policy), "Debating a Research Agenda for Children for the next Five Years," *Social Policy Journal of New Zealand*, Issue 15, December 2000, 41-54

Robert Stephens, "The Social Impact of Reform: Poverty in Aotearoa/New Zealand," *Social Policy and Administration*, Vol.34, No.1, March 2000, 64-86

Serena Stier, "Children's Rights and Society's Duties," *Journal of Social Issues*, Vol. 34, No. 2, 1978, 46-58

George Weigel, "Are Human Rights Still Universal?" *Commentary*, February 1995, 41-45

Lianne Woodward, David Fergusson, and L.J. Horwood, "Risk Factors and Life Processes Associated with Teenage Pregnancy: Results of a Prospective Study From Birth to 20 Years," *Journal of Marriage and Family*, Vol 63, No. 4, 2001, 1170

V.L. Worsfold, "A Philosophical Justification for Children's Rights," *Harvard Educational Review*, Vol. 44, No. 1, 1974, 142-157

Unpublished Theses and Research papers

Bruce Abramson, "Why is the US Having so much Trouble Ratifying the Convention on the Rights of the Child?: a framework for understanding the ratification debate," Unpublished manuscript, January 2004

_____, "Clearing up Three Misunderstandings about the Convention on the Rights of the Child," Unpublished manuscript, November 2004

J.M. Beagle, "Children of the State: A Study of the New Zealand Industrial School System 1880-1925," Unpublished MA thesis (Education), University of Auckland, 1974

Don Browning, "Meaning of Family in the Universal Declaration of Human Rights," paper presented to the Asia/Pacific Family Dialogue for The Doha International Conference for the Family, Kuala Lumpur, 12 October 2004

D.M. Crowther (ed), "Street Society in Christchurch, Psychological Report No. 3." Christchurch: Department of Psychology, Canterbury University, 1956

Dugald McDonald, "The Governing of Children: Social policy for children and young persons in New Zealand 1840—1982," Unpublished PhD thesis (Sociology), University of Canterbury, 1988

Richard McLeod, "UNCROC: Implications for Domestic Law," Unpublished LLM thesis, Victoria University, 1995

Fiona Mackenzie, "The Impact of Postmodernism upon the Doctrine of the Best Interests of the Child," Unpublished LLB (Hons) dissertation, University of Otago, 2001

Lynne Milne, "The Plunket Society: an experiment in infant welfare." Unpublished BA (Hons) dissertation (History), Otago University, 1976

Arika Morita, "Family Dissolution and the Concept of Children's Rights: an historical and culture-comparative analysis," Unpublished paper delivered to the World Congress of Families, Prague, March 1997

Vanessa Pupavac, "Children's Rights and the Infantilisation of Citizenship: Children's Rights and New Concepts of Citizenship," Unpublished paper, University of Nottingham, 1999

Video Kit

Jenny Rankine, (Lee Chisholm, Jessie McArthur, Kim Myhill, Sue Rouse and Helen Schamroth, eds), *Safe Before Five*. Auckland: Te Auenga Inc., 1991

INDEX

———————— • ————————